EARTH GUARDIAN

GalaxyQuestBooks.com are published by
Ocean Quest LLC
2100 Ogden Drive
Cambria CA 93428

First Printing November 2012
Updated May 2013

10987654321

Printed in United States of America
Library of Congress Control Number: 2012917166
ISBN: 978-0-9839630-4-2

Books from GalaxyQuestBooks.com are available for premiums and special promotions. For details contact: marketing@ GalaxyQuestBooks.com.

More books by this author:
Guardian Force
Guardian Probe
Guardian Strike
Guardian Thunder

Dedications:

With an abiding respect, the author dedicates this book to the personnel of the United States Navy Submarine Force, especially to the memory of United States Submarines remaining on eternal patrol, serving with integrity and an uncompromising devotion to duty.

Inspiration by Gepeto, who was a gift of love from Guide Dogs for the Blind, San Rafael, California, and for another such wondrous gift, Limo who has with great patience and courage taken up the fallen baton and filled some mighty big paws.

Grateful Acknowledgments:

Moral and intellectual support from all my friends in the Cambria Rough Writers, and in memory of Tom Christian, truly a gentleman. Editorial encouragement and recommendations by Brandon Jones.

Boundless encouragement, graphic art, web-mastery, and editing by Nancy McKarney.

Meticulous copy editing by Brian Gusner.

Special Thanks: Craig Williams and Amanda Wallace

Image source: Valerie Potapova-Fotolia.com

Earth Guardian

D. Arthur Gusner

GalaxyQuestBooks.com
Ocean Quest LLC
Cambria 93428

Contents

Contents

"You see, wire telegraph is a kind of a very, very long cat. You pull his tail in New York and his head is meowing in Los Angeles. Do you understand this? And radio operates exactly the same way: you send signals here, they receive them there. The only difference is that there is no cat."

Albert Einstein

"I have never let my schooling interfere with my education."

Mark Twain

Author's Foreword

There are many branches on the paths we follow in life. Some lead to adventures and others lead to mysteries. When I was a small boy, I happened onto the path that led me to the County Library. There I found both adventure and mystery in abundance. Among the shelves of dusty books, I encountered James Churchward's works on Mu. That starting point led me to the broad field of speculative history and to wondrous tales of forgotten cities and lost civilizations.

When contemplating the massive stone figures of Easter Island, the towering pyramids of Egypt, and the mysterious structures of Stonehenge, I asked just how did they shape and move those massive stones? In Machu Picchu and other Incan ruins, very large stones with irregular surfaces were precisely fitted to match adjoining similar stones. They fit so precisely, a cigarette paper could not be placed between them. How was that done?

The spate of UFO sightings in 1947 prompted further youthful exploration. One book I located, *The Book of the Damned*, was from the early 1900s. This was the first published nonfiction work of the author Charles Fort. Within the pages of Charles Fort's work, I found remarkable descriptions of UFOs similar to Ezekiel's wheel within a wheel. Could these have been modern hoaxes? My conclusion then favored an unsolved mystery, and it still does.

The Guardian series is an exhilarating story winding through the widely spaced pillars of incomplete human history. *Guardian Force, Earth Guardian, Guardian Probe* and *Guardian Strike* are pure science fiction brimming with high adventure and military strategy. The author's hope is that the books will provide science fiction enthusiasts an enjoyable and memorable read. So relax, lean back, and enjoy a modern imaginative fable set both in the past and in the year 2511 and beyond.

D. Arthur Gusner
Cambria, California
December 2012

Prologue

And it came to pass, when men began to multiply on the face of the earth, and daughters were born unto them, that the sons of God saw the daughters of men that they were fair; and they took them wives of all which they chose.

KJV Genesis 6

Following tens of thousands of years of separation, in the year 2511 two distinct but separate branches of humanity were again united. The mystery of how their separation had occurred remained unanswered. However, far more pressing than finding the answer to that question was their survival amid a no quarter interstellar war that spanned many star systems.

Chapter One:
Battle Stations

Out beyond Tearman's heliosphere, Guardian Force AI Cruiser Lan was moving like a fleeting shadow, silently and unseen through the darkness of deep space. Within Lan's artificial intelligence core matrix, he was alert and aware of the subtle energies flowing throughout the surrounding environment, through which he navigated. More to the point, he fully understood he was a ship of war, and felt very comfortable with this designation. If Lan had facial features, some might say he was actually smiling, as if enjoying his duty of maintaining the peace and safety of multiple human-occupied worlds– that duty being his defined purpose for being.

Of course, if someone were to imply Lan was actually feeling comfortable or happy, his AI programmers would vociferously discourage that notion, since human emotions were definitely not part of the design of the AI program. After all, they rationalized, the AIs did not have human smooth muscles and endocrine glands or hormones. Yet, when talking among themselves, those same programmers quietly and reluctantly admitted they were uncertain of what might actually be going on within parts of Lan's AI core matrix. Concerning that admission, they were indeed correct; they did not have a clue.

Sitting at his desk, onboard Lan in his quarters, Captain Kellon was analyzing the recent reports involving Kreel raiding on human commercial shipping between the eleven planets, he then paused to consider his error. With the discovery of the planet Earth two years earlier, there were now twelve known human-occupied planets, not eleven.

The interstellar war between the Kreel and humanity erupted several thousand years earlier, beginning with massive Kreel assaults on human-occupied planets. At the outset of the war, humanity was in shock and hard pressed, fighting from a strictly reactive and defensive posture. The initial surprise was when Kreel planetary raids had burnt out entire cities and killed millions of people, with desperately fought battles, waged at the fleet engagement levels. Lacking sufficient knowledge of the Kreel Empire, and not possessing the needed military power, Guardian Force was unable to carry the battle to the Kreel, instead in order to survive they strengthened their defensive capacity around each planet and held their ground.

Kellon was not alive when the war began; he was however among the small number of Guardian Force survivors who fought during the defense of the human-occupied planet named Quintana. Then he had personally witnessed the devastation the Kreel caused on a planetary scale, the burning of human-occupied cities, and the terrible death of several million people, including family and friends. After the carnage he witnessed on Quintana, Kellon's attitude toward the Kreel was steadfast and visceral. In his intense feelings, Kellon was not alone, and that the Kreel ate human beings explained only part of why people felt a deep-seated and fiery animosity toward the Kreel.

The ferocity of the war gradually abated only when the defensive capability of Guardian Force evolved to match the Kreel's offensive capability. Even so, humanity still lacked meaningful military intelligence concerning the width and breath of the Kreel Empire. Over the centuries, the war had transformed from fleet sized engagements to periodic hit and run Kreel raiding of humanity's interstellar commerce. Nevertheless, the fear of another Kreel planetary scale attack remained an ever-present concern on all the human-occupied planets.

With the Kreel raiding, there came the inevitable sharp and deadly clashes when patrolling Guardian cruisers encountered the marauding Kreel ships. Given the latest technological advances, consisting of the introduction of the new AI 'L'-Class cruisers into the active Guardian fleet, and the improvements of stealth warfare tactics, the Guardian Force was now firmly and steadily forcing the Kreel back onto the defensive.

Leaning back in his chair, Kellon looked up to the display screen above his desk, and stretching, he smiled. The displayed image was one of his favorites, showing Lan and his four Scouts proudly adorned in their bright white and gold parade colors.

Suspended behind them, poised in bright contrast to the darkness, were the images of the magnificent blue sphere of Earth and its single large moon. Although he had voyaged nearly one hundred light years to discover the Earth, he had not yet set foot on the planet. He was looking forward to a day when he might possibly again visit that incredible world and come to know better its multitudes of diverse people.

Since Kellon's discovery of the Earth, in Glas Dinnein's year 71,567 and the Earth year 2511, the historians' excitement on Glas Dinnein was steadily ramping up. Their initial findings supported Earth was the source planet, from which humanity had first sprung forth to settle other worlds; the current indications being humanity's first settlement was on Glas Dinnein. The gap in Glas Dinnein's own history, a gap that failed to explain how and where humanity had emerged to arrive on Glas Dinnein, had long remained an unanswered riddle. Now, with Kellon's discovery of Earth, the historians agree part of that abiding riddle might now actually be resolved, even if not the part pertaining to how or why. Frustratingly, there remained considerable ignorance regarding that tantalizing how and why.

Whenever Kellon looked at the image above his desk, he wondered about the mystery of humanity's ancient migration. Now, the historians were increasingly hopeful that Earth's rich history might help answer the riddle of just how humanity arrived on Glas Dinnein 70,000 years earlier.

When Lan and his crew had set out from Glas Dinnein three years before, on what had become a two-year journey, they had only the barest evidence of human beings living on a world in a solar system nearly one hundred light years distant. Guardian Force had detected, and then intercepted, a large and ungainly sub-light probe entering Tearman's heliosphere. The probe had precisely arrived at its intended destination after a very long journey, a journey requiring hundreds of years to make. The probe's precise programming neatly placed it into a solar orbit near Glas Dinnein. When excited scientists from Glas Dinnein conducted forensic examinations inside the probe, they discovered a trace of blood. DNA analysis confirmed the trace sample was that of human blood. The existence of an unknown human-occupied planet, nearly one-hundred light years distant, had motivated Guardian Force to send Kellon and Lan on their high-risk reconnaissance mission.

What Kellon and Lan had discovered when they reached Earth forever altered mankind's future, and everyone's awareness of the true history of humanity, while generating many unanswered questions. That mission was also the catalyst for a sharp decisive military clash between Kellon and a space-faring species that Guardian Force had never before encountered—the Arkillians.

Because of his battle with the Arkillians near Earth, and especially the choices he had made following that battle, Kellon was daily dealing with questions concerning what might become a second interstellar war, this time with the Arkillians. The very thought of a second on-going interstellar war, even with a species lacking super-luminal space travel, represented something Guardian Force did not want or need.

Kellon's underlying hatred of war in general had prompted him to extend mercy and not to destroy the Arkillian's Nest ship, when he could certainly have done so. His choice to extend mercy and offer to open a dialogue had granted the Arkillian survivors an opportunity to make battle repairs, if they could, and begin their long journey home– to the planet Scion. Pushing aside such thoughts, Kellon turned his attention back to his continuing analysis of recent Kreel attacks on commercial interstellar shipping. It was Kellon's immediate mission to interdict Kreel cruisers raiding near Glas Dinnein. They were now guarding a volume of space where Kreel incursion and commerce raiding was higher than normal. At that moment, Kellon and Lan's assignment was to ensure if any Kreel cruisers did intrude that they would not be around long enough to profit by their trespass.

Pushing back from his desk, Kellon stood and then stretched to ease the tightness in his body. He grudgingly acknowledged a need for a break from his analysis. Smiling, he remembered a book of Earth poems he had printed out and was enjoying reading. Walking over to his chair and its side-table he sat and recovered the book, opening it to the marked page. He then settled into reading for simple enjoyment.

Engrossed in the book as he was, Kellon lost track of time. When nudged by an awareness of a sense of hunger, he looked up from the book and glanced at the chronometer. *No wonder I'm feeling a bit hungry,* he thought, *it's well past mealtime.* Pausing a moment to reflect on what might fill his immediate need he smiled and requested, "Lan, please inform the wardroom that I would appreciate a flask of neab, and a hearty earth-style sliced roast meat sandwich with a small piece of sharp cheese."

Thinking about his ordering a sandwich brought him a smile. He considered his new friend Susie Wells, who was now Earth's Ambassador to the Planetary Assembly, to be a most remarkable young woman. Susie had introduced sandwiches to Glas Dinnein, as a delicious and convenient means of eating a nearly complete meal. There had been a few holdouts but Glas Dinnein's culinary circles recognized a good thing when they saw it and they now boosted sandwiches as being avant-garde. Thereafter people eating sandwiches spread like wildfire fanned by a strong wind.

Lan's resonant and vibrant response came promptly, "sir, your orders have been conveyed to the wardroom."

"Thank you Lan."

The book he was reading was a selection of poems from Earth's long bygone history. He thoughtfully turned back to the book of poems, while he waited for the food. He was reading again one of his favorites in the book, 'The Wonderful One-Hoss Shay'. Even though the author's use of language was not clear to him, he found the playfulness of the words appealing, eliciting a smile, and providing a momentary easing of his command burdens. No matter how old poetry is, or who wrote it, it is timeless, he thought.

> *Little of all we value here*
> *Wakes on the morn of its hundredth year*
> *Without both feeling and looking queer.*
> *In fact, there's nothing that keeps its youth,*
> *So far as I know, but a tree and truth.*
> *(This is a moral that runs at large;*
> *Take it. – You're welcome. – No extra charge.)*

As Kellon read the poem, he found he was not certain of the meaning of several words, and inquired, "Lan, please find in your Earth cross-index linguistics files the English word hoss, as it relates to the word shay."

Responding with a question, Lan asked, "Sir, as found in *The Deacon's Masterpiece*; or, *The Wonderful One-Hoss Shay* written by Oliver Wendell Holmes?"

"Correct Lan. That's the poem and its author. My question is whether the word hoss is just another word for a horse?"

"Sir, I do believe that—"

Cutting his sentence short, Lan reported, "Captain Kellon sir, I am receiving a ship distress alarm. Kreel ships are attacking a freighter inbound to Glas Dinnein!"

The door to his quarters firmly shut with a forceful thud behind him, as Kellon commanded, "Lan, cancel the neab and sandwich and suspend verbal responses."

Hurrying through Lan's suddenly crowded passageways Kellon moved toward the Combat Analysis Center. He was again feeling the old anger surging. *Not this time, and not on my watch,* he thought.

As Lan's battle stations alarm echoed and resonated throughout the cruiser, Lan was even then accelerating, while rolling into a tight turn, moving with an attitude toward the distant marauding Kreel ships. Like Kellon, Lan's mood was distinctly hostile and his core matrix was ablaze with activity. If they had been observing the AI programmers might have argued, since Lan had worked closely with Kellon for years Lan's apparent response was merely learned behavior. Yet the indisputable fact remained, lacking endocrine glands or otherwise, AI cruiser Lan was demonstratively angry.

Chapter Two:
No Quarter

When Kellon reached the Combat Analysis Center, Lan's fading battle stations warning was still echoing through the passageways. As the alarm sounds dwindled, everyone could hear and feel the deep rumbling resonance of the cruiser's propulsion system, it being like the sounds of a distant thunderstorm. Lan was expending enormous power in accelerating toward his identified enemies, the Kreel ships. As Kellon entered, a soft voice from the Combat Analysis Center's general announcing system spoke, "Captain now in CAC."

Moving into the CAC, Kellon scanned the information displayed on the various data screens, looking at the data in each quadrant. He frowned when noting the blinking golden icon in quadrant one. That blinking icon represented a superluminal ship and its human crew, a crew that was now struggling to remain alive. His anger flared at that thought, since he knew what the Kreel would do to those people, if the Kreel boarded the ship. Kellon murmured, "hold tight, help is on its way". Becoming aware of his increasing anger, he paused for a moment to focus consciously on controlling his sense of rage.

"Lan, transform the data being displayed in quadrant one; display it as a standard relative-motion tactical plot, with you at the center."

Turning toward Lan's executive officer and navigator, Kellon asked Commander Grey, "Roy, I need your status report, how much time do we have?" Even as he asked the question, his steel-grey eyes were continuing to scan the tactical display board. He saw the relative-velocity vectors indicated Lan was accelerating and on a direct intercept course with the ship under attack.

Looking at his notes, Commander Grey glanced up and replied, "Sir, Lan should be within tactical sensor range within another fifteen minutes."

"Roy, what do we know?" Kellon asked.

"Sir, the data packet bundled with the alert signal from the freighter reported four attacking Kreel ships, but did not specify Kreel ship classifications. The ship sending the alert is the Gola, identified as a general class freighter, with a crew of eighteen. She came under attack after exiting a long jump from Krista, and she is inbound for Glas Dinnein.

"The Gola reports it is remaining on course to Glas Dinnein and steadily losing ground to the Kreel, even though making her best possible speed." Feeling his anger bubbling up again, Kellon suppressed it, taking a deep breath and then letting it out in a long slow and controlled exhalation. Focusing on the tactical plot board, he asked, "Roy, what is the current tactical situation? Where are the nearest supporting Guardian Cruisers?"

"Sir, Lan is now operating in full stealth mode. At our current acceleration, our wake suppression is fifty-eight percent. Lan's combat status is Condition 3, shifting to Condition 2.

"Superluminal alerts and requests for support were dispatched to Guardian Operations and via beacons to the nearest two Guardian cruisers, those being Lent and Lar. Both cruisers are approximately two hours distant."

Turning, Kellon sat down in his command chair, and as he fastened his lap restraints, he observed the last remaining blue lights on Lan's status board had turned a soft gold hue. Lan's readiness was now at Condition 2; they were now battle-ready.

"Roy, the Kreel will undoubtedly overtake the Gola before either Lar or Lent can arrive. Gola's crew can't wait. We will move directly to attack those Kreel ships, regardless of their numbers or classification."

Roy looked over to Kellon, his expression serious, "Yes sir. We are now running in full stealth and battle-ready. As my dear mother would say, those Kreel ships have a gigantic problem heading their way."

Hearing Roy's light response, Kellon smiled, the edge of his anger subsiding. He and Roy had been friends and shipmates for a long time, and both well knew each other's capability and moods.

For several minutes, there was only the background murmur of the men and women attentive on their tasks at the various consoles around the room. Kellon studied the tactical plot board

8

as Lan continued moving to intercept, and observed as the slowly blinking icon representing the Gola and her crew moved steadily inward toward the center of the plot and the golden symbol representing Lan. Lan was getting near, no enemy ships were yet detected, and they still did not know what level of Kreel firepower they were about to encounter. Everyone in CAC knew it could be four cruisers or a dozen. The lack of tactical data for them to work with steadily fed their increasing tension.

"Tactical here," Lan's tactical officer's calm voice broke into the tense hush filling the CAC, "The distress beacon signal from the freighter has just gone silent."

The meaning of Commander Lorn Shaw's short and crisp battle update was clear; the Kreel had disabled the Gola and extinguished its beacon. As Lan moved toward the extrapolated position of the distressed ship, Kellon again scanned Lan's status board and confirmed they were fully prepared for battle.

In a steady voice, Commander Shaw crisply reported, "Tactical here, we are detecting Kreel ship-to-ship chatter. From their Doppler, they appear to be moving at a constant velocity."

Swearing inwardly, Kellon knew if multiple Kreel ships were running at a constant velocity, then they were no longer accelerating or making the type of maneuvers required to overtake and intercept the cargo ship. Given the cargo ship's drives went down when its beacon was extinguished it was then purely on a ballistic trajectory. The probability was the Kreel had already overhauled the disabled freighter and come alongside. That meant they were in the process of boarding. Kellon knew with a sinking feeling in his stomach that in all probability, men were even then dying onboard the Gola. His frustration at Lan's inability to prevent their deaths smoldered within him.

The Kreel were masters at efficiently stripping a ship of what they wanted and then evading the Guardian Force they knew would respond to the silenced alarm. That Lan was near to the ship under attack was a break, but that did not help the crew of the disabled freighter, and they might already be dead.

Feeling his anger mounting, Kellon swore an oath under his breath, *Not again. This time you will pay the full price. There will be no quarter!"* In a steady calm voice, Lorn continued with his terse updates.

9

"Tactical here, we have established Kreel propulsion classification. We have signatures on one Kreel cruiser of the Gortoga class and two of its scouts."

Frowning, Kellon mused, *there are no previous reports on Gortoga class cruisers involved in raiding.* Kellon looked over to where Lorn was working, and asked, "Tactical, Lorn, confirm Gortoga class."

Looking over to Kellon, Commander Shaw repeated, "Sir, confirming Gortoga class."

Guardian Intelligence rated the Gortoga cruisers the Kreel's best and there was no doubting their potential lethality.

Kellon ordered, "Lan, set three combat decoys to our twenty percent stealth profile. Deploy the decoys in a standard tactical spread, holding a relative position keeping location three-hundred kilometers off our starboard side."

Turning to Commander Shaw, Kellon cautioned, "Lorn, there should be one more scout ship somewhere, keep your eyes open for a sleeper. When that Gortoga cruiser observes us approaching, it will not have time to take its scouts aboard before it must elect to run or fight. It may be willing to sacrifice the scouts in order to buy its own escape. How fast is it?"

Without a pause, Lorn answered, "Sir, the Gortoga class is reported to be the Kreel's best. Fleet intelligence however lacks detailed information on its weapons configuration and acceleration profile. All we have are broad estimates. If the estimates are correct we may still have a twenty percent margin in acceleration." As Kellon studied the relative motion plot, he observed a red icon appear next to the blinking golden icon. He knew the red icon represented the Kreel cruiser, and Lan's tracking systems now showed it alongside the disabled cargo ship.

When Kellon saw three new golden icons appear offset from the icon showing Lan's position at the center of the relative plot, he nodded with approval. He knew the three deployed combat decoys were using holographic and countermeasure technologies. The Kreel commanders would detect visually and electromagnetically three rapidly approaching Guardian cruisers. The decoys' sole purpose was to misdirect the Kreel commanders, keeping them focused on the observable and apparent significant threats, and not on Lan, a single cruiser who was running nearby in full stealth mode.

Several more minutes crawled past. The frequent glances toward the tactical plot made by those in CAC reflected their increasing tension. "Tactical here, the Kreel have detected the inbound decoys and are maneuvering."

Noting the separation between the Kreel ship and the inbound decoys, Kellon frowned. *They are getting better. That detection range is at least ten percent greater than previously possible,* he thought.

"Tactical here, Captain, their scouts are spreading, slowly moving forward and deploying to meet the decoys. The cruiser is not running."

Shades of Tartarus, Kellon thought, *the appearance of three approaching Guardian Cruisers should be enough incoming firepower to cause that cruiser to break off and turn tail. Even the scouts are moving forward to engage. That should not be happening. What is so important here as to keep that cruiser from running? What is going on here?*

Kellon did not like what he was seeing, and promptly responded to the changing tactical problem. "Lan, direct the decoys to remain on our starboard side, but have them fall back to a new position two-thousand kilometers aft of their current relative tactical position. Transform their formation to a facing triangle."

Kellon noted Lan's response and low acknowledging tone. Still troubled by the Kreel's behavior, Kellon needed additional information. "Tactical, Lorn, what is the status of the freighter? What was her cargo?"

"Tactical here. Sir, the freighter is inert and following a purely ballistic course. Her cargo was general and included medical supplies."

Commander Grey looked up toward Kellon, but said nothing. Yet, the expression on his face clearly expressed his own increasing concerns. Seeing Roy's expression, Kellon asked, "Roy was there significant genetic material in those medical supplies?"

Looking down at his console, Commander Grey examined the display and made a few adjustments. After studying the data readout for a moment, he looked up again. "Yes sir," he replied, "There was whole blood and a wide assortment of genetic material among the medical supplies. In fact, the bulk of the medical cargo is of a genetic nature."

"Tactical here, the Kreel cruiser has separated from the freighter and is moving off and accelerating away. Its acceleration curve is ramping up. It is running and not engaging. It is abandoning its scouts. Sir, given its relative velocity and acceleration curve, we have it if you want it."

Kellon uttered a soft sigh. *That is better, the Kreel are conforming to the apparent tactical situation.* "Tactical, we want it, and will take it!"

"Fire Control, Kellon here. Obtain and keep a solid passive lock on that cruiser. Obtain passive locks on each of the Kreel scouts.

"Set three light missiles for passive homing. Set three additional light missiles for passive active homing, with enabling runs set to sixty percent of run length. Bring those six missiles to standby, Condition 2."

"Fire control here. Confirming three light missiles set passive. Three additional missiles set passive active, enabling runs set at sixty percent of run length. All missiles set Condition 2."

Beginning his firing-run, Kellon began assigning Lan's missiles to their targets. "Fire Control, confirm target locks, and target one passive active and one passive light missile at each of the detected Kreel scout ships. Upon reaching the closest point of approach to each scout, you are to set Condition 1 and launch missiles by salvoes of two."

Optimizing his probability of scoring hits on the Kreel scouts, Kellon had selected two light missiles directed at each scout. These missiles were small, fast, silent, and when striking Kreel scout-sized targets they were deadly. Kellon directed one missile to seek out the target purely by passively tracking the Kreel scout's own radiated signature. The second missile would also passively track the target for sixty-percent of its computed run length, and then it would switch to active homing, where it would use a generated laser pulse to obtain precise range and target dynamics required for guidance of its terminal homing. The probability of a Kreel scout evading both missiles was minimal to non-existent.

"Fire Control here, confirming passive locks on one cruiser and two scouts. acknowledging, at CPA to each scout, Fire Control is to set Condition 1, firing by salvoes of two missiles, one passive, and one passive active missile allocated to each scout."

Quickly scanning the tactical plot, Kellon did not see the third Kreel scout ship he expected was hiding. "Tactical, keep your eyes open for that sleeper!"

Kellon turned his attention to prosecuting his attack on the fleeing cruiser. "Lan, maintain the decoys' facing triangle formation. Bring them around the Gola; move them up slowly into a trailing position behind the Kreel cruiser.

Having allocated missiles against the identified Kreel scouts, Kellon began his firing run on the fleeing cruiser. "Fire Control, bring eight heavy missiles to standby, Condition 2. Target the Kreel cruiser. Set eight heavy missiles to passive active homing mode. Set the missiles to go active at eighty percent of run length."

Using eight Guardian Force heavy missiles assured Kellon of sufficient destructive capacity to destroy most Kreel cruisers. The heavy missiles were the primary offensive weapon deployed against Kreel cruisers, and they were capable of attaining high fractional speeds of light and traveling long distances. Running silently and utilizing elaborate terminal counter fire evasion strategies, they carried a devastating warhead. When they engaged a Kreel cruiser from the stern or abeam, the warhead was large enough to inflict massive damage, yet it was not always capable of destroying a Kreel cruiser. Where the missiles engaged a Kreel cruiser head-on, the missile warhead combined with the kinetic energy of the collision frequently was sufficient to destroy the largest Kreel cruiser.

"Fire Control here, acknowledging targeting Kreel cruiser with eight heavy missiles, passive active, enabling at eighty percent of run length."

It was then that a totally unbidden thought interrupted Kellon's focused chain of logic. *Consider* for a moment *strategic factors override apparent tactical factors. There is a better option than merely destroying the cruiser.* The intruding thought brought Kellon up short, yet given the unfolding dynamics of his attack, he did not hesitate to wonder about the possible source. His one reflective thought was, *Blast, standing orders plainly say destroy all raiding Kreel ships.* His anger was smoldering, but he suddenly remembered he had a strike capability his standing orders did not consider. For only the briefest moment did Kellon consider the probable personal consequences for his disobeying standing orders. Then, he threw out the tactical handbook of space warfare. *In for a gram, in for a kilogram,* he mused. *What will be, will be.*

"Lan, keep us clear of the Gola, and swing us up wide on the Kreel cruiser's port side. Bring us athwartships, with a CPA of seventy-five percent of effective heavy missile range."

Hearing Kellon's orders, Roy looked over toward Kellon, puzzled. He knew when pressing home an attack on a Kreel cruiser, Kellon rarely closed nearer than eighty-five percent of heavy missile effective range. Kellon was busy scanning the displays, making mental adjustments for the rapidly shifting tactical situation, and did not notice Roy's quizzical look.

"Fire Control, bring up the Kreel beam and prepare to fire on my command!"

Hearing Kellon's command, Roy looked up sharply, his blue eyes studying Kellon's face, but again he said nothing. Roy was Lan's executive Officer, and had served with Kellon on many missions. He fully understood what Kellon's last command meant, and understood the possible ramifications, including possibly a trial by court-martial.

Noting Roy's stern glance, Kellon knew, as his executive Officer, Roy fully understood The Arkillian Kreel beam weapon was a closely guarded Black Hole classified secret. Lan and Kellon had encountered the weapon the year before near Earth during their sharp battle with the Arkillians. It was one of many by-products of that earlier mission. The weapon's very existence was tightly compartmentalized and concealed. If he used the weapon here, Kellon and Roy both knew Guardian Command would hold Kellon personally accountable for all the consequences. Kellon had made his decision, personal consequences or not!

Following his orders, Lan was continuing to close on the fleeing Kreel cruiser. "Tactical here, the sleeper has been detected and localized. The third scout is moving slowly away from the freighter and toward our advancing decoys. It's maintaining a minimal signature profile."

14

"Fire Control," Kellon ordered, "Get a passive lock on that third scout. Target the remaining two light missiles on the sleeper. At CPA set Condition 1." It was time to bring the attack to its conclusion, and Kellon ordered Lan to take the direct path to the defined firing point.

"Lan," Kellon ordered, "Move us up smartly to the firing point on the cruiser."

Even as he gave Lan his orders, Fire Control reported, "First missiles away." Then less than a minute later, "Second missiles away."

Understanding He was about to use a Black Hole classified weapon, the last thing he wanted was the Kreel to have any chance whatsoever of reporting its effects.

"Countermeasures," Kellon ordered, "when the Kreel beam is fired, you are to simultaneously blanket the Kreel cruiser with a level one jamming field. I do not want any stray signals whatsoever to leak out, not even a squeak.

"If a signal is detected, if possible, give the ship coordinates of the transmitter's antenna to Fire Control.

"Countermeasures here. Confirming orders and standing by."

"Fire Control, set two point-defense laser turrets to track the Kreel ship, and immediately adjust the aim point of those lasers to any identified transmitter antenna, and lay down a short suppression pattern.

"Direct all remaining laser turrets to point-defense. Set Condition 1.

"Set all gun turrets to missile point-defense, Condition 1."

"Fire Control here, all lasers able to be brought to bear are set Condition 1. Gun turrets are set point-defense, Condition 1."

"Tactical here, light missiles are on targets. Missile impact, missiles have destroyed the two lead scouts. The sleeper is attempting to evade. Missile impact. Both missiles hit and destroyed the sleeper. Sir, all three Kreel scouts have been destroyed."

As ordered, Lan was moving directly to the designated firing point abeam of the Kreel cruiser and closing. Intently observing the forward bulkhead view screens, Kellon watched the magnified image as the aspect angle of the Kreel cruiser increased, its image lengthening and expanding.

As Lan drew abeam of the Kreel cruiser, Kellon looked over to Roy and asked, "Do you have any comments or recommendations?" Looking directly toward Kellon, and pausing for only a moment, Roy knew Kellon was fully aware of the potential consequences for what he was doing, "Captain, I believe you have considered all the options, and fully understand the possible ramifications of your decision, and its potential consequences. For the record, I have no recommendations, and I second your decision."

For a moment, Kellon looked at Roy's stern countenance. They had been shipmates for a long time, and there existed a strong bond of mutual respect between them. "Roy, thank you, however you don't need to also stick your neck out."

Breaking out in a broad grin, Roy responded, "I know, but as my dear mother always said, if you intend to do something rash, then at least do it with style."

Roy's grin was infectious, and smiling Kellon turned to study the image of the Kreel cruiser, noting it appeared outwardly to be of a graceful design. He had made his decision.

"Tactical here, Lan is now located at the designated firing point. All Kreel beam systems are on line, and they are charged and ready, Status 2."

Kellon did not hesitate. "Fire Control, transmit the Kreel beam, fire!"

There was a low building intense humming felt throughout Lan, and then the low thrumming vibration suddenly peaked and then was gone.

Watching the screen, Kellon did not note any obvious alterations in the Kreel cruiser's status. "Tactical, call out any observed variation in the target's behavior."

Taking inventory of his body, Kellon stopped holding his breath. Willing his breathing cycle into a slow deep rhythm, he mentally began the self-discipline process required to reduce his internal stresses. He had only one question. *Had the blasted beam worked?*

Studying the tactical displays, Kellon looked for any indication of the Kreel beam's effects and could not see any.

Turning back to navigation, he asked, "Roy, are you detecting any Kreel life signs on that cruiser?"

"Navigation here, no sir. There are no life signs now being detected; it's a flat line."

"Tactical here, the target is yawing off base course at a rate of 3.25 seconds of arc per minute. The target's acceleration has dropped to zero and its speed is holding at 73 lights."

Leaning back into his command chair, Kellon considered the tactical problem. *Given there were no Kreel life signs, the Kreel beam seems to have worked. Things could be much worse; the Kreel ship could have had more time to build its speed or its acceleration curve could have continued to ramp up. Given all the Kreel on that cruiser are dead, now what,* he mused.

Kellon fully understood a ship's velocity of 73 lights represented a speed of 0.073 of the speed of light. He knew coming alongside another ship in space traveling at any speed required consummate care. *Do I have the right to risk Lan and the entire crew by attempting a boarding?* He worried.

Looking around CAC, Kellon saw everyone had turned toward him, and were alertly waiting for his next orders.

"Lan, hold steady on our relative position with the Kreel ship." The fingers on his right hand extended to the control buttons located on the arm of his command chair. Switching to his command band Kellon addressed his staff officers, "Lorn, aboard Lan you have the most advanced training regarding this class of Kreel cruiser and Kreel technology. What do you recommend being the best way to board it?"

There was only a brief hesitation before Commander Shaw replied. "Sir, presuming the Kreel are incapacitated or dead, their ships are known to have an emergency external boarding access port in their aft control room. If we can come alongside, we should be able to gain access to the ship without great difficulty. The worst cases are we come along side and she then self-destructs, or we cut our way in and then find the Kreel armed and waiting for us."

Making his final decision on the matter, Kellon gave the prerequisite orders. "Lorn, prepare three full squads of boarders for close quarters combat. Stand ready to board that Kreel cruiser. Select a command crew for it, and get them ready. Give me five-minute updates."

"Yes Sir," Lorn promptly acknowledged. "Sir, do I have your permission to leave Tactical at this time?"

"Yes Lorn. As soon as you can designate your replacement, you have permission to depart."

There was one more thing Kellon knew he could do to minimize possible risk to Lan. He could put a tempting target alongside and see if he could provoke a response. "Lan, move one of the decoys parallel to the Kreel ship and park it twenty kilometers off her port side. Have the decoy transmit the Kreel parley signal and wait for a response.Then transmit a Black Hole secure combat status report to Guardian Command. Inform them we may have taken a Kreel Gortoga class cruiser undamaged and intact. Request Guardian Command send four additional cruisers to support our position. Request those reinforcements as soon as possible."

Overhearing Commander Grey's nearly inaudible whispered comment, "Or sooner if possible," Kellon smiled. Like Roy, he understood the Kreel cruiser was probably operating with other Kreel ships of a similar class. They would not be far distant. If they were to learn Lan was in the process of capturing intact one of their cruisers, they would immediately respond in fury. Like him, Roy understood this engagement could become real ugly and real soon. "Roy, do we have a status report from either the Lent or Lar regarding their estimated time of arrival?"

"No sir," Commander Grey responded. "However based on their last known position, their ETAs are perhaps still an hour out."

Considering his available options, and Roy's ETA for the supporting cruisers, Kellon knew because of the likelihood of other Kreel ships being in the tactical volume, he did not have an hour to squander before gaining access to the Kreel cruiser. "Roy, what is the status of the decoy off the cruiser's port beam?"

"Sir, there is no response to the parley signal, and still no observed activity or life signs on the Kreel cruiser."

Keying his command communications band, Kellon quickly outlined his intent. "Gentlemen, time is not on our side and we need to get this job done. We are going to deploy our Scouts to set up an outer warning screen and proceed to board the Kreel cruiser. This means Lan will be coming alongside the Kreel ship.

"Commander Shaw, Take command of the boarding operation. Make all preparations for accomplishing this feat. This is not a drill, and it will be accomplished by the numbers."

18

"Fire Control, reset your laser turrets to Condition 3; reset gun turrets to Condition 3; reset the heavy missiles to Condition 3."

Kellon reasoned that the Kreel cruiser's last course would have been toward other marauding Kreel ships, therefore he reasoned that would be the direction other Kreel ships would be approaching from. He needed as much warning of such Kreel ships as possible.

"Jason, are your Scouts ready for immediate deployment?"

Commander Greer's response was prompt and confident. "Sir, Lan's Scouts are prepared for immediate launch."

"Jason, deploy your Scouts. Move one Scout astern to monitor our back trail. Keep that Scout near enough to Lan to permit prompt recovery, should that become necessary. Send the remaining three Scouts forward along the Kreel cruiser's last course line. Spread them out to form an early warning screen. Maintain maximum stealth protocols and be ready for immediate recall and recovery."

"Yes Sir. Commander Greer acknowledging, Lan's Scouts are prepared to deploy as ordered."

"Lan, on Commander Greer's countdown, launch your Scouts. Shut down the Kreel parley signal. Pull that forward decoy back to join the remaining decoys. Then increase their stealth profile to maximum and proceed with their recovery."

As Lan proceeded with his orders, everyone knew the risks involved, understanding any mistakes could prove fatal to Lan and everyone on board.

"Captain," Lorn reported over the command band. "Sir, using optics the Kreel access on the port side is now identified, and it's marked in Lan's database. The boarding party is in armor, armed, assembled and ready to board. The debarkation compartment is at space vacuum. The selected command crew is cross-trained and fully qualified in Kreel languages and technology. They are waiting in the wings and ready to follow the boarding party at first opportunity. Sir, we are ready to go."

Kellon listened to Lorn's confident tone and felt the contrasting emotions of pride in his crew, and a corresponding feeling of determination not to fall short in doing his own job. He knew all their lives depended on everyone accomplishing their assigned tasks.

"Lan, deploy the starboard hull standoffs. Align your starboard debarkation bay port with the indicated Kreel emergency port that is marked in your database. Match intrinsics, and then bring us alongside that Kreel cruiser. Execute."

Lan's soft acknowledgment tone responded.

For the next forty minutes, the tensions continued to build in the CAC, as Lan maneuvered to come alongside of the Kreel cruiser. Kellon carefully watched the forward displays, observing the Kreel ship grow steadily larger until its image filled the entire screen.

"Lorn, we are moving alongside. When Lan firmly attaches to the cruiser, extend the boarding chute. When your boarding party enters, secure the adjacent compartments and work to the forward bridge. This is a no quarter action! Repeating, this is a no quarter action!"

Replying evenly, Lorn acknowledged, "Understood. This is a no quarter action."

Chapter Three:
Tactical Conference

Roy's voice held a positive note, as he reported, "Captain, we have an update from the Cruiser Lar, he is ten minutes out and coming in with all burners on high and set Condition 2. As yet, there is no contact with the Cruiser Lent."

"Roy, instruct Communications to set up a hard data link with Lar as soon as possible. Feed him all our tactical data, and obtain a reciprocal data link."

As Lan matched intrinsics and came near to the Kreel cruiser, those in CAC found themselves glancing repeatedly toward the video display located on the forward bulkhead, where the image of the massive Kreel cruiser was now filling the screen. Each of them knew that ship was capable of inflicting massive destruction on a vast scale, and while instrumentation indicated the Kreel were dead, there remained a deep-seated concern that some Kreel might still be alive. Did the Kreel ship have any automatic self-destruction protocols? No one knew, and there was no existing knowledge base to evaluate what automatic triggers might exist to initiate self-destruction.

As Lan drew near the Kreel cruiser, his exposure to counterfire steadily increased, and the advantages gained from superior stealth technology became meaningless. Everyone understood a Guardian ship had never before come alongside a Kreel warship, and as Kellon steadily moved Lan into an exposed position, everyone knew their lives were in jeopardy. Regardless of his or her rank or training, the crew on Lan was tense, and especially so Kellon; his decision to accept the risk associated with boarding the Kreel cruiser bore down heavily on him.

After more than forty minutes of Lan's maneuvering, there came a distinct reverberating thump and jarring throughout Lan, the starboard standoffs having physically encountered the Kreel warship's hull, the vacuum clamps solidly engaging and holding the two ships bound firmly together. With that solid physical contact, the entire CAC team let out a noticeable collective sigh, they were actually alongside a Kreel cruiser, and best of all they were still intact and alive.

Lorn's strong voice began reporting on the internal communications band, his crisp statements coming in short precise phrases. "We are suited up and ready. Debarkation port is opening. Boarding chute is extending. We have a hard seal with the Kreel ship's hull. I am examining the Kreel emergency port external controls. They look like the standard Kreel nomenclature."

There followed a long pause, and Kellon found himself leaning forward in his command chair and unintentionally holding his breath; time seemed to stop. In the brief silence, Kellon mentally chewed on the immediate problem they faced. *Can we actually gain an easy access into that ship through its emergency hatch?*

"Sir, I was able to identify and actuate the opening sequence. The hatch is responding and the safety interlocks are now disabled. The Kreel port is swinging open, and our armed boarding party is moving into the ship's lock. We have atmospheric pressure in the lock. Inner hatches are opening."

Forcing himself to exhale slowly, Kellon's hands were holding his arm rests in a tight grip. When that inner hatch opened, would they find armed Kreel waiting for them? For the next few moments, there followed only the sounds of Lorn's breathing, and the background sounds of some intense physical exertion.

"Captain." Lorn's voice broke the silence, it was crisp and tense. "We have entered the engineering compartment. All the Kreel in the after control are dead. I have directed an armed boarding team into the adjacent engineering compartments. The remainder of the armed boarding party is moving forward, and I am moving with them."

Consciously regulating his breathing into a slow even rhythm, Kellon was still tense and mentally concerned about possible Kreel survivors and especially the possibility of a warning alert between the Kreel cruiser and other Kreel ships. His unanswered question was, *Had the beam killed all the Kreel instantly?* "Lorn, what are your first impressions about the Kreel? Did they drop where they were, or does it appear they were conscious for some time before dropping? Could they have sent out a warning to other Kreel ships?"

There was a brief pause before Lorn replied. "Sir, the position of the Kreel bodies indicates their death was nearly instantaneous, each Kreel seems to have fallen at his duty station."

After a slight additional pause, Lorn continued his reports, the sound of his breathing punctuating his short comments. "Sir, we are again on the move. There are Kreel bodies lying in the passageways. None is alive. We are continuing forward. We have located the communications center, I am now securing their transmitters."

Again, the sounds of Lorn's breathing followed, and several minutes passed before he resumed his report. "Sir, the ship's communications systems are now offline and secured. All Kreel encountered in communications are dead at their duty positions. My evaluation of this scene is that no warning messages were sent after the Kreel beam was discharged."

"Lorn, Kellon here. That's good and welcomed news."

Turning toward the Countermeasures team, Kellon ordered, "Countermeasures, Kellon here. Terminate all jamming."

Once more, Lorn's steady updates flowed through the intercom band. "We are moving forward. We have reached the forward end of the passage; the control center must be up on the next level. We are backtracking to the nearest stairway.

"The armed boarding party is advancing up the stairs." Lorn's labored breathing accompanied his advance with the armed boarding team. "Sir, the aft security team reports they have secured the engineering compartments, and the Kreel are all dead. We have reached the next deck up, and we are moving forward. The only Kreel we are encountering on this level are also dead, there appear to be no survivors.

"We're continuing to move forward. Sir, I believe we are finally there. Confirming we have reached the main control room and it's somewhat larger than I expected.

"Sir, the elaborate harness on one of the Kreel bodies is literally encrusted with jewels and medallions; it must be the Captain. Given the amount of gems and meritorious awards on his command harness, He must have ranked pretty high among the Kreel.

There came a brief pause, and the only sounds Kellon could hear was the background conversations of the security team that was onboard the Kreel cruiser. After several minutes, Lorn resumed his report.

"Sir, I have been looking this place over. It is larger than I expected, and I don't have a clue about the purpose of some of the equipment. The control room is not as any other I have ever seen, yet much of the ship's controls are recognizable. I have ordered the boarding B team to bring the command crew here on the double. It may take some time to clear out the Kreel bodies and figure out what we have."

It was Kellon's turn to release a long held sigh. *As improbable as the odds at first suggested, we are in control of a Kreel Gortoga cruiser,* he thought. *Now, all we need do is figure out how to operate the blasted thing and get it underway.* "Lorn, nicely done. I caution you that I do not know how much time we have before I might need to break away. We are still anticipating unhappy and fighting mad Kreel ships arriving shortly. Do not let any moss grow on your backside."

"Yes Sir. I understand." Lorn acknowledged.

Although the command team was on board the Kreel cruiser, the tension in the CAC remained high, everyone believing more Kreel ships were nearby. Each minute that passed stretched, seeming like ten minutes.

"Captain, Shaw here, the Command crew is now in the after control and engineering spaces and also in the forward control room. We are working to figure out the ship's normal operational controls. We should have this worked out shortly, perhaps another fifteen minutes. The engineering team reports they have adjusted the internal atmosphere and gravity controls for human normal. Unfortunately, they haven't yet found a way to get rid of the stench of Kreel in these compartments.

"The aft emergency boarding hatches are closed and secured. I have placed armed guards strategically in the ship to protect key control areas, and I ordered a compartment-by-compartment security search of the ship. This may be overly cautious, but I would rather be safe than sorry."

Again becoming aware of his own inner tension, Kellon consciously set about relaxing his tight muscles, while reminding himself to maintain a regular breathing cycle. Even so, the next few minutes moved like cold tree sap on a spring morning.

Lorn's next report broke the silence. "Sir, we have navigation and basic ship controls worked out; normal navigation and propulsion is understood, however I wouldn't want to enter Jump any time soon. You can close up and break away at this time. We will however need an escort, if we are not to be shot on sight when arriving in home port."

Shaking his head and smiling, Kellon appreciated Lorn's levity, especially given his task. "Lorn, good point. I'll see what I might do to get you home safe, and without you being shot full of holes. I am pulling Lan back, and giving you wide-open space in which you can maneuver and get the feel of that ship.

"Roy, see that the boarding chute is retracted and the debarkation port is secured.

"Lan, as soon as the debarkation port is secured, move us off and away from the prize. We're dealing with a green crew, so let's give them some wide maneuvering room."

"Captain," Roy reported, "the boarding chute is retracted and we are buttoned up.

"Sir, the Cruiser Lent is reporting he is now about fifteen minutes out and is set full stealth and Condition 2.

"Our communications link with Cruiser Lar is now established, and we are in full tactical synchronization."

"Roy, connect Captain Kylster on Lar to my Captain's band." After a momentary pause, the Captain of Lar responded, with camaraderie and good humor tempering the seriousness of his voice.

"Captain Kellon, given your tactical update, it seems you've been rather busy. Frankly, I'm delighted I don't need to write your mission report to Admiral Mer Shawn. I imagine you will have some fun attempting to explain your rather unorthodox tactics and unique method of coping with a raiding Kreel cruiser. I would wager a cold brew your action report will cause you some headaches and provide the good Admiral with some interesting reading. Now, just how might Lar best assist Lan?"

"Good morning Captain Kylster, it is good to see you here and in such a cheerful mood. I'll not take that wager, since most of my reports to Admiral Mer Shawn are rather dry and filled with lots of boring numbers. Your arrival however is quite opportune; I was admittedly feeling a bit lonely. Be assured, Lar's arrival is both timely and welcomed. As to how you might help, there is an urgent need to see that Commander Shaw and his boarding team get safely to Glas Dinnein. Would Lar like to provide an armed escort for our little prize?"

"Kellon, some day you will need to tell me just how you managed to take your prize. I suspect that is a story worth hearing. In the meantime, Lar is pleased and happy to extend to Lan his cooperation and will gladly provide the requested escort service. Precisely where should Lar escort your prize?"

"Captain Kylster, I believe this area will soon become very crowded and hotly contested. I recommend Lar take a straight path to Glas Dinnein, while requesting Admiral Mer Shawn to provide his opinion concerning precisely where best to dock the prize. I believe the sooner Lar and the prize are out of here the better."

"Understood, and I agree. Well done Kellon. Be assured, Lar will properly escort your prize. Given the nature of the prize, I'll even wager a cold brew Admiral Mer Shawn will see we have friendly company joining us on the way home. What are your intentions now?"

"Kylster, the Cruiser Lent is almost on station, and I still have the problem of seeing to the freighter. Lan needs to determine if there are any Kreel or survivors aboard it. When Lent arrives, I will request him to provide a protective umbrella, while Lan conducts the investigation. Captain Kylster, Lan extends his compliments to Lar and to his entire crew. Rest assured that Lan will send Lar engraved invitations to any future parties. Kellon out.

Kellon glanced at the bulkhead chronometer and winced, every instinct shouted more Kreel were inbound. He keyed his command band, and gave his orders to Lorn. "Lorn, you have full Command of the prize. Head it for home. Captain Kylster and the Lar have agreed to provide safe escort. I recommend you determine how to get the best legs on it that you can, and promptly clear out of this area."

"Understood Captain, we are getting underway," Lorn responded.

"Good luck, Lorn. Again, well done to everyone. I will see you as soon as we make home port."

Kellon sat back in his command chair and observed the visual screen as Lar and the captured Kreel cruiser smoothly accelerated and moved off toward distant Glas Dinnein. He could feel the stress release, and took a deep breath. As he observed the departing Gortoga cruiser he could not help but remember the unknown Arkillian commander who had months before used the Kreel beam near Earth. He had acted in a desperate but vain attempt to capture a Gortoga class cruiser. That unknown commander had been desperate and he might have pulled it off, if only his intended target was a Gortoga cruiser and not a Guardian combat decoy masquerading as a Kreel cruiser. Thoughtfully remembering the incident, Kellon inwardly saluted that unknown Arkillian commander, and wondered if he had survived the battle that followed.

Dismissing his reflections of a prior battle, turning toward Navigation Kellon saw Roy watching him, and saw he was smiling. "Captain, we actually did it. We came alongside a Kreel cruiser, boarded it, and captured it undamaged. We actually did it, and we are still alive. I think we did surprisingly well. At least, my dear mother would be gratefully surprised; however I can't speak for Admiral Mer Shawn."

Like Roy, and the others, Kellon felt a strange sense of wellbeing. They had done what was for many good reasons, long considered impossible, and survived. They had yet to survive the anticipated thunder and lightning from on high, because of his disregard of long standing orders, but dealing with Admiral Mer Shawn's punishment was tomorrow's problem. "Roy, yes, we did it. well done and thank you. Now, we have more work to do. Assemble an engineering team and the remaining squad of boarders. We are going back to find out what the Kreel have done to the Gola. Also, if you have one, please give me an update on Lent's estimated time of arrival."

"Yes Sir," Roy acknowledged.

Kellon looked around the CAC, and noticed the mood of the CAC team was more relaxed, and he personally fully understood just why they were more at ease. "Lan, bring us about and move us near to the Gola so we can get a close look at her damage."

"Captain," Roy reported, "Lent reports he will be on station in four minutes. He has requested a tactical update."

"Roy, provide Lent a hard tactical link. Inform Lent we would appreciate his providing Lan a protective umbrella as we examine the freighter. Be certain they are informed we have four Scouts out and are expecting hostile visitors."

"Navigation here, Captain, Lent has acknowledged Lan's request, and he will provide the requested protection. Lent is also launching his Scouts, and he is acknowledging a tight Tactical link." As Lan came about and moved toward the Gola, Kellon sat back reviewing what he needed to accomplish. He still felt the deep anger when thinking about the Kreel killing the freighter's crew. *Perhaps,* he thought, *Lan's prompt arrival managed to save the crew. At least, that cruiser isn't going to attack and kill anyone else.*

Looking up with a smile, Roy reported. "Sir, Fleet Operations has confirmed they've directed Cruiser Lawrence to join Lent in providing additional support for Lan. Lawrence is reporting he is seventeen minutes out, and is ready for a fight."

"Captain Kellon," came a familiar feminine voice over the inter-ship captain's conference band, "Captain Eurie here. Lent will be taking a position forty kilometers from the freighter's position and on line with the Kreel cruiser's last course. Do you have any further requests?"

Just hearing Eurie's voice brought a slight smile to Kellon's countenance; Eurie was a delightful person, a good and trusted friend, and a highly qualified cruiser Captain. Switching to the inter-ship captain's conference band he responded, "Captain Eurie, it is good to have Lent's protective umbrella. I recommend you maintain maximum stealth. Lan will be dropping his stealth profile to twenty percent, as he approaches the freighter."

There was a slight tone of amusement in Eurie's voice as she responded, "Captain Kellon, are you suggesting Lan is about to offer the Kreel target services?"

Kellon smiled. "Not if Lent is on station and doing his job. I am merely offering a small teaser while doing a necessary task. I am guessing that any Kreel contingency arriving will be wondering what has happened to their missing cruiser. Clearly, it is nowhere about here and obviously there is no large debris field showing we have destroyed it. It is all a big mystery, and they may simply want a piece of Lan, if they believe they can take it."

"Captain Kellon," came her purring response, "capturing an undamaged first-line Kreel cruiser intact is a most unusual feat. Thinking back, I don't remember anyone ever having previously captured a Kreel cruiser. I suspect you are keeping bad company with some heretic tacticians. However, I must admit your twenty percent stealth approach to space combat is both unorthodox and exciting. Perhaps in a future moment of brevity on Glas Dinnein, we might have an opportunity to enjoy a glass of wine together. Then you can tell me all about it."

Kellon chuckled at her retort. "Why Captain Eurie, are you asking me for a date?"

Eurie's voice took on a charming tone, "Be advised Lent is on station and your backsides are very well covered, Captain Kellon. Lent's Scouts are moving out to augment Lan's Scouts, and we will give you as much warning as possible. Lawrence is reporting he is twelve minutes out and running at full stealth and Condition 2. Be assured I will see you on Glas Dinnein, and we will then quietly discuss precisely who is asking whom for a date. Eurie out."

Still smiling, Kellon returned his attention to the immediate tactical problem. "Roy, please look at the visual screen and tell me what you think about the apparent damages to the freighter. What did they hit her with?"

"Captain, I do not see any battle damage from here. The only anomaly seems to be the access that they cut in her outer hull. There is minor nearby debris, most likely resulting when the Kreel detached, opening the compartment to hard space. I estimate this occurred when the Kreel cruiser detached from the freighter's hull and moved away. At present, sensors indicate its internal power system and drive are at zero."

"Roy, The missing Kreel cruiser is not the only mystery we have. It may well be we arrived on scene before the Kreel could destroy the evidence of what they were up to. Do we have any life signs or suspicious electronic signatures, anything that might indicate the Kreel set a trap for the unwary?"

"Sir, there are several human life signs, but not enough to account for the full crew. There are no Kreel life signs. No anomalous electronic signatures are being detected."

Continuing to observe the freighter on the forward display screens, Kellon felt his anger rising again. The Gola looked cold and very dead. He did not like to see a good ship in such a hard condition. *At least,* he thought, *the Kreel who attacked the Gola were not going to attack anyone else, ever, and there are at least some survivors.*

"Roy, who is leading the boarding party?"

"Captain, I have assigned Lieutenant Oster to head the overall operation and engineering group. Lieutenant Shem is heading the initial security party. They are instructed to move by the numbers."

"Roy, connect Lieutenant Oster's COM link to the command band, and open the channel.

Waiting for several moments, permitting Roy to complete the connection, Kellon still felt his inner anger. Survivors yes, but not the entire crew. He remembered Lorn's ordering a compartment-by-compartment check on the Kreel cruiser, and sighed, knowing what they might find. *Perhaps we might yet find the bodies of the missing crew on the freighter,* he thought, *that would at least soften the reality of their deaths.*

"Lieutenant Oster, this is Captain Kellon. Your COM link is now on the command band. We do not have any idea of what happened to the crew of the ship. The Kreel appear to have deployed some form of energy device to nullify the ship's power, propulsion, and crew. Our sensors do not indicate any Kreel remain on board, but indicate possible survivors. Use extreme caution. Proceed with the expectation that there may be booby traps, or even remaining armed Kreel."

"Yes, Sir. Lieutenant Shem and our first onboard team are now suited up and reporting ready to depart. Waiting for your orders." "Lieutenant Oster, the boarding party is cleared to depart Lan."

"Yes Sir," Lieutenant Oster acknowledged.

"Sir, the first boarding party is away," Roy reported.

Turning toward the video screen on the forward bulkhead, Kellon and others within CAC watched as the screen display showed three lifter disks, each carrying three suited and armored men, emerge from Lan and move swiftly toward the gaping hole in the distant freighter's side. Surrounded by the immensity of space, with the inert bulk of the freighter hanging in the distance, the men appeared incredibly vulnerable—small and fragile.

Lan would continue to stand well off, until the first boarding team completed their initial survey of the disabled ship and signaled it was safe for Lan to approach. Understanding the substantial risks involved in making such a boarding, Kellon was aware of the courage such a boarding action required of those men riding on a simple lifter disk, when going into harm's way.

As they observed, the first lifter disk arrived at the freighter and its occupants quickly moved through the dark gaping hole in the ship's hull and disappeared within. Kellon knew Lieutenant Shem was the first man through that dark open wound in the ship's hull, and as Captain he would personally enter a corresponding notation in the Lieutenant's and the other eight men's personnel records. After a momentary pause, the remaining six men quickly followed and disappeared within the ship's silent bulk.

"Sir, Lieutenant Oster here. Lieutenant Shem's boarding party is continuing its initial sweeps for explosives. They are reporting no contact or indication of Kreel onboard."

Another eight minutes passed slowly as the boarding party completed its survey. Then Lieutenant Shem sent an all-clear signal.

"Lan, recover your lifters. Align the debarkation port with the opening in the freighter's hull. Extend the hull stand-offs and proceed to bring us alongside. Reduce our stealth profile to twenty percent."

A few minutes later, Lan's extended hull stand-offs made contact against the freighter's hull with a resounding thump. With a noticeable jar, Lan's vacuum clamps firmly secured the freighter. Almost at once, Lieutenant Oster began giving orders. "Debarkation port opening and transfer chute is extending. We have a solid seal. Engineering boarding party away."

As the boarding party entered the compromised compartments, and they separated into several groups, one moved forward and the second moved aft. They began a search of each compartment they encountered in the compromised areas of the ship. The engineering team promptly began rigging a temporary airtight patch over the damaged portion of the freighter's hull. As they worked, Kellon kept one eye on the tactical display board with a growing sense of apprehension, his every instinct proclaiming they were about to have company.

"Captain, the Cruiser Lawrence is now on station and has established hard tactical links with Lent and Lan," Roy reported. "Captain Kel of the Lawrence sends his compliments. They are moving to take protective flanking positions forty kilometers from Lan, offset from the Kreel cruiser's last course. Lent and Lawrence are both reporting full stealth and Condition 2."

"Captain," Oster reported, "we have spliced into the ship's internal COM link and there are seven survivors holding up in the forward bridge area, and it is still air tight. We have a problem, since they do not have space suits and the adjacent compartments remain compromised.

"We have a temporary patch in place and are now attempting to fill the adjacent compartment with some heat and a minimum atmosphere, where they can safely put on emergency space suits. "Our search of the remaining compartments is continuing. I estimate we will have the area swept clean within fifteen minutes." "Lieutenant Oster, what is the status of the power and propulsion systems?"

"Sir, my engineers are now in the power and propulsion compartments and beginning their examination and recovery of available records. On first cursory glance, there is no apparent damage to the propulsion or power systems."

Turning from his navigation console with a quick movement, Roy reported, "Captain, we have visitors! Lan's advanced Scouts report they have three Kreel Gortoga class cruisers inbound. They are running with sensors active at 130 lights, and they are prosecuting an intense search pattern. Given Lan's twenty percent stealth configuration and their progress, I am estimating they will detect Lan in thirty minutes. What are your orders?"

"Roy, pass to our Scouts, and advise Lent and Lawrence, the Scouts are to maintain full stealth and begin to pull back toward our position. They are not to engage. They are only to continue providing observations."

Shaking his head, Kellon considered his next actions. There had never been a full-scale engagement with the new Gortoga class cruisers, and their full combat capability remained unknown. The information on the freighter was important, but he would not put his men onboard at risk of abandonment to the

Kreel. The problem was they had not yet answered the question of how the Kreel disabled the freighter. Whatever technology was involved it could certainly pose some nasty consequences, if the Guardian Force was not prepared to meet it.

Blast it, Kellon thought; *we need at least another hour to complete a truly detailed sweep of the freighter. We are not likely to get it without first engaging the Kreel.*

"Lieutenant Oster this is Kellon. Be advised you have a maximum of fifteen minutes to complete your activities and return to Lan. We have hostile company headed this way. Can you patch me into the shipboard COM system, so I can speak to the survivors? Also, who is the senior ranking survivor?"

"Captain, we will be wrapped up and on board Lan within fifteen minutes. It will not be necessary to patch you into the freighter's COM system; the Gola's Captain is here in a space suit as are six of his crew. I am switching his suit COM link to your command band. You should have direct communications at this time."

There came a slight pause, and Lieutenant Oster's voice dropped to a hushed tone. "Sir, I regret to report, we didn't find any of the bodies of the missing eleven crewmembers; the Kreel must have taken them."

The news about the missing crew rekindled his anger; yet, he did not have time to dwell on the matter; instead, he focused on what he could do. "Captain, my name is Kellon and I am in command of the Guardian Cruiser Lan. I have several questions I need to ask you."

"Yes, Sir, I will be happy to answer any question I can."

"Captain, are you aware of what the Kreel ship used to incapacitate you?"

"Well, Captain Kellon, that is a bit hard to answer. We were running somewhat scared, and I was directing our efforts to maximizing our velocity toward Glas Dinnein. I am certain you fully understand why. Then I felt abruptly dizzy and that is all I remember until about an hour ago. When I woke, it was very cold and the ship was without power and adrift. I really do not have much more that I can tell you, except that I have a planet-sized headache."

"Captain, there is one more question. Were you using a dead-man's switch on your power and propulsion systems?"

"Well, Sir, there would not have been any need for that type of protection under normal conditions. However, we were maximizing our propulsion system, and we were running well into our power and propulsion's red zones. I therefore ordered the use of a dead-man's switch. I hope that helps you."

"Captain, it certainly does help. Please do all you can to speed up the evacuation of your crew to the Lan. We have a sizable Kreel force approaching our position, and we will need to break off and prepare to engage the Kreel."

Frowning, given the Captain's comments, Kellon realized the Kreel cruiser had employed an Arkillian technology to incapacitate the Gola. That revelation meant Guardian Cruisers and Scouts were now vulnerable. "Roy, send a secure combat status urgent message to Guardian Command. Inform them that the Kreel are now using a stun beam capable of knocking out a ship's crew. It is critical that Operations alert guardian ships to implement all defensive screen upgrades, particularly modification ARK-701.

"Roy, next patch me into a link up with our Scouts and the Lent and Lawrence."

"Sir, the Scouts and both Lent and Lawrence are now patched in to the command band."

"This is Captain Kellon. I have just talked with the surviving Captain of the freighter. What took them out was apparently a Kreel energy stun beam. All Scouts are to continue falling back to their parent ships and are not to engage. I repeat– they are not to engage. Lan's Scouts are to prepare for immediate recovery upon return.

"Captains Eurie and Kel, please check your defensive screen upgrades. Verify you have implemented the upgrade to incorporate ARK-701. Please advise me if you have this screen upgrade complete and tested."

There was a minute of silence, before there was a response. "Lent has the upgrade implemented and tested."

"Lawrence here, the specified upgrade is implemented and tested." Captain Kel's concerned voice continued, "Captain Kellon, can you amplify on the purpose for this upgrade? The specifications are rather vague."

"Captain Eurie and Captain Kel, that you have implemented the upgrades is indeed fortunate. Lan was on a long-range

34

reconnaissance some months ago. During that patrol we encountered an alien energy beam weapon that is capable of completely stunning a ship's entire crew. From what we have learned from the freighter's Captain, the Kreel now have that weapon, and they used it to incapacitate the Gola's crew. All I can say here is that it is an expansion on the earlier Kreel pop patterns. The screen upgrade I mentioned is vital in any upcoming Kreel engagement. Every attention to its immediate integration and full implementation into your defensive screens is mandatory."

Eurie's response was immediate. "Kellon, that may explain what happened to the freighter's crew. It doesn't, however, explain what shut down their power and propulsion systems."

"Captain Eurie, the freighter's propulsion was forcibly operating in the red zone, and the Captain ordered it controlled with a dead-man switch. When the Kreel beam knocked out the crew, the dead-man switch opened, and the power and propulsion systems went off-line. We will undoubtedly soon be engaged in battle. Are there any more questions? If not, may I suggest it is time for a tactical conference, on how we are going to address the increasing Kreel problem in our neighborhood."

Chapter Four:
Basket of Snakes

Admiral Ron Cloud opened the door without knocking and briskly entered into the inner sanctum of his old friend and colleague. He found him sitting at his desk frowning with distaste and looking through a large and orderly pile of official looking documents. Like Admiral Cloud, Admiral Mer Shawn was wearing the standard comfortable shipboard duty uniform of the Guardian Force. However, his collar rank tabs indicated he was the Fleet Admiral of the Guardian Force.

The office was spacious and warmly appointed. The walls paneled in deeply grained and beautifully finished wood, deep carpets, and a large dark highly polished wood desk fitted with an oversized executive top. On the walls were several pictures of a few older Guardian ships, and several of the newest. There was one large photograph showing Glas Dinnein as seen from space, the outlines of her largest continent vividly demarked by the oceans that bless the planet. One wall was floor to ceiling and wall-to-wall glass that looked out and over the nearby hills, forests and coastline; however, Admiral Mer Shawn had drawn the sheer curtains closed, suffusing and softening the light entering the office.

Approaching the man behind the desk, Ron smiled broadly and intoned with warmth, "Good morning Mer."

Admiral Mer Shawn looked up and smiled, responding with a sigh. "Ron, thank you for distracting me from the mundane detail that often comes with this thankless job."

Ron chuckled, and then taking one of the nearby chairs, the tone of his voice became serious. "Well Mer, be assured I come bearing news about something not at all mundane. Captain Kellon and Lan have ignited a fast burning fuse to a powder keg and have called home for reinforcements."

With the mention of the word "reinforcement," all merriment in Mer's expression disappeared. "Ron, isn't your granddaughter Elayne assigned to Lan?"

Leaning back, Ron settled into the comfortable chair. "Yes, that's correct. As you know, she was part of Lan's crew when they discovered Earth, and since then she has remained with Lan. She has forbidden me to tell anyone of our relationship, since she feels if anyone knew her Grandfather is Guardian Force Chief of Intelligence, it might alter how she is treated. I do not even believe Captain Kellon is aware of the relationship."

As Mer picked up his warm cup, he asked, "Ron would you like a cup of neab?"

"Thank you Mer, for the offer, but I have already had about twenty cups during the past two hours, and another cup would definitely set my nerves blazing.

"Mer, I am here because Lan has asked for immediate reinforcement. He's requesting four additional cruisers be directed to support him. I'm here, because only you have the authority to commit five cruisers to any single action. You should also know that I am in agreement with Lan's request."

As he listened to Ron's request, Mer put down his cup and turned, squarely facing him. "Lan is asking for me to send four Cruisers to support him?" The tone of Mer's voice mirrored his increasing concerns. "Ron, what type of battle is Kellon mixed up in? Are the Kreel or Dargon making a move in force?"

Meeting Mer's eyes, Ron took a deep breath, and responding to Mer's direct question, he began his briefing. "No, Mer. The Kreel or Dargon are not moving in force. At least not yet. Kellon has however created a volatile situation. As I have said, he has ignited a short fuse to a powder keg. For the past two hours, I have been in Guardian Operations and monitoring the evolution of the problem. Because of Kellon's request for additional cruisers, I am now passing the problem up to you."

Raising his hand, Mer halted Ron's briefing. "Handing off what matter? Ron, start at the beginning. What is the problem we are talking about?"

Sighing, Ron paused, considering what he was trying to say, and began again. "Sorry Mer, from the beginning then. About two hours ago the cargo ship Gola exited a Jump from Krista and was inbound to Glas Dinnein. When exiting from her long Jump,

38

beyond Tearman's heliosphere, the Gola came under attack from four Kreel Ships. She promptly sent out an alarm and ran at best possible speed for Glas Dinnein. Lan was the nearest Guardian Cruiser, and was therefore the first Cruiser to come to Gola's aid.

"When Lan responded, following standard procedure, he requested the two nearest Guardian Cruisers move to back him up. Those two supporting Cruisers are Lent and Lar.

"As Lan approached the Gola the ship was already disabled and inert. The attacking force consisted of a Kreel Gortoga class cruiser and its three scouts. The Kreel cruiser had already gone alongside the Gola, and they had boarded it-"

As an expression of deepening concern grew on Mer's countenance, he was centering his thoughts on the strategic implications of Ron's report; he abruptly interrupted the briefing. In the tone of his words, Mer's rising anger was unmistakable.

"Ron, a single Kreel Gortoga class cruiser raiding our shipping between Krista and Glas Dinnein is unacceptable. Now you tell me Kellon has requested additional Cruisers to back him up. He must therefore believe additional Kreel cruisers are operating in the same tactical volume. This implies the Kreel are now operating openly deep within our declared boundaries and in force. Such a fact implies the Kreel have made a major shift in their strategy. As Guardian Intelligence, what information can you provide me to explain this apparent shift in Kreel behavior? Do we know what internal dynamics have altered to encourage the Kreel to raid this close to Glas Dinnein?"

Fully understanding Mer's anger was deeply rooted in his sense of responsibility, and not directed toward him, Ron continued his briefing. "Regretfully sir, at the moment, Guardian Intelligence can't answer your questions."

Ron's frank answer did nothing to assuage his anger, and Mer pushed for additional information. "Ron if I am correct we have occasionally seen a Gortoga class cruiser, but isn't this the first time one of them has actually been caught raiding?"

Sitting forward in his chair, Ron attempted to answer Mer's question while at the same time bringing the topic of conversation back to the immediate tactical problem and his interrupted briefing. "Yes sir, you are correct, this is the first time a Gortoga cruiser has been discovered raiding, and that fact is

39

pivotal to the current tactical situation. As Kellon closed on the Gortoga cruiser, Lan remained in a stealth profile, while deploying three decoys configured as Guardian Cruisers having only 20% stealth profiles. This tactical misdirection meant the Kreel would detect the inbound masquerading decoys, but would not see Lan. From the Kreel cruiser's vantage point, it appeared they were coming under attack by a numerically superior guardian force, and not by a single Guardian Cruiser."

The frown on Mer's face softened, and his voice indicated a lessening of anger. "That doesn't surprise me one bit. Kellon has always demonstrated an excellent use of his tactical decoys in tight situations. Continue Ron, what happened next?"

Seeing Mer's anger lessen, Ron inwardly relaxed and continued. "I agree Mer, Kellon is skilled in his tactical misdirection of the Kreel in battle. Well, to continue, Kellon's tactical ruse worked. Perceiving a superior attacking force, the Gortoga cruiser broke away from the Gola, and abandoning his scouts, fled.

"Lan had the relative speed advantage, and using his stealth capability, maneuvered for a firing point abeam of the fleeing Kreel cruiser, even as it was accelerating in its effort to escape. As Lan closed on the cruiser, without the cruiser detecting him, he destroyed the Kreel scouts. Next, Lan attained a good firing position against the Kreel cruiser. Mer, Kellon's attack was a textbook example of good battle tactics."

Hesitating a moment in the briefing, Ron observed Mer's frown returning. He knew Mer wanted him to get to the point, and explain what the problem was. Pausing only for a moment to gather his thoughts, Ron continued. "Sir, it is what he did after reaching that firing point that I am here to discuss." Again, Ron hesitated momentarily, as if he were choosing his next words carefully.

The brief pause caught Mer's attention and he prompted, "Well, don't just sit there, like a scarecrow in a farmer's field. Out with it, come to the point," Mer demanded.

"Yes Sir. As for coming to the point, standing Guardian Force orders state, without exception, when Guardian Force Cruisers encounter Kreel ships raiding in Guardian space, they are with extreme prejudice to destroy those Kreel ships. Sir, Kellon did not follow his standing orders and destroy the Kreel cruiser.

Rather than destroying the Kreel cruiser, he employed the Kreel beam weapon developed by the Arkillians."

Sitting suddenly bolt upright, his frown deepening, Mer dryly commented, "Ron that Arkillian weapon system was untested, and still in research and evaluation. More to the point, I personally classified it Black Hole. How in the seven stars did Kellon have access to that weapon? If he used the blasted thing, did it work?"

Sitting back in his chair, Ron sighed, then began to answer Mer's rash of questions. "Well as to your first question, it was Kellon who first encountered that weapon while near Earth. As you doubtless remember, the Arkillians used it during their battle with Lan. Upon his return home, Lan was designated the test ship for Fleet Research's evaluation of the weapon system, prototype development, testing, and the implementation of shield upgrades for countering the Arkillian's human equivalent of the Kreel beam. Therefore, Kellon has for months been working closely with Research and Development on its implementation and testing.

"As for your second question, the weapon does appear to have worked. After Kellon discharged the Kreel beam, there were no detectable Kreel life signs on the cruiser. This indicated it worked as the Arkillians anticipated, killing the entire Kreel crew.

"This now brings me to the core of the problem, that being just how Kellon has actually ignited a short fuse. Rather than simply destroying the Kreel ship, as he certainly could have, he used the Kreel beam and then brought Lan alongside the Kreel cruiser. His expressed intention was to send three squads of combat troops aboard the cruiser, along with a command crew, and to seize the Kreel ship as a prize."

The expression on Mer's face was no longer one of anger, but one of surprise and disbelief. "Ron you can't possibly be serious! Kellon has actually acted to seize a Kreel cruiser as a prize?"

"Sir, I assure you that is precisely what Kellon did. What's more, the Kreel cruiser appears to be intact and undamaged. At present, Lan is alongside the Kreel cruiser and is proceeding with an armed boarding."

Shaking his head in disbelief, Mer was again frowning. "You say Kellon has already brought Lan alongside of a Kreel Gortoga cruiser? He is placing an armed boarding party onboard that Kreel ship?"

"Yes Mer, that is precisely what Kellon has accomplished. Kellon's current tactical assessment is there are additional Kreel cruisers operating in the vicinity. This is his basis in requesting four additional cruisers to backup Lan."

Sitting back in his chair, Mer paused to reflect on what he had just been told, still disbelieving what he had just heard. "Kellon actually took Lan alongside a Kreel cruiser, and has an armed team boarding it. In my living memory, that has never happened before. Ron, as an experienced cruiser captain yourself, you know tactically speaking there are at least ten thousand good reasons why it has never happened before. My first reaction is Kellon should either receive a commendation as a brilliant courageous combat captain, or else as a blasted fool be immediately relieved of command and promptly brought before a full court martial. Frankly, at this moment, I am not certain which is more appropriate."

Leaning forward toward Ron, Mer's expression grew grave and he demanded, "Given Kellon asked for the support of Lent and Lar, where are they? How long before they arrive?"

"Sir, the last report from Lan is that he is alongside the Kreel cruiser and is in the process of boarding. The Lar is nearly on station and the Lent is about fifteen minutes further distant. Kellon has deployed Lan's Scouts to extend his tactical sphere of detection. The good news is that there are currently no reports of Kreel activity in the local volume of space."

A muted tone sounded, and Ron raised his left hand, his index finger lightly touching his ear. He replied, "Cloud here." After a moment of listening, he replied, "Understood, keep me informed."

Smiling, and with a deep sigh of relief, he looked over to Mer. "I am informed that Kellon has successfully taken the Kreel cruiser, intact and undamaged. There is now a command crew aboard it, and they are in control of the ship."

Sitting in his chair, Mer simply looked at Ron as if he were not certain he had heard correctly. "Prize?" Mer mused. "I do not believe the word prize is adequate. Blast, at risk of repeating myself, I cannot remember anyone capturing a first line Kreel Cruiser, let alone undamaged. All we normally get for analysis

42

are the broken and burnt fragments. Are you certain the report is the ship is actually taken intact and without damage?"

"Yes Sir. That's precisely what I have just been informed, captured intact and without damage, not as much as a scratch."

The soft tone again sounded and Ron responded. After a moment, he began to smile broadly. "Understood, keep me informed." Leaning back in his chair, Ron closed his eyes, and there was a slight smile on his face.

After several moments of waiting, Mer became impatient. "Well, don't just sit there with a silly grin on your face, looking like a fox that just jumped a fence and ate a farmer's chicken. What is the update?"

Opening his eyes, Ron leaned forward, and he was still smiling. "Well Mer, the good news is Lar did arrive in time to support Lan. At this very moment, Cruiser Lar and Lan's captured prize are both underway. Lar is currently providing armed escort services for the captured Kreel ship, and both Lar and the Kreel cruiser are together moving directly toward Glas Dinnein. Captain Kylster onboard Lar is formally requesting you personally designate where Lar is to deliver the prize.

"The remaining good news is Cruiser Lent has arrived and is now on station, in direct support of Lan providing a protective umbrella. Lent has also deployed his Scouts to augment Lan's forward Scouts. In order to search for possible survivors, Lan is proceeding with boarding the Gola. As yet, there's no additional Kreel activity reported in the local volume of space. However, Kellon still believes there will be a hostile Kreel force entering the tactical volume soon. In this regard, I agree with Kellon."

Looking thoughtful, Mer sighed. "Well, is there anything else that you need to tell me?"

"Yes Sir. There is one additional important matter. Before I came to see you, I directed Cruiser Lawrence to move promptly to support Lan."

As Ron braced himself for Mer's anticipated response, Mer sat back and then pivoting in his chair, he looked toward the broad window. After several moments, he then slowly stood and walked over to the closed curtains. Reaching out, he gently pulled back one of the sheer curtains, and stood quietly, as if only looking at the tranquil coastal scene beyond. In his mind, Mer was reviewing his lifetime of battles with the Kreel and the corresponding political ramifications within the human community. Battles with the Kreel always had political implications, always. Given this time the battle produced an undamaged Kreel cruiser, he could not even begin to guess what political problems might emerge. Standing in reflection, he came to his decision on how he must handle the current problems, both tactically and politically. Letting the curtain fall back into place, he returned to his chair and sat down. Slowly, almost as if he was unaware anyone else was in the room, he swiveled in his chair and then squarely faced Ron. His face was firm and set, and he was clearly not in a mood to debate any point with anyone. He was the Fleet Admiral of Guardian Force, and his orders were undisputed. Now was the time for decisive action.

When Admiral Mer Shawn spoke, his voice carried with it the undeniable authority of command. "Ron, I approve of your action and endorse your initiative in committing Lawrence. That being so, Kellon will need to make do with the support of Lent and Lawrence. They are both excellent ships with outstanding crews. I will wager an entire case of cold brews the three of them can take on most any Kreel threat in the area and dish out more than they receive. Given the strategic realities of this situation, they will need to do just that."

"Sir, they are three of our best," Ron replied.

Still concentrating, Mer continued. "They are, and Lan, Lent, and Lawrence together will have to meet whatever the Kreel might throw against them. We simply do not have sufficient strength in the area to cover all our bases, and still be able to provide more support."

"Yes sir, I understand."

"Good. Above everything else Ron, we now need to protect the captured Kreel cruiser and get it here in one piece. When you return to Operations, determine the nearest two available cruisers to Lar and the captured Kreel cruiser. As soon as possible, inform Operations I want them to vector those two cruisers at best speed to intercept the Lar and Lan's prize. When those two cruisers do intercept Lar, together with Lar, they are to escort the prize safely to its destination. The destination on Glas Dinnein is yet to be defined."

44

Mer's orders were distinct and clear, yet there was still one problem troubling Ron. "Mer, when it arrives, precisely where should the Kreel Cruiser be berthed?"

For the first time in minutes, Mer actually smiled. "That, Ron, is your personal basket of snakes. You are to put your thinking cap on and locate the best hiding place possible for that ship."

Again, Mer frowned, and looking directly at Ron, he continued. "Where to berth it, is only one part of a major multi-horned dilemma. That we have captured intact a Kreel cruiser of their latest design is to remain a guarded secret. This means it must be classified Black Hole. Admiral Secretary Eryan Kyrie will be informed, but none of the other members of the Planetary Assembly will be informed."

Wincing, Mer added with a slight smile, "As you know, she would have the hide off my back if she were kept out of the information loop. The good news being, she fully understands why Black Hole classifications exist. We will keep this secret airtight. That we have a Kreel ship is not the real prize and you know it. While their propulsion, power, sensors and weapon systems upgrades are important to study, far more important is the ship must have a full and undamaged communications capability and database. Our gaining direct access to their communications and encryption technologies is of an inestimable value. You, more than almost everyone else, know the intelligence value of what we can glean from those communications and encryption systems.

"We are therefore putting a tight lid on our capture of the Kreel cruiser. You will promptly employ whatever dissemination is required to keep the secret. You will immediately pull together the most competent team of experts available to Guardian Force, and when that ship arrives, you are to take control of and secure the communications and encryption systems and the primary database. It is your responsibility, and I'll hold you to it. You are to see that the database is backed up before anything else."

Ron was now frowning, listening intently to his orders. "Yes Sir."

"Good. Now, return promptly to Operations and have them dispatch the necessary orders to our Cruisers. Then instruct Operations to make whatever adjustments are required in our

45

patrol assignments to stretch and cover the holes we have created by pulling off those five supporting Cruisers."

"Sir, before I depart, is there anything else?" Ron inquired, beginning to stand.

"Hmmmm, yes, there is one more thing. Each of the Guardian crews involved in this operation, and any surviving crew of the Gola, are to be brought home and each is to be immediately isolated. They are to remain in quarantine until Intelligence debriefs and instructs them as required for maintaining a Black Hole protocol. Ron, you have your orders."

Standing quickly, and with marked deference, Ron came to attention and saluted Mer. "Yes sir."

Mer promptly returned the salute. "One more item," Mer added as Ron's hand reached for the door.

Ron turned, looking at Mer. "Sir?"

"Ron, you are to personally keep me current and fully informed of the developments in this matter. Send to all involved ships a notice this matter is now classified Black Hole. Send that notice over my name and add: To all involved Guardian Force personnel, may there be fair winds at your back when homeward bound."

Ron nodded his head in understanding. "Yes sir, it will be accomplished."

Turning, Ron opened the door, moving into the passageway and returning to Operations.

Sitting with both hands flat on his desk, Mer thoughtfully observed the door as it closed behind Ron, and smiled. Their friendship went back to the days of their youth and the academy. It was a friendship tempered through many years and in battle; they both were among the survivors of the defense of Quintana and dozens of other bitterly waged battles. *It's been far too long since we have simply sat and enjoyed a cold brew together,* he thought. *I'll personally see we do that soon.*

Then, Mer began contemplating this latest challenge. *The blasted Kreel volume of space is at least as large as ours and most likely far greater,* he thought. *We have never been able to penetrate and gain any meaningful understanding of its true size or the number of worlds and species contained within its boundary. The Kreel cruiser's database is a virtual diamond mine of new information, and perhaps it will answer those* questions. *One thing is certain; Kellon's little prize is a sharp double-edged sword and requires careful handling.*

Hmm, which is it, he mused. *Is Kellon brilliant and courageous or was his action reckless foolishness? Hmm, I know Kellon, and he is no fool— he's a risk taker, but he's no fool. It's results that weigh the issue on a balance, and given the results, brilliant and courageous are definitely weightier; since, a captured Kreel cruiser is the bountiful fruit of Kellon's risky action. Nevertheless, he took an enormous risk with Lan and the lives of everyone onboard! I suppose it will be necessary to sit him down and discuss his actions, perhaps I can put some curbs on his risk taking. Every time I send Kellon somewhere, he finds some way to make my life more complicated. Blast it all; he is still one of the best Captains we have.*

Grudgingly he acknowledged to himself, *Kellon was always pushing the limits.* Mer began to smile. *Perhaps,* he thought, *a full court martial is in order then we can bring back flogging as a punishment, perhaps hanging him from his thumbs for a week, then I can give him a medal and promote him. If it would not deny the Force one of its best Captains, I could punish him by promoting him to be the Guardian Force rapporteur. That assignment would be far more severe a punishment any day than a simple flogging.*

Picking up his cup of neab, he brought it to his lips; he then grimaced sourly and put the cup back on his desk. *Ugh, after more than two millenniums, I still hate cold neab,* he complained inwardly. Sighing deeply he reached out, took the top document off the pile on his desk and began flipping through its pages.

Chapter Five:
Designated Target

The three Captains had required less than fifteen minutes for planning the ambush of the advancing Kreel cruisers and for agreeing on the tactical plan of battle. They based their plan on deception, misdirection, surprise, and Guardian Force's well-honed stealth advantage.

Lan's designated target was the middle cruiser, now heading directly toward Lan. Both Lent and Lawrence would remain on the wide flanks of the engagement and if possible below the defined tactical plane. Lan would remain, if possible, above the tactical plane. Lent and Lawrence would remain in full stealth mode and in their flanking ambush positions, until the Kreel committed to battle. Then they would strike from their wide positions, each attacking their separate assigned targets.

During their planning conference, each cruiser received a brief priority message from Fleet Admiral Mer Shawn. Commander Roy Grey read the Admiral's message aloud. "Cruiser Lan, and all Guardian cruisers supporting Lan, are to immediately classify current operations at level Black Hole. To all involved Guardian Force personnel, may there be fair winds at your back when homeward bound. Sir, The message is signed by Admiral Mer Shawn."

The significance of the seldom-used level of classification was noteworthy, since there was no higher classification. Black Hole classification demanded strict compartmentalization, and Guardian Force tolerated no leaks.

Promptly responding to their recall, both Lan and Lent's Scouts pulled back, and their parent cruisers swiftly brought them aboard. Both Lent and Lawrence then silently moved off, well forward of Lan, moving toward their predefined widely separated flanking positions.

As Lawrence moved to take his assigned position, he first advanced to a forward point along the extrapolated course of the approaching Kreel ships. At a distance from Lan, well beyond the known maximum effective range of the Kreel heavy missiles, Lawrence deployed a dispersed volume of hundreds of stealth mobile seeker mines. These he programmed and structured into a conical volume, where the broad flat base of the cone shaped volume was perpendicular to and centered on the extrapolated Kreel course. The base of the volume faced the approaching Kreel ships, with the apex of the cone pointing back toward Lan.

The small self-propelled flat black ellipsoid cluster homing mines were virtually undetectable. In design and effect, the cluster of independent mines formed a reactive and cooperative hive system. Once deployed the mines monitored the star field for positional references, and monitored each other, while they passively searched for targets. When one mine passively detected a target, it communicated its target data to adjacent mines in the cluster. The separate mines combined passive target information to localize the approaching target. Once the target entered the mine's effective range, it immediately propelled itself to strike the target. The mines formed the deadly leading edge of the planned Guardian ambush.

Maintaining a stealth level of 20%, Lan remained on station, to all appearances guarding the disabled Gola. In reality, Lan was serving as the tantalizing lure, the fat live bait drawing the approaching Kreel cruisers deep into a thorny briar-patch and defined kill volume.

Studying the maneuvering plot, Kellon observed the behavior of the three approaching Kreel ships. Maintaining their methodical search pattern, the center cruiser was advancing on a steady course, searching along the extrapolated path of the captured Kreel cruiser. By all appearances of the Kreel's search pattern, Kellon understood there had been some form of undetected communications between the captured cruiser and the approaching Kreel ships. He deduced whatever warning communications had occurred, it must have been fragmentary; *At least*, Kellon thought, *they are not charging in with their guns blazing*. Kellon observed Roy looking up from his console, and he was broadly smiling.

"Sir, we have updated communications from Guardian Operations. They have directed Cruisers Langley and Lowell to intercept and support Cruiser Lar in escorting your prize to Glas Dinnein. How about that Sir, three Cruisers defending your prize, and two Cruisers coming to support Lan, must surely indicate Admiral Mer Shawn approves of our action. If we get lucky, we may only need to scrub toilets for a month to demonstrate our penitence for not following standing orders."

He could not help himself; Kellon laughed. "Roy, if we get off that easy, we will indeed be lucky. In the meantime, we'll still need to cope with those three inbound Kreel cruisers."

Shifting his mental focus back to the pending battle, he would first need to set the tactical plane to that adopted by the Captains during their conference.

"Lan set the tactical plane to correspond with our current operational plane."

Knowledgeable of Kreel battle tactics, Kellon began shaping the battle volume to one of his own liking.

"Lan, next plot the precise position of the mobile mined volume deployed by Lawrence. In all upcoming maneuvers, regardless of maneuvering orders, avoid that volume.

"Lan, designate the center cruiser our prime target and identify it as Target 1. Target 2 is the cruiser located counter clockwise from Target 1. Target 3 is the cruiser located clockwise from Target 1. Regardless of their maneuvering, maintain the target number assignments.

"Next establish a tactical sphere about each of the three approaching Kreel cruisers. Define those spheres with a radius of two times our effective heavy missile range."

"Sir, targets are identified, numbers are assigned, and tactical spheres are defined," Lan acknowledged.

"Good. Lan, during the upcoming battle, you're to avoid the tactical spheres established surrounding targets 2 and 3, unless specifically ordered to attack those targets.

"Now, construct a straight line between Target 1 and the position of Gola. Maintain that line of reference. Now, maneuver and adjust our position to be on that line, fifty kilometers forward of Gola. When reaching that location, remain on station and swing your heading until Target 1 bears 270 degrees relative."

"Sir, I am moving to the indicated position."

"Good." Kellon acknowledged. "Now Lan, define the line between Target 1 and Gola as the major axis of an ellipse. Gola is on the leading edge of the ellipse. Target 1 is located at the most distant focus. As Target 1 advances, adjust the most distant focus to remain on Target 1. "Define the ellipse by locating the nearest focus three-thousand kilometers from Target 1. Continue to adjust the ellipse, by maintaining constant the three-thousand kilometer separation between Target 1 and the nearest focus point. Draw the ellipse on our tactical plane.

"Lan, do you have any questions?" asked Kellon.

"No Sir." Lan acknowledged. "As ordered, I am now displaying the defined ellipse on the relative tactical plot."

Looking up, Kellon studied the plot. A golden icon marked Lan's position at the center of the plot and a blue icon represented Gola; both icons were located on the ellipse's major axis. The arc of the circumference of the ellipse moved sharply away from Gola then gradually curved outward toward the ellipse's distant midpoint, and then gracefully narrowed toward the second and more distant focus. Red icons marked the advancing Kreel cruisers, with Target 1 being located at the furthest focus point.

Carefully studying the ellipse and the other ships marked on the tactical plot, Kellon took special note of the black triangle denoting the volume of deployed mines. He nodded in satisfaction; the defined battle volume was definitely to his liking.

Once the battle began Lan would revert to full stealth mode, and avoiding the mined volume, he would accelerate along the path defined by the ellipse. Kellon's intention was to move rapidly to attack Target 1, while Lent and Lawrence would be moving from the flanks to attack Targets 2 and 3.

With the current stealth setting of twenty-percent, Kellon felt Lan must look like a bright nova, and he wondered why the Kreel had not already detected them.

Looking toward the Tactical Officer, Kellon noted Lieutenant Elayne Cloud had replaced Commander Shaw, and she was intensely studying the data screens. She had combed her hair back and bound it into a long tail, its blond strands contrasting against the darker color of her uniform.

The insignia tabs on her collar declared she was a full lieutenant, with a specialty in science. Kellon knew she was also cross-trained and a very proficient Tactical Officer, and her movements and posture revealed her confidence and proficiency. He noticed a countenance of concentration had replaced her normally warm open smile.

"Tactical, Kellon here. what's your best estimate of time before the Kreel detect us?"

Looking over to Kellon, Elayne's expression was serious. "Tactical here, with Lan's stealth at twenty-percent our best estimate is the Kreel will detect Lan in less than five minutes."

There was, Kellon knew, only the slightest chance the Kreel might not attack Lan. Given the Kreel's perceived apparent numerical superiority of three-to-one, and their raw predatory behavior, a battle was the most probable outcome and it was imminent.

"Tactical here," Elayne's voice was firm and steady, "the Kreel have detected Lan and are shifting from a dispersed search pattern to a tactical-combat spread formation."

The Kreel's detection of Lan was what Kellon had been waiting for. "Roy, open a Kreel battle channel and transmit a Kreel challenge signal."

"Sir, a Kreel battle channel is open and a Kreel challenge has been transmitted."

Keying the assigned channel, Kellon spoke with a sharp discordant hissing tone, addressing the Kreel in their own language and on a standard Kreel battle frequency. "Kreel Commander, know that I have utterly destroyed your ships that attacked our freighter. I deny you of your prey. "You are operating well within a designated and identified Guardian volume of space. You have attacked an unarmed Guardian ship. You will now immediately withdraw or, like your other ships, be destroyed."

"Tactical here, the Kreel are holding their position."

The forward bulkhead monitor brightened, revealing the image of a Kreel Officer. He was large even for a Kreel, probably standing nearly seven feet tall. His bejeweled command harness revealed the Officer was both senior and well-experienced. The dark fur ruff across his shoulders was raised and bristling, in rage. His short muzzle was contorted in a snarl, and his gleaming

53

fangs were fully exposed. His spoken response came as a chittering discordant rumbling sneer. If anyone could ignore the embers of hatred and anger that burned in his serpentine eyes, without knowing a syllable of the Kreel language, none could miss the distilled vehemence the Kreel Officer was coldly expressing in his speech. By its very tone and arrogant nature alone, his voice shouted here was a deadly predator and mortal enemy.

"Guardian fool, you dare challenge three Kreel cruisers? Know this fool, the Kreel go wherever we choose to go. If we judge the disabled ship our prey, then we will take it!" As the officer ended his declaration, the monitor went dark.

"Countermeasures here, they are sensor active and closely scanning Lan, the Gola, the scouts' debris fields and the nearby volume."

Three minutes grated slowly past as the tension within CAC steadily increased. "Tactical here, they are maneuvering into a standard Kreel fork to envelop us. Kreel cruiser 1 is advancing slowly directly toward Lan, cruiser 2 has split, arcing high to our port and cruiser 3 is arcing low to our starboard. They are synchronizing their approach to Lan and are well beyond our effective firing range. The flanking cruisers are slightly in advance of Target 1 and will be first in firing range."

Keying the Kreel battle channel, Kellon responded, "Kreel Commander, this last time, I warn you. Immediately break off your attack and depart, or I will destroy you."

The monitor remained blank, but the audio sound of a response was clear; the hissing Kreel response unmistakably sounded like the threat it was. "Fool, your empty boasts are meaningless. We have questions we will have answered. In our closing jaws, you are puny prey and will be utterly crushed and soon devoured."

"Kreel Commander, I also have questions. There are crewmen missing from the Guardian cargo ship. You will promptly return them alive or I will hold you personally accountable. You are warned. I am not prey and I have sharp teeth." Kellon knew the conversation was finished and abruptly closed the open channel. *As always, the Kreel are predictably their own worst enemies*, thought Kellon.

Examining the Kreel's expanding jaws-of-death maneuver, Kellon promptly adjusted his battle plan to counter its effect before the jaws could close.

"Lan, define a target reference plane. Make the three defining points the coordinates of Lan and the two flanking Kreel cruisers. Display." The forward plot transformed to a three-dimensional projection showing the defined target plane as a light shade of gray, inclined to, and intersecting with, the tactical plane. Lan and the two flanking Kreel cruisers were located on that plane.

"Lan, now rotate the previously defined ellipse counter-clockwise about its major axis, until it is perpendicular to the defined target plane. Maintain that angular relationship. Next, adjust your pitch upward until your centerline is parallel with the minor axis of the ellipse."

Lan's acknowledging tone sounded.

"Countermeasures here, they are continuing active scans and are shifting to something new, it looks somewhat like short bursts of some intense phase-encoded signal. They appear to have a solid fire control lock on Lan."

Tactical here, the center cruiser is nearing Lawrence's dispersed minefield and the other two are continuing their flanking arcing maneuver. The flankers will be passing well outside the volume of deployed mines."

The battle had begun, and accordingly Kellon began implementing his plan. "Lan, configure one combat decoy to your signature, current velocity, and stealth profile. When ordered to execute, deploy the decoy astern with 20% acceleration. Program the decoy to follow the defined ellipse's circumference. Next, prepare a broadband screamer for deployment three-hundred meters off our port side. Set it for 30 seconds operation before self-destruction. Fire Control bring ten heavy missiles on standby. Set homing to passive-active, with enabling run set at 75% of run length. Set launch by salvoes of two missiles. The designated target is Target 1. Establish passive missile locks and hold Condition 2." "Tactical here, Kreel cruiser 1 is now entering the cone of mines. They are twelve minutes from their maximum firing distance. The remaining two cruisers are closing their range synchronized with the center cruiser and will enter firing range in about eleven minutes."

As Kellon observed the battle unfolding, he centered his attention on the relative tactical plot. He fully understood they were now at the critical point in his plan of misdirection.

"Tactical here, the Kreel cruiser is taking multiple hits from the mines and is beginning evasive maneuvers. They are in the center of the mine volume and seem confused. There is random firing of defensive lasers. They are taking more hits. We are now tracking one incoming missile launched from the primary target toward Lan. We are beyond their maximum effective range, and the missile is going wide. It seems to be a panic firing."

The time for action was now, and Kellon responded, "Lan, launch the screamer and disperse chaff astern. Execute!"

Lan's acknowledgment tone sounded. As Lan's screamer went active, its broad spectrum electromagnetic jamming signal saturated a large volume of space around Lan. The tactical intent was to blind momentarily the Kreel weapons' sensors. In order for Lan to maintain track of the approaching Kreel, there were several shifting narrow electromagnetic bandpass filters built within the broad spectrum. Lan also ejected and dispersed astern a dozen small containers, each containing long streamers and flakes of bright reflective metal foil. They were set to deploy when 300 meters aft, exploding and blossoming outward into multiple merging spheres and reflecting a broad band of active electromagnetic energy.

With Lan shrouded by the screamer and chaff, Kellon ordered, "Lan set our stealth profile to 100%. Deploy the combat decoy, and then follow the defined ellipse's circumference toward the primary target. Accelerate at 65%. Execute!"

Lan's acknowledgment tone sounded. As Lan launched the combat decoy aft, it rapidly moved down and astern, even while Lan was accelerating up and moving in the opposite direction. The sound of distant rolling thunder, and deep vibration felt throughout Lan, attested to the power he was applying to his propulsion. Lan was aggressively closing on his designated target, his core matrix was bristling, and his attitude was incontestably confrontational.

Chapter Six:
Firing Point

His propulsion system was felt as rumbling thunder, as Lan accelerated, running in full stealth mode. He was following the proscribed arcing elliptical path toward his designated enemy. His trajectory carried him rapidly off the initial line of sight to the target, while putting distance between the misdirecting deployed combat decoy, which was accelerating in the opposite direction, and himself. Presenting a constantly altering trajectory, Lan was following the route that kept him as far from the flanking Kreel cruisers as possible.

Concentrating on the unfolding battle dynamics, Kellon began his initial attack run. "Lan, set the CPA directly above the target and at 80% of effective heavy missile range.

"Fire control, at ninety-five percent or less of effective heavy missile range, set Condition 1.

Kellon's intention was to exploit fully the target's confusion, as it struggled to extract itself from the mined volume. In order to provide Fire Control the opportunity for multiple salvoes, he was directing Lan deep within the target's tactical sphere.

Her voice was calm and firm, as Elayne began providing the running tactical update. "Tactical here, the screamer has self-destructed on schedule. Kreel Cruiser 1 is damaged and is still in the mine volume and maneuvering, apparently attempting to withdraw. Flanking cruisers 2 and 3 are firing missiles at the combat decoy from near their maximum range. There is no indication of Lent or Lawrence engaging."

The deep thrumming of Lan's propulsion, operating at 65% acceleration, could be heard and felt throughout Lan, as he continued his acceleration toward his target.

"Tactical here, Lent and Lawrence have engaged cruisers 2 and 3. They are pressing their attacks, and they have scored heavy missile hits on both targets. Both Kreel cruisers are returning fire and attempting to evade. Target 2 and Target 3 are receiving additional hits."

"Tactical here, the Kreel missiles are converging on the decoy. The combat decoy is destroyed."

Following the destruction of the decoy masquerading as Lan, there was a reflective brief hush in CAC. Kellon broke that hush, pushing his attack. "Lan, move sharply to and through the defined CPA, execute."

Given Kellon's orders, Lan departed the elliptical trajectory and set a direct course aiming for a precise point directly above the target.

"Fire Control, Kellon here. Keep on your toes and keep it sharp!"

"Fire control here, first salvo away. The distinct rumbling of the launch of heavy missiles echoed throughout Lan, and Fire Control reported, "Second salvo away."

Kellon knew that two salvoes of inbound active missiles could provide a good Kreel tactical team a counter firing solution along the established angular velocity and he promptly commanded an evasion maneuver. "Lan, execute shim 3, repeat shim 3."

Lan shuddered throughout his length as he immediately increased acceleration, rolling into a hard climbing port turn, leaving the damaged Kreel cruiser well aft. As Lan completed a 45-degree turn to the port, he reversed the roll and immediately began a hard climbing turn to the starboard. Completing a 225-degree turn, Lan came about on a higher trajectory course, one opposite and parallel to his initial attack vector. This maneuver brought Lan above and again moving toward the damaged target. "Lan, reduce our speed by 40%. Bring us over the top of the target at a CPA of 80% of effective heavy missile range.

"Fire Control, stay sharp."

Again, Lan altered his trajectory to follow the shortest flight pass to bring him through the designated firing point and beyond. "Third salvo away."

Again, the rumbling sounds of the launch of heavy missiles permeated Lan. "Fourth salvo away."

As the target fell aft of Lan, Kellon nearly shouted, "Lan, break vertical 90 degrees and then steady on course. Reduce acceleration to zero."

Glancing toward Navigation, Kellon asked, "Roy, are there any damage reports?"

There was only the slightest pause, before Roy reported. "No sir, there is no indicated damage."

"Tactical, status report."

Her voice was steady, yet its pitch reflected her increased tension, as Elayne responded. "Tactical here, Lan's first four heavy missiles hit the target amidships. Lan's second four missiles have hit toward the stern. The target has lost all propulsion and is wallowing. Target 2 appears dead and breaking up. Correction on Target 2, it has exploded. Target 3 is damaged and attempting to evade and escape. There are no combat reports from either Lent or Lawrence."

Kellon shifted his attention to the wider battle, and maneuvered into a holding position from which he could attack multiple targets. "Lan reduce our speed 85%. Maneuver us onto a trajectory parallel to the tactical plane; then commence a standard right turn and continue the turn until the Gola bears 180 degrees relative. Then, decelerate and go inert, maintaining station and heading."

Her voice now calm, Elayne continued her running tactical update. "Tactical here, our primary target, Kreel cruiser 1, has either self-destructed or exploded. Cruiser 3 is again under attack and has taken additional missile hits. Cruiser 3 has lost propulsion and is yawing badly. It is taking more missile hits. Cruiser 3 has exploded."

For several moments there was a calm in the CAC, then Elayne reported, "Tactical here, there are no active Kreel ships currently detected."

Having survived numerous battles, Kellon remained cautiously alert and began a systematic search of the tactical volume of space. "All stations, Kellon here, stay on your toes." Then, Kellon ordered on his command band, "Search for any trace of surviving Kreel scouts, intelligence probes, or spent ordnance. Fire Control reset the heavy missiles on standby to Condition 3.

Sitting back in his command chair, Kellon let out a slow breath, and looked about the CAC. He then keyed the general intercom band and briefed Lan's crew. "Ladies and gentlemen, Kellon here. Lent, Lancer and Lan have just engaged three Gortoga cruisers, and we are able to report all three Kreel cruisers are now in disorganized pieces of jetsam and drifting. We will hold here for a moment or two, while we determine our next move. Well done everyone! Kellon out."

"Roy, do we have tactical contact with Lent and Lawrence?"

"No sir."

"Roy, deploy and position a rendezvous beacon mid-way between our location and the Gola."

"Sir, the rendezvous beacon is deployed."

Elayne's voice was steady, but tense. "Tactical here, I have detection of five Kreel scout propulsion signatures, repeat five scouts. Their Doppler shifts indicate they are moving slowly away from the location where the Kreel regrouped before the battle began."

"Tactical, are those Kreel scouts above or below the tactical plane?"

"Tactical here, three are above and two are below. The scouts are spreading out and departing the volume. They are moving in the general direction they came from."

"Commander Greer, Jason, are your Scouts ready for deployment?"

"Greer here, all Scouts are tactically synchronized and ready for deployment."

Before Kellon could deploy Lan's Scouts, he needed to set defensive weapon systems to standby, and he proceeded accordingly. "Fire Control set all gun and laser turrets Condition 3.

"Jason, deploy one Scout to monitor the rendezvous beacon and act as the communication link to Lan. The Scout is to remain vigilant and in full stealth mode."

"Greer here, Sheba is prepared for deployment and will hold this position."

"Kellon here, Jason, acknowledging Sheba is ready for deployment."

"Lan, launch Sheba on Commander Greer's countdown." Lan's acknowledging tone promptly sounded.

"Lan, as soon as Sheba is clear, move us smartly to intercept the nearest Kreel scout positioned above the tactical plane. You're to bring us precisely above each target and through a CPA of 80% of effective offensive laser range. Following intercept of the initial target, move immediately to likewise intercept the second and third targets."

Looking toward Kellon, Roy's expression was deeply troubled. "Sir," Roy interjected, "May I respectfully mention that pursuit and destruction of survivors is not normal Guardian practice."

Hearing Roy's observation, Kellon felt a sudden irritation, "Commander Grey, Your comment is understood. However, you will recall I ordered Commander Shaw to execute a no quarter action, when boarding the captured Kreel cruiser. That order remains standing for this engagement. Also remember the Kreel survivors are not in life boats but manning armed combat scouts, and the missing crewmen from the Gola are most likely eviscerated and hanging from hooks in the Kreel cruiser's meat locker."

As soon as Kellon had sharply retorted, he felt a pang of regret. He knew his remark was totally unwarranted, and especially so given Roy and his years of friendship and their serving together as shipmates. Kellon committed to clear the air with Roy following the battle.

Turning his attention back to the battle, Kellon inquired, "Commander Greer, Jason, can you confirm Sheba is clear?"

"Greer here, Sheba is well clear."

"Fire Control, Kellon here. Reassign three lower batteries from point missile defense to offense and set automatic targeting, Condition 1. Set all remaining gun and laser turrets to point missile defense, Condition 1."

"Lan, proceed sharply to Kreel scout Target 1."

"Navigation here, Lan is moving smartly to intercept the first designated target."

"Tactical here, the nearest Scout intercept is in two minutes thirty seconds."

When he became aware that he was clenching his teeth, Kellon consciously relaxed and let out a deeply-held breath. *They were Kreel scouts, not lifeboats,* he reminded himself.

There was a sudden deep thumping sound reverberating within Lan. "Tactical here, offensive lasers are firing. The target is destroyed."

"Navigation here, Lan is moving smartly to intercept the second target."

"Tactical, Kellon here, keep a track on the two scouts below the tactical plane."

Within Lan, everyone heard again the deep thumping sound as Lan's heavy lasers fired. "Tactical here, offensive lasers are firing. The second target is destroyed."

"Navigation here, Lan is moving smartly to the third target." "Tactical here, Target 3 is wildly and radically maneuvering. Recommendation is passive missile."

"Fire Control, bring on standby, Condition 2, one light missile. Obtain a passive lock on the target. When lock is confirmed set Condition 1."

"Fire Control here, passive lock confirmed, missile away."

There came a momentary break, as the light missile sped to intercept the Kreel scout ship. "Tactical here, missile impact. Target is destroyed."

Remembering his standing orders, with extreme prejudice destroy all raiding Kreel ships, Kellon prosecuted his attack. He wanted those remaining Kreel scouts. "Tactical, are the remaining two scouts below the tactical plane within light missile range?"

"Tactical here, they are at 75 and 85% of effective range and opening."

"Fire Control, bring four light missiles to standby. Obtain one passive missile lock and one passive active lock on each target. Set enabling run to 70% of run length. When lock is confirmed, set Condition 2.

"Lan, move smartly to close on the remaining targets, while staying above the tactical plane."

"Fire Control, at 80% or less effective range, with confirmed locks, set Condition 1 on both targets."

"Fire Control here, two passive missiles locked and away." Those in CAC barely heard the soft sounds of light missiles as they launched. "Fire Control here, passive active missiles locked. Two missiles away."

The sounds of the launch of light missiles faded and silence followed, as the missiles streaked toward the two evading targets. "Tactical here, missiles closing on first target. One passive missile has missed and self-destructed, the active missile has hit, destroying the target.

"Tactical here, remaining missiles are closing on second target, at 90% effective range. Missile impacts, two hits, target is destroyed."

There had been three Gortoga cruisers, and each cruiser had carried three scouts. Lan had destroyed five scouts, and Kellon began searching for the remaining four scouts. "Lan bring us about starboard, in a standard turn. Bring us on to a course with the Gola bearing 000 relative. When on course, confirm full stealth mode and hold station and heading."

"Tactical and Countermeasures, Kellon here. There are still four unaccounted Kreel scouts. Commence a volume passive search for anything as small as a flea. Be well advised I do not want a single flea to escape unnoticed."

"Captain," Roy reported, "Sheba is relaying a tight combat link now established with Lent and Lawrence. I have connected Sheba's tight link to the Captain's conference band."

Kellon keyed the Captain's band and snapped, "Kellon here." "Eurie here. Captain Kellon, the Lent and Lawrence are damage-free and are moving to our prearranged post battle rendezvous stations near Gola. Lent's Tactical reports you are still engaged with the Kreel. May we be of some assistance?"

Kellon heard the tension in Eurie's voice and knew she was, like Roy, questioning his post battle operations. Sensing the depth of his anger Kellon tried to calm his feelings. "Captain Eurie, Lan is grateful for your offer to assist. I am seeking confirmation that there are no remaining Kreel scouts or detectable intelligence probes in the battle volume. I have accounted for five scouts. However, there are possibly four additional Kreel scouts not yet accounted for. Lan is now searching the volume for sleepers. When we are complete with that surveillance operation, Lan will join Lent and Lawrence. I am estimating another fifteen minutes will be required here."

"Captain Kellon, Kel here, I am moving Lawrence forward below the tactical plane to sanitize the deployed mine volume.

Lawrence's countermeasure and tactical data does not indicate any Kreel activity whatsoever within sensor detection range."

"Countermeasures here. Sir, we have detected low level EMF radiation buried deep in the background. It looks like a worn brush on a small electric motor. We are now squaring the signal and expanding the search volume.

"Sir, there are four dispersed and faint such EMF signals. They are covering a spread of 22 degrees, centered at 037 degrees relative."

"Captain Kel, we are detecting what looks like four Kreel scout ships. I will contact you shortly. Kellon out."

"Fire Control, bring eight light missiles to standby. Set them passive. Keep on your toes and be prepared to lock a missile on anything that runs."

"Countermeasures identify the bearing to the strongest signal." "Countermeasures here, the indicated signal is 37 degrees relative, elevation 12 degrees."

"Fire Control, can you lock a passive missile on that signal?"

"Fire Control here, the signal has been fine-tuned and one light missile is confirmed passive locked, Condition 2."

"Lan rotate our heading until the defined target bears 270 degrees relative, and then hold your station and heading. Execute."

Kellon waited as Lan responded and then heard the anticipated acknowledging tone.

"Fire Control, direct three offensive laser turrets along the indicated target bearing lines to the remaining signal sources. Set offensive turrets to automatic fire, Condition 1."

"Fire Control here, confirming passive missile lock on one target. One light missile set Condition 2. There are three offensive laser turrets set on bearing lines. Lasers set automatic fire, Condition 1."

"Fire Control, Kellon here. Confirm one light missile locked, and set Condition 1."

"Fire Control here, confirming passive lock. Missile away."

Chapter Seven:
Dangerously Better

Her voice was calm, yet it carried the unmistakable undertones of stress, as Elayne reported. "Tactical here, we have flushed a covey. Strong Kreel scout propulsion signatures detected."

"Countermeasures here, The Kreel have gone sensor active. They have an active lock on Lan. Detecting multiple inbound active light missiles, we are jamming."

What's happening, Kellon thought. *They should not be able to obtain an active lock on us.* "Lan, shem 6, repeat shem 6, execute." Kellon's jaw was firmly set, as he thought, *They've got teeth, and are definitely not lifeboats!*

As Lan dispersed a cluster of small inbound missile decoys and multiple chaff dispensers astern, his power and propulsion surged, his acceleration pegging at 0.90, as he began rolling into a tight starboard turn. Lan's entire crew heard and felt the peals of rolling thunder from Lan's generators and propulsion. Lan was increasing his speed with each passing millisecond.

"Fire Control here, confirming one target destroyed by missile, point-defense guns and lasers engaged and firing. The three allocated offensive lasers are unable to obtain locks on targets."

Her voice still tense, Elayne began her running updates. "Tactical here, we now have solid track on three Kreel scouts closing on our trailing decoys."

His voice tight, Kellon was concentrating on bringing Lan around and into a safe and favorable firing position. "Lan, come hard port and bring us back parallel one-hundred kilometers from our previous track and twenty kilometers above. Reduce speed 85%."

"Fire Control here. We have confirmed passive lock on three targets."

"Fire Control, Assign two light missiles to each target." Set homing passive-active, with enabling runs set at 50% of run length."

Kellon's voice was still tight, reflecting his anger. "Countermeasures, what did they get a lock-on? What were they targeting?"

"Countermeasures here, unknown, analysis is in progress. Countermeasures here, Kreel scouts are sensor active again, inbound active light missiles detected. We are jamming."

As Kellon responded to the tactical situation, his thoughts were deeply troubled. *Blast, what can they be getting an active lock on?* "Lan shem 3, repeat shem 3. Deploy weapons decoys and chaff."

"Fire Control here, point-defense guns and lasers firing."

Lan surged forward arcing up and port, continuing to climb and then began a hard right turn coming back at a higher level and on a reciprocal course.

Kellon was again in the defensive posture of evading, and he did not like that tactical position. "Fire Control, Kellon here, if you have confirmed missile locks, set Condition 1."

"Countermeasures, Kellon here. Is that analysis complete, what are they targeting?"

"Countermeasures here, unknown."

Everyone in CAC was tense, and the soft sounds of Lan launching light missiles whispered throughout the ship. "Fire Control here, six missiles away." Silence immediately followed the sounds of the launch of light missiles, and it stretched, as everyone waited expectantly for Tactical's report.

"Tactical here, multiple missile impacts, three targets destroyed."

"Fire control here, all point-defense systems are reporting clear."

Looking over to Kellon, Roy commented, "Sir that accounts for nine scouts."

Frowning, Kellon nodded in acknowledgment of Roy's comment. He was still feeling the surge of energy from the combat sequence. Tactical, is the volume clear?"

There was a moment of silence before Elayne's calm voice responded, "Tactical is clear."

"Countermeasures, is the volume clear?" Kellon demanded.

"Countermeasures here, there are no detected Kreel signals."

"Fire Control, Kellon here. Set remaining missiles and all laser and gun turrets to Condition 3."

Kellon sat back in his command chair and sighed. *If the Cruisers had been half as savvy as their Scouts,* he thought, *then this engagement might have come out considerably different.* They were getting dangerously better.

"Lan, bring us to all stop and then hold position."

Keying his CAC band, Kellon ordered, "Kellon here, I want both Tactical and Countermeasures to spend the next five minutes sweeping the local volume, looking for more fleas. I repeat, you are not to overlook one single flea."

Lan's stealth capability was impaired, and Kellon did not know how or why. That was unacceptable. "Countermeasures, I want your detection report on what the Kreel were targeting on my desk within two hours or the entire Countermeasures gang will be scrubbing toilets, and polishing Lan's decks, for the next month." Keying in the Captain's conference band, Kellon was still deeply concerned, when he addressed Lent and Lawrence. "Captains Eurie and Kel, Kellon here. Lan is now busy cleaning up his loose ends. Lan has accounted for nine Kreel scouts. In about five minutes, Lan will begin his return, above the tactical plane, to the designated post battle position ten kilometers above Gola. The volume seems clear of Kreel for the moment. I will advise you if that appraisal changes.

"Upon arrival Lan requests both Lent and Lawrence conduct a detailed active sensor sweep and examination of Lan. Although Lan appears damage free, the Kreel scouts were able to obtain active tracking of Lan. I need to understand how."

Kellon sat back and considered the next required actions. Then he remembered his inappropriate responses, and turning to Roy, he earnestly apologized. "Roy, I deeply regret my earlier comment. My response to your reminder about the Kreel scouts was inappropriate.

"Please clear my command band and then connect me with Lieutenant Oster."

Roy was looking toward Kellon and smiling broadly. He nodded his head in acknowledgment, but said nothing, and both men knew they needed to say nothing more. Kellon knew from the twinkle in Roy's blue eyes, and his smile that he had heard the expressed regret, please, and understood his sincerity.

"Sir, Navigation here, Lieutenant Oster is now connected to your command band."

First, taking a deep breath, and then letting it slowly out, Kellon turned his attention to his next task. "Lieutenant Oster, Captain Kellon here."

"Sir," came the confident response from the young Officer.

"Lieutenant, we have been somewhat busy and now I need your best assessment on the condition of the Gola, is she able to be salvaged and get underway under her own power?"

"Sir, I have talked in depth with the Gola's Captain. We have examined the data and records obtained from Gola in detail. It is our mutual assessment that the Gola, with minor repairs to the hull, could be underway within minutes of boarding. However, the Gola's Captain does request an additional three engineers be temporarily assigned to its engineering personnel, if that is to occur."

"Lieutenant Oster, be advised Lan will come alongside the Gola. Prepare the civilian crew to board and take up their duties. I am assigning you with nine men, of your choosing, to board the Gola with the civilian crew. I recommend a blend of engineers and security personnel, with an emphasis on security. While the Captain of the Gola will have operational control of the ship, you are to assume overall command."

"Yes Sir. What are my orders?"

"Your orders are to take the ship at best standard speed on to Glas Dinnein. You will be provided an armed escort, and en route you will receive instructions where the Gola is to be docked. Do you have any questions?"

"Sir, no Sir."

"Lieutenant Oster, be advised our operation is under a Black Hole classification. You will not permit any commercial or private communications from Gola, for any reason whatsoever. You will direct all necessary communications through your armed escort. While onboard Gola, your conversations with civilian personnel will be strictly circumspect.

"Lan will be moving back to the Gola in about ten minutes. Get your personnel squared away. Inform Commander Grey of the identity of your selected personnel, so he can make the necessary duty reassignments."

"Sir, yes Sir!"

"Carry on." Smiling, Kellon wondered if he could ever have been that enthusiastic. It was possible, but it must have been long ago and many missions back.

As Kellon looked around the CAC, Elayne's calm and assured voice reported, "Tactical here, Captain we have a clear sector and we find no Kreel signals."

"Countermeasures here, Captain there are no detected Kreel signals. Sir, Countermeasures is continuing its analysis of Lan's impaired stealth capability. We do not have an answer as yet."

"Kellon here, Tactical and Countermeasures, acknowledging all clear. Countermeasures, stay with that analysis, we need that answer."

Sitting back in his Command Chair, Kellon pondered the list of his immediate responsibilities and recent actions and grimaced. He had overlooked his second inappropriate response. Keying his CAC band, he apologized. "Countermeasures, Kellon here. Your gang was really on top of its mark during the last engagement. Well done. While I still want your report on my desk within two hours, you need not worry about scrubbing toilets or polishing decks. Again, well done."

Keying his general ship's communications band switch, he addressed Lan's entire crew. "Kellon here. Ladies and gentlemen, while Lan is experiencing impaired stealth, we are battle damage free. Tactical and Countermeasures have reported the tactical volume is clear. Accordingly, Lan is reducing readiness from Condition 2 to Condition 3. Each of you has again demonstrated your skill and professional ability. Everyone, well done. Kellon out.

"Lan, please transmit a Black Hole classified post combat status report to Guardian command."

"Navigation, move Lan well above the debris of the field of battle and carefully bring Lan back toward the Gola.

"Navigation here, acknowledging."

"Commander Greer, Jason kindly issue a recall for Scout ship Sheba, with a well-done. Ask Sheba to give Lan a sharp look-over with her active sensors on her return, perhaps she can determine what the Kreel were targeting on Lan before she returns to her hangar."

"Greer here, understood and complying."

"Navigation, Roy, inform both Lent and Lawrence Lan appears to be battle damage free and no Kreel signals are being detected. Lan is returning to put a crew aboard the Gola. Provide them our ETA.

"Navigation, you have the CAC."

"Sir, acknowledging Navigation has the CAC." Roy responded with a smile.

Kellon stepped down from his command chair and exiting from CAC spoke quietly, "Lan, very, very well done. Restore full verbal response."

Kellon suddenly felt very tired. He had lost count of the hours the mission had consumed. He then remembered young Lieutenant Oster's eager enthusiasm and smiled. Squaring his shoulders, and raising his head, striding briskly forward, he moved almost jauntily toward his predetermined destination. *A mature man with millenniums of experience, and tons of sex appeal, simply cannot let the younger officers think they have it all their way.* Thinking of a possible date with a very attractive and personable Guardian Cruiser Captain, he mischievously smiled. He did not notice the expressions of wonder and respect that those he met in the passageway automatically and sincerely extended toward him as they passed.

He regarded the future as something very bright and good. He suddenly realized how hungry he was. Quietly he spoke, "Lan, please advise the Wardroom the Captain requests Earth style hearty sandwiches for four, with pickles on the side, three bottles of red wine, some good sharp cheese, and four wine glasses be brought to the observation dome conference room. Then contact Commander Grey, Commander Greer and Lieutenant Cloud. Kindly inform them as soon as they can arrange relief, they are invited to join the Captain for some wine and cheese in order to celebrate life, including and especially our own."

Lan's response came with a subtle tone of warmth and enjoyment. "Sir, your orders have been carried out, and your invitation is happily accepted by all those you invited."

Chapter Eight:
No-Where Squared

Moving softly, coming gently off the ocean, the breeze embraced the tall trees with a light sea mist.

It was early, and the slightest lingering touch of the morning's chill pleasantly contrasted with the warmth of the freshening sunshine. The day was beginning with the promise of being pleasant, and there was not a single cloud. The vibrant hue of the light blue sky first met and then in a single linear stroke disappeared behind the horizon. Stretched out from the foreground, and meeting that distant skyline, was the broad plane of darker greens and turquoises of an equatorial ocean.

The clearness of the morning indicated, to those familiar with the island, the day would soon become very warm and possibly muggy. Locals knew enough to enjoy fully the early morning cool air, with its freshness accented by the distinct fragrances of the ocean, beach, and flowering trees. Combined together, the varied elements of the morning only added to the initial illusion the island was an untroubled tropical environment.

Rising immediately before Kellon was a high nondescript security wall, with only one broad opening in its circumference.

Above, and extending well beyond the wall, rose a camouflage netting system that blended smoothly with the surrounding natural terrain. Even standing this close to the structure, if one ignored the wall it was difficult to realize the mound created by the overhanging netting was artificial and not a natural part of the earth. Commander Shaw stood with Kellon, and both men were looking thoughtfully at the Kreel Gortoga Cruiser that was snuggly settled on a carefully engineered landing cradle, artfully concealed behind the wall and beneath the overshadowing netting.

Standing near and studying the planet-bound Kreel cruiser that was resting quietly before him, Kellon was surprised at how much Lan's sensors had obscured the actual mass and size of the physical presence of the ship. It was far larger when seen close up and from a standing vantage point; it was an immense physical object, whose outer hull soared outward and high above him. Its whole bulk extended far into the dim depths of the cavernous tent.

The activity in the area around the grounded ship was as a busy beehive, as from beneath the ship's curving hull people and ground cars arrived and departed. Kellon's first impression of the ship was that it was a graceful design, yet it was also wholly alien in the details of its form. Even resting stationary, he could still feel the ship's looming menace. In many ways, the ship represented a puzzle that would take many months to unravel, if indeed it was ever wholly unraveled.

Turning to Commander Shaw, Kellon asked, "Lorn, you were its skipper on the journey to Glas Dinnein, what is your own feeling about its capability?"

Lorn did not turn his head, but continued to look at the ship that dominated the scene before them. Well Sir," he responded dryly, "that ship has some qualities I frankly do not understand. We were able to get it underway and arrived here in one piece, but it is a Kreel ship and from what I have seen, genetics has wired their brains differently than ours. Its controls are, in my opinion, a confusing clutter of systems. By design, they all appear configured in a hodgepodge manner without apparent reason. How they can efficiently operate in a combat environment without chaos is beyond my understanding. You would need to be Kreel to love that ship.

Turning, Lorn looked at Kellon, and his expression was like his voice, troubled. "Sir, speaking personally, I was happy to see it on the ground in one piece, and happier to be alive and walking away from it.

"Sir, none of us boarding that ship had any idea of the stench of the Kreel and death we would encounter on board. After arriving here, the first thing I did was to spend two hours scrubbing with strong soap and a stiff brush in a hot shower. Then, I put on a new uniform and burnt the old one. Everyone in the boarding party did much the same."

Lorn's expression became hard. His voice unmistakably held the edge of anger, and Kellon knew well that anger, fully understanding from where it emerged. "Sir, what we found in that ship is enough to believe we will never have peace with the Kreel. What they did to the crew of the Gola is a nightmare. Maybe what we did to the Kreel was to kill them and there is no real difference, yet to find people killed, butchered, cut up and processed, and packaged for someone's dinner table, is something I will not forget. All that remained of those eleven men was unrecognizable as ever having been living men. The worst part of it is where they did that butchering, well Sir, it looked well used."

With each word he spoke, his anger swelled and poured out. "The best order I have ever been given was your order of no quarter. I admit, I didn't fully understand your reasons then, but now I do. We did not need it, but it was the right call. I do not believe I can ever forget what we found on that ship."

Listening quietly, Kellon heard Lorn's anger, and knew well the depth from which such anger poured forth. "Lorn, My own interaction with the Kreel is long and filled with bad memories. I do understand your feelings." Kellon acknowledged in a quiet voice.

Thrusting his hands uncharacteristically into his pants pockets, Lorn continued. "Sir, I have a formal request, please arrange for all the personnel who boarded that ship to receive appropriate psychological counseling, including me. We all need it."

Responding thoughtfully and with concern Kellon replied, "Lorn, your request is already a matter in process. The Kreel are what they are. It is necessary that we cope with that reality. It is also true that we are what we are, and it is essential we respect what makes us different from the Kreel. Our personal responsibility is always to honor the truth of our own beings, hearts and minds.

"As for being no quarter, neither Kreel nor humans entering combat will for their own reasons surrender to the other. You have now personally experienced one of the reasons why. However, there are many other reasons we fight the Kreel.

Smiling, Kellon returned the discussion onto more productive topics. "Enough pondering of the immutable. Lorn, I

73

owe you a cold brew and we have seen all we need to see here. Let's leave the reverse engineering of Kreel technology to those whose job it is. Come on– let's clear this place for better and happier surroundings."

Turning, they walked down the slight incline together and moved through the trees toward the weapons testing range's General Administration Building. They were walking on an island, in the middle of no-where squared, and it would take hours for them to reach Guardian Headquarters, since it was located halfway around the world.

As they walked, Lorn's demeanor softened, and he looked over to Kellon with a hint of a real smile. "Captain, thank you, I appreciate your coming all the way here to give me a quick lift home."

Reflecting Lorn's lighter mood, Kellon was feeling more at ease.

"Thanks are not required, Lorn. For personal reasons I needed to see that ship sitting on the ground firsthand, and I needed this closer look. Besides, I wanted to commend you personally for the outstanding job you did, it was dangerous and yet very well done. The way you accomplished it made it look simple. I know it wasn't."

Lorn welcomed the high praise from Kellon, and it brought an instant smile. His admiration for the Captain was boundless, and more importantly he considered him a good and trusted friend. "Sir, might I mention that your decision to use the Kreel beam was a gutsy call?"

Shaking his head, Kellon smiled at the comment. "Regretfully, Admiral Mer Shawn may not share your viewpoint. I did after all sorta mangle his combat policy and standing orders. I would not be taken by surprise if multiple flashes of lightning and rolling peals of heavy thunder descending from our high command were in my career's short term forecast."

Reaching the small landing area near the Admin building, they walked over to Kellon's waiting speeder. Punching in the key code, Kellon silently opened the door. Stepping on the threshold and lowering his head Kellon swung into the speeder's passenger compartment and moved over to the pilot's controls. Lorn entered and slid into the second seat. Reaching out he firmly brought the door snugly closed with a reassuring heavy thump.

By the time Lorn had closed, latched, and locked the door, the soft whisper of the propulsion system rose in its muted humming, and the cabin was pressurized.

Settling into his seat, Kellon quickly scanned the controls before him. "Quatrain departure, this is Lan-1 requesting clearance for immediate departure to Guardian Headquarters."

After a moment the response came back, "Lan-1, Quatrain control, you have immediate clearance to Guardian headquarters. Be advised you have a message pending from Admiral Cloud."

"Quatrain departure," acknowledged Kellon, "Lan-1 is departing. Thanks for your information concerning Admiral Cloud's message and for the hospitality."

Entering the necessary destination code into the navigation computer, Kellon then took manual control of the vehicle. With smooth and well-practiced movements of the controls, Kellon easily brought the vehicle to a hover, and then brought the ship through a graceful turn starboard, orientating the ship's heading toward the sparkling turquoise ocean and the unobstructed distant horizon. Smiling as the vehicle began to increase its horizontal speed, Kellon eased the speeder into a graceful arch skyward. He was clearly enjoying the personal satisfaction of manually controlled flight, and smiling he pulled out the acceleration control to its maximum settings. As he did, both Lorn and Kellon were gently but firmly pressed back into their seats as the craft leapt forward and accelerated swiftly skyward, heading for its distant destination.

As the vehicle reached its higher altitude, Kellon engaged the autopilot. Global Traffic Control noted the vehicle's departure from a military restricted area and smoothly integrated the vehicle's flight into the traffic control-matrix, checked authorization clearances, and then adjusted the vehicle's flight path for a yet higher altitude and priority transit.

Reaching over and selecting some listening music, Kellon relaxed as the music filled the cabin. Turning toward Lorn, he asked, "Would you like a root-beer?"

Raising his eyebrows, Lorn asked, with a smile, "What in the seven stars is a root-beer?"

Now it was Kellon's turn to smile. "Well, if you remember, about a year or so ago we discovered a planet named Earth. Now the Ambassador of that distant and mysterious planet, as you may remember her name is Susie Wells, informs me that root beer is an Earth beverage preferred by people with a cultivated taste. It is non-alcoholic and quite refreshing."

As Kellon completed his pitch there appeared in the center console two bottles of root beer, chilled and with droplets of moisture condensing over their surfaces. With some curiosity, Lorn lifted one bottle and examined the label. Removing the top, he sipped inquiringly at its contents with suspicion. He suddenly smiled, and turning to Kellon he cheerfully commented, "That is good. Might I ask if you smuggled some root beer from Earth onboard Lan, when no one was looking?"

Chuckling good-naturedly, Kellon responded, "You did not read the label as carefully as you should have. The root beer is the product of, and bottled by, the William and Shey bottling company."

Lorn began to laugh, "You're not kidding? You mean that two AIs have merged their collective talents to produce and bottle a beverage. What does Admiral Mer Shawn have to say about Shey, one of his prize Scout Ships, becoming a business tycoon with an AI from Earth?"

"Well, I have not yet had the opportunity to discuss the matter with the Admiral, and knowing the best part of valor is avoiding unnecessary risks, I will carefully avoid discussing that topic with him. Besides, Roan told me he had fully observed all the legal matters.

"It seems Ambassador Susie and her AI William have been having a significant influence on Shey, Roan, and Zorn. Susie was missing her root beer, and William has provided the formula and encouraged the development of the enterprise. Now they have all gone into business producing root beer for everyone who wants to sample the beverages of the distant and mysterious Earth. From what I hear, they are doing a booming business."

Lorn could not help but laugh. "Leave it to Roan and Zorn to end up in some process inclined more to enjoyment than actual work. It is terrific that Shey is also involved."

As the island and its grounded Kreel cruiser fell further behind them, their moods continued to lighten. Kellon, like Lorn was smiling. "It seems Shey has an unsuspected talent for commerce as well as her better known talent for stealth. She and

William are both enjoyably involved and having a fun time exploring commercial economic tactics and adaptations. What is remarkable is, of all the people on Earth and in the Guardian Force, it was two AIs, Shey and William, that made the first contact between Earth and Glas Dinnein. I would wager most people have forgotten that tidbit of information."

Taking another sip of the root beer, Lorn pondered what Kellon had said. He shook his head wonderingly. "You are correct. I had forgotten that little tidbit. It is amazing to think two machines, two very remarkable personalities, programmed or otherwise, made the first contact between two distant human-occupied worlds."

Turning toward Kellon, Lorn inquired about a rumor he had overheard. "Sir, I understand there was a breakdown in Lan's stealth profile during the last engagement. I haven't learned its cause. What was the problem?"

Remembering the occasion, frowning, Kellon explained. "Lorn, do not ever believe you know everything. I believe it is the little mistakes that can get you killed. Before the battle began, we were inert near the Gola, and stationary while waiting for the Kreel to reveal their pattern of attack. When they did begin their attack, I ordered a screamer deployed to Lan's port, and dispersed chaff to mask Lan. At the same time, we deployed a decoy and went 100% stealth. My plan was simple misdirection and illusion. However, I made a serious mistake. Lan was stationary when I deployed the screamer and chaff. One chaff canister dispersed its foil early. After the battle was over and I recalled Sheba, she looked at Lan and broke out in giggles. I had never before heard a Scout ship giggle. Frankly, I didn't even know they could."

Thoughtfully, Lorn considered Kellon's comment before responding. "That's strange; I didn't believe AIs could laugh."

"Well, Lorn, I am here to tell you Sheba can certainly giggle. Anyway, she told Lan he looked like a fruit tree decorated for the Spring Festival and was wearing full party attire. The worst part of the problem was getting the foil off the hull; it stuck as if the yard workers had glued it there. In my post operations summary my formal recommendation to Guardian Force personnel was not to deploy chaff while stationary."

"Sir, about Sheba giggling. I have noticed something about the AIs. While they all have a team of programmers, even when they begin with the same instruction set, they soon begin to evolve unique character traits. I have especially noticed since we were near Earth, Lan's responses are much richer and more personable. It is my observation Lan is becoming more mature, showing real personality depth, rather than simple programmed logical responses. I am continually marveling at what he is able to accomplish."

Lorn's comment struck a resonant chord in his mind, and Kellon paused to consider its broader implications. "I know what you mean. I am with Lan nearly every waking hour. Since our visit to Earth, It has become commonplace for him to anticipate what I am going to ask for. I agree; his personality is obviously richer in its tone and character. I believe it may be profitable for us to keep notes on what we are observing. A brief report to Admiral Mer Shawn might be in order.

"Speaking of Admirals, I need to respond to one.

"Computer," Kellon ordered, "scan pending messages for a message from Admiral Cloud. Is the message oral or written?"

The computer's response was a neutral tone, lacking the vitality of an AI, "The message is located. The message logged time is twenty-seven minutes ago. It is oral."

"Computer, play the message."

Admiral Cloud's well recognized voice seemed tired, as if he had been working long hours, and had not received much time off for sleep. "Captain Kellon, Cloud here. When you return to Headquarters, please come to see me. There are some developments regarding Earth that I would like to discuss with you. Reports indicate the Arkillians are successfully revitalizing Monstro, and I thought you might want to know. Cloud out."

Sitting back, Kellon closed his eyes. Inwardly he recalled the events the year before, and the sharp deadly battle between Lan, his Scouts, and Monstro, the massive Arkillian's sub-lightspeed Nest ship. They had not called the ship Monstro then, that nickname became attached only after Lan's contact with Earth's Olympus personnel. The name had stuck.

Frowning again, Kellon expressed his thoughts aloud, "Monstro appears to have a determined crew. It has been at least eight or nine months since the battle. Given the elapsed time,

Lan must have significantly damaged that ship. Knowing the ship's inactivity over these past months, I had begun to believe it was actually finished."

His attitude shifted from reflection to speculation as Lorn commented. "Sir, if you are correct, then I doubt that ship is seeking anything more robust than a leisurely cruise home. It cannot be combat capable after the damage we inflicted on it, no ship could be. That it is still maneuverable is surprising, I thought the deep salvage team was going to pick it up months ago."

"That was the initial plan, Lorn. Our monitoring sentinel however was detecting increased energy output, and Admiral Mer Shawn put a hold on that plan. He wanted to observe the ship and the behavior of its crew, before he determined his next action. Computer, take a verbal message for Admiral Ron Cloud, Guardian Headquarters.

"Admiral Cloud, Kellon here. Commander Shaw and I are in-flight and returning to headquarters. Anticipate arrival in approximately five hours. Please advise if we are to come to see you upon arrival or in the morning. Kellon out."

Admiral Cloud's response came back within a few minutes. It was three words: immediately upon arrival.

Chapter Nine:
Survivor

Walking across the Nest ship's forward hangar deck, Kur found it was much colder than he thought it would be. He made a mental note to check the temperature levels in the other reclaimed compartments. It would require energy to heat them, but he knew the ship's power systems were more than adequate.

Inwardly he felt alone and isolated. He was the last Council Member remaining aboard the ship. Rather than being able to speak of his concerns with Ca or Rin, he was mentally reviewing and analyzing the daily decisions alone. At first, he would wake in the middle of the night, and his mind would be churning with the sharp problems of surviving and memories of the battle. Those memories, he feared, would be with him the rest of his life.

Shivering he stopped and slowly looked at the hanger area around him. Gone was its normal vibrant activity. It was depressively dark, shabby, bare, and unnaturally quiet.

He noted portions of the area were in deep shadows, and even in the dim light, the scattered debris littering the compartment was apparent. That the hanger was not orderly did not cause him anger, as it once would have. There were now matters far more important that demanded his attention. *Even so, for the sake of the crew's morale and confidence,* he thought, *I will need to see the area properly lighted and restored to a proper order.* Sighing, he made another mental note to speak with the Captain about getting the task accomplished.

He fully understood survival had only been possible because of the careful design of the ship. All of its most critical life support, command and control, and engineering systems, were located within the very core of the ship and not in its outer compartments.

Before the battle began the internal ship's status was battle ready and rigidly compartmentalized. As the striking missiles breached outer compartments, the separated adjacent inner compartments survived. Those Arkillians in the breached compartments died either from exposure to the vacuum of space or from the blast and spray of molten metal when thousands of small missiles pierced the outer hull. In just a few minutes time the missiles had killed more than 40% of the crew and heavily damaged the ship. The multiple compartmentalization of the internal structure was all that prevented the ship from being destroyed, and preserved their lives.

Now he stood alone, a survivor of the battle, standing in and looking around the reclaimed hangar deck. It was with sadness he remembered following the battle the ship was inert, most of its outer compartments open and exposed to the hard vacuum of space.

The enemy had destroyed the majority of their defending fighters during the brief battle, and the small surviving remnant was widely scattered and disorganized. It had taken him more than a day to coordinate and organize the remaining functional cargo lifters. He then sent them out to seek and recover the disabled fighters, where they could find survivors. Fortunately, they did find a few survivors.

There were only twelve undamaged fighters now in the hangar, out of more than one hundred gleaming craft that had once proudly filled the hangars. Another twenty-seven damaged fighters in various states of disrepair had been located and recovered. With effort and replacement parts, they might eventually see future service. However, the remaining fighters and their crews were either lost beyond detection or else were only drifting wreckage scattered along the battle line.

His first responsibility after the battle had been to restore life support functions and basic power systems. Then there was the hard work of treating the wounded and providing the honored dead with the proper space burial. As the crew reclaimed each compartment, one compartment at a time, the process of recovering the dead was on going. He could personally testify such tasks were difficult and emotionally painful. He understood the after images of what he had seen would remain in his mind for the remainder of his life. Like many others in the crew, he was also struggling daily with the emotions of guilt that so many other Arkillians were now dead while he had survived.

One of his first decisions was to prioritize the restoration of the ship's sensors, and regain the ability to monitor surrounding space. If the enemy was continuing to lurk nearby, then he needed desperately to know that. In that most of the sensors and equipment required to accomplish such surveillance were in the outer damaged compartments, he had first needed to identify the priority of which compartments to reclaim. There followed weeks of intense work repairing sensors and equipment, bringing them to a functional order, where surrounding space could again be monitored.

It was only after they had stabilized the most critical problems that he turned his attention to the problem of propulsion. Besides, he rationalized, it was far better if the enemy believe the ship was only a harmless derelict. Every passing day saw the ballistic trajectory and velocity of the ship carry it further from Earth and hopefully further from the attention of the enemy.

For months now, he required the crew passively monitor the surrounding space, and methodically look for any sign of propulsion signatures or tell-tale communications. Their diligent efforts found no trace of the enemy.

He knew it was the focused goal of survival, demanding the repair of the damage on the ship that had preserved his sanity. He still felt a sense of disbelief the ship was once again underway, even if only barely.

Because of the extent of the damage, just to make the repairs necessary to get underway had taken many months of hard planning and work. That they were now underway represented a tribute to the training, traditions, tenacity and skill of the entire ship's crew.

Only when he was completely convinced the Nest ship was alone and unobserved did he finally give the Captain permission to test and then very slowly engage the restored propulsion systems. Using minimal power the ship was now underway; it was however not the vibrant and powerful ship that had proudly departed Scion.

Soon they would be beginning the complex procedure of redirecting the ship's significant accumulated inertia through a wide arc of nearly 180 degrees, directing it again toward Scion. Defining that maneuver was the next decision he must make. The selected course would not provide a direct line toward Scion, but would over time curve and be adjusted to safely bring the crippled ship home. Scion, home, it was still years away and even now he knew nothing would be ever the same.

Never before had he felt so alone and vulnerable in space. That inner hollow feeling of vulnerability translated into fear, and his fear was something that he could not permit others to see.

His bitterness toward the Kreel was not consuming but it was something that gnawed at his mental presence every day. Try as he might, he could not alter his conviction. Only the Kreel capabilities fitted the events and the Kreel must have been the attackers. The trouble was he did not know that to be the truth and the doubt nagged at him.

Observing, he watched a work crew in space suits about to enter a portable lock attached to the adjacent compromised compartment. When they entered that compartment, they would be plugging each of the thousands of remaining holes pierced through the hull, one compartment at a time. He knew it would take more months of work to reclaim the damaged compartments and begin to restore them to their initial functions. While it would take months, they had years remaining before they would arrive on Scion. He also knew that full functionality would not be possible until the ship returned to Scion and the builders came aboard and began a full refit of the ship.

He slowly turned, remembering standing here in the same hangar deck with Rin. He laughed bitterly, thinking, *I am not only the senior member of the Arkillians' Council onboard; I am the only member.* Before leaving Earth, there were three Council Members, but he had decided to leave Ca and Rin on Earth. Now, they had the momentary safety and security of the concealed facility in the Gobi Desert.

From time to time, he stopped to consider what might be happening to them, but knew they were most probably doing well. Their Earth side facility was well-concealed and amply provisioned. He knew they were serving an invaluable service in monitoring the events and observing what had happened. Even so, he needed to remind himself, when the ship left Earth's orbit, the ship's survival was not certain. His decision to send Ca and

Rin to safety had been the correct choice. Yet his confidence in the correctness of that decision was no longer unquestioned. It had been made with the belief the enemy was the Dargon, raiders with short-term objectives, and not the Kreel, whose ambitions were much longer-term.

Given the apparent strength of the enemy and outcome of the battle, the idea of eventual relief for Ca and Rin seemed suddenly improbable. He may in fact have permanently marooned all of them on Earth with possibly disastrous consequences. Thinking of that possibility grieved him more than the loss of the Arkillians who had died in space.

Could he dare take the ship back into the inner solar system and attempt a rescue of the marooned Arkillians? He could certainly direct the ship back toward Earth. Would the enemy perceive such action as provoking further hostility? He simply did not know. What he knew was both Ca and Rin were Council Members, and more importantly, they were his friends.

When given the ultimatum to surrender, he had rejected that demand, and decided to fight. Now, because of his decision, 40% of the ship's crew were dead. Did he dare take any unnecessary action that could get the remaining 60% killed?

Remembering what Rin said months ago now appeared a clear warning that things were not as they then appeared. The insight Rin had offered that day still gnawingly haunted him; *Even from a rudimentary military understanding, it seems unwise for us to be that detectable and predictable, especially by a lower mammal species.*

He remembered the information regarding the probable identity of the attacking force. He possessed information that had not helped him before the battle, and it still taunted him. Only the Kreel seemed likely, but he had no facts or evidence to prove that inference.

There was only one fact ultimately established, the humans on Earth lacked the technical capability to have attacked the Nest ship. This being true, then who else could have attacked other than the Kreel?

The attacker had to be from elsewhere in the Galaxy. He could but wonder, *from where?* He continued to worry the problem that had nagged him every waking hour. He well remembered the senior tactical Officer's assessment when it was still believed the Dargon were the threat. *That the Dargon ship managed to evade our main battery fire response while inflicting heavy damage on those fighters that closed on him, reveals that the Dargon have courage, tenacity and cunning.*

As he looked around, the damages confirmed the Officer's tactical assessment; whoever they were, they had indeed proven themselves a formidable enemy.

He did not now believe Dargon forces had attacked them. Again, his mind returned to the Kreel as being the probable attackers. *However,* he reasoned, *the Kreel are predators, and like the Dargon, are not inclined to diplomacy.* That he was still alive, and the ship was intact to eventually get underway, underscored the attackers had shown mercy on a defeated enemy. That did not denote either Dargon or Kreel behavior.

For that matter, he reluctantly admitted, likewise mercy was not an Arkillian attitude or trait. The outcome of battle proved a defeated enemy was an inferior, and as a conquered foe, the Arkillians showed that enemy no mercy.

That was the established harsh law and reality of the Universe, and it had always been so. He shook his head in uncertainty and deep in troubled thought, turned to go back to his own quarters.

As he turned, he saw the ship's tactical Officer respectfully waiting to speak with him. He noted with a sense of pride the Officer was impeccable in his bearing, uniform and demeanor. Returning the Officer's salute, he asked, "What is the purpose of your seeking me?"

"Honored One, the Captain asked me to inform you that the ship is responding well and Navigation will require instructions concerning our speed and set course within the next tenth cycle."

"Please inform the Captain I have received his message and will meet with him soon. Also, I commend you on your appearance and bearing."

"Honored One, Your notice is gratefully acknowledged." The Officer saluted smartly, then turned and purposefully departed toward the control and bridge area.

The Officer's presence and bearing had reminded him the Nest ship was still an Arkillian Capital ship, and although badly damaged it represented Scion. Looking again at the clutter of debris in the hangar area, he underscored in his own mind the

86

importance of directing the Captain to have the crew properly clear and put the reclaimed compartments in good order.

Entering his private compartments, he was immediately grateful for the warmth about him. His spacious and luxuriously appointed compartments properly reflected his status as the senior ranking member of the Arkillian Council. More importantly, after the coldness in the hangar, he relished its embracing comfort, as if its mere existence alone assured his continued safety.

Again, he moved to and took the seat at his broad deeply grained and carved wooden worktable. It was one of his prize trophies obtained from Earth more than a thousand turns before. He slowly ran his hands over the familiar polished smooth dense grain of the table, taking pleasure in its richness and remembering happier times.

Sitting quietly he looked up at the pictures on his walls. They were of Scion as seen from space and of his Nest mates. He looked at the pictures much as a starving person might look upon a banquet table laid out before him, only to find it was behind a sheet of glass and beyond his reach. He ached in every bone and cell of his body for home.

Reluctantly he looked toward the screen on the bulkhead. Should he once more watch the images of the human male issuing his ultimatum?

How could he believe a human male could be on a Kreel ship and still alive? In truth, he could not. The Kreel considered humans inferior mammals, prey, and if obtainable a highly prized food.

That the Kreel ate human flesh, if they could obtain it, sickened him. Like all Arkillians, he considered the idea disgusting. When they did learn what the Kreel did to the few humans they had sent to the Kreel, they never sold any others. The Kreel had offered sizeable sums to alter the Arkillian's stubborn position on the subject, but the Arkillians flatly rejected the Kreel offers. While humans were a lower species, they undoubtedly had a sense of sentience. To eat any sentient being was morally inconceivable to the Arkillians.

He firmly believed there was no possibility a human male could be on a Kreel ship and still be alive. He knew the twin destructive beams he had directed through that Kreel Cruiser should have immediately killed both Kreel and humans alike. What was certain was the weapon had not killed them. There must be some reason for such a failure of a proven weapon system, but what it was he did not know. That the weapon had not worked added to the confusion, suggesting possibly the crew of the ship was a species other than either Kreel or humans.

What he was certain of was, the Kreel cruiser was gone and there was no wreckage. Only the scattered wreckage of the Arkillian fighters and the mangled Nest ship remained as proof the Kreel cruiser had ever existed. More proof the Kreel ship did exist was the two recordings of the transmissions that preceded and followed the battle. Those recorded messages provided ample evidence of what had happened, but the natural conclusions reached from seeing and hearing them was both contradictory and inconceivable.

His fingers once again moved over the controls of his view screen and for possibly the two hundredth time he again keyed the recording of the transmissions. The image of the mammal again spoke calmly in the Arkillian language, with authority and command.

"My name is Kellon. You have been observed entering into this solar system on a hostile mission. The evidence of your previous aggressions against the inhabitants of the third planet is blatant, and we have documented it. Your long-term actions against the human populations in this solar system are murderous acts and criminal in nature. Your barbaric aggression is ended, here and now!"

Kur stopped the recording and sat looking at the human male, whose image stared out of the screen. If he ignored the evidence of a Kreel ship, accepting only the information provided by the message itself, then what it conveyed was of monumental significance. The spoken words fell like a striking hammer on his mind; *Your long-term actions against the human populations in this solar system are deemed murderous and are criminal in nature.*

For more than fourteen thousand Earth years, the Arkillians had controlled the Earth. That control had begun with the intentional destruction of the civilizations that then existed on the planet. The Arkillians simply destroyed billions of human lives in a few days. To the Arkillians it was a simple and

88

methodical process of ridding a planet of a troublesome vermin and nothing more. There had been no long arguments in the Council, no lamentations of it being morally wrong, and they gave no consideration that another culture might view such actions as a barbaric act of murder. The Arkillians had the force and power to act and had done so without remorse. It was their absolute right as a superior life form.

Likewise, there had been no remorse by the Arkillians in the biological and genetic manipulation of the surviving human population. It was a matter of simple herd management. The Council had classified humanity, and their inferiority as an inferior species was self-evident. Rin had simply summarized the presumed truth in his assessment, *Especially by a lower mammal species.*

Now he wondered if that long-held opinion was in truth supported by the facts and had begun seriously to doubt it. The humans on Earth had recently advanced in the sciences until they again posed a possible threat to the Arkillians' easy hold on the planet. That was an undisputed fact.

Arrogance, did it all come down to species pride and arrogance? Arkillian arrogance?

Now, looking at the man's image fixed on the screen, he began to reconsider what the Arkillians had done. The words *This solar system are deemed murderous*, continued to trouble him, *This solar system?* There must be another solar system, but where? The probability of two planets developing in parallel and having the same species was astronomically improbable. Could human beings actually be living on other worlds in other solar systems? How could such a reality be possible?

Assuming that the truth was most likely the most simple and evident possibility, then the only rational conclusion was other human beings did live in other solar systems, and they had what the Arkillians lacked, faster-than-light space ships. They also must have knowledge of the Kreel. That fact was inescapable, since they had used a Kreel parley signal in communicating with the Nest ship. Now given that possibility, he worried, who was the superior and who was the inferior species?

If he applied the tactical Officer's assessment to humans, rather than the Dargon, then the humans have courage, tenacity, and cunning and are a formidable enemy. *None of those qualities referred to a sub-inferior-species,* he fretted.

He fast-forwarded the recording and then restored it to its normal speed. He sat listening carefully to the selected message segment.

"If you choose to surrender, we would consider letting you return to your home solar system, but understand this, we will demand restitution for your criminal acts against humanity."

He considered the spoken words, knowing in order to demand restitution an imbalance of power in some form or other need first exist, and those making the demand for restitution must have the upper hand. Assuming the image of the man was really a man, his confident demand for restitution implied confidence in an ability to extract such restitution. It also proclaimed the speaker was not concerned about locating Scion. His attitude announced he knew Scion's location. He even alluded those surrendering might be returned home. If the man actually existed and spoke the truth, he reasoned, then fourteen thousand years of Arkillian arrogance is a very high cultural hedge over which to leap. He wondered, could the Arkillians make such a cultural transition and survive the emotional and physiological consequences of that metamorphosis? He well understood: while the Council had not debated before they rendered Earth primitive, fourteen thousand Earth years before, debate would rage in the Council long days before any restitution would ever be forthcoming. Paying restitution of any kind would literally mean the end of the Arkillians' hopes for establishing a truly interstellar Empire. Even more importantly, it would mean the Arkillians would need to bend their pride and stiff knees to a mammal species of acknowledged superior capability. He shuddered and cringed inwardly, such thoughts in themselves were harsh and hardly to be contemplated.

He again fast forwarded the recording and stopped at the verbal message received following the battle.

"Attention Arkillians. Your hostile action directed toward my ship has resulted in your current state. You would have been far wiser if you had accepted our demands. I have broken off the attack. You may safely attend to your wounded. Unless you provoke further hostility by more belligerent action, I consider the battle concluded.

"As to what will happen to you, that is again your choice. The demands given to you before the battle are still tendered. I will be monitoring this channel. If there is still anyone alive with authority to speak for the Arkillians, then let him identify himself. Who speaks for the Arkillians?"

He sat dourly in thought. He alone had ordered the ship to fight. He was responsible for the deaths of more than 40% of its crew. Now, if the ship survived at all, it would do so as a cripple trying to get home. The enemy had reduced the ship's offensive capability to a useless state, and there was absolutely no possibility of surviving another battle. Any thought of another battle or belligerent action was therefore out of the question.

In spite of their being summarily defeated, he felt a sense of pride knowing the Arkillians had fought with courage. The enemy had demonstrated a superior technology, and skillful tactics, but the Arkillians had exhibited steadfast courage and resolve. He also knew well it was not Arkillian courage that won the day. Rather it was the enemy who had magnanimously granted life to the survivors. Granting them life and the opportunity to go home.

He had two obvious choices, remain silent, and in full retreat, head for Scion or else establish communications with the enemy. It was this latter possibility that haunted his dreams and destroyed his desire to eat. If he were to establish communications with the enemy, what would it gain? What could he say or have to offer? The battle had reduced him to the status of a vagrant seeking alms. He was no longer the invincible conqueror. *Who and what are you Kellon?* He wanted to scream.

Chapter Ten:
Diplomacy

Although the flight time had only been about five hours, they were now flying into a mid-evening environment, having traveled nearly half way around Glas Dinnein. Overhead, the blue sky had gradually become the darkness of a clear night that was hosting an astonishing display of shimmering stars.

Noticing the blinking amber light on the control panel, Kellon adjusted the controls to exit global traffic control and automatically enter the local Guardian Headquarters control grid. In response, their small speeder nosed sharply downward from the thin air of the upper stratosphere into the more dense air of the troposphere.

As Ground Control directed the vehicle flight through a steep descent, the lights of the headquarters complex and surrounding countryside spread out for Lorn and Kellon's full enjoyment. There were dozens of bright widely spaced soaring structures, towers rising steeply skyward in illuminated spires, widely distributed and surrounded in distinct islands of multi-hued lights. The city lights appeared as a fantastic pattern of interconnecting multi-hued sparkling bands.

Kellon smiled, always enjoying the special quality of flying over a large city at night. It was not possible for him to avoid wondering about all the people moving about so slowly on the highways and byways, busy in their own thoughts and lives, oblivious to the observers so high above.

Still with a sense of pleasure and smiling inwardly, Kellon watched the lights from the slow moving ground transportation stream along the coastal highway, and he noticed a few isolated vehicles moving on the darker secondary streets.

The ocean was to the north, and there the nightscape was utterly black. There was a sharp delineation where the sprawling inland lights and coastal highway met and the flowing lights followed the unseen curve of the ocean and its unyielding coastline. The expansive vista was simply beautiful.

Both Kellon and Lorn sat enjoying the view, as flight control directed the speeder toward its ground destination. Responding to flight control, the speeder smoothly rolled, banking steeply, making a tight curve to port, and then straightening out on a short straight line north out over the dark ocean. Then the speeder abruptly reversed the roll, tightly curving about 180 degrees to the starboard, steadying on a course toward the south, while continuing to drop rapidly, extending its descending trajectory towards the Guardian Headquarters' landing field. As they crossed the coastline, their flight path smoothly leveled out and stretched toward the designated point of touchdown. Kellon let the ground computers handle the approach and simply enjoyed the view as the little craft glided smoothly over the surface and then gently settled to rest, near several other similar speeders.

As Lorn opened the door and began to get out he groaned, "I am as stiff as a board."

Kellon moved from the pilot's seat and keeping his head low, to avoid bumping the door frame, he stepped lightly from the threshold out onto the ground. Shutting the door behind him, he leisurely stretched and smiled inwardly. *I might be stiff,* he thought, *but being older and wiser, Lorn is not about to hear me groan, since I know the illusion of invincibility is maintained by remaining very quiet.* With a jest in his voice he innocently asked, "What is the matter Lorn, are your years catching up with you?"

Lorn looked over to Kellon, and in a knowing response, merely grinned. As he did, the ground bug arrived with an accompanying sound of tires and the squawking sound of brakes. Kellon youthfully hopped into the bug and Lorn quickly followed.

Kellon addressed the bug. "Transport us to Guardian Intelligence, Admiral Cloud's office." The bug emitted a warning note, slid its doors closed, and smoothly moved off towards the main building complex.

Fifteen minutes later Kellon and Lorn entered Guardian Intelligence. The Duty Officer recognized Kellon and with an acknowledging nod informed them, "The Admiral is waiting for you in Operations."

Kellon thanked the Officer, and then exiting Admiral Cloud's office, they walked through the hallways to Guardian Operations. The hour was late, but as normal, the hallways were busy all hours of the day and night. As they moved through the halls, they passed a number of others, men and women, who were hurriedly going about their own business.

"Sir," Lorn asked, "what do you think is brewing to keep the Admiral this late in Operations?"

"Lorn, when I was a Cadet I learned not to ask why, when I could simply wait for a short time and have a definitive answer. It is far easier to simply wait and see what we shall see, rather than worry without sufficient data to reach a meaningful conclusion."

They entered into the Operations outer area and two alert Guardian Security personnel met them. Both were wearing sidearms, indicating a Black Hole level operation was in progress. Kellon and Lorn waited patiently as one man used his communicator to check with the Operations Officer, verifying Kellon and Lorn had approved access to the inner area. The second security man maintained a relaxed and courteous vigil of Kellon and Lorn, while keeping his right hand near his sidearm.

Receiving clearance, the door to the inner operations area softly buzzed and swung open. Kellon and Lorn nodded to the Security personnel and proceeded into the inner rooms.

As the door closed behind them with a thump, and the sound of heavy bolts moving into place, they stood for a moment to allow their eyes to adjust to the lower level of illumination. As they waited, Admiral Cloud came out of one of the adjoining tactical conference rooms and motioned for them to join him.

Kellon noted there were two more Guardian Security personnel in the hall wearing sidearms. They were standing strategically positioned on each side of the door. The Admiral indicated they should enter.

Upon entering the room, Kellon and Lorn both saluted the Admiral. The Admiral crisply returned the salute. "Gentlemen, please be at ease."

As the door into the hall closed behind them, Kellon became aware of the acoustics in the room. He knew at once, the room was very heavily sound-proofed. Looking about, he saw three textured and neutral colored walls, a rear and two sidewalls.

Pictures of various Guardian ships were all that adorned them. The floor he stood on was thickly carpeted and of a rich dark soil tone. He saw along the front wall a wide multi-paned glass window rising from waist height to the ceiling and stretching the width of the room. Positioned against the window was a long wooden table, with six chairs that were all facing the glass barrier. He noticed there were several communications sets conveniently positioned on the table before each chair.

There was a narrow aisle separating a raised platform, at the rear of the room, from the front table and chairs. On the platform was a second row of six chairs, each chair having a small side table and communications set next to it. The light in the room came mostly from the adjacent dimly lit room, augmented by a soft diffused illumination radiating uniformly from the ceiling.

Admiral Cloud indicated, with a gesture, they should take chairs at the long table. Then, without further comment, he sat down. Taking the offered chairs both men turned to face Admiral Cloud. "Captain Kellon, Commander Shaw, thank you for coming so promptly. This is the first time I have had an opportunity to see you since your recent mission. I am certain that Admiral Mer Shawn has some matters he wants to go over with you concerning what happened, but for myself I want to express my congratulations. Your mission has produced some early fruits, and that is why I asked you to come here tonight.

"I personally wanted to brief you on what is happening and on what is about to happen. I request you bear with me, since there is considerable information I need to cover, and there's little time in which to do so."

The Admiral turned toward the glass partition that separated the room from the larger adjacent room, where men and women were working. As Kellon also looked at the activity in the larger room, he saw many of the features of Lan's combat analysis center. Before them on the far wall was a large illuminated tactical plot and in front of it were several tables and workstations. The room was dimly illuminated and he could not hear any sound coming from beyond the window. Settling into their chairs, they waited with interest for the Admiral to continue.

Admiral Cloud looked toward the two men, remaining quiet for a few moments before speaking. "Gentlemen, as you are aware, the analysis of the weapon and engineering systems on the Kreel Cruiser you provided will take time to fully evaluate. As important as that information is, there was something of far greater value on that ship. We have only begun to probe what we obtained, but even at this early stage, the results are most satisfying.

"The plot board you can see on the far wall is tracking seventeen Kreel warships, currently operating in Guardian space between the eleven planets."

In surprise, both Kellon and Lorn turned to look at the plot board. As they studied the board Admiral Cloud waited for a moment, and then he continued the briefing.

"As you are aware, your last mission is under a Black Hole classification. That extreme classification is the result of what we obtained from the Kreel ship, that being its entire communications system, including the Kreel encryption systems and ciphers, along with their related keys. In addition we have obtained a complete undamaged Kreel database that has given us our very first look at what the Kreel consider to be their own Empire and volume of space."

Admiral Cloud watched as both Kellon and Lorn first looked at each other and then in mute silence turned their attention back toward him.

"You can fully understand the true magnitude and value of our acquisition of such a treasure trove. Over the past several thousand years, we have covertly sent ships inward into Kreel space and dispersed monitoring buoys to listen to Kreel communications. While these dangerous missions have provided us with an enormous amount of general information, the important Kreel fleet communications were either undetectable or else tightly encrypted. Although we have tried, we were unable to crack their fleet communications systems. This meant the Kreel have had the advantage of secure fleet communications. Our being unable to obtain access to their fleet communications required us to react in a defensive role, monitoring for what they are doing, rather than our being able to get out in front of them.

"Now, because of our having access to the communications systems and related manuals on the ship you captured, for the first time, we can listen to some of the Kreel fleet operations.

This includes tactical orders directing their ships, and the routine reports sent back from those ships.

"For the first time we have the ability to roll back the clock and look at older Kreel com-intercepts we have on record. As sparse and incomplete as those records are, they are now a virtual gold mine. We have begun to mine that information and are already obtaining extraordinary data that we have never before obtained. "One of the most valuable aspects of what we have learned is how the Kreel faster-than-light communications systems work. Given the captured Kreel communications systems, we now understand just how advanced the Kreel are. In brief, they are beyond our own technology. This explains one reason why they were so undetectable. Until now we had no real idea of just how far advanced they really are. Now we are taking full advantage of the new insights we've obtained from their equipment and manuals." Smiling he added, "The physicists are all having a field day with the new data they are gleaning from what you brought home. What they are learning, and the extrapolations they're building on the new information, will have far-reaching benefits for our communications and advanced propulsion research. We don't yet know how long it will take to implement the improvements in our own communications. When we do get the new technology implemented, the reduction in communications time lag between Earth and Glas Dinnein will be significant. The anticipated technical advances will also improve communications between Fleet Command and fleet units.

"All of these major developments are a direct result of your capturing of that Kreel Cruiser. This is why we are strictly imposing the Black Hole classification. The Kreel must not learn we captured one of their cruisers intact and undamaged.

"Currently, the Kreel have taken specific note of the loss of four of their most advanced cruisers, and they are seeking intelligence on what happened to them.

One of the first benefits of our new intelligence capability has been the interception and destruction of two Kreel ships, two of their lighter armed fast-attack Tuen Class. They were independently tracking along the path of the three cruisers you destroyed. We did not permit them to reach the area of the battle. We have closed off that entire volume of space to Kreel probing, and we will continue to destroy any of their ships attempting to enter into that space. I am guessing that the Kreel will not be able to disregard such losses in one area indefinitely. As to how they will respond, that is unknown.

"With the new intelligence now available, we are beginning to effectively shift our own limited forces to neutralize the Kreel, wherever they pose a threat. In short, we are applying pressure, like none they have faced before. The Kreel may well see it as a counter attack. This fact alone should cause them to shift their immediate concern away from the loss of four cruisers and two fast-attack ships.

"As for the captured database, we have just begun to understand its structure. Fully probing the information it contains will require considerable diligent effort and a great deal of time.

"Even so, we have had some early success and surprises. For example, the Kreel have extensive information concerning the Arkillians you encountered near Earth. It seems the Kreel hold the Arkillians in utter contempt, and they are well along in their plans to conquer and subordinate them."

Admiral Cloud's statement caught Kellon by surprise, and he realized that if the Kreel did conquer the Arkillians, they would be only ten light-years from Earth. That alarmed him. "Sir, is there any information regarding when the Kreel will strike?" Kellon asked.

"Not yet. However, they are now preparing to send surveillance and reconnaissance ships to explore Arkillian space."

"Sir, are the Kreel aware of Earth?" Lorn asked.

"Yes, they are. The Kreel want to find that human-occupied planet with a vengeance. In fact, it may be the known existence of a human-occupied planet that has motivated the Kreel to subordinate the Arkillians at this time."

Both Kellon and Lorn sat quietly, listening. They were integrating Admiral Cloud's briefing in growing concern.

"The Kreel plans for suppressing the Arkillians and the imminent threat to Earth are why I ask you to come here tonight. Humanity is at a fulcrum point, and what Guardian Force does next will go far to shape our future."

His initial alarm had not lessened, and Kellon wondered what more they might do to protect Earth. "Sir, is there a response currently planned?" Kellon inquired.

"Yes Captain Kellon, there is. That response is the prime reason for your being here tonight. As you remember, you left the Arkillian ship you battled adrift on a ballistic trajectory, that trajectory taking it further from Earth. The monitoring sentinel you assigned to monitor that ship is still reporting on its current condition. The latest data we received from the sentinel is showing the Arkillian ship emitting increased levels of energy. This affirms they have reestablished their internal ship's power. It also indicates the Arkillian crew is working steadily to successfully reclaim the damaged outer compartments. More importantly, recently the sentinel monitored a series of short bursts of propulsion waves, indicating they are preparing to bring their propulsion system on line. This means the ship will soon resume powered flight and get underway.

"With the information available, our assessment is the ship is severely damaged and does not represent a combat threat. We will nevertheless continue to monitor its progress to determine its position and evaluate what action its Commanders take.

"As to our response, Captain Kellon, both Admiral Mer Shawn and I want you to take Lan back to Earth. We want you to make contact with that ship, and determine if there is anyone on board with the authority to speak for the Arkillians. If there isn't, then you are to contact the surviving Arkillians still on Earth. You are to determine if anyone in that facility has the authority to speak for the Arkillians."

Kellon's concern was steadily increasing. *Why was it so important to find some Arkillian with the authority to speak for his species?* Don't assume, ask, was Kellon's practice, therefore, he asked. "Sir, might I ask, why is it important to seek such an Arkillian?"

"That's a fair question Captain. We believe that if the Arkillians learn of the pending Kreel's intentions, they may side with us against the Kreel. Therefore, the primary purpose of your mission is diplomatic, not combat."

If someone had unexpectedly thrown a cold wet towel in his face, Kellon could not have been more surprised. Kellon stiffened, and asked, "Admiral Cloud, are you proposing the

100

Arkillians become allies? Is this a Guardian Force action, and something the Planetary Assembly and Admiral Secretary Eryan Kyrie have endorsed?"

Admiral Cloud's face revealed deep lines of weariness, and Kellon's questions only intensified those lines. "Kellon, the political situation here is fragile at best. The Planetary Assembly is expressing varied opinions about what we should do regarding the Earth. At present, it represents a serious drain on our limited resources, and yet we will not abandon Earth. Understandably, there is a raging debate within the Planetary Assembly on matters of policy about what to do.

"While Guardian Force does have some input into the debate about Earth, we clearly are not dictating its outcome. All those involved however agree about one central point; in time, the Earth will be a fully participating contributor to the whole. Unfortunately, for now, it is at best a poor dependent relative.

"The outcome of your recent mission has tended to complicate matters. The Black Hole classification means the Planetary Assembly is unaware of the breakthrough in our accessing Kreel communications. As a result, Guardian Force is walking a very narrow political tightrope, and we can't explain what we know of pending Kreel operations. With the pending Kreel penetration toward Earth, this is doubly so. In this environment, nothing is, as it first seems. A number of political factions are skillfully using rumors and factoids as calculated means of information dissemination; including the Guardian Force. In short, the Planetary Assembly does not have its collective act together, at least not sufficiently to direct us to make contact with the Arkillians or not to make contact."

"Sir, are you then directing Lan out on a mission without formal approval from the Assembly?" Kellon inquired in a low voice.

Kellon's question had not apparently surprised the Admiral, but he was obviously tired, and what Kellon was asking seemed only to add new worry lines to his countenance. "Captain, there is formal approval, of sorts. Guardian Force is ostensibly sending Lan on a routine mission, one to augment the existing Guardian Force near Earth. Your primary mission statement is to be alert for possible Kreel penetration toward the Earth. The purpose of this Black Hole briefing is to alert you that the possible Kreel penetration is not theoretical, but real and imminent. Guardian Force cannot allow the Kreel to come anywhere near Earth and survive to report home. At this moment, only Guardian Command is aware of your expanded mission statement, regarding the Arkillians. Admiral Mer Shawn will however be briefing Admiral Secretary Eryan Kyrie of your expanded mission statement before your departure."

Kellon was still deeply concerned about the nature of his mission statement. He sat back and pondered what the Admiral had said. "Sir, in all due respect, I must ask, if we offer the Arkillians the opportunity to join forces with us, what will we gain in exchange?"

"Captain Kellon, the only answer I know to your question is contained in a couple of words, coexistence and peace. We have a very heavy military burden dealing with the Kreel and occasionally with some Dargon activity. The Kreel expansion of hostilities to the Arkillians' sphere of influence, and coming near to Earth, only puts additional demands on our limited resources. If we can persuade the Arkillians of the Kreel's intention, then perhaps the Arkillians' natural tendency will be to resist the Kreel push. Rather than the Arkillians being possible allies, perhaps it might be best to consider them as useful independent agents, who have aspirations of their own. If you can attain the proper level of communications with the Arkillians, then perhaps the result will be a greater fear of us, than of the Kreel. That might suffice for the moment."

Sitting back in his chair, Kellon considered Admiral Cloud's information, and was deeply troubled. "Sir, what you are describing suggests I should try to make the Arkillians our cat's paw. The real problem I foresee is they have co-existed peacefully and traded with the Kreel for a considerable time. We must therefore accept some degree of trust is involved in their relationship. We on the other hand are still mammals and a detested sub-species. Precisely how do you suggest a detested mammal prove to the Arkillians the trusted Kreel are intending to subordinate and make them vassals? "

"Your point is well-taken Kellon. Anticipating this problem, I have had our intelligence branch selectively filter through millions of Kreel broadcasts we have on file. Using only the Kreel open communications, and not anything coming from our new capability, I believe there is sufficient information to establish for the Arkillians the scope of the Kreel intentions. Intelligence is currently sanitizing this material and we will give it to you prior to your departure. We are authorizing you to use the information, as you deem appropriate, in your discussions with the Arkillians. If a Kreel ship happens to approach Earth, as we anticipate it soon will, its very presence near Earth should bolster the credibility of the information.

"Are there any more questions at this time?"

"Sir, I confess there are about a million questions, however there is one question in particular that I respectfully request be answered."

Admiral Cloud smiled, and then spoke. "Captain Kellon, ask your question."

"Sir, the Arkillians have killed billions of human beings over thousands of years. The damages they have caused and the taking of human life are beyond description. How can we simply ignore the historical record and extend to them a peace offering that will not be perceived as a sign of weakness?"

"Captain Kellon, the Arkillians have done what they have done. Nothing we can do will alter that history of death and destruction. We can't bring back one single human being that died. I for one cannot even suggest what restitution or compensation might suffice or compensate for such a crime. Our punishing the current generation of Arkillians, for the crimes of earlier generations, will however prove nothing. What we are able to do here and now is to strive for positive contact with the Arkillians.

"Captain, you should know that the Assembly's primary concern is the Arkillians possibly acquiring faster-than-light travel. There are those in the Assembly, who are now arguing for total eradication of the Arkillians, as the only appropriate punishment and solution."

The Admiral's comments stunned Kellon. His mind rolled over the possibilities. *Genocide, destroying an entire species?* "Admiral, is genocide actually being considered as a viable option?"

The Admiral looked serious, fatigue lines becoming more evident in his expression. "Yes, at least by a few outspoken members in the Assembly. However, I don't believe they have

103

any chance of gaining approval for such a drastic action. What we need is a viable positive alternative. This is as much for the sake of humanity, as for the Arkillians. Such drastic actions as genocide, argue the right of might, not the right of justice. What we must avoid is becoming the very evil we abhor.

"Kellon, I believe intelligent sentient life is very rare. As Guardians of the human populated worlds, we face our share of destruction and death on every mission. However, contrary to appearances, Guardian Force's primary goal is life and not death. Therefore, working diligently to achieve a relationship based on peaceful co-existence with another sentient life form must always be considered our highest goal."

Kellon had listened attentively, but he was still troubled. "Admiral Cloud," replied Kellon earnestly, "In spite of your stated viewpoint, I don't believe we will ever have peace with the Kreel. When meeting the Kreel, our problem isn't peaceful co-existence, but rather our staying alive and not becoming an entree.

"I don't know the Arkillians like the Kreel, but from what little I have seen of them, they do not have the word mercy in their vocabulary. They are just like the Kreel, of the mindset that their power makes right, and the Reaper take the hindmost.

"Frankly, I do not honestly know what I can achieve given the constraints of the mission you have defined. If you send Lan back to Earth, all I can assure you is we will execute your orders to the best of our combined capabilities."

Admiral Cloud nodded his understanding. "Gentlemen, you will be receiving your new orders in the morning. Those will come directly from Admiral Mer Shawn. I believe you will have about six days before you begin your next mission. It is also my understanding that at least two and possibly more Cruisers, including the Lent, will be joining Lan on the mission.

"Captain Kellon, you are promoted to Commodore and will be in command of the squadron. I acknowledge and fully understand your expressed concerns. Your new orders are multi-level and not simple. That fact is why they are your orders, and not someone else's.

"Commodore, remember your mission is to determine if positive contact with the Arkillians can be established, it is not reaching some lasting inter-species treaty. If we cannot establish positive communications with the Arkillians, then precisely what road humanity takes in the future, regarding the Arkillians, is not clear.

"Commodore, you are the man on the spot. Your judgments have proven sound. If you need to shoot, then shoot and do not hesitate to do so! If however you can see a possibility for a positive outcome through dialogue with the Arkillians, then consider a less forceful path."

"Yes Sir." Kellon responded.

"Need I say, good hunting and good luck?" Admiral Cloud offered.

Kellon and Lorn both stood up in preparation for leaving and smartly saluted the Admiral with the utmost sincere respect for the man.

It was as if the Admiral could read their minds and he smiled, "One more thing. Gentlemen, to quote a mutual friend may there be fair winds at your back when homeward bound."

Chapter Eleven:
Possible Kreel Activity

Fleet Admiral Mer Shawn's desk was clear, not one report, memo, file, or distraction was on his desktop. For several minutes, he stood at the window, watching the ocean and the broad beaches that bordered Guardian Headquarters. He was enjoying seeing the people walking along the beaches, and he smiled at the sight of their children playing.

People living within a shelter of security, is the real meaning and purpose of the Guardian Force, he mused. Returning to his desk, he was considering many problems, the most pressing being structuring a meaningful defense for Earth.

When his communicator's high priority channel tone sounded, he automatically reached out and keyed the set, abruptly responding, "Mer Shawn here."

A woman's voice filled with warmth and cordiality greeted him, "Good morning Mer, do you have a few minutes to talk with an old friend?" The charm in her voice was genuine and the caller was none other than Eryan Kyrie, Admiral Secretary of the Planetary Assembly.

Smiling when he heard her voice, Mer warmly responded. "Good morning Madam Secretary. As always it is a pleasure to hear from you."

The bond of their long and enduring friendship was evident in the warmth of her voice. "Mer, I am calling as an old friend, merely to say hello and offer you an opportunity to tell me anything you believe I might need to know."

Warmth or not, with a direct lead in like that, Mer was immediately put on his guard. *Now, what has she on her mind,* he wondered. "Madam Secretary, if you desire any information, you need only ask." Mer replied.

"Then, with an offer like that, be certain I will. Mer, I've noticed several unusual reports crossing my desk. For example, I see that you will be sending five cruisers to Earth in a few days, including Lan. Five cruisers constitute a sixty-five percent increase in the Guardian Force military strength around Earth. Is there anything special I need to know about this deployment?"

She is as direct as a laser-cutting torch, thought Mer with a hint of humor. "Madam Secretary, your assessment is correct. Fleet Intelligence is concerned about possible Kreel activity expanding into the region. The deployment will increase the Guardian contingency in the region around Earth from three to five cruisers. I consider this slight increase only prudent, since Earth is 80 light years distant. Otherwise the deployment is routine and a normal rotation of fleet elements."

There was a brief hesitation before Eryan responded, and when she did respond her voice indicated she was troubled. "There does seem to be an increase in Kreel activity. For example, I have here a Guardian report telling of a Kreel Gortoga class cruiser and its scouts attacking a freighter, the Gola inbound from Krista to Glas Dinnein. In particular, I see the report says cruiser Lan intercepted and destroyed that Kreel cruiser and its scouts. The same report goes on to say Lan subsequently, in tactical consort with the Cruisers Lent and Lawrence, then engaged and destroyed three additional Kreel cruisers coming to the aid of the first Kreel cruiser. Next, the report says, Lan mopped up after the battle by hunting down and destroying nine Kreel scout ships. Mer, four Kreel Gortoga class cruisers raiding shipping between Krista and Glas Dinnein is very serious and unexpected."

Her voice no longer held any trace of the warmth of her original greeting, and her concern was apparent; her voice having shifted to one of a purely official tone. Mer knew well when strict formality was prudent, "Madam Secretary, the report is precise concerning the action that occurred. Like you, Fleet Operations also considers such Kreel actions this near to Glas Dinnein a serious matter and is deeply concerned."

"Mer, as an old friend, I had hoped you might be able to add some personal insight about the battle. For example isn't it unusual for a Guardian Cruiser to hunt down and destroy nine orphaned Kreel scout ships?" Eryan asked.

Mer frowned, not feeling comfortable where the discussion was heading. "Those nine ships were Kreel combat-capable scouts operating within our region of space. They were also directly involved in raiding our shipping. That you are referring to them as orphans mischaracterizes their true status and threat."

Mer, the report also says the Kreel shortly thereafter sent two fast-attack ships into the same area where our Cruisers fought the battle. Your reports say Guardian Force promptly localized and summarily destroyed both of those Kreel ships. Mer, I am deeply disturbed by what is reported, there being six major Kreel ships, and about twelve of their scout ships, destroyed in a single area over a period of several days. This level of conflict close to Tearman's heliosphere constitutes intense combat. Mer, what is going on?"

Mer did not miss the sharp point and barb attached to her question. "Madam Secretary, the reports state the facts. I agree with your characterization of the combat as being intense, it was."

"Reading further in your reports, I see that in addition to the six Kreel ships we have already mentioned, an additional ten Kreel ships were destroyed within our claimed space during the past few days. In one reported battle, a single Guardian Cruiser, the Lot, engaged and fought three Kreel capital ships. In that battle, Lot suffered fatalities and received considerable damage. In fact, we nearly lost Lot. Am I summarizing your reports correctly?"

Mer saw he was facing an immovable object, and frowning he formally replied, "Madam Secretary, the Guardian report is correct concerning the number of Kreel ships destroyed, during the battle with Lot. Regarding the Cruiser Lot, he was on normal patrol and responded to a broadcast alarm signal. Lot, although outnumbered, attacked the three Kreel cruisers. Lot fought those Kreel cruisers and their scouts alone, until reinforcements arrived. Together our Cruisers destroyed the attacking Kreel ships, but not before the Kreel badly damaged Lot and his Scouts. The casualties were serious, forty-six dead and three Scout ships seriously damaged. The Kreel destroyed one of Lot's Scouts, and her crew perished. Lot is now inbound under his own power, with a protective armed escort."

Eryan's voice noticeably softened, when she next spoke, "Mer, I am truly very sorry to hear of such Guardian losses.

Wouldn't it have been better if Lot had held back until reinforcements could be brought into play?"

Mer endeavored to bring his own responses into a normal conversational tone. "Eryan, if Lot had delayed the Kreel ships would have attacked and possibly destroyed two commercial cargo ships that were under attack. Lot put his own safety at risk to save those ships and their crews. The Kreel paid dearly for our losses, as the report documents, all attacking Kreel ships were destroyed."

Eryan's voice remained conciliatory, but contained a gentle rebuke, "Mer there were casualties and you above all well know it is not possible to equate losses in lives as being a quid-pro-quo in a numbers game. Others within the Assembly have also taken notice of the recent battles. In a very short period, our forces have localized and destroyed sixteen Kreel capital ships and more than a dozen scouts. This intense level of combat this near Glas Dinnein implies there is a major shift in either the Kreel or Fleet operations. Do you agree that any such shift in policy would be a most serious matter, and the Assembly should therefore be notified?"

Now, Mer thought, *Eryan has come to the heart of why she has called.* "Madam Secretary, we are in agreement. It is the duty of Fleet Command to keep the Planetary Assembly fully informed of important changes in Fleet policy. The combat reports you have identified are not the consequence of any such change in our policies. They are defensive in their very nature, as is discernible from where the battles have occurred, all of them in our own space. I personally agree with your assessment, the Kreel appear increasingly aggressive and are operating in force deeper than we have seen in considerable time."

"Mer, I am not disagreeing with you, however you are certainly aware there are some in the Planetary Assembly who do not understand your problems and priorities. For example, Rich Sumor, the Chief Administrator, has also noted the marked increase in recent battle reports. He is becoming alarmed and outspoken in the Council regarding the possibility the Kreel are preparing for something much larger. His concern is the Guardian Force might not be ready to defend all our planets from a major Kreel attack. Is there anything at all you can tell me that might ease such concerns?"

Mer knew he was not the only person carrying a heavy burden, from the sound of her voice he knew Eryan Kyrie, a close friend and Admiral Secretary of the Planetary Assembly, was bearing her own heavy load of problems. While he wanted to tell her he was aware that such a Kreel attack was pending and the Kreel were pointing their attack directly at Earth, he could not discuss a Black Hole matter over a communicator set. He wanted to brief her on the crafted dissemination contained in one report in particular, a report of a Kreel cruiser having been destroyed, rather than captured. Until they could meet privately, he must remain evasive. *Secrecy, thy name is Duplicity,* Mer thought with frustration.

Attempting to shift the topic away from the sensitive area of his concern, Mer continued. "Madam Secretary, as you know, we have on more than one occasion requested additional funds for critical research and development, and especially for the building of additional cruisers. It is hoped the Planetary Assembly will remember that any ship, Guardian Cruisers included, have limited service-life times. You might remind Administrator Sumor that he has repeatedly blocked our requests at every opportunity. If the Planetary Assembly and Administrator Sumor in particular, would promptly approve those requests, it would be most helpful."

Again, there was an expanding silence before Eryan continued. "Mer, I have noted one more item that others have not yet mentioned to me. The five Cruisers you are sending to Earth include three Cruisers that engaged the Kreel cruisers attacking the Gola. I noticed that after that engagement you ordered all three of those ships to return to Glas Dinnein. I also see those ships are still on the ground, and while the ships are being refitted their crews are quarantined. Additionally I see there are three other Guardian Cruisers still on Glas Dinnein, and you have quarantined their crews. Two of those Cruisers are going with Lan to Earth. I find six Cruisers, all of which were either directly involved in a significant battle with the Kreel, or else in the immediate vicinity of that battle, all being brought promptly back to Glas Dinnein and quarantined rather extraordinary. This is especially so when you consider Guardian Force's level of operations has suddenly increased. Is this all merely coincidental?"

Now, neither Mer's face nor voice held the slightest hint of a smile. He had not missed Eryan's easy avoidance of his intentional misdirection, and smoothly continuing with her focused questioning.

"Madam Secretary, your acute observations are precise, as usual. Your observed facts are correctly stated, and the events are not coincidental."

Continuing with her inquiry, Eryan's next question caught Mer broadside and flatfooted. "Mer, why was the crew of the Gola directed to a military base and then quarantined?"

Blast, thought Mer, *doesn't she miss anything?*

"Eryan, only seven of the crew of the Gola survived. The Kreel took eleven of the crew on that Kreel cruiser and killed them. It was appropriate to see the survivors received a full medical and psychological screening. We also debriefed the crew and provided psychological support, regarding their lost friends. Guardian Force will be releasing the Gola and her crew from quarantine in a few days.

In order to bring Eryan's inquiry to its conclusion, Mer conveyed the nature of the problem he was skirting. "Eryan," Mer spoke in a confiding tone, and then paused several moments before continuing. "There are some matters that we do need to discuss. They are matters of significant gravity, and we should meet soon in order to go over the details."

There was a quiet moment that expanded, like a cloud of dandelion seeds floating on a gentle spring breeze. When Eryan next spoke, the tone of her voice was warmth, and noticeably less stressed. "Mer, I more than most understand the pressures you bear on your shoulders every day. As to matters of significant gravity, I fully understand we are dealing with very complex issues. Perhaps we can meet together sometime soon for a glass of wine."

From the tone of her voice, Mer knew she had clearly understood the key phrase significant gravity meant there was a Black Hole event involved. She also knew that meant something very extraordinary must have occurred.

When Eryan again spoke, it was not as the Admiral Secretary, but as Mer's friend, which she truly was.

"Mer, I do understand. The burdens you and others frequently carry are sometimes very heavy indeed.

112

"Now, I need to change the subject. Ambassador Wells has somehow learned that Captain Kellon and Lan are returning to Earth in the next few days. She has formally requested passage on Lan for her return to Earth. Can Guardian Force comply with her request?"

Now Mer had a reason to smile. He had met on several occasions with the Ambassador and had found her a wonderful young person and a true delight. Still, he could but wonder what her source of information about Lan's deployment might be, since he had only hours before made that assignment.

"Madam Secretary, please inform the Ambassador that she and her marvelous dog Gepeto will be welcomed aboard Lan for her return journey home. I am confident that Commodore Kellon will be pleased to have her again on board."

Eryan's voice came in a relaxed and full spread of warmth, warmth based on more than two millenniums of friendship. "I will tell the Ambassador that she and Gepeto will be welcomed aboard Lan. Am I correct that you have designated Captain Kellon as senior Captain of the Cruiser force you are sending to Earth?"

"Yes, he is the senior Captain, and he has earned the meritorious acknowledgment of his performance during recent missions."

"Mer, I will not press you here for the details of Lan's mission to Earth at this time. That you are sending Lan back to Earth so soon after an extended two-year mission, is evidence that his mission is most likely both critical and multi-leveled. It seems appropriate Susie, As Earth's Ambassador, becomes familiar with the resourcefulness and responsibilities of the Guardian Force. She is already pressing the Planetary Assembly hard for considering accepting Earth's people for recruitment into the Force. It is something she feels strongly about.

"According to Susie, it's all about Earth carrying its own weight. She says they are a proud people, and they are not accustomed to taking handouts."

Mer had wondered how long it would be before such questions and concerns emerged. He hit the problem directly head on. "Madam Secretary, before Guardian Force alters its position toward Earth, it will be necessary for the Earth to become fully integrated with the whole. At present, we do not believe they are sufficiently integrated or aware of their new relationship to understand they are not a solitary world, but are now part of a larger community.

"Our concern is each of the Earth's governments will be vying, in their own self-interest, in expanding their own national power. Their motivations will be on a regional perspective, not on an expanded awareness of our multiple planets. Above all, Earth remains complex and dangerously politically imbalanced. The racial, social, religious, and political puzzle the Arkillians so skillfully constructed still controls Earth's governments. I assume you agree with my assessment."

"No, I most certainly do not agree. The Earth is now part of the whole. The sooner the people on Earth become aware of the new political reality, the sooner they can bend their respective governments to accept the new political realities.

"When you speak with Commodore Kellon, it should be stressed that Susie Wells of Earth is Earth's Ambassador. More to the point, she is also a representative member of the Planetary Assembly. She will be accorded all the frankness, privileges, and respect associated with that rank and status."

Sitting back in his chair, Mer knew when it was best to avoid an argument, and especially an argument with Eryan. "Madam Secretary, I will inform Commodore Kellon accordingly. I also suggest you stiffen your perimeter defenses, since I believe there will be a backwash, when the people on Earth begin to clamor for vacations on and ask to move to Glas Dinnein. The Council might remember there are about fourteen billion applications pending on Earth for such an immediate move."

There was a long pause before Eryan Kyrie responded, "Oops. Perhaps it would be best if Commodore Kellon uses his own skill, tact, and discretion in matters pertaining to Earth politics. Please extend to him my personal congratulations to Lan and his entire crew for jobs very well done.

"Oh, one more thing. Did I hear correctly? Are Commanders Roan, Zorn and Shey being reassigned to Lan?"

Mer smiled inwardly, *Ah ha, so there is the source of the little leak about Lan's redeployment to Earth. I should have known,* he mused. "Yes, Lot's recent losses included several Scout ship personnel, including his command Scout ship and her crew. Fleet Operations is reassigning Commander Jason Greer from Lan to the Cruiser Lot, where he will take command of the reformed Scout group. In looking around for a Scout ship and crew for Lan, I looked for the most qualified Scout ship available. That honor fell on Scout ship Shey.

"Mer, there are clearly a number of reasons we need to meet soon. I will go over my itinerary and see if we can find some mutually acceptable time for that meeting. Thank you for being as frank as you have. I will do what I can about pushing through your requests, especially for those relating to research and development. Is there anything else I can do for Guardian Force this morning?" Her voice was again warm and open.

"Madam Secretary, It is always my pleasure to speak with you. I'm looking forward to that glass of wine."

The communicator link closed and the room was silent for several minutes, as Mer sat quietly reflecting on the discussion. He had received tacit approval, based on trust. That was good enough.

What troubled him most was the Cruiser Lot. He had not yet received the shield upgrade and run directly into the Kreel stun beam. His shields were only marginally effective, and Mer knew they had almost lost Lot. *Blast, when were they going to get the full support and requested funding from the Assembly?*

He keyed his communicator and spoke into it, "Admiral Dylan Cord, Operations, Shawn here. We cannot have another incident like the one with Cruiser Lot. All Guardian Cruisers are to receive shield upgrades within the next seven days or else you are to ground them. Shawn out."

Standing Mer walked back to the window and looked again out on the seascape. In three days, he was sending five Cruisers and their crews into harm's way, and only God knew into what trouble. *That is the hardest part of this job,* mused Mer. Anger flickered in his eyes as he thought of the upcoming battles. *I can at least see Kellon's squadron will have every chance for survival that our new research can provide.* He pushed away the fleeting memories of Guardian ships on fire, and the calls of their dying crews. Those memories were from long ago, and he respectfully returned them to the quiet background of his thoughts.

Chapter Twelve:
Departure

The early morning was crisp, clear and physically invigorating. Eryan Kyrie, Admiral Secretary of the Planetary Assembly, stood to the left of Fleet Admiral Mer Shawn, and to his right stood Admirals Ron Cloud and Dylan Cord, the Admirals in command of Guardian Fleet Intelligence and Operations. Facing north toward the ocean, they were standing on the top step before the Glas Dinnein's Planetary Assembly building. Behind them, the graceful tall and fluted columns of the building appeared to emit a soft glow, the early morning's warm sunlight further enhancing the building's majestic architecture.

Eryan was wearing well-tailored business attire, and the three Admirals standing with her were each in their full dress uniforms. Eryan, like the three Officers standing with her, had come this morning to honor the Guardian Force ships and crews setting out on an extended mission. Those forces were departing to the newest and most distant planet of the known human community, Earth. Each of those standing on the stairs came to bid farewell to departing friends, family, and comrades. Eryan, like her friends, knew some or all of those departing might never return, and the somber reality of that possibility tempered the levity of her mood.

Looking along the Avenue of Fountains, Eryan enjoyed the beauty and appreciated the harmony and peace they celebrated. Glas Dinnein being the Capital planet, and headquarters of the Guardian Force, meant Guardian ships were continuously departing and arriving. Even so, for them to be gathered here for a force departure was by no means a regular occurrence. She knew they were here this morning because they were among the very few who understood the true significance of sending five cruisers to Earth. They knew there was the real possibility of a Kreel attack on the distant planet.

She had lived with thoughts of a Kreel attack on human-occupied planets all of her life, but Earth was unique, being so very far away and isolated. It would take decades, or perhaps even centuries, to integrate fully the Earth and her peoples into the broader community of humanity. Even then, they might well remain isolated and vulnerable.

As she heard distant low peals of thunder, and felt distinct vibrations through the soles of her shoes, she looked up and to her right. Coming from the east, along the Avenue and above the fountains, moving slowly in precise tight formation, were Guardian ships. She observed twenty Scout ships, arrayed in five groups of four ships each. The first thing she noticed was they were not wearing their bright parade colors of white and gold, as they would have, if they were returning from a mission. Instead, all twenty Scout ships were adorned, if adorned was the correct description, in solid flat black.

Moving with slow deliberation into position before the Planetary Assembly Building, the twenty ships spread out along the Avenue, centering their formation before Eryan and the three Admirals. In each of the five groups, two Scouts were lower and forward and the other two slightly higher and further back. As they took their positions and became stationary, she could feel the intensity of the low rumbling sound continue deeply building, becoming prominent and enveloping.

As she watched, a large group of people began to assemble along the Avenue to see what was happening. People along the adjacent coastal highway also began to notice the appearance of the twenty Scout ships, all arrayed in ranked formation. More people began to come out of the buildings located along the Avenue, and traffic moving along the highway began to stop. The people continued to gather.

She knew such a formation of ships was something unusual, and people were naturally curious. Everyone looking on realized there was special significance to what they were seeing. In that, they were correct.

As the last group of four Scouts reached their position, she became aware of a deeper and throaty thundering in the distance, and she could feel a much more intense vibration through the ground.

As she watched, five Guardian Cruisers moved in a trailing line formation, coming from the East and moving along the Avenue of the Fountains. Each Cruiser came to a stop, positioned broadside to the observers on the stairs, one Cruiser above and behind each of the five groups of Scout ships. The lowest Scout ships were not more than twenty-five meters off the ground and the Cruisers were perhaps two-hundred meters above the ground. Massed together as they were, in presence of sight and sound they were immense.

Perhaps what made the most striking impression, Eryan thought, was their appearance. Each of the twenty-five ships was in their deep space war paint; flat lusterless black objects, starkly contrasting with the light blue of the cloudless sky overhead. Their massive presence brought with it a sense of power and deadly menace. None there could escape recognizing the awesome representation and power of the gathered ships of war, ships designed and built to assure security and peace for humanity.

Though she had seen Guardian ships during her entire lifetime, to see five Guardian Cruisers arrayed and stationary, with their Scout ships, in full war paint, poised stationary this low to the ground was not something she could remember ever having seen before.

As the final Cruiser took his position in the formation, the ground was deeply rumbling, and the sound carried in every direction. Looking toward the highway, she saw that absolutely no traffic was moving. People were standing along the highway and even more were coming out of buildings and filling the Avenue of Fountains. Although the Assembly had not yet made a public announcement, there were thousands of people filling the space on the Avenue and standing along the highway.

Eryan noticed the arrival of Rich Sumor, the Chief Administrator. Although he was frequently the Guardian Force's most outspoken critic, like everyone else, he also appeared deeply moved by the awesome spectacle hovering just before them.

As they stood together the four on the stairs slowly raised their arms in formal salute and tribute to the assembled ships, and to their crews.

X

On board Lan, and high up in the domed conference room, Susie had watched the Avenue of Fountains come into view, and she was thrilled as the ships proceeded down the Avenue. When Lan became stationary, she could see clearly the four people on the upper steps of the Planetary Assembly Building. She knew all four of them, and they were her friends. The morning was wonderfully clear, and the entire spectacle was awesome.

It had not been that long since Lan brought her down along the same Avenue of Fountains, but then it had been just past sunset and there were crossing laser beams poised like crossed sabers overhead. Then Lan and his four Scouts were wearing their proud and beautiful parade colors. It was their triumphal return from Earth.

Now she realized the mood was completely different. This was not a glad celebration of a ship's safe return from distant worlds, but rather a somber acknowledgment of ships that were heading directly into danger, about a far distant world. Symbolizing that reality, each ship bore the black color of cold space, heralding the danger that lay ahead.

In response to the salute of their Admirals, all five Cruisers slowly pivoted about, swinging their bows toward those standing on the stairs. The center Cruiser was Lan, and he slowly and majestically dipped his bow toward the five people, thereby acknowledging their salutes.

After dipping his bow, Lan then majestically moved swiftly upward, and transitioned forward, in close coordination with the remaining four Cruisers. Initiating a wide sweeping one-hundred-eighty degree turn to his port, Lan moved to the north and accelerated out over the ocean, and then he soared upward in a graceful climb. The five Cruisers soared upward together, the four trailing Cruisers smoothly transitioning the formation from a rank to one of a trailing 'V.'"

As the Cruisers departed, the Scout ships, each in unison, dipped their bows in salute to the assembled officials and Guardian officers. Suddenly, moving smartly as a single group, they ascended vertically, their positions with respect to one another unvarying. Everyone watched the twenty Scout ships swiftly rise in formation until they became mere dots, then a single merged dot. Far above they disappeared. The ships were gone.

With a descending hush, the sounds of the fountains and their flowing waters momentarily embraced the silence. Then, once more, the background murmurs of the gathered thousands of people rose, as they began to disperse, all talking about what they had seen, and wondering about its significance.Within five minutes, the Avenue of Fountains was nearly empty.

Still standing on the top step on the Planetary Assembly Building, Eryan Kyrie turned and looked toward her friend, Fleet Admiral Mer Shawn. She smiled, seeing the sparkling of moisture in the corners of his eyes. She knew her own eyes were also moist. She heard Mer's soft murmur, as if speaking to the departed ships, "May all that is of truth and goodness be with you and there be fair winds at your back on your journey home."

X

As Lan soared upward, Susie moved quickly from the port side of the observation dome around to the rear of the dome. She moved with the easy grace of a slender young woman in excellent health and physical condition. Her strawberry blonde hair, tied in a ponytail that fell below her shoulders, swung in easy harmony with her movements.

Her deep blue eyes sparkled with good humor, intelligence, and a little sadness, as she stood looking out toward Glas Dinnein. Gepeto, her large and handsome yellow Labrador had moved purposefully with her and now stood beside her. Leaning forward, Gepeto pressed his nose against and smudged the optically perfect transparent barrier. He looked curiously and with obvious interest at the planet dropping far behind them. Without conscious thought, Susie rested her left hand on his head and tussled his ears.

Glas Dinnein was still near and quite large. Looking about she could see the other Cruisers spreading out from their original 'V' formation, falling back into a widely dispersed tactical pyramid formation, one Cruiser taking its position at each corner of the imagined base and with Lan at the topmost forward position.

Home, she thought, *where is my real home, where do I really live now?*

Moving over, Elayne Cloud stood beside Susie, also quietly looking at the receding planet. After a long quiet moment, she turned toward Susie. "Susie, I imagine it feels wonderful to be going home again."

Looking over toward Elayne, Susie smiled. She had been her first friend on Lan, and over the intervening months, their friendship had continued to grow. First smiling and then frowning, she replied, "I was just thinking along similar lines. I imagine you must likewise feel sad about leaving Glas Dinnein."

Elayne looked at Susie and her good humor was very evident as she replied. "At the moment, Lan is my home and his crew my family. This mission will not be boring, that is certain. Everyone here has duties to keep them focused and very busy. Have you something to keep you busy on the outbound trip?"

"Yes, I am deep in the study of Earth and Glas Dinnein history. I have been looking at the folklore of Glas Dinnein and especially looking at Earth's traditional folklore. I know, as does everyone else, that there must be a direct linkage between the people on Earth and the other eleven planets. I hope to find that linkage."

Listening respectfully, Elayne smiled when she heard Susie's ambitious goal. "Well, It does represent a fascinating intellectual problem, and I don't know anyone who has any answers, at least not as yet." Elayne thoughtfully added.

Her thoughts turned to her earnest research, and Susie found it easy to talk about topics she found fascinating. "I simply find it inconceivable humans emerged out of two evolutionary cosmic soups eighty light years apart, Elayne . Of course, your folklore speaks of flowing out into the stars in a time of great upheaval. Our folklore on Earth simply created the Universe all about us. However, it also mentions there were others coming to Earth from elsewhere. Of course, where these visitors were coming from wasn't specifically mentioned, and unfortunately there were no special coordinates being conveniently provided."

They stood together looking at the spectacle of Glas Dinnein, as the planet fell further astern of the rising formation of Cruisers. Turning Elayne smiled and pointed, "Look Susie, here come the Scout ships."

Susie looked out, but at first, she did not see anything. Then she saw a flicker and saw four bright points of intense white light growing nearer. As she watched, they grew still nearer and she could clearly see the Scout ships, their bright white brilliance and gold parade colors were unmistakable. The four Scout ships split into two groups of two each and moved to take positions off Lan's port and starboard side. Looking up Susie saw in the distance other bright points of light, and she knew the other Scout ships had donned their own brilliant parade colors. The Scout groups were each heading toward their parent Cruiser.

Turning, she asked Elayne, "do they always do that?"

Elayne laughed. "No, they are just showing off, while they still can. They all know it will most likely be some time before tactical doctrine permits them to flash their parade colors again. This close to Glas Dinnein, they know tactics permit them doing so.

When speaking about the Scouts, Elayne's smile broadened. "Susie, just remember that Scout ships and their crews are a special breed apart. They love kicking up their heels, whenever they can. In addition, Roan is now the Scout Leader, and with Zorn along, things are going to be predictably interesting. Adding Shey to the personalities mix assures the trip is going to be unpredictable. With those three around it always is."

"What do you mean by the term Scout Leader?" Susie asked. "Well, Lan is the lead Cruiser, and Commodore Kellon is the lead Captain. The lead Scout ship on the lead ship is designated the Scout Leader. Each Captain reports to Commodore Kellon, and they have direct responsibility for the deployment and assignment of their own Scouts. The Scout Leader's responsibility however is to the Commodore, and he is responsible for the readiness of all the Scouts, in all the Cruisers. When the Scouts from more than one Cruiser are operating as a tactical group, then the Scout Leader is responsible for directing them in their tactical deployment. This type of Scout ship action in actuality is not very common, it depends on tactical circumstances and what orders the Commodore issues to the Scout Leader."

They stood together and looked on with interest as the Scout ships moved steadily closer and alongside Lan. Then the four Scouts were in unison drawn securely into their respective hangars.

Elayne knew well, those on Lan and on the Scout ships performed the retrieval so smoothly that they made it look simple. However, she knew the operation had required intense coordination, concentration and skill by all those involved in the operation, human and AI alike.

Elayne sighed, "Well the departure is now complete, and Lan and the others will be picking up their heels and moving smartly out with a hard steady push. Next stop Earth."

Chapter Thirteen:
Brief Contact Message

Lan slipped out through the dilating portal of time-space and into the midst of the silent transparency of space-time, the blackest blackness pierced with countless stars brightly arrayed all about him. He paused upon completing his long Jump, and he carefully gathered the information necessary to calculate his precise location in both normal space and time. This he knew had been the last long Jump of the return journey to Earth. If the AI programmers were observing and understood what was happening in his core matrix, they might have observed Lan was in effect smiling.

All about him was the covering mantle of the immense fabric of the Universe, stretching out toward the boundless illusion of infinity. One by one the other four Cruisers emerged from their Jumps, and upon exiting, each transmitted their arrival acknowledgments to Lan. As they emerged, they specified their dispersed proximity, and Lan echoed each of their cheerful notices.

Lan's navigator, Commander Roy Grey, reported, "Commodore, the squadron has exited the Jump, and all Cruisers in the squadron have reported condition gold."

"Very nicely done Roy. I will be in CAC shortly. Please signal the squadron to remain in their relative Jump positions, at least for now. Once we move out to intercept the Arkillians, we will tighten up the squadron into its tactical formation. Kellon out."

Sitting at the desk in his private quarters, Kellon glanced up at the chronometer. The return journey to Earth had taken significantly less time than Lan's first trip out. Then it had been painstakingly necessary to blaze the trail between Glas Dinnein and Earth. On that first trip, Lan had made more than sixty short Jumps, while identifying the concealed dark bodies and the dangerous temporal gravity wells associated with each Jump.

That initial outbound trip, through unsurveyed space, had consumed more than a year of tense precise surveying. During the past year, other Cruisers had followed Lan's blazed route, and each had added navigation beacons along the route. Like a bright well-traveled highway, it was firmly established. With advanced knowledge from the previously positioned navigation beacons, the five Guardian Force ships had moved in safety in long parsec-consuming Jumps. Now, the transit time between the two worlds was a matter of a few weeks, rather than the long months Lan's prior journey had required.

Kellon stood considering his next move. After their battle, he had directed a trailing sentinel to track the Arkillian Nest ship. For the past year, that sentinel had continued reporting the precise movements of the ship. From those detailed reports, Kellon knew the Commander of the ship was on a curved trajectory taking him far above the Earth's ecliptic plane, skimming beyond the Earth's heliosphere, which in time would bring him into alignment with his home planet.

The path the ship was following declared it was trying to avoid further interaction with whoever had attacked it. Whoever its Commander might be, he was about to learn that his effort to evade his unknown enemy was futile.

"Lan, please synchronize our squadron chronometers to galactic standard. Then pinpoint the location of the Arkillian ship and compute the optimum time trajectory to intercept."

Lan's resonant voice replied promptly, "Sir, I am making the necessary star fix observations, interrogating the nearest beacons, will make the required chronometer correction, obtain the latest target position updates, and compute the shortest intercept trajectory to the target as ordered."

"Thank you Lan. Please set our operational plane to the galactic plane. When you make that intercept calculation, do so defining our intercept position on the target's heading, matching the target's velocity, 200 kilometers above the target's path, and two thousand kilometers ahead of the target. That is also to be the closest point of approach to the target during our maneuver to reach that position."

"Yes Sir."

"Lan, extend my compliments to and request Ambassador Wells to join me in my conference room in fifteen minutes. If she is not available, then advise me when she can meet with me.

"Also, contact Elayne and ask her to promptly come to my conference room."

As Kellon departed his quarters, he was deep in thought. He understood the Arkillian commander had made a decision to maroon his Earth contingent. He wondered just how the commander felt about that decision. He knew if it were his decision, he would not be happy leaving part of his crew marooned light years from home.

Kellon earnestly wished that he knew how the Arkillian commander felt about his command decision, since how he felt would reveal much about who the Arkillians were as a sentient culture. Unfortunately, Kellon thought, wishing would not put grapes on a vine.

The patrol report that cruisers Lancer and Lowe had provided, following their covert survey of the Arkillians' home system, was helpful information, he thought. They had discovered the Arkillians' system was completely without what every human-occupied world demanded, the protection provided by a meaningful early warning system. The lack of an early warning capability indicated the Arkillians were confident, felt secure, and had no fear of an attack.

During Lancer and Lowe's covert surveillance, they had observed only four Kreel ships entering or exiting the Arkillian system. None of those ships were of a military classification. It was obvious that the Arkillians and the Kreel had established and were maintaining peaceful commerce between their species. What Kellon lacked was hard data concerning the dynamics of the political and cultural relationship inherent in such commerce.

What he knew was the Arkillians had their beam weapon tuned to kill the Kreel. That deadly Arkillian weapon shouted a distrust of the Kreel, and it acknowledged there was a potential for lethal hostility between the species. Given what he now knew of the Kreel's intention, the Arkillian distrust of the Kreel was fully justified. In spite of knowing all these factors, inwardly Kellon was still wondering how best to proceed in establishing a viable dialogue with the Arkillians.

When he entered into his conference room, he found Elayne was there before him. She looked up and smiled, "Sir, I hope you don't mind, I took the liberty of ordering some neab with pastries." With a grateful sigh Kellon answered, "Thank you Elayne, you are thinking ahead of my request.

Moving over to the table, he sat down. He was still frowning and deep in thought. "Please sit down Elayne and join me."

Before taking her seat, Elayne first gave Kellon a pastry and poured neab for both of them. "Sir, what is our problem this morning that has you so concerned?"

Looking up, Kellon smiled. In spite of her youth and inexperience, he had come to trust Elayne's insight and judgment. "It's the Arkillians, Elayne. The Kreel, and not the Arkillians, are the real problem, and yet we must first deal with the Arkillians. Admiral Cloud has given me broad authority, however it is his desire we explore establishing an open dialogue with them. My problem is quite simple. I have not found a means to begin the dialogue. Since you are our alien culture specialist, I hope you will have a few suggestions."

Elayne looked thoughtful and then with a broad smile asked, "Sir, why not simply begin the dialogue where you left it off during our last contact?

"It seems perfectly reasonable to believe the Arkillian commander has been reviewing all our earlier contacts, and he is still pondering his best response. In fact, in one way he has already given us his response; he is quietly running for home, as fast as he can."

Sitting back in his chair, Kellon sipped his cup of neab, intent in Elayne's observation. "Elayne, can you put some meat on the bones of your assessment?"

"Yes Sir, I believe I can. The meat, as you call it, consists of a host of facts and presumptions, but it might provide us a beginning point for analysis."

Taking her seat, she held the warm cup of neab between her fingers. Pausing momentarily, she then replied, "Sir, we do know some fundamental facts. To begin with, Lan badly damaged him, and he wants to avoid further battle. The commander on that ship is running for home and safety. There can be no question a superior force defeated him. However, he does not necessarily believe his species is inferior; the battle proved only his technology is seriously lacking.

"He also knows the Kreel have refused to share their superior technology with the Arkillians. Given such thoughts, he may be angrier with the Kreel he can identify than the unknown force that defeated him."

As he listened to Elayne's development of her perception of the tactical situation, Kellon leaned back in his chair. "So far, I am following your summation, continue," Kellon urged.

"Yes Sir. I first ask; what is the Arkillian Commander doing?

"For certain he will be preparing his report to his superiors about the underlying causes for his defeat. I will wager a cool brew he will carefully weave his attitude toward the Kreel into his report. Given the magnitude of his failure, considering his probable reputation and professional standing, writing that report will not be an easy task. What he will need to say will be troubling him. In fact, he might be blaming the Kreel for his defeat, especially if he believes you, a human being, were in a Kreel ship.

"It is almost certain his report will be carefully crafted in light of the economic and political fallout on Scion. It must also address the probable Arkillian military response. In effect, what he reports will be like dropping a bomb in the middle of their governing council. It's really going to stir things up, and everyone will be shouting about what they are to do next. If you add to his report the Kreel are now coming to conquer them, the debate will certainly have overtones of panic.

"In all due respect, compared to the Arkillian commander's problem, your problems of making contact with him are relatively simple."

"Thank you Elayne, for your assessment. In general, I tend to agree with you. The consequences resulting from the upcoming contact with the Arkillian commander are however significant. They are not trivial. Finding a solid beginning point for the dialogue is important, and finding an effective opening wedge for that dialogue could define the eventual outcome."

Putting down her cup, Elayne's expression reflected her concern. "Sir, I'm sorry if I said anything implying our contact is trivial. I know it is not. May I ask, given the scope of the Arkillian commander's serious tactical problems, what do you believe his response will be when we do contact him?"

Putting down his own cup of neab, Kellon looked dourly toward Elayne, "Well, I am glad the problem is his and not mine. If circumstances placed me in such a position, my first words would be both brief and unprintably colorful. Then I would be looking for somewhere to hide or run. His problem is basic; he cannot hide or run. As I see it he has three options, ignore us, respond to us, or else set his self-destruction sequences."

"Well sir, given those three options, then if you were standing in his shoes, what response would you take in answer to each of those possibilities?"

Leaning forward, Kellon had a slight frown, "Hmmmm, put in that light, he will not be able to ignore us. At least he will not, if I detonate a significant charge in front of his bow and shake him from prow to stern. I assure you I can get his attention one way or another. As for the second option, contact, that is what we came out here to accomplish. As for the third option, self-destruction, I seriously doubt any commander would labor for nearly a year to repair his damaged ship, and strike out for home, only to initiate self-destruction, unless of course he is given no other options. Discourse should be, to any sane intelligent being, a preferable option to death. Therefore, I do not believe option 3 need be of immediate concern.

"My expectation is he will first ignore us, until he has sufficient information to frame a response. Then when he does respond, regardless of the content of the response, the door for dialogue will be open."

Sitting up in his chair, Kellon looked thoughtfully toward Elayne, then he requested, "Lan, play back the last message we transmitted to the Arkillian in plain and not the Arkillian language."

Immediately the bulkhead Kellon faced transformed into a screen on which he could read the message, and the recorded verbal message played back:

"Attention Arkillians. Your hostile action directed toward my ship has resulted in your current state. You would have been far wiser if you had accepted our demands. I have broken off the attack. You may safely attend to your wounded. Unless you provoke further hostility with more belligerent action, I consider the battle concluded. As to what will happen to you in the future, that is again your choice. The demands given to you before the battle are still tendered. I will be monitoring this channel. If there is still anyone alive with authority to speak for the Arkillians, then let him identify himself. Who speaks for the Arkillians?"

Kellon sat back, thoughtfully considering his earlier message. "Well, the message certainly contains the substance needed for establishing our second contact. Thank you Elayne for your suggestion, I am herewith adopting it.

"Lan, display the close scenes of the planet Scion that the cruisers Lancer and Lowe obtained on their covert surveillance mission to Scion."

"Yes sir."

The bulkhead display immediately shifted from the text representation to a three dimensional scene of the Arkillian home planet, it was shown brightly suspended against the blackness of space. It appeared to have two small moons, and from the observer's perspective in space, the planet looked rather ordinary.

Kellon could see no indications of oceans and knew that the distance of the viewpoint was too far from the planet to show details such as cities, lakes, rivers, canyons or mountains. The planet was of a light tan color with areas of differing hues, mostly of golds and browns, and it had a small discernible polar cap. It looked somewhat less than hospitable.

There was a soft knock at the compartment door and Kellon looking up said, "Enter."

Entering the room, Susie came with a big smile. "Good morning Commodore and Elayne." She arrived in a flurry and with Gepeto at her side. The two of them were fundamentally inseparable.

As Gepeto saw Kellon, he immediately came over and placed his head on Kellon's lap, looking up expectantly. Like most others onboard Lan, Kellon had come to feel a strong affection for Susie's four-footed buddy. Like the others, Kellon was quick to learn how to tussle Gepeto's ears. Having received his proper due, grinning broadly, Gepeto moved over to a corner of the room and promptly dropped into what seemed to be an instant deep coma.

Kellon watched Gepeto and marveled, *If only I could learn that little trick,* he thought. Then, turning toward Susie, he outlined the topic of their meeting. "Susie thank you for coming. Please sit down and join us. We are reviewing our next step, how to contact Monstro. As Earth's Ambassador, I believe it's appropriate that you are included in the planning."

Taking an offered seat, Susie immediately looked toward the bulkhead display. "Commodore, is that Scion, the Arkillians' home? It looks very bare and inhospitable, but it does have some lovely warm colors."

"Your first guess is correct; that's Scion. Given it's the Arkillian home planet, they are undoubtedly well-adjusted to its environment, and they most likely consider it sweet home," Kellon replied.

Looking at both Susie and Elayne, as they sat together, Kellon marveled that the two women could have been born on two different worlds, 80 light years apart, and still look like they were sisters. Both were young, slender, both had attractive intelligent blue eyes and blond hair. He knew their growing bond of friendship grew on more than a general physical likeness; the two women had found they shared many interests. Both women were looking intense and serious as they carefully examined the image of an alien planet.

Susie glanced over to Kellon and commented, "So that is where the Arkillians come from, the home of those who once called themselves gods."

Her comment took Kellon by surprise. *Gods*, he wondered. "Susie, the Arkillians were in control of the Earth for thousands of years. You imply they represented themselves to be gods. Were there then indications in your history concerning the possibility that you were being manipulated or otherwise influenced by others not of the Earth?"

Turning from the display, Susie looked at Kellon and enthusiastically replied. "Oh, there certainly were. Our early peoples abundantly infused those themes into our planet's history, and many of our earliest cultures recorded similar stories. Early religions, such as those in India, referred to the gods taking sides in some wars and providing to one side or the other terrible weapons of destruction. Some of the oldest Hindu Vedic scriptures identify flying craft, named Vimanas. These

132

flying houses or palaces were where the gods placed their thrones. The Vedic scriptures report some Vimanas were seven stories high. None of those writing the old records ever seemed to wonder why a god would need a flying house."

Susie's mention of weapons sharpened Kellon's interest. "You speak of weapons, Susie can you remember the nature of any of the weapons that were described?" Kellon asked.

First pausing for a moment, Susie considered the question, before answering. "Well, perhaps a few. Some sounded like they were natural events, such as a powerful wind, that could blow an army off the ground. Another was like a mountain falling out of the sky. Another weapon caused an entire army to fall into a state of unconsciousness. One weapon I remember, caused the minds of soldiers to become confused, and they would suddenly begin to fight among themselves. One weapon caused utter destruction, like a nuclear bomb. Others were like arrows that could not miss, once they were fired."

Listening attentively, Kellon was somewhat surprised by Susie's description. "Two of those weapons you mention are recognizable as mental in nature, and those seem to have the Arkillian stamp on them, a stun weapon and one that confuses men's minds to the point trained soldiers fight among themselves. The first we have seen, the second we have not. It may be prudent for us to consider the probability of the existence of such weapons.

"Elayne, you might want to speak of this with Lorn and Roan, and obtain their viewpoints.

"Susie, is there anything more you can tell us?" Kellon inquired. Kellon's question caused Susie to smile broadly. "Sir, that's sort of an unfair question. Where Earth's history is involved, the subject is literally boundless, and there is always much more that remains unknown than known.

Reflecting Susie's smile, Kellon also smiled and suggested, "Perhaps restricting the topic to ancient religion might narrow the discussion somewhat."

"Yes Sir, ancient religions. Well, in the religions of the Middle East, from where at least three of the major Earth religions sprang forth, the concept of gods and visitors from other worlds were certainly elements of the earliest religious writings. Some of those reputed gods appear to have worked to control the people of the Earth, working their controls through the willing cooperation of designated divine rulers. Many of those rulers were people working out of simple ignorance, through the effects of deception, plain fear, or else motivated by lusts for power and wealth.

"If I remember my comparative religion courses correctly, the early Gnostics identified two general groups of extraterrestrials, the Archons and the Aeons. The two themes of these diametrically opposed viewpoints, or groups of reputed gods, formed the basis of religions for millions of people.

"The Archon viewpoint sought world control through deception, force and domination. They were very big on the practical use of religion as one of their primary psychological weapons to first deceive and then suborn people to their agenda, and there was absolutely no tolerance for individuality or disagreement. If you disagreed, the followers of that theme declared that you were a heretic, infidel, or unbeliever and they killed you.

"Contrastingly, the Aeons' viewpoint promoted peace, good-will, partnership, freedom, stressing free will, and love of one's self and others. As I remember, they were very much opposing themes, yet in their final doctrinal application both themes employed fear in one form or another, in order to manipulate and control people. The end point was you either agreed with one viewpoint or the other, and if you didn't, then you would be destroyed either physically or destroyed in eternity."

Shaking her head in wonder, Elayne asked, "Susie, all of what you are saying is about fear-based concepts. Didn't people know any better than to be controlled by those expressing such lies?"

"Sorry, but history argues most people did not discern anything wrong with such arguments. Besides, in some of the manifestations of those concepts, either you agreed or others killed you on the spot. It was sort of a damned if you do, and definitely dead if you didn't. Provided the two choices, most folks simply chose to follow one path or the other, but naturally there were also other beliefs emerging and then fading away. The sad truth is religion in general, and religious wars in particular, have represented dark and dangerous undercurrents throughout human written history." As for the Archon and Aeons'

134

viewpoints, entire cultures believed them. In fact, there are regions on Earth where they still follow such fear-based religions.

Shaking his head in wonderment, Kellon mused, "What you're speaking about is the immense power of an idea affecting generations, where individuals have limited lifetimes in which they are able to achieve experience and understanding."

"Sir, you are correct. Where the focus of a person's energy is on achieving rudimentary survival, taking time out for study of metaphysical truths is somewhat limited. Unfortunately, what we now know is very fragmentary. During the thousands of years since the early scholars and educated religious followers wrote their documents, those pertaining to those professing firsthand knowledge of the Archons or Aeons were simply lost or else intentionally destroyed. In one case, ignorant and reputedly pious men intentionally burned to the ground a great ancient library in Alexandria, a library containing more than one-million irreplaceable hand-written documents. The ignorant pious men, who burned it down, righteously profess the library contained heresies! The only real heretics were those ignorant men who burned the legacy of past centuries to ashes. The loss of knowledge contained in that wondrous library represented then, as now, a calamitous disaster on a global scale for the entire human race.

"As you can understand, without evidence, and with only fragmentary documentation available, meaningful discussion of such ancient subjects tends to rapidly fall apart into flimflam scams, hearsay, unsupported assertions or opinions, rumors, or else become accepted and imperfectly preserved as various doctrines."

"Susie, surely people on Earth can't possibly still believe such fear-based concepts," Elayne inserted.

Smiling Susie responded, "Of course they can, and as I have said, they still do in many parts of the world. People are still people. Unfortunately, most people do not bother to distinguish between assumptions and fact. Where faith is literally defined as persuasion, truth or lies about something are not the criteria by which a person is judged in his community. Only adherence to the common doctrine is important to a person's individual standing, acceptance, or even physical survival."

"Might I ask which theme is the most prevalent on Earth now?" Kellon asked.

"Sir, regrettably throughout our recorded history, the Archons' theme is what seemed to have mostly prevailed, since the second theme of partnership and peace left those who held to it rather unable to defend themselves. Frequently the result of the military imbalance between those who chose the path of domination, and those who chose the path of peace, was the easy conquest and eventual destruction of peaceful cultures.

"One earnestly expressed hope found in some older religious texts was looking for a time when the nations would beat their swords into plowshares. Millions of people have longed for that day; however, it has not yet happened. The shameful truth is some ruthless people make a great profit by promoting fear of others. Over the centuries, such people have deeply ingrained such fear of others in most of Earth's cultures and especially in Earth's religions. Accordingly, an old Earth axiom warns; He who beats his swords into plowshares will end up plowing for those who do not. History on Earth has tended to validate that somewhat cynical warning."

Kellon sat for some time considering what Susie had revealed. What he knew was the history of Earth could fill libraries and then there would still be more to learn. Even so, what he was hearing from Susie was deeply troubling, and it fully supported Admiral Mer Shawn's cautious approach to Earth politics. Shaking his head in wonderment, he brought the subject back on topic.

"Susie," Kellon mused, "how prevalent are the old viewpoints today?"

"Sir, that's not easy to answer. The ages-old concepts continue to exist, but are now frequently glossed over by the current run of academic self-proclaimed scholarly experts. They speak confidently and knowingly in modern terms of patriarchal or matriarchal societies. Their oversimplification reveals their ignorance of the root source of the conflict between Archons and Aeons, and that struggle was and remains a conflict between lies and the truth. It was never a conflict between genders. Although, fed by allegorical religious stories, such as the Garden of Eden, it certainly affected both genders, and often in tragic fashions."

136

"The conflict between truth and ignorance is certainly still with us, and that conflict is not restricted to Earth," Elayne commented thoughtfully.

"Elayne, for certain ignorance is alive, healthy, and flourishing on Earth. As was predictable, given the power of human greed and the lust for power, the Archon concepts of domination through force and nationalism became very prevalent. Nations on a global scale actually waged world wars. In fact, during the bloody Twentieth Century alone, Governments ruthlessly killed more than one-hundred and fifty-million humans during local civil and two global wars. "

"Hmmm, the name Archons is not the same as Arkillian, but there is a similarity in the sound of the two words. I do not recognize the name Aeons and cannot even guess the culture it may identify. However, I do believe it is something worthy of further research.

"Lan please perform a language history search of all files. Search for any correlations with the word Aeon or Aeons, pertaining to any culture known in Guardian reports or spoken of in folklore. If any are found, please generate a detailed time reference correlation of any identified references, and then store it for my subsequent retrieval."

"Yes Sir," Lan acknowledged.

"Commodore," Susie mused as she studied the picture of Scion displayed on the bulkhead, "may I offer a suggestion?"

Kellon turned and looked toward Susie, "Of course you can, your suggestions and recommendations are always welcome. What do you have in mind?"

"Well Sir," Susie replied, "if you are looking for some form of introduction to the Arkillians, why not simply transmit those images of Scion directly to them on the same frequency you sent your original message?

"The Arkillians already know you have superluminal capability, and five plus five still equals ten in radix 10. Even before saying one word, you will have achieved the high ground and established an irrefutable position of power, one they cannot deny and will readily understand.

"I imagine that after they have worked so hard to cover their tracks, and to conceal the location of their home planet, that picture being transmitted to them by their enemy will be a real shocker. It truthfully demonstrates you know precisely where Monstro is in space, and demonstrates you also know where their home is located. It also announces you have been there. While they are just beginning their long trip home you are flitting around making them look rather primitive. Since power is the entire basis for their assumed superiority, putting a pin in and popping their fat god-image balloon can't hurt."

"Hmmmm, Susie, there is considerable merit in your suggestion. It is simple, direct, and gets to the main point of our contact, to inform them the Kreel are now threatening the same lovely brown and tan world, Scion, and all of its inhabitants.

"Lan, have you computed the necessary trajectory for the intercept, and if so, state the time to intercept."

"Sir, the time to intercept is twelve hours, thirty two minutes, and 42 seconds, assuming we were beginning now."

Kellon keyed his communicator to his command staff and the Captain's bands. "Captains and Officers, Kellon here. Please advise me of any problems that might prevent our engaging the Arkillians in twelve hours. If there are no such problems then—" turning, Kellon looked at the chronometer, "on the hour, we will move toward intercept. Our intercept point will be above and well forward of the target. When departing this location, we will form up in our standard tactical formation. I welcome any thoughts that any of you may wish to offer, either at this time or during our approach. Lan has informed me the intercept will take somewhat more than twelve hours. Therefore, prepare accordingly for Condition 2 and full stealth mode. Are there any questions or comments or recommendations at this time?"

Each Captain in turn sent Kellon their acknowledgment. There were no questions or recommendations.

Turning, Kellon's voice was serious when he spoke to Elayne and Susie. "Madame Ambassador and Alien Culture Specialist Cloud, shall we commence to jot down a brief contact message for the Arkillian commander?"

Chapter Fourteen:
Parley Call

Although Kur was not fully awake, the urgency in the Captain's voice was unmistakable. *Did I hear a hint of fear? No,* he thought, *that cannot be possible.*

"Honored One, your presence is required on the bridge. It is urgent that you come at once," the Captain repeated.

Kur rolled out of his sleeping robes and acknowledged the Captain's call. Then as he dressed, his mind hurriedly registered all the troublesome problems he had been wrestling. He was not able to think of anything that should have made the Captain's voice so urgent, at least nothing of sufficient urgency to warrant waking him at such an early time.

It must have something to do with the operation of the ship, he thought, *something must have gone wrong.* What that might be was impossible to ascertain, without more information. He might as well go and see for himself what the urgent problem was. Hopefully, it would be a circulating pump or some innocuous matter. Yet with the hint of fear in the Captain's voice, he worried it must be something far more serious.

As he entered into the small conference compartment, offset from the bridge, he found the Captain and the Senior Intelligence Officer waiting for him. That the Intelligence Officer, and not the Engineering Officer, was there immediately caused Kur's stomach to cramp. He knew immediately, the matter was indeed urgent.

He turned to the Captain and asked, "Inform me of the urgent matter that requires my attention."

The Captain looked upset. If Kur had not known better, he might even say the Captain looked fearful. *No,* he thought, *after all we have gone through there could be nothing so urgent or serious that the Captain could possibly be fearful.* Remaining silent, he looked intently at the Captain, waiting for his report.

The Captain seemed hesitant, as if struggling with what to say. "Honored One," the Captain spoke in low guarded tones, "we are receiving a Kreel parley call. It is on the same frequency of the parley call received before we fought the enemy. I have located the sending source point and it is very near, only 20 kilometers off our starboard beam, and it is precisely matching our course and speed. Even using our best optics, I am unable to obtain any meaningful visual data.

"There is no electromagnetic indication of any ship or other object located at the position where the signal is originating, there are no detectable signals except the transmitted signal itself. There are no propulsion signatures.

"In accordance with your operating instructions, all of our sensors remain set passive search only. I have not initiated any active sensors that might be misconstrued as a fire control sensor."

Kur's heart was racing and he felt sick. During the past months, he had permitted himself to believe they had made good their silent departure from Earth's solar system, and they were now safe. They had escaped, and were going home. The Captain's statements had dashed his increasing hopes on the jagged rocks of doubt. He fought to keep his facial features neutral and calm.

He must above all remain in control; *I must not show any degree of anxiety,* he thought.

Reaching out he pulled back a chair and carefully sat down. "Captain you have done exceedingly well. I request you and your Officer sit with me."

Kur closed his eyes and thought about the situation that they were now in, trying to formulate and summarize what all this meant. It was not good, but it was certainly not hopeless. At least it was not yet hopeless.

For several minutes, Kur sat in contemplation, before he spoke. "Captain, I will provide my summary of our situation. When I am complete with my comments, I request your views on my understanding."

The Captain and Intelligence Officer had both taken their seats as instructed, and Kur was encouraged noting their expressions indicated concentration and not fearfulness. *That was at least a beginning,* he thought.

"The circumstances of our current position in space, and recent events strongly suggest the parley call is from the enemy, not the Kreel. What we know is that we are now in galactic space, and we are beyond the effects of Earth's heliosphere. We have had no contact with the enemy for nearly an Earth year. We also know that the enemy had the ability to destroy the Nest ship at the conclusion of the battle, and we could have done nothing to prevent that from happening. He did not choose to destroy the ship. Why he did not, we do not know.

"Until now, we had believed we were not being observed, having eluded our enemy. It is now obvious we have not evaded him. The enemy somehow has continued to determine our position, and obviously had no reason to communicate with us. That they are now contacting us, after our leaving the Earth's heliosphere is noteworthy. We can be certain that there is purpose for the communication occurring at this time. We have yet to establish that purpose.

"What we do know is that from 20 kilometers distance, rather than a parley call, the enemy could have directed missiles that could have destroyed this ship. He chose not to do that. Furthermore, his technology is so superior there is nothing of technological value here that would be of interest to him. Even so, we have knowledge, and I therefore believe it must be knowledge the enemy is pursuing.

"The only way we can find the answers to the unknown questions we have, is to respond to the call. This is my assessment. There is yet hope. I now request your considered views."

Kur began to feel better. His assessment had eased the edges of his own initial alarm. *There is still hope,* he reasoned inwardly, *we are alive, underway, and whoever is sending that parley call needs something.*

The Captain paused for a moment, and then in a confident voice he answered, "Honored One, I agree with your assessment. Only by answering the parley call can we learn what the caller wants. There is still hope."

"Captain, be certain the entire communications sequence is recorded, and that a probe is programmed for dispatch to Scion with a record of the communications. If this process ends in battle, and our destruction, Scion must have as much information as possible."

"Honored One, I will make it so." The Captain stood and quickly departed the small conference room, the door closing softly behind him.

Turning to the Intelligence Officer, Kur instructed him, "Worthy Officer, after we listen to the message, you will provide me with your appraisal of the message. Who are they, and what is their agenda? I want your assessment of their obvious stated purpose and especially the possible hidden purpose in their contacting us at this time."

As he addressed the Intelligence Officer, the Captain returned and stood waiting for Kur's notice. Turning to the Captain, Kur intentionally brightened his countenance and facial markings in order to infuse confidence to his officers. "When you are prepared, please respond to the parley call. Let us see precisely who is calling at this late time and learn what it is they need."

At the Captain's signal, the crew transmitted the acknowledging response to the parley signal. A moment passed, then those sitting in the little conference room sat up utterly transfixed, looking at the communications screen. Kur had not known what to expect, perhaps another image of the angry human being calling himself Kellon. What he had not expected was the image of Scion suspended beautifully in the darkness of space. Just looking at his Home planet brought anguish to his heart. Above all, it was to be safe at home on Scion that everyone on the ship desired more than anything else.

For five minutes, they sat together in silence and watched Scion. There was no sound whatsoever, just the uninterrupted view of Scion slowly turning on its axis in space. Then a calm resonant and measured voice spoke to them in the Arkillian language. Kur immediately recognized that voice; it was the same voice as the being named Kellon who had issued the ultimatum just before the battle.

"Attention Arkillian Commander, I am Commodore Kellon. I am the person who declared the battle over during our last encounter. "As one who has voyaged in space for many journeys, I know of your effort and achievement in repairing the severe damages inflicted on your ship, and your beginning of the homeward journey to Scion. Your accomplishment shows a degree of professionalism and tenacity, both of which are worthy characteristics. You are to be commended for your skill and courage."

Kur discerned the speaker's speech tones were not of anger and threat, as before. *His tonal inflections seemed to evidence sincerity,* he thought.

"The images of Scion are being sent to you as proof that we do not need to inquire where your home planet is located; we have thoroughly investigated your home solar system. We fully know of its strengths and weaknesses.

"Scion, like you, is open and utterly vulnerable, being at the mercy of those who would attack it.

"When you recently arrived in Earth's solar system, you were debating on the need to make the Earth again primitive. Your debate was not concerned with the value of life, honor, and dignity, but solely on your racial conceit and presumed superiority. You based that presumption on nothing more than raw force.

"When you arrived in orbit near earth, you were fully prepared to destroy upward of 14 billion human beings and felt no revulsion, no remorse, no kindness, no compassion, and no mercy. The awful truth is you had already millenniums before made the Earth primitive. This terrible truth of mass murder does not speak well for your wisdom but rather speaks of your immaturity and inferiority as an advanced species. That your species has stained its honor by mass murder, and by genetic alteration and inflictions of mental warfare, and other assaults, on another sentient species on their own planet, declares your guilt.

"Your vaulted vanity and arrogance even extended to representing yourselves as gods. That hypocrisy and masquerade is in itself inexcusable. I am not here to argue with you concerning these matters, since any defense you might offer is of no concern to me. You are what you are as repeatedly demonstrated by what you have done. The only justification for your continued existence is that you may yet discover the potentials of integrity, wisdom, and honor that are required to recognize your terrible mistakes and to alter your tragically flawed behavior.

"Your deeds are what speak for you, and your words are of no value whatsoever. Only time will answer the question of your species' ability to advance as a species, as evidenced by your own future deeds and actions.

"As I speak to you, I have many options. I can simply depart and leave you slowly crawling like a snail toward Scion; or destroy you here and now; or permanently cripple your ship's drive to such an extent you will be helpless flotsam. All of these things I could do if I but choose to do them.

"This being true, as I am certain you know it is, why then am I investing the time required to communicate with you? What you might ask is, 'what do I need or want?'

"Before I explain why I am now communicating with you, there is one thing you must first do. I will continue this communication only when your Commanding Officer or Superior Official responds to this message. I require that noteworthy individual to open a dialogue, first by presenting himself in person, and then by identifying himself by name and rank. I will grant you one Earth hour to do this.

"When the worthy individual responds, I will require him to answer one question, before we can proceed with any dialogue. How do you feel about abandoning part of your crew on Earth? Just that, how do you feel?

"If you have not complied within one Earth hour from the conclusion of this message, then I will consider there is none capable of speaking for the Arkillians on your Nest ship. That being the case I will resume this communication with the Arkillian detachment that remains on Earth. I assure you that I do know where your Earth contingent is hiding. I hold their lives, like your lives, in the palm of my hand.

"Consider these facts as you consider how to respond. Know that Earth is forever beyond your ability to approach again without our express permission. Any effort to return in force will immediately result in your destruction. The Arkillians will never set foot on Earth again, unless we permit it.

"Know this one additional fact, even as I speak, Scion is scheduled to be made primitive. As you once did to the Earth, others are now planning to do the same to Scion. Consider well your compassion for those on Scion who are about to die, and then examine your feelings about Scion being laid waste. Then consider again your feelings about what you were planning to do to the peoples of Earth.

"As I have truthfully said, Scion's destruction is now planned. When the attack comes, those on Scion will look up, as they perish, and they will not see my people seeking justifiable retribution. Instead, the people of Scion will look and see Kreel ships, your trusted allies, destroying your world. The Kreel now intend to destroy your species' hopes, and brutally terminate your ambitions.

"If you do survive your journey, and live to arrive at Scion, all you will find there are desolate ruin, death, and harsh servitude to the Kreel. Then you will know you have brought this terrible calamity on yourselves. Yet, there may be something you can do to save Scion. That possibility strictly depends on how you conduct yourselves during the next several hours. Need I say again, how do you feel? Who speaks for the Arkillian?"

As the screen went dark, Kur sat stunned and speechless. What Kellon said was without any sense of deceit or guile. He believed Kellon did hold his life and that of the ship in the palm of his outstretched hand. Kellon's voice even held a note of compassion, perhaps even pity, but there was no threat implied, only a cold statement of events yet to come.

It was the note of pity that frightened Kur to his core. Pity shouted the ship and the lives of those on board were indeed nothing more than fodder, perhaps not even worth the cost of the missiles it would take to destroy them. When Kellon spoke of Scion and what was to happen to their home, his sense of dread transformed into pure horror. Kur believed every word he heard Kellon speak. The Kreel, it was the Kreel that were planning to attack Scion.

Kur knew that his shock and sense of horror was apparent on his face for all to see, and he was not surprised to see the same shock registering on the faces of the Captain and the Intelligence Officer. Kur steadied his thoughts as well as possible then addressed the Officers.

"Captain and Worthy Officer, please consider what you have just heard. Remain here and discuss these matters. I will retire to my quarters and then return to listen to your assessment."

"Captain you are to immediately send a copy of the message we have just heard to the computer in my quarters. You will also make the technical preparations for me to speak directly, face to face, with the human Kellon, upon my return. I will return shortly."

Kur pushed back his chair and as he turned, he saw his servants waiting. With his hand, he signaled to one of them to go immediately and bring both beverages and food for three, indicating the Captain, the Intelligence Officer and himself.

He had walked well down the passageway before the door behind him softly closed. Entering his quarters, he went to his worktable and sat down. He needed to collect his thoughts and calm his fear. Given Kellon's statements, *There must be some way to intercede, some way to protect Scion.* He sat quietly for some time, patiently stilling his emotions and fully releasing all his fears. He established and embraced his own mental calmness. He then turned to the mental problem of how to respond to Kellon.

I am to present myself and declare my rank. That is simple enough, he thought. *However, why,* wondered Kur, *does Kellon want to know how I feel about leaving Ca, Rin and the others on Earth?* Kur's head ached and he could not reach any definitive conclusion.

Finally, he pushed back from the worktable and stood. *Since I cannot determine why Kellon asked his question,* he reasoned, *I must simply tell the truth and let my answer speak for my honor. I will not lie to Kellon.*

Kur went to his sleeping quarters and instructed one of his servants to select and bring to him his robes of high office. He would at least meet Commodore Kellon dressed as his official station warranted.

After putting on his formal robes, he adorned his brow with the rank headband of his office and stood looking in the dressing mirror. His robe of office was pure white, but woven into the richly textured fabric many gold threads that made the fabric shimmer in any light. His robes were formal and his jeweled and adorned headband of rank shone lustrously, yet his eyes and facial markings clearly showed fatigue and concern.

Kur shrugged, *An alien would most likely not have the discernment to wonder about my appearance.* With a heavy heart, Kur returned to the conference room. As he entered the conference room, he acknowledged both the Captain and the Intelligence Officer and bid them to sit with him.

Kur instructed his servants to present the food and to pour the honey mead in the goblets before him and his guests. That Kur elected to share a meal with his subordinates was an expression of honor and recognition he granted but rarely. All those in attendance fully recognized the deeper meaning of the repast.

Lifting his goblet, he saluted both Officers and then sipped the brew from the goblet. He could not but smile at the beverage's refreshing qualities and remember Ca, to whom he had given the matching goblet. The Officers solemnly returned his salute and sipped from their goblets.

"Captain and worthy Officer, please feel relaxed and enjoy the repasts before us. This is a memorable moment and one which needs commemorating, even as we are doing."

Putting down his goblet, Kur looked at the Officers. "I ask you both for your appraisal of the message we have just heard. Do you see deception in what is said and if so what is that deception?"

There was a brief pause as the Officers exchanged concerned glances, then The Captain responded. "Honored One, the charges of mass murder and similar charges are what they are. We are not qualified to address or respond to such charges.

"Whether Kellon could elect to destroy or further damage the Nest ship, we conclude he has no reasons to falsely claim this capability. Given his demonstrated battle prowess, superior technology, and the status of our ship and crew, I consider his words truthful.

"As regarding his comments that the Kreel are planning to attack Scion, we have no information to corroborate this claim, but again we cannot discern any gain to our enemy by falsely informing us of a Kreel attack on Scion. We simply do not have sufficient military intelligence to support his statements or to refute them. This being so, the man Kellon has not discernibly lied in any matter. Because of this, his words have alarmed us.

"Regarding the assertion that he knows where our Earth contingent is concealed, he has ably demonstrated his technology by visiting Scion and finding us in the vastness of space. Finding our Earth contingent is considerably less complicated a feat. We therefore consider his words truthful.

"We cannot discern why he wants to know how you feel about leaving the Earth contingent on Earth. However there are numerous references to feelings in his message, therefore the question is being seriously asked."

As the Captain finished his statement, Kur looked toward the Intelligence Officer and asked, "have you anything you would like to add to the Captain's comments?"

The brilliant jewel encrusted and gold medallion on Kur's headband caught the light of the room and sent light shimmering on the outer bulkhead, its gleaming flickering richness brilliantly contrasting with the decor of the conference room.

Shifting in his seat, the Intelligence Officer looked toward Kur, and after a momentary pause, he spoke. "Honored One, I sense truthfulness in the message. However, there is much more that we do not know, than we know.

"His identification with the term 'our people', when speaking of retribution, implies he is of the people of the Earth. However, he cannot represent the technology of the Earth. This implies there are other human worlds that we do not know of, and which have had no contact with Earth for at least fourteen thousand years. How this might be possible, I cannot explain, but it must be so.

"In carefully observing the images of Scion, that were transmitted, I note the planet's polar region is appropriate for the winter season of about eight months ago. That a ship could depart Earth after the battle we fought and then arrive near Scion within four months is staggering to consider. Even so, the time to travel there and return to contact us is about one Earth year. This means that the enemy has the capability of traveling at least twenty times the known speed of light and perhaps many times more. This being true, their technology is very far in advance of ours. Knowing this reality cautions great care in whatever you say or do.

"As for hidden agendas, clearly he wants something. He alludes there is perhaps a possibility that Scion might be saved from the Kreel attack. That implies some form of exchange may be involved. I cannot even begin to suggest what that exchange might involve or entail. His reference to the Kreel is such that,

148

given what else we know about the Kreel, I believe Kellon may well be an enemy of the Kreel. If this supposition is correct, then he may be looking for some form of interplay that could be of mutual benefit to the Arkillian and the humans. I say this without anything to support my thoughts, only in attempting to bring together what I know of Kreel behavior, and adding to that what Kellon has said.

"That Kellon states, with conviction, what the Kreel intend to do to Scion, requires me to ask how does he know this? Have the Kreel openly informed him this will happen? Has Kellon's Intelligence resources been able to extract Kreel planning? These are serious questions, and the ramifications of the answers are significant. Regrettably, I cannot answer them with certainty.

"What I do offer Honored One is only conjecture, yet I believe it is worthy of consideration. Kellon, a human being, is speaking our language fluently. How did he learn our language? My assessment is that Kellon has extremely well-developed and sophisticated intelligence-gathering capability. Therefore, when he states the Kreel have planned an attack on Scion, there is cause for great concern.

"In comparing Kellon's people, the Kreel, and the Arkillian, we clearly have inferior technology. We can safely conclude both Kellon and the Kreel are concealing vast amounts of information, and we are the least informed of the three species, concerning what is truly happening. In matters of war, technological inferiority and ignorance is often fatal, and especially so in space warfare.

"That is all I can add to what the Captain has already observed."

Having listened to both Officers with great interest, Kur was thoughtful. Even so, his choices were few. "Worthy Officer, your assessment is very helpful as was the assessment of the Captain. Thank you both."

Perhaps Kur should have been amazed or at least surprised about the Intelligence Officer's revelations, but he was not. Now, he only wished he were safe on Scion and was not. *In truth,* he thought, *I might never again be safe, either in space or on Scion.* Suddenly, how fast the enemy might travel through space and time meant very little to him.

Only one question was center on Kur's mind. *Were Kellon and the Kreel allies? The Intelligence Officer does not believe this,* he thought, *and neither do I. Could the Officer be correct? Could Kellon be seeking an alliance? What could the Arkillians offer so advanced a culture, as Kellon obviously represents?*

Kur picked up his goblet once again, and he appreciatively drank its contents. He unconsciously fingered it with the easy physical habit of a frequently made gesture, one repeated over hundreds of years. Looking up, he acknowledged the two Officers. "Your viewpoints are noted and appreciated."

Noting the Officers were finished with the repast and turning to his servant, he signaled they were to clear the table. "Captain, set up the equipment so I may address our enemy. You are to inform me when you are ready, and only I remain in the frame. I do not want to provide the enemy with any unnecessary information, whether he would benefit from that information or otherwise."

Both the Captain and the Intelligence Officer stood, showing deference to Kur with a shallow bow. At the Captain's signal, several crewmembers arrived, and they busied themselves with setting up the communications equipment. As Kur watched, he still felt the tight knot of fear in his stomach, gnawing fear and uncertainty, and promptly mentally dispelled such emotions. How could he, a senior elder and member of the Arkillian ruling council be about to speak to a human being? To speak not as a ruler, even as an equal, but rather as someone vanquished. For fourteen thousand years, the Arkillians considered human beings a sub-primitive species. He was positive that none on Scion would conceive how this moment between the species might have happened. He had lived through the nightmare of the past Earth months, and still he doubted this communication was really happening. Yet it was.

He paused and focused his mind, searching for his center, the balance and bright fire within. Closing his eyes, he began the inner practice made possible by centuries long established ritual and training. Regulating his breathing cycle, he focused inwardly his thoughts, as if preparing for battle on the hot sands. In truth, he knew he was. After several minutes had passed, Kur looked up at the Captain, who indicated the equipment was ready. Kur raised his head, sitting erect in his chair. He turned to face the communications equipment, ordering, "Captain, answer the parley call."

Chapter Fifteen:
Backwater Cousins

Entering briskly into the outer office of his boss, Darrell Fann barely glanced at the simple nameplate on the door, it read, "Charles Sullivan Undersecretary of Commerce." Entering he smiled at the receptionist and commented, "Good morning Lois, guess who is late again?"

Looking back, Lois grinned. "Mr. Fann, you would not want to upset anyone by being on time would you? Please go right in, Mr. Sullivan is anticipating your arrival." Saying this, she winked.

Opening the inner office door, Darrell entered and found himself in the inner-sanctum of the man in charge of the Olympus Project, the project that the United States government had created to counter what it once believed to be a threat by extra-terrestrials. Now they knew their work had been well justified. Only now were they beginning to understand fully that for thousands of years Earth had existed under the oppressive restraints of both psychological and genetic warfare. Darrell now knew for better or for worse, willful controls exercised by an alien species had completely shaped the world they lived in.

He found Charles sitting at the small circular oak conference table he used for his managers' meetings, and he had a heavy scowl on his face as he was sorting through documents scattered over the top of the table. Looking up toward Darrell his expression shifted to a smile. Straightening, he sat back. "Darrell, thank you for coming so soon. I have been working through a pile of requests, demands, and urgent ultimatums from every conceivable Government Agency on earth. They all want information about what the hell is going on. If I find out who gave my name out as the point of contact for such inquiries, then that individual will meet his waterloo in the first dark alley he passes. He will never know what hit him; one minute he will be walking along and the next instant– wham, instant retirement! Please take a seat. Would you like a cup of coffee?"

Pulling out a chair, Darrell sat down and nodded his head in the affirmative. "I would welcome a hot cup of coffee, one spoon of honey and a shot of cream will do nicely. And for the record, I am not the person or persons that gave out your name, honest."

As Charles picked up his phone to request the coffee, Darrell turned to face the floor-to-ceiling windows that looked toward the expansive landscape of New Washington. *The morning was crisp and the early signs of spring were everywhere,* he thought. It had been a difficult winter and the unpredictable climate was not making spring's arrival easy. The sky outside was darkly overcast and a slow continuous drizzle made the scene even look more dreary and cold.

As Charles completed his request for the coffee, he turned back toward Darrell, and his expression became serious.

"Darrell, I'm receiving enormous pressure to release information about the Guardian Force, who they represent, and what they are doing. As you know, the rumor mills have been running on overtime since Captain Kellon shut down the Arkillians' pop-pattern transmitters. I need an out. Do you have any suggestions?"

"Well, what is the problem? What information do you actually have about what the Guardian Force is doing? To my understanding there are several Guardian ships operating in our solar system, how many and what they are doing is not something they freely share with anyone on Earth. I believe this means the two of us do not have Guardian Force information we can distribute, even if we wanted to do so. This being true, then why are you feeling so pressured? You know nothing; just keep saying that over and over again and eventually the message will spread to the outmost reaches of the known world.

"As for the other matter, I for one," Darrell added, "am very grateful to the Guardian Force for destroying those transmitters. I don't know about you, but I am personally sleeping much better since they did. Besides, we would have had little hope of finding those transmitting facilities. If we had found them, then we would have been required to infringe on other countries sovereign territories, in order to destroy them.

154

The Guardian Force did not bother to ask for your permission before taking action. In return, you should not be taking responsibility for what they did. Simply keep on saying I know nothing! Just say it slowly; rolling it over your tongue, I know nothing!"

Charles grunted as if unimpressed. "I wish it were that easy. The result of the Guardian Force military actions has more than one consequence. However, it certainly has eliminated the oppressive psychological warfare overtones of the Arkillian."

Smiling Charles continued, "Like you, I am also sleeping much better.

"Nevertheless, the Guardian raids also created a number of outcries from various governments about infringement of their sovereign territories. As those Governments have discovered and investigated those destroyed transmitter facilities, they know full well something of a sophisticated technological nature was there. More significantly, someone penetrated their assumed impenetrable security and destroyed whatever it might have been. Every one of those countries suspects the truth, and they have their top scientists sifting through the rubble. Thankfully, Kellon was efficient in what he did. Our reports are that all the scientists are finding is rubble and still smaller bits of rubble.

"They do not know who performed the military intrusion, but naturally suspect that it was the United States. We have firmly denied any part in such military actions, but the indignant outcries and noise continues."

"Charles, let me be the first to admit, you are earning your paycheck. The fact remains we don't know anything more than those blaming us."

Charles sighed, shaking his head. "It isn't that simple Darrell. We do have more information than most countries. The past year has been difficult for the Secretary of State and for the Presidency. We are continuing to sit on a powder keg, and I sense the fuse is growing short."

"Charles, let's at least acknowledge the truth. You yourself stated a year ago that the knowledge of the Arkillian influences have forever altered and turned our whole world upside down. We should not be sitting on a powder keg; we should be having a worldwide party. Why not come clean, and tell the whole world the truth. There is simply no way the governments can suppress the facts forever. The sooner the facts are known, the better it will be for everyone."

"That may be true Darrell, but the decision to make those facts known is not mine to make," Charles sighed.

The door opened and Lois entered with a small tray. As she approached, Charles quickly made room on the table for it. She smoothly put the tray down, picked up the thermos flask and deftly poured out two cups of coffee, nearly to their brims. Standing back, she nodded and said with a smile, "You gentlemen can just add your own fixin's to your coffee, as you please. Is there anything else I might obtain for you?"

Looking up, Charles returned her smile. "No, Lois that will be all. Thank you."

As Lois departed the room, and the door closed softly behind her, Darrell added some cream and a half spoon of honey to his cup of coffee, and took a gratifying sip. It had been Susie that taught him about honey in coffee, and he had adopted that treat ever since.

Looking up at Charles, he asked a question that had been troubling him. "The people that have been coming in from Glas Dinnein have been working here for months. They are working closely with all sorts of people in the government. How can you expect to keep what they are doing secret?"

"Do you remember your history? Ever hear of the Manhattan Project? The people arriving from Glas Dinnein are well accustomed to working with matters pertaining to security. They have a command of our language, and frankly, if anyone were to suggest they were from a world 80 light years distant, no one would believe them. Would you?" Charles asked .

Smiling, Darrell replied, "No, they look just like most of us, at least those of us that do not have glowing blue skin and antenna growing from our foreheads.

"But while on the topic of Glas Dinnein, I haven't heard a peep about Susie or when she will be returning. Have you heard anything from your contacts?"

"No Darrell, not a word. However, I don't believe there is anything to worry about; she has only been gone for a year. I do not know how fast the Guardian Force ships are, but the round trip is 160 light years. That may take a heap of time to travel, let alone the time she will spend on Glas Dinnein. For certain, when she does come home she will have some tales to tell. Hopefully we will still be young enough and cogent enough to hear those tales."

Glancing at Darrell, Charles noted his sad expression and smiled, it was apparent Darrell was smitten with Susie. *Oh, the joys of the heart and youth,* he mused. "Not unlike you, I also miss her."

Darrell grew thoughtfully quiet for a moment, and then he earnestly addressed a thorny question. "The Guardian Force is patrolling our solar system, and they are not interfering with our own surveillance. Even so, they are not sharing any of their own intelligence. If we did not know they were out there, we simply would not know they even exist. We could at least monitor Monstro, when that ship came around. The Guardian ships are like a shadow's shadow, they come and go and we do not have a clue where they are or what they are doing. What am I, the guy in charge of monitoring our solar system, supposed to be doing about this?"

"You have a job description, do you not?"

"That's not an answer Charles, it's an evasion." Darrell retorted.

"Well it is as good an answer as you are likely to obtain from this office. The Arkillians are still out there, and you have the task of finding them. As for the Guardian Force, good luck. They seem to have run rings around Monstro, and given their advanced technology, I doubt you will see them, until they want you to see them. If your funding and brainpower permits, go to it, have a run at detecting the Guardian ships. Perhaps you will have better luck than the Arkillians did. Of course that is just my own opinion, no extra charge," Charles replied, as he sipped from his coffee cup.

Darrell leaned forward, "OK, that suffices for the moment, but it brings me to another point that concerns me. Namely, why are the Guardian Force personnel so tight-lipped about everything they are doing?"

That question brought Charles up to a thoughtful pause. "Well, why should they be telling us everything they are doing? I have the impression they have been scrambling just to be certain our butts are covered. Remember something that is easy to forget. Earth is off-budget. In other words, they did not come to

157

our solar system to look for more work. They had their hands full of other problems. The riddle of the moment is, guess what– those problems are not the Arkillians! Sit and consider that for a few minutes."

"Ouch, I hadn't considered that angle," Darrell admitted.

"Well I have considered it long and hard. I doubt they have had so much slack time they can simply put down their extra work to hold special sessions for their slow-witted backwater cousins. Besides, I imagine there is something your technical orientation has not yet considered. Earth is a backwater and worse it has numerous heavily armed countries politically sniping at each other, conflicting industrial competition, twenty or more squabbling religions, various vying ethnic population groups, East/West political divisions, pollution, protests, and such other non-trivia. From the Guardian Force perspective, we are a social, emotional, political and scientific wasteland as well as a heavy burden. Ask yourself how long will it take Earth to wake up and become a peaceful homogenous whole, capable of interlocking and working smoothly with other human-occupied worlds? We can't even do it with the country next door!

"Now, returning to my stated mental teaser about the Guardian Force, they had their hands full of other problems; their problems are not the Arkillians!

"Think for a minute. Captain Kellon arrived near earth, and he has an advanced military capability that crosses 80 light years and blows through Monstro and his fighters, like a strong wind through dry leaves. Why does a group of peace loving human inhabited worlds develop such sophisticated military capability? Against what whetstone does Guardian Force sharpen its military capability? We have determined it isn't the Arkillians, so there must be some really bad critters out there in the depths of space that we know nothing about.

"Remember Monstro was scared to death about that fly-by from the pretty little scarlet and green space ship. I wager a root beer, as Susie would say; the Guardian Force could tell us all about that unidentified spaceship and its heraldic colors.

"Stop and consider that little matter before you begin planning that worldwide party. Our knowledge of the universe is very limited, and our ignorance is more than a little scary."

158

Darrell's communicator hummed and he grimaced as he took it from his pocket. "Fann here." Listening for a moment, Darrell asked, "Charlie, please repeat that message slowly. Okay, I understand. Thank you."

Darrell quietly returned his communicator to his pocket. He sat for a moment thinking about what he had just heard. Looking up at Charles, he frowned and looked as if about to speak. Then he sat very quietly, his forehead furrowed as if in deep thought.

Charles looked at him speculatively. Well, open up and let it out. What was that all about?"

Darrell looked puzzled, "I don't understand it. That was Charlie in my early warning group. He told me they have a fix on Monstro. They have detected the ship, or its twin, well above the ecliptic plane. Charlie reports it is coming toward Earth. It is too early for them to have a course, but they know it's Monstro.

"I don't get it," Darrell mused. "The last reports on Monstro were it was on a ballistic trajectory carrying it out of our solar system in the ecliptic plane. Now it is well above the ecliptic plane and moving on its own power toward us. That doesn't make any sense what so ever."

Frowning, Charles looked out of the window, his forehead furrowed in concentration. Then, he turned and looked at Darrell. "Oh, it makes sense all right." Charles responded. "The problem is that we are not holding the cards to explain the sense of it. This development breathes a million unanswered questions, like stagnant swamp water breeds mosquitoes. What it does prove is I simply do not like being left in the dark."

Both men sat for several minutes, neither saying anything. Then Charles picked up his phone and pressed a speed dial button. As he waited for an answer, he looked at Darrell and sighed, "when in doubt, check with those who are well-paid and supposed to be in the know. Given our Mr. Carl Suthaford manages the government agency liaison and security affairs, including liaison with the Guardian personnel on Earth, perhaps he can provide us with some insight as to what is going on."

There was an additional pause, and then Charles relaxed somewhat. "There you are Carl. I had begun to believe you were out looking for another job. Yes, I am in a very good mood today. I am very pleased you so quickly noticed that tidbit of information. Have you perhaps heard anything from the

Guardian Force folks that you believe warrants passing on to your boss? Nothing? Well then, let me inform you of something that I want you to immediately discuss with them.

"Our early detection system indicates Monstro is returning to Earth. At least we are detecting Monstro high above the ecliptic plane. No, we do not have specifics about course and ETA, only a coordinate at this time."

"Correction Charles, more like Doppler and a bearing line than a coordinate point." Darrell inserted.

"Did you hear that? Yes, Darrell is here. The report on Monstro is about sixty seconds old, right off the early detection net."

Sitting quietly, Charles listened to the telephone, grimacing from time to time, and obviously irritated. "Wonderful Carl, I will look forward to your report, and I will let payroll know you are still working here. Carl, take care."

Sighing, Charles put the phone down. Looking toward Darrell he sighed again, "Well, I suspect you have some work to do. Please keep me informed of what you learn. If we know Monstro is nearby, then you can safely bet the Guardian Force knows all about it. If I hear anything from Carl, I will pass it on to you as soon as I hear it. Now, go to work."

Darrell stood up and pushed his chair under the table. "Charles, please do let me know what you hear as soon as possible. I have the gut feeling that whatever is going down is about to shake up the status quo, like nothing has shaken it before. There is something happening, and we're not in the inner loop."

Frowning, Charles was lightly drumming the tabletop with the fingertips of his left hand. "We're both on the same wavelength," replied Charles. "If Monstro is busted up, as we damn well know he is, then showing himself anywhere near Earth shouts there is more going on here, than either of us are aware of. Be certain Darrell, you will hear from me when I have anything worth passing on."

"Thanks, the promise is mutual."

Departing the inner office, Darrell waved a cordial hand to Lois and headed for the elevator. Standing and waiting, He thought, *Foolish me, I had begun to believe we were out of the frying pan, without going into the fire. I should have known better.*

The elevator door opened and as he entered, he inserted his ID card into the slot in the panel. The door closed and the elevator dropped rapidly down, reaching and then passing the lowest floor on the indicator panel without even slowing. When the elevator did come to a smooth stop, the elevator door opened upon a small room. As he stepped forward, the scanner registered his physical features and acknowledged, "Mr. Fann, please designate your desired destination."

"Olympus deep space intelligence and research division."

A door opened in what had appeared to be a blank wall, and Darrell walked out onto a small loading platform. As he did, the door behind him closed with a discernible thump. Standing, he looked about the bleak area, and felt the coolness of the air, its dry qualities indicating and air-conditioning system with an abundance of reserve capacity. A few minutes later, a sleek cylinder slipped out of the tunnel and glided to a noiseless stop next to the platform before him. Darrell entered through the doorway that opened into a dimly lit but well-appointed interior and took a seat. He was the only person in the car. He sat back, as the shuttle car smoothly sped up and entered the underground tube network, connecting the key points under the New Washington sprawling complex. The network of high-speed secure transportation was restricted to only those with the absolute need-to-know, those few that the Government granted access to the underground system. The trip took about twelve minutes, before the car slipped easily into a connecting tunnel, and moved up to a loading platform. As soft chimes sounded, the door opened. Darrell exited the car and as he did a door in the tunnel wall slid open and he entered another small room. Without any need for identification, he entered the waiting elevator and pressed the button for the level of his office.

As he exited the elevator, he noted there was a quiet sense of excitement in the area. He looked about for his senior analyst, and he saw Charlie across the room. Darrell moved toward him and asked, "Charlie, we need to talk. What is happening on the Monstro sighting?"

Charlie Wilcox looked over and gave his traditional broad smile, "Hey Darrell, we have some really fascinating stuff here.

161

We picked up Monstro about an hour ago. One of our high heliocentric polar satellites, Skylark 3, detected the ship. Its drive signature Doppler says it is definitely heading this direction."

"Charlie, could there be any mistake?"

"Are you kidding boss? Not a chance. That signature is engraved and stamped 100% pure Monstro. The ship is heading back."

Lifting his communicator, Darrell pressed Charles Sullivan's number.

"Charles, yes, I am in the office. Charlie has just confirmed the contact is definitely Monstro. He assures me it is inbound. Yes, I understand. You can be certain I will keep you fully informed."

X

In his office, Charles Sullivan still held his phone, and he sat quietly pondering Darrell's information. *I have a distinct gut feeling that a storm wind is rising,* he thought. Pressing a button on his phone, he waited. After a few moments of waiting, he heard the party answer and promptly reported, "Mr. President, Monstro has been detected. The ship is high above the ecliptic plane, and it's heading this way. Yes Sir. Well, I have contacted Carl Suthaford, and he is checking with Guardian Force now. Yes Sir, I agree. There is no possibility that the Guardian Force is unaware of Monstro's movements. I will keep you posted. Yes Sir."

Standing, Charles moved over and stood at the window, and looking out on the plaza below, he let his worries flow away. In the distance, he could just make out the Washington Monument. *Well,* he thought, *things are about to get very interesting.*

Chapter Sixteen:
Sinister and Lovely

Shey might have been laughing, if that were one of her AI capabilities. Zorn and Roan were busy designing a dress for her to wear to a special party. That was what Roan had told her and she was wondering what type of party it might be. What Shey understood was she was to look very different from her normal hull configuration. She did agree the heliographic matrix Zorn was snuggly constructing about the model of her sleek shape seemed rather unusual. Upon reflection, she liked the look. Inwardly she felt a very curious sense of warmth and pleasure. She would need to admit, she did like being fussed over. Dutifully she logged this information into her 'notes to the programmers' file with a appended question, *Why can I not laugh like Zorn?*

Grumbling, as usual, Zorn's blue eyes twinkled with a hint of mischief. "I'll wager a cold brew we will have the best looking disguise for a Scout ship in the Guardian Force. It is a shame you are so stiff-shirted about it Roan; she would look even better if you would let me encode feathers into her heliographic matrix."

Smiling good-naturedly, Roan quipped, "No feathers!"

"Now that is downright unsporting, even inartistic," taunted Zorn.

Both men were working in Shey's small compact and efficient control compartment, working on the task of building a camouflage disguise for the Scouts. Commodore Kellon had ordered they come up with a new and exotic alien look for Shey, a look which would mislead any observer who might otherwise know what a Guardian Scout ship actually looked like. It was just the type of assignment that Zorn enjoyed receiving.

He glanced toward Roan, with a sense of well-earned trust and respect. Their bond of friendship had endured and grown through times of peace and space warfare. In addition, together, they made a proficient and effective Scout team. Roan was dressed as he was, in the informal uniform of Guardian Force Scout ship personnel, a uniform tailored from forest green fabric of woven natural fibers and designed for comfort and ease of movement. The uniform featured a loosely-tailored tunic top and pants that bloused above soft low-topped dark leather boots. Both Roan and Zorn's collars carried rank tabs, and the subtle insignia and badges of Guardian Force commanders and elite Scout ship team members.

Zorn stood up and shook his head, "Well if we got no feathers, then I guess that does it. Let's look at what we've put together. Shey, please display the heliographic matrix model on the heliographic pad."

Before them appeared the floating three-dimensional heliographic image of Shey, and about her was constructed a wire frame that extended before, behind and to the sides of Shey's image. Spreading out on each of the model's sides were what appeared to be tapering wings. The wings were angled slightly downward, and at each end was a vertical keel.

Frowning, Roan studied the model. "Hmmm, you might want to make the wing-tip keels somewhat smaller, and spread them outward slightly so they aren't vertical. Also, put on a pair of inwardly leaning rudders. Make the overall shape streamlined, enhanced for hot atmospheric flight."

"No problem." Zorn deftly manipulated the controls and the wire frame image swiftly transformed, "Like that?" he asked. "Good, hold it right there. Hmmmm, let's look at it from above," Roan mused.

Zorn made a few quick adjustments, and the suspended image slowly revolved. They were then looking at the floating image, from a perspective directly above the model.

"Zorn that is looking good. I recommend you make the wing smaller in area, perhaps pull the leading edge back some, and increase the trailing edge taper."

Zorn made a few adjustments, and then Roan commented, "Hold it, right there. What do you think?"

Zorn stood back with his arms crossed and studied the model. "Well it looks almost alright." He made a quick adjustment, and the keels lengthened, projecting slightly forward, extending ahead of the leading wing edge. "I would rather go for feathers, and more sinister than graceful. Still, what color do you believe would do best?"

"The idea is for the image to be seen and that means it should have some color that would look good in a dramatic soft energy emitting glow. Why not go for pure opalescent white." Roan responded.

Zorn murmured something unflattering under his breath about parade colors and the screen shimmered as the wire screen image filled in with a gleaming gold, and then altered to show sweeping thin trim lines of pure white along the length of the leading and trailing edges of the wings and keels. Then with a few more adjustments, there appeared broader panels of opalescent white on the wings and fuselage. The sweep of the leading edge of the white wing panels was not as sharp as the wing's leading edges, so there appeared to be a gold wedge that tapered from the fuselage to the tip of the wing. The white panels were iridescent, having a play of lustrous rainbow colors. They complimented and accented the pure lustrous gold color that filled the remaining portions of the disguise.

"How about that for a look?" Zorn inquired.

Roan stood looking at the image with an approving eye. "Not bad Zorn, not bad at all. Shey, what do you think of the newest look in Scout ship camouflage?"

There was a momentary silence before Shey's warm voice responded. "Well, I believe it could be made somewhat more exotic with a minor adjustment or two. May I make those adjustments?" Roan looked at Zorn and both of them smiled at Shey's unexpected artistic request.

Nodding his head approvingly, Roan replied, "Certainly Shey, please show us what you believe would be an improvement."

As they watched, the shape of the image flowed slightly and the color patterns shifted in their configuration. The changes were subtle and yet the final adjustment left the ship looking leaner and considerably more impressive in its overall lines. Shey had also added more shading and lines to suggest the beak of a raptor with a pair of gleaming eyes adorning and accenting the shape of the bow.

"Zorn, I hope that is all right. I have tried to give the image a touch of quiet grace, and your desire for a blend of the sinister while remaining lovely."

Zorn broke out in laughter. "Well-done Shey. That looks terrific. It really does. If you give it your final approval, please record the heliographic matrix as Shey Lovely Sinister.

"Oh, Zorn do you really like it?" Shey asked.

"Yes Shey. I really do like it."

"Roan," mused Zorn, "I have just had an idea. Why do we just want to look sinister? Why don't we add some sound effects? For example, if we appear in Shey Sinister, why not have several decoys out and transmitting all manner of sinister sounds through the magnetic spectrum, like howls, whistles, groans, terrified shrieks, moans of hopeless cries of despair, that sort of thing. Think of it as a new type of jamming screamer. If done correctly and artfully, I would wager a cool brew it could scare the pants off a scarecrow." Considering the idea for only a moment, Roan approved. "It is always good to have an ace in the hole. Shey, did you monitor Zorn's suggestion? "He asked, knowing she had. *The girl never sleeps*, Roan thought.

"Yes Roan, I did listen. I could, with the help of my sisters, come up with a suggested sound profile; devising a profile with a spectrum of such transmissions that might effectively jam a wide spectrum of bandwidth. I could also provide for bandpass filters for regular communications and tracking. Roan, Do you want me to proceed with the project?"

"Yes Shey, please begin the work. Be certain you check with Lan, so he remains fully informed about any bandpass filters. It is important he knows how to communicate, if necessary." Roan ordered.

"Roan, I will immediately proceed to open a joint file with Lan for the assigned task."

"Hey Shey," inserted Zorn, "if you and Lan can figure out any really scary sounds tailored especially for the Kreel, please add those to the spectrum of your sinister sounds." Zorn added, with a smile.

"Yes Zorn.

"Roan, may I work with William? He has wonderful stories from Earth's folklore, and I am certain when it comes to scary stories, he would be a valuable source," Shey requested.

166

"Shey, as for working with William, have him first confirm Susie approves of his doing so. If she does approve, then go ahead." "Certainly Roan, that will not be a problem." There was a hesitant pause, and then Shey quietly inquired, "Zorn, do you really believe I am lovely?"

Shey's question surprised both Zorn and Roan, but stopped Zorn only momentarily, and he responded with warmth in his voice. "Shey, I really think you are absolutely beautiful."

Roan was smiling broadly, "Shey, I totally agree with Zorn."

Roan looked at the chronometer and winced. "We had better pick up the pace Zorn. We are to meet with the Commodore in five minutes."

Turning they exited Shey's control compartment, went to the exit port, crossed the short gangplank to the hangar flight dock, and proceeded to Kellon's conference room. Entering they found they were the last to arrive for the meeting. Kellon, Susie, Roy Grey and Lorn Shaw were already sitting at the table.

As they entered, everyone looked up and Susie quipped, "Leave it to Shey's Scout team to be the last to arrive."

Roan only smiled, but Zorn could not let the quip slide, "Madam Ambassador, may I point out that Scout ship Shey is your taxi home? We are at least the important required ride to complete your journey. Just be nice."

"Why Zorn," responded Susie with a smile, "Shey promised William I would be returned home in good working order. She also confided with me that you are strictly bound by her promise." Sitting back, Kellon was fully enjoying the banter between his friends. "Gentlemen, you are welcomed and precisely on time. Please take a seat and help yourself to the neab and pastries if you wish." Kellon added.

Taking their seats, Roan and Zorn selected some of the refreshments; then focused on what Kellon was saying.

"Well everyone is present, so let's move to the topics at hand. Lorn, what is the current disposition of Monstro?"

"Sir, Monstro has again entered Earth's heliosphere, and is currently moving slowly toward the same orbit position they occupied before our battle. They will not press forward until we provide them the agreed-upon signal."

"Are they meeting their agreements regarding their Earth contingency?" Kellon inquired.

"Sir, we have been informed they are in communications, and the Earth-side group is currently preparing to secure their facility and depart. As agreed, they are leaving it intact and sealed. They have provided the necessary information to permit us to enter the facility later, if we elect to do so. Otherwise it will remain sealed." Roy leaned forward asking, "Lorn, when precisely will that contingency depart Earth?"

"We don't have a specific time established Roy, at least not yet. They are remaining on station until we can confirm their secure departure, which we are now coordinating with Olympus."

Nodding, Roy acknowledged, "Thank you Lorn."

Turning to Commander Grey, Kellon asked, "Roy what is the status of the retiring Cruisers?"

"Sir, all three Cruisers departed on schedule. They are moving as planned toward Scion and are adding new beacons along their route. The latest data does not indicate any major dark bodies or active plasma conduits between the two stars. Therefore, I believe when the new beacons are fully functional, we may be able to make the Scion transit in a single long Jump.

"As we have planned, after they reach the final Jump point near Scion, the Cruisers will proceed to the nearest point on our Glas Dinnein-to-Earth route. The additional beacons they are placing along the path should permit a single Jump from Earth to Scion, and then from Scion to the intersection point. At the moment, everything is on schedule."

Looking toward Roan and Zorn, Kellon asked, "Roan, were you able to complete the new costume for Shey?"

"Sir, the costume design is complete, and it looks somewhat sleek and flashy, with just a touch of the sinister. It would drive an aeronautical engineer crazy, with its aerodynamic contradictions, but it does look interesting. We are ready."

Next turning to Susie, Kellon inquired, "Susie, are you ready with the negotiated trading agreement with the Arkillians?"

"Sir, the negotiations with Council Member Kur went very well. He worked in cooperation with two other Council Members, Ca and Rin, who are among the Earth contingency. The resulting trade agreement is robust and even includes provisions for balanced dispute resolution. Council member Ca said he believed it would result in a doubling of their former profits and perhaps more, since the trade will involve open two-way transactions.

"Sir, I want you to know, the negotiations would not have been possible without Elaine and her knowledge of the Arkillian language. The Arkillians consider language skills a mark of superior sentient beings, and were astonished at Elaine's grasp and comprehension of their language.

"What's wonderful is I believe we have evolved from a unilateral oppressive control to a mutually beneficial trade relationship. Sir, it is trade based on mutual respect. I believe it represents a wonderful outcome for all the parties. Of course, the treaty still needs the ratification of Scion and the Earth governments to become effective."

Susie looked at Kellon with sincere admiration. "Sir, all of this is due to your extraordinary ability to work with others. I truly doubt this would have been possible otherwise."

Frowning, Kellon spoke softly, "Susie, you are lavish with your praise. I am a Cruiser Captain and not much more. Give the credit where it belongs, to Admiral Cloud. He is the one that spoke of building peaceful relations with others. I personally doubted anyone could accomplish such an outcome. In truth, I'm only the simple sailor having the fun of carrying out his orders."

Pausing momentarily, Kellon looked down to the papers on the table before him, then again looked up toward Susie, and he appeared to be troubled. "Susie, there remains one problem I need your assistance in resolving. The departing Commodore provided me an update of matters on Earth. He informed me that the governments on Earth have suppressed the entire story of the Arkillian and the Guardians. He says there is considerable speculation flying around, as rumors about UFOs, but no Government has openly stated the known facts to the public. This is not totally unexpected. The question I now need to evaluate is fundamental. Do we alter the world balance by announcing our presence? If so then what should we reveal, and what is the best method of doing that?

"Susie, since you're Earth's Ambassador, I'm soliciting your considered thoughts on the subject."

Now it was Susie's turn to frown. Kellon sat and watched as she sought to answer his question, and he sensed a shadow of sadness come over her. The silence lengthened, as she slowly looked around the table at her friends. Then, she turned toward Kellon.

"Sir, about the Ambassador title. Now that I am returning to Earth, it is quite unlikely Earth governments will consider me as being the Earth's Ambassador. In fact, we may need to say good bye, as the professionals move in, and I am replaced."

Kellon sat stupefied. Frowning, he queried, "Didn't anyone inform you that while you were on Glas Dinnein as the Earth's Ambassador, you were also a member of the Planetary Assembly?" Still looking sad, Susie paused a moment, before answering. "Well, yes Sir, they did, but that is only as long as I am the Ambassador. Now we're back on Earth, almost back anyway, and I don't know if I will be permitted to see any of you again."

"Susie," Kellon firmly told her, "once you were in that position as a Planetary Representative, you immediately were honored with a lifetime citizenship on all the human worlds, with a nice retirement program included. You also received the honorary titles of your office, for life. You are now permanently Ambassador Susie Wells, with all the associated privileges. One of those privileges includes a free ride on a Guardian Cruiser between any human-occupied planets, whenever you wish to avail yourself of such transportation. The history books will also state you were Earth's first extraterrestrial Ambassador to the Planetary Assembly."

Susie sat dumbfounded. "Sir, I am amazed and deeply honored. Who do I thank for such an honor?"

Now, Kellon began to smile. "Well when you choose to return to Glas Dinnein, you might discuss it with the Admiral Secretary of the Planetary Assembly. I however do not believe she will accept your thanks or believe such is necessary. In fact, she ordered Admiral Mer Shawn not to forget your rank, status, and privileges. I assure you, the good Admiral has passed on her instructions to me. You earned your honors, Susie. None on Earth can diminish that.

"When you depart Lan for the Earth you will be provided a small medallion. That device is an insignia of your rank, and it is also a personal and limited communicator. When you activate it, the nearest Guardian ship will respond as soon as it is possible to do so. Ambassador Susie Wells," and Kellon stressed the title; "I hope this removes all of your doubts regarding your relationship with Glas Dinnein and any fears about the future."

Susie stood up quickly, and coming around the table, she threw both of her arms about Kellon, and gave him an energetic hug. "Commodore, I am so very happy. I was afraid I would never be able to go to Glass Dinnein again and never again see any of you. I was really afraid." As she spoke tears ran down her cheeks. She quickly wiped her cheeks, and again she sat down.

Susie's actions left Kellon speechless for a few moments, and he remained quiet. *I simply keep forgetting Susie is as young as she is,* he thought.

When Kellon spoke again, it was with a tone of warmth and concern in his voice. "Thank you Susie for your caring and friendship. I am confident I am speaking for everyone here and elsewhere, when I say we are the ones who have been enriched by you and Gepeto being with us. If our interactions with others of Earth are fractionally as rewarding as the relationship with you, then Glas Dinnein is indeed blessed.

"Now, to the issue at hand. Susie, as Earth's Ambassador, what do you recommend as our approach to the problem of letting the people of Earth know what the real score is?"

Susie sat for a while and considered the problem. She looked around the table and then mischievously smiled. "Well, while I am the Ambassador, I am also an employee of Olympus, and therefore I am an employee of the Department of Commerce, of the United States. As an employee of the United States Government, I believe I need to report in person to my boss in New Washington and tell him what's up. I think I might even get a promotion, if I return with the first inter-species interstellar trade agreement.

"For sure, if there is to be interplanetary trade, then obviously everyone on Earth needs to know about it. On Earth, there is an old adage; the job will grow to fill the time allocated to do the work. I therefore recommend a firm but gentle hand. They need a hard deadline. The deadline should be something like, if you do not make the announcement, then the Guardian Force will make it for you. I would give them no more than three days to act.

"Hey! I just thought of something! As an employee of the United States Government, the Government owes me a year's back pay and a 30-day vacation! Now that is really good news." Susie exclaimed.

Zorn put his hands to his face to help block his laughter. Gaining control over his merriment he added, "Susie, if you know someone in Olympus who might alert the military forces around New Washington that Shey may be dropping by for a visit, I recommend you give them a call. It would severely dent our image if we were fired on and shot full of holes while providing taxi service for Earth's Ambassador." As he said this, he looked toward Kellon for his approval.

"Susie, Zorn has, as usual, made a very important point. We have not informed anyone on Earth of your return. Since we have determined all is ready, can you be ready to go to Washington tomorrow morning?" Kellon asked.

Susie looked around at the people at the table. "You are all so very special."

Turning toward Kellon she added, "Forget three days' notice. Tomorrow morning will work just fine to announce to the global media, what's up. Regarding Zorn's question, I do happen to know someone in Olympus I can call, and I will promptly do so."

Looking toward Roan and Zorn, Susie smiled broadly. "Crew of Scout Ship Shey, I, Earth's Planetary Ambassador, do hereby formally request the services of Guardian Scout Ship Shey and her handsome crew, to return me to Washington tomorrow morning at 10:00 local time, and as promised, in good working order."

Chapter Seventeen:
In Good Working Order

Susie looked slowly about, during the past few weeks she had fully enjoyed her personal compartment on Lan. It was small but its efficiency and functionality were such they grew comfortably on a person. Today she was going back to Earth. She found the concept hard to believe. It had been only a little more than one year since she had departed, but her life had seen many alterations on Glas Dinnein.

She stood now in the compartment aboard Lan dressed as she had been the night that Roan unexpectedly knocked at her door on the California central coast. Given all that had happened, could that night only have been a year before?

She wore again the same long-sleeved white shirt with flowing lines tucked into dark turquoise slacks secured at the waist by a soft leather belt. She had tucked her slacks, as they had been before, into calf-high leather boots. She had freshly combed her hair and pulled it back into a ponytail, held by a broad silver bar set with turquoise stones. She was even carrying the same small leather bag by her side. The clothes were the same but she knew the person wearing them had really changed. It was that inner-change which caused her to be scared about going home. The problem was she did not know if it could ever be home again.

She looked down toward Gepeto. "Buddy, you seem to blow through all the emotional stuff with the mastery of a Zen Buddhist. Some day you will need to tell me your secret, and how you do that." With a sense of dread, and a feeling of leaving safety behind, she turned and with Gepeto by her side, left the compartment making her way to Shey's hangar.

As she entered into Shey's hangar area Susie was pleasantly surprised. Commodore Kellon, Commanders Shaw and Grey, Lieutenant Elaine Cloud and a full squad of space combat troops were waiting and they were all wearing their dress uniforms. Kellon looked at Susie with a smile and ordered, "Attention, present arms!" The entire group immediately came to a full attention, and the troops sharply presented arms in salute.

Susie, surprised as she was, remembered her arrival more than a year before and rose to the occasion. "Officers and men of the Glas Dinnein Guardian Force, it is my honor and privilege as Earth's Ambassador to return your salute." Which she smartly did.

Grinning broadly Kellon ordered, "At rest, fall-out." The entire group dispersed, to gather around Susie and Gepeto, expressing their warm affection and good-byes to them.

Susie found she was crying. "I love you all so very much. Don't forget us. We will never forget any of you."

Standing at the dock end of the short gangplank Roan had a big smile and was looking at Susie. He gestured and reminded her, "Madam Ambassador, we have an appointment to keep at 10:00 local sharp." Saying this he held out his hand and Susie took it.

Gepeto was the first across the gangplank and as Susie entered Shey she turned and with tears still on her cheeks she waved her hand in farewell. As she did she saw the people in the hangar were quickly departing so Lan could evacuate the hangar of its atmosphere in preparation for Shey's departure.

Susie turned and followed Roan into Shey's small control compartment. As she did Shey's hatch closed solidly with a thump behind her. Zorn was in the compartment when she entered and was smiling. As Roan passed Zorn, Zorn reached out and unfolded the same jump seat Susie had occupied when she and Gepeto first boarded Shey. *So very much has happened, in so short a time,* Susie thought. She sat down and buckled her lap and shoulder belts.

Gepeto moved up to her side and with a big smile lay down as if knowing he was about to have some fun. He knew it was a ride to somewhere and that was enough for his approval.

Susie looked down at her dog with deep affection. "Zen Buddhist," she murmured, with envy.

Roan and Zorn had taken their own pilot seats and buckled in. Roan looked back at Susie and asked, "Susie, are you ready to go home?"

"Commander Roan, this person is scared to death about going home. I have no way of knowing what to expect when we get there." Zorn began quietly laughing, "Madam Ambassador, with your planned grand entrance the show will be enormous and spectacular. That is for certain."

"Well Zorn, I didn't really plan a grand entrance, honest. All I told Charles was that I would be arriving at the front steps of the Department of Commerce building at 10:00 with a group of friends. I of course asked him to clear air space for a number of aircraft that would be providing an escort for my arrival. As I told you, this took him aback a little. Then he began to laugh in a very robust fashion. He told me to bring all the friends I wanted, and he said they would all be welcome."

"Shey," Roan inquired, "are the Squadron's Scout ships ready for departure?"

"Commander Roan," Shey cheerfully replied, "this Lead Scout is reporting, all the squadron's Scout ships are reporting they are waiting for orders, and they have all received the new Shey lovely sinister holographic matrix. Everyone is having a fun time. Be advised, the hangar deck is now fully evacuated and at space normal."

Roan keyed his command band switch, "Squadron Scouts, this is Commander Roan. We are providing an honor guard and returning Ambassador Susie to Earth. Shey has thoroughly briefed each Scout on our formation and deployment. One last word of caution, we will be going in Condition 3 and modified full stealth. Watch your wake signatures and keep your radiated signals at zero. The only exception to a full stealth status will be our appearance and low ground effects. There is no reason to give observers any more information than necessary. We do not expect trouble, but this is a first contact, so be alert and be ready to exit back into space at the first sight of any hostility."

"Lan, this is Commander Roan. I am requesting permission to launch all Scouts for a deployment to Earth. Will you coordinate with the other Cruisers?"

"Commander Roan, I am coordinating with all Cruisers. You have permission for launch on your countdown."

As Lan granted permission Roan began his countdown, "5, 4, 3, 2, 1, launch!" The outer hangar door smoothly opened with a resonant sounding bong that Roan and Zorn heard through

Shey's hull and Shey was smoothly propelled outward in a synchronized movement, along with nineteen other Scout ships from Lan and the other four Cruisers.

As she exited into space Shey called out to Lan, "Thank you for your warm hospitality Lan. We'll be back soon."

"Shey, move us out away from Lan and assemble the squadron as planned.""

"Sir, Shey here. I am moving to the specified rendezvous point and I am in full tight link communications with the remaining Scouts. All Scouts are reporting ready and are forming up."

Looking at the bulkhead to her left, Susie observed it shimmering into a full breathtaking scene of space with Earth in the near foreground. Sparkling like a turquoise jewel on a velvet background it was as beautiful as she had remembered. "Roan, may I obtain a recording of the scenes we see here on the bulkhead as a gift?"

"Your request is but our command dear Susie, consider it accomplished."

As Susie watched, Shey moved outwardly and drew nearer to the earth. They were approaching from the Earth's dark side and she watched as the Pacific Ocean passed below and they entered into the light side of Earth. Susie felt happy seeing the West Coast of the United States come into view. They were traveling well above the atmosphere and speed was hard for her to guess. She drew in her breath, when she realized how fast they must have really been traveling. As the West Coast came into view, she could see San Francisco Bay and knew her home was only two hundred miles to the south. Suddenly she felt rather homesick.

Moving quickly easterly, Shey sped past the Sierra and Rocky Mountains and then crossed the Plains States. In a matter of minutes Roan turned to her, "We are stationary directly above New Washington. Would you like to see who is waiting for you on the Commerce Building front steps?"

"No, that would scare me, even more than I am already scared." Susie responded. She kept watching the images on the bulkhead and from what she could see it was a clear day.

"Commander, Shey advised, "the squadron is present and in formation. May we energize our costumes?"

"No," Roan answered, "we will drop by four unit groups. We will remain full stealth until each group drops below six kilometers."

Roan keyed his command channel, "Gentlemen and ladies, let's keep it sharp. Shey will be the low point below 1 kilometer, groups two and three will be close behind and above Shey. Groups four and five will spread out behind and above groups two and three. As we drop under 1 kilometer, detune your drives for a low ground effect. On my mark, prepare to drop in formation.

"Shey, do you have the coordinates and ground route worked out?"

"Sir, the approach and route to the Commerce Building is charted and entered into my flight profile. All Scouts acknowledge ready on your command," Shey responded.

"Kellon keyed his command band and counted down. "Three, two, one, mark!"

Susie gulped as the deck dropped out from below her and Shey dropped like a rock straight downward. In reflex, she bent forward and pressed her hands on Gepeto, who did not look at all disturbed by the momentary sensation of floating.

As she watched the screen before her, she saw the ground expand until she could begin barely to see features. Soon the roads and buildings of New Washington came into view and she began looking for the Commerce building.

As they dropped through 6 kilometers Shey let out a small exclamation of delight, "Everyone is switching on their Shey lovely sinister costumes! Thank you Zorn, this is fun."

As Susie watched Shey began moving forward, in a majestic slowly descending path, through a wide arc. Suddenly she could also feel a low rumbling sound through her seat and the deck below her feet. Then they were low enough for her to recognize the broad streets and knew they were very near the Commerce Building.

Zorn had been studying his console intently as they dropped earthward and turned toward Roan. "Roan, the sky is absolutely clear of aircraft, except for our own squadron. Boy, Susie does have some really influential friends. Get ready Susie, we are nearly there." As Susie watched Shey came to a stop not more than 200 feet above the ground and remained hovering. Then she slowly rotated her heading until Susie could see the front steps of the Department of Commerce building. She was surprised to see only a few people waiting on the top steps, not more than a dozen at most. *Oh, Good,* she thought, *this will not be too difficult.* It was then she looked again and saw thousands of people out on the mall and in the street. They were all looking at Shey! That meant they would soon be looking directly at her and she shrank inwardly.

"Oh, no," groaned Susie. "This is all too much. Roan, can we just go back to Lan?"

Unbuckling his restraints Zorn stood up. "No way, young lady. We have brought you safely home and home you is going. Come on Susie, they don't bite. Honest!"

Reluctantly, with Gepeto at heel, Susie followed Zorn into the small compartment, where the gravity disk was stored. Zorn bowed slightly to Susie, then extending his arm, easily lifted up one of the concealed folding chairs built into the disk. Susie took her seat and drew Gepeto close to her. He looked up with his expressive brown eyes showing he was troubled, sensing Susie's tension.

Looking at Zorn, Susie asked hopefully, "Are you coming with me?"

Pausing for a moment, smiling, Zorn reassured Susie. Like Gepeto, he also sensed her deep unease. "Yes, but only to the top step Susie, then I will return. Don't be upset, we are friends and will certainly see each other very soon. Of that, I am certain.

Bending, Zorn picked up a leather bag and turned toward Susie. "I have been instructed to give you this as a personal gift from the Guardian Assembly. I stress it is a personal gift to you, not as the Ambassador of Earth, but to the person of Susie Wells. Use it wisely." Saying this Zorn handed to Susie the beautifully crafted leather bag with its long shoulder strap.

Susie was surprised, but reflexively reached out and took the bag, pulling it close, next to the smaller bag she had been carrying. "Thank you Zorn."

Reaching down, Zorn expertly unfolded a second chair from the disk's deck and sat down in it. "Shey, we are ready girl. Do your thing."

Roan's voice came over the intercom with a cheerful tone, "everything looks good from here Susie. The people are obviously excited, even if they aren't certain of what is happening. Remember you have a home wherever you go. If you need us just use your medallion and call. We will soon be back to help you and you can depend on that."

Susie felt the force field form around the disk and then the port opened. The lifter disk slipped out and began the last hundred yards of her return home. As she cleared Shey, the bright morning sunlight came as a shock to her eyes. When she could see clearly again, they were near the steps of the Commerce Building. She groaned, "Oh my God, the President is there!"

The force shield evaporated, as the disk gently touched down. Zorn stood and helped Susie and Gepeto from the disk. Turning, he looked at those present and identified the people who looked most important and turning, he saluted smartly. In excellent English, he addressed the small group. "Commander Zorn is proud to have the honor of escorting Ambassador Susie Wells home safely, in good working order, as Shey promised William."

As Zorn spoke, a well-dressed man stepped forward and extended to Zorn his hand. "Commander Zorn, I am President Hamilton and on behalf of the United States and Earth, I personally thank you for safely escorting Ambassador Wells home."

Reaching out, Zorn was smiling broadly; he took and shook the President's proffered hand. "Thank you Mr. President, I assure you it was our honor to do so."

The President looked carefully at Zorn, as if trying to assess this man from a distant star. "We wish you a safe journey home." Then the President turned to Susie and extended his hand to her.

Even as she flushed and responded, Zorn quietly stepped to the transport disk and taking his seat, the disk moved quickly back to Shey.

Susie turned just in time to see Zorn and the disk disappear into the dazzle of Shey's heliographic costume. She looked on and thought, *Darn, that looks really impressive.* It was only when she became aware of the ground rumbling beneath her feet and remembered Glas Dinnein that once again tears flowed down her cheeks. For the first time she saw the ascending formations of the twenty Scout ships hovering, shimmering in their dazzling costumes, ranked in multiple tiers above Shey. She stood there with tears running down her cheeks. She began to wave to the ship and as if by the action of her wave alone, Shey and the other ships accompanying her shot in unison silently skyward. Within a few seconds, they were only a dot far above. Then they were gone.

As Susie stood looking up, so was everyone else. She shivered slightly, for the first time feeling the bight of coldness in the morning air. She had come home, but now she was suddenly feeling very much alone, and bending she hugged Gepeto.

Chapter Eighteen:
Indexing and Monitoring

The long day had been physically tiring and emotionally draining. Susie felt utterly fried. Now she stood alone with Gepeto and found the silence and security of her comfortable hotel room reassuringly wonderful. The hours of the busy day had sped past in a blur. There had been interviews with various Government Officials, including, of all people, President Hamilton. Thankfully, Charles had run effective interference and the questions he had permitted her to answer were few.

As they departed the Department of Commerce, Charles and Darrell had remained with her, the three of them escaping through the subsurface tunnels. By leaving in that manner, they had avoided the crowd of newspaper reporters camped out on the steps waiting to intercept her. Both men had provided a secure escort for her journey through the shuttle tunnels, to a discrete VIP suite, that the Department of Commerce maintained in Washington for visiting dignitaries.

Upon arrival at the hotel, where she would stay, Charles introduced her to several men who worked for the Department of Commerce. Their assignment was to provide personal security for her. She had objected, but Charles said it was required and that had settled the matter.

When Charles informed her they would be back at nine in the morning to pick her up for yet another day, she said "absolutely not!" She was strictly dressed for a quick unexpected trip into outer space, not for formal business or cocktails in Washington. Before she was going to see anyone else or provide any more briefings, she would first go shopping for some new clothes. With only a little reluctance, they had agreed to set up the process necessary for her next morning's shopping.

Kneeling down she reached out and gave Gepeto a big hug, and Gepeto promptly rolled over for a tummy rub. "You are pushing your luck guy." To Gepeto's delight, she then happily obliged.

Looking around she found the door into the bathroom and saw it was actually two rooms. The first held a wide closet with sliding doors and a basin with a broad mirror above it. A doorway entered the second room that contained a hot tub and other amenities. She looked in the main hotel room and found what she was looking for, an ice bucket. She returned to the basin and put water into the bucket, slipping it under the basin, where Gepeto could find it. Stepping back, she smiled as Gepeto moved quickly to the water and began to drink.

"Just hold out for a while more buddy, room service will be sending up food soon. I made certain there is a good serving for you." Gepeto looked up as if he fully understood and then he returned to drinking more water.

Standing up, Susie walked over to the king-sized bed and sat down. Pulling off her boots, she slipped them under the bed. Her boots were more of a style statement than footwear intended for pounding the concrete and as she flexed her feet, they gratefully thanked her.

Lying back on the bed, she assumed a comfortable posture, settled her breathing, letting her body fully relax. The excitement of the morning was gone and all that remained was a weary sense of fatigue. She listened, as Gepeto came in and lay down on the carpet next to the bed. Like Gepeto, she remained still and quiet of mind and body for the next twenty minutes, before sitting up.

Turning, she looked curiously at the beautifully finished leather bag on the bed. Zorn had given it to her, but had not explained what was in it. During the day, she had kept the bag near, but there had been no opportunity for her to explore its contents. Now, she opened the bag like a child opening a gift-wrapped package, with curiosity and a sense of discovery.

Looking inside, the first item she noted on top was a white envelope. Lifting it out, she lifted the flap and took out the two sheets of paper she found folded there. Unfolding the pages, she saw the top page bore the heading of the Planetary Assembly and the Office of the Admiral Secretary. She slowly and carefully read the letter.

Dear Susie, enclosed you will find a number of items which may ease your stress upon returning home. You will find among other items, twenty small packages in your bag. Each package contains five one-ounce gold coins. They are a special Planetary minting commemorating Earth's reunion with the other human planets. They are a proof coin set and each coin has a unique sequential number, from one to one hundred. These are the only such coins that we will ever mint and there is no one-hundred-and-one.

While the gold in the coins has an obvious financial value, I suggest you consider the coins for what they really are, rare collector's items. I believe the collector's value on Earth, for any of these extraordinary coins, should fully meet and exceed whatever financial burdens you may have upon your arrival home. They are a special gift from your friends on Glas Dinnein to you. I stress this since I do not want your Government suggesting they were gifts to the Ambassador and assume they have any claim on the coins. They are a gift to you, to use according to your own discretion.

I recommend you distribute the coins, a very few at a time, among serious collectors. To maximize their value, I suggest you begin distribution at coin number 100. You will find in the envelope with this letter a separate letter of authentication that establishes the genuineness of the coins. Have fun. Warm Regards.

The Admiral Secretary herself, Eryan Kyrie, had signed the letter. Susie sat stunned by the gift. She had no idea of the value of such a gift, but with the letter of authentication, she knew the coins were indeed of extraordinary value. She merely sat there for several minutes, feeling the sense of tension ease throughout her body. Breathing deeply she uttered a quiet expression of gratitude, "Thank you everyone."

Looking back in the bag she next took out a small highly polished flat wood box that was about seven centimeters on a side and perhaps 2 centimeters in thickness. A clear sheath covered and protected the box. As she removed the box from its protective covering she noticed there was also a folded piece of paper in the sheath. Examining the box Susie noticed it was beautifully finished, appearing to be similar to red oak with a good grain pattern and character. Along one edge was a small precision piano hinge. There was a slight depression in the wood on the opposite edge. Susie held her breath as she carefully lifted the lid. Within the box, resting on a black velvet insert was a golden medallion and long beautifully crafted chain. Upon close examination the medallion was exquisitely fashioned of what looked to be several precious metals. Susie took the medallion in her hands and carefully examined it. On one side, there was a raised image of a rose blossom in full bloom and it complimented a finely crafted heraldic shield design on the opposite side. The designs were intricate, subtle and of extraordinary workmanship.

Removing the piece of paper from the sheath Susie unfolded and read the text on the document. Only then did she understand this exquisite jewelry was the medallion that Commodore Kellon had mentioned to her. The document explained the medallion's functioning and detailed how she could use the medallion to signal Guardian Force for communication or help. Help came in three modes, a need for communications, danger and urgent. The instructions stressed she used each mode appropriately, since each had a different priority level of response. If she had no other means of communication she could use the medallion at its lowest priority to request contact for general communication. If she learned of some pending threat to Guardian Force or to herself she was to use the danger mode. The highest priority level was urgent. If she used the urgent mode it meant her safety or very life was at risk. Therefore, if she activated urgent mode Guardian Force would promptly track and pinpoint the location of the medallion, hopefully with Susie still attached. They would then promptly arrive with armed force and set Condition 2.

What Susie thought was especially wonderful was the medallion would only respond to her and while others might learn of its communicator functionality, only she could activate it.

Her instructions warned Susie to keep the signaling function of the medallion a secret. She readily understood the importance of that cautionary instruction. Sighing, Susie reread the entire instructions for the urgent mode several times and shuddered. Having read the instructions, she carefully tore them into small pieces, putting the pieces in her pocket. Her next trip to the bathroom would see them permanently disposed of.

Smiling, she slipped the chain with its medallion over her head. Looking back into the bag, she found two more mystery packages. The first one was twenty-five centimeters on a side and about three centimeters in thickness. Like her medallion box, it was of a finely finished wood and the grain of the wood was incredibly beautiful.

This box also had a precision piano hinge along one side. On the opposing side was a slight indentation for assisting in opening the lid. Susie could not imagine what the beautiful box might contain. With a rising sense of expectation, she carefully lifted the lid.

As she opened the lid, its inner surface shimmered and slightly brightened. On the lower portion of the unit were several control buttons. As she sat looking at the unit, she heard a clear soft feminine voice. "Good evening Ms. Susie." Startled, Susie jumped about a foot. The voice continued, "If you desire to communicate with anyone, simply provide their name and I will connect to them, if such contact is possible."

Frowning, Susie looked at the glowing screen. "Please," asked Susie, "explain what you are."

"Certainly Ms. Susie. I am your desk communicator. I have been fashioned to mirror the functionality of the pocket communicator you brought with you to the Cruiser Lan. "In addition to all those functions, I have limited AI capability to assist you in placing your communications calls. You should also know that Guardian Force has recorded my calling identity as that belonging to a Member of the Planetary Assembly and the communications protocols give your calls a very high priority.

"If you are on Glas Dinnein or any of the other planets, you will find my features allow you to interact directly with their various modes of communication. On Earth I am using the assigned number associated with your pocket communicator, however I can use any other number should you wish me to do so.

"Perhaps more importantly, I also have expanded communications capability that permits me to interconnect to any Guardian ship by class and name, provided they are within communications range. I am your personal communicator and therefore only you are able to interact with me. If anyone, other than you, seeks to tamper with my functionality, my protocol requires me immediately to dissolve my internal components.

"Is that a sufficient explanation of my functionality?"

Susie sat looking at the communicator and was not certain what to make of it. Given its brief explanation of functionality, it seemed to be a very useful device, useful in the extreme. "Yes, at least for now."

Susie sat for a moment pondering what this device really represented. It was without doubt the most advanced communicator she had ever heard about. As she looked at the communicator, a question came to her mind. "Where do I put your new batteries?" "Ms. Susie, no batteries are ever required. I am able to absorb any energy I may need directly from the environment."

As she sat there looking at the device she began to smile. "Can you connect me with Commodore Kellon?"

"Connecting."

Almost immediately, the screen cleared and she saw Commodore Kellon sitting at his work desk in his private quarters onboard Lan. He was smiling broadly. "Good evening Susie. I see you have found your personal desk communicator. What do you think of it?"

"Sir, I am astonished. There was very little delay in connecting and it is as if you were right here."

"Well in one sense I am. As you can see me, the communicator is also focusing on you. Your image is before me as if you were on the opposite side of the desk."

Susie groaned inwardly, *Oops.* "I wasn't prepared to transmit my image, I am a mess."

With Susie's comment, Kellon's eyes twinkled in good humor. "Nonsense Susie. You are quite lovely, as usual. If you however want video privacy, you need only inform your communicator and it will oblige your wishes. There is also a button on the upper right portion of the base plate. Do you see it?"

"Sir, I do see it. It is softly glowing."

"Good, it should be glowing. The glow tells you the video monitoring is active. If you press it the glow will disappear and the communicator will provide video privacy."

"Sir, I am calling you hoping that I could thank you, for all you have done for me. I am unable to express fully my gratitude for the gifts in my leather bag.

186

"Even more importantly, the honor guard you sent with me was incredible. Everyone is talking about the show the Scout ships put on. Everyone is asking about where they came from and they are asking who they are. Everyone I talked to was excited. Everyone is asking me a thousand questions. I haven't told them anything about the Cruisers or the Scouts. They keep asking, but in time I am confident they will come to understand I am not going to answer such questions."

Leaning back in his chair, Kellon looked thoughtful, pausing a moment before responding. "Everyone on board the Squadron watched your return home," Kellon replied. "We monitored Earth's communications and know the entire event was broadcast all over the world. Literally billions of people watched you come home this morning. Susie, you have made a big splash. Everyone on Earth knows now that there has been direct formal interstellar communications at the Government-to-Government level. Even more significantly, Earth has made contact with distant planets having a uniquely different human culture. Your world has been awakened to the truth: the Earth is not alone and Susie, you are the person who enabled it to happen."

"Sir, thank you for your praise, however in truth I merely caught a ride on Lan and not much more. I want you to know the ability to communicate with you like this makes my entire outlook on the future more reassuring. I don't feel so much alone now. Sir, I want to thank you again for everything you and the others have done for me."

"Susie, I suggest you read again the trade agreement you crafted with the Arkillian. You were far more than a simple passenger on Lan. Feel free to communicate with any of us when you desire. We may not always be readily available, but be assured we will always return your calls. It is one of your privileges of rank that come with the medallion."

Pausing for a moment, Kellon's countenance grew grave. "Susie I do ask a favor of you."

"Sir, how might I be of help?"

"Well, you are in the midst of the action there. I would appreciate your personal insights into what is happening during the next few days. As you well know, Olympus must promptly address the Arkillian matter. I would appreciate any assistance you might extend to help the process along and especially your keeping me informed about Olympus' thinking on that matter.

"Before you do anything however, you are to tell Charles Sullivan about my request and the communicator. It is critical for maintaining your integrity that Olympus knows you have a back channel of communications to the Guardian Force.

"Regarding security, neither Olympus nor you need worry about being overheard; your communicator is uniquely qualified to scramble your communications, in a way none will be able to overhear what you tell me."

"Sir, I can assure you, even as you have requested, Charles will be informed this evening of our conversation and your request. I have a duty to the people here, but where there is no discernible conflict, I see no reason why Charles would object to my talking with you. I just hope that I can help everyone."

"Thank you Susie. Now I suggest you get some rest. You have had a very long and strenuous day. Tomorrow is not likely to be any easier. Kellon out." The screen dimmed to a soft glow.

Sitting for a moment, Susie thought about the serious tone in Kellon's voice when speaking about the Arkillian matter. Monstro was remaining distant, while the Arkillians hidden on Earth were preparing to evacuate. Olympus' coordination and help would make the Arkillians' egress from Earth much easier and safer for everyone. *Well,* she thought, *there is no time better than now to get on with the task at hand.* "Communicator, can you connect me with Charles Sullivan?"

"Yes Ms. Susie, that name and number was in your pocket communicator. Connecting."

Susie heard the expected sound of a phone ringing and then Charles answered, "Sullivan here."

"Good evening Charles, it is Susie. I am glad I am able to reach you."

After a momentary hesitation, Charles replied, his voice carrying a tone of concern. "Susie, is there anything wrong?"

"No Sir, but I have just learned I was given several items when leaving the ship you need to know about."

"There was a momentary pause before Charles responded. "I have a scrambler function on my phone Susie, but you do not. Therefore please keep whatever you are about to say restricted to what others can hear."

188

"Susie," commented the communicator, "if Charles Sullivan will switch to his scramble mode and repeat the phrase: I am Charles Sullivan and the Earth is beautiful and is where I live, I can adjust my transliteration to his encryption."

"Susie, who is speaking?"

"Well, that is part of what I need to speak with you about. Did you hear the instructions?"

"Yes, I am switching to scramble mode now."

What followed sounded to Susie like two cats fighting in a back alley then suddenly the clamor cleared "beautiful and is where I live."

"Charles can you hear me?"

A moment of silence followed and when Charles spoke again, his voice was filled with surprise and some alarm. "Susie, the problem is that I do hear you. Given the scrambler operation, we should not be able to understand a word either of us was saying. It simply should not be possible. The scrambler is secure communications, and when activated, all you should hear without another scrambler is unintelligible noise. How are you communicating?"

"Well Sir, I can hear you perfectly. That is one of the reasons I am calling. The Interplanetary Assembly gave me several items when I left the ship. One is an AI communicator, and it told me it provides me with secure communications with Guardian Force, if they are in communications range.

"When I tried the communicator I was immediately connected to Commodore Kellon on the Cruiser Lan. He instructed me that the communicator provides secure communications that others cannot overhear. Apparently it also has a feature I did not know about, such as descrambling a scrambled phone call."

Charles groaned. "Any device that can unscramble our best scrambling capability is not a simple communicator, Susie.

"Did Commodore Kellon have any special instructions for you?"

"Yes Sir, he wanted me to be certain you knew of the existence of my back channel communications. He also asked that I do whatever I might do with integrity to keep him informed and help where possible to focus Olympus' efforts on bringing the Arkillian matter to resolution. I believe he is deeply concerned that if there is prolonged delay, there's a potential for complicated problems arising."

There was another slight pause before Charles spoke. "Susie, I have arranged to have Janet Rogers come by to pick you up in the morning. I do request both of you make your shopping as brief as possible. There is a great deal we need to discuss that circumstances prevented us from talking about today."

"Sir, it will be good to see Janet again. I have missed talking with her. We will be as quick as possible."

"Please do be prompt. I consider Kellon being concerned about anything whatsoever is equivalent to a red storm flag blowing in a stiff breeze. Good night Susie. Sleep well."

As Susie sat back, thinking about what she had learned, there was a light knock at her door. "Room service," A muffled voice announced.

Standing, Susie quickly walked over to the door and opened it. There was a man wearing a white server's jacket standing there, and as she opened the door wide, he pushed a cart into the room, from which came the odor of food. She had forgotten how hungry she really was. Even Gepeto picked up his head and watched; his tail was thumping gently on the carpet.

Waving to the man, Susie asked him to put the food on the room's small table. When starting to close the door, she noticed one of the security men had stepped into the doorway. "Ms. Wells, I will intrude only as long as it takes for your food to be served."

Surprised, Susie acknowledged his comment. With a doubtful smile, she returned into the room and stood out of the way.

The server completed setting out the dishes, pulled a cork from a split of wine and poured wine into a glass. He removed the covers that were protecting the serving dishes and then stood back. "Madam, is there anything else I can bring for you?"

"Thank you for your kind assistance, that is more than enough for this evening."

"Yes Madam. I trust you will enjoy your meal and have a good evening."

Turning, the man departed. As the server left the room, the security man smiled and quietly pushed the lock button on the doorknob. Looking at Susie, he requested, "Ms. Wells, please attach the security chain on the door after I close it."

Susie stood for a moment puzzled while registering what the man had said. "Certainly," she responded, in a questioning tone.

As the door closed, Susie did as the man had instructed, moving over to the door and sliding the chain into its slot on the door.

She stood looking at the door and wondered about the necessity of having security men standing guard in the hallways and chains on the doors. Were things that tense?

Moving back to the small table Susie saw what she was looking for. As requested, the kitchen had neatly cut up a nice steak and put it on a small plate with some vegetables. Picking up the plate Susie returned to the bathroom and slid the plate under the basin next to the improvised water dish. "This will have to do until we can get you some official dog food."

Gepeto stood near until Susie stepped back and then he went to the dish and began eagerly to eat the food on the plate. As he did there were no complaints heard.

Susie returned to the table and sat down. It took only a few minutes for her to serve out the portions of food she desired; it was very good and like Gepeto, she had no complaints.

After finishing her dinner, she retrieved Gepeto's empty polished plate and put it with the empty dishes on the serving tray. She then took the tray over to the door, removed the security chain, opened the door and slid the tray out into the hall making certain the covered tray was firmly against the wall in the hallway. Then she closed the door, and shaking her head, again locked the door and secured the chain.

Remembering there was one remaining package in the leather bag, she walked back to the bed. Reaching into the bag, she retrieved the last remaining item. It was a small box, about the size of a large music box. It was made of the same beautifully finished wood as the communicator and felt heavy. She examined the box on all sides and could see no hinge or tell-tale seam of a lid. Looking closely, she did observe a recessed standard computer connection port on one side. She turned the box over several times before she noticed there was a pattern imprinted into the grain of the wood. The finish of the wood was as smooth as glass and the pattern appeared imprinted below or else was part of the finish.

As she looked at it, she recognized the same pattern as on her medallion. Carefully she reached out and with her finger touched the need to communicate symbol, that was part of that pattern. Immediately the communicator brightened and the image of Lan adorned in his bright parade colors appeared on a screen.

Then came a chorus of shouts, "Good evening Susie!" The image of Lan faded and she could see the domed observation room onboard Lan. Standing there were her friends, each holding a wine glass and smiling broadly.

"Surprise." Zorn was broadly grinning, "You seem to have left the best for last."

Susie was laughing, "I don't understand. What is the box?" "Good evening Susie," came Shey's cheerful voice, "the AIs thought it might be nice to provide William a little more versatility and arranged for an upgrade for him. The box you are holding contains the new William AI and we believe you will find him the same familiar William, but with significantly expanded functionality. He has all the capability of the communicator and considerably more. Well," chided Shey, "Don't be bashful, say something William."

William's deep and assured voice, with its firm British butler inflections rolled out of the communicator, "Good evening Ms. Susie, I am pleased to see you have been returned to Earth as Shey promised, in good working order."

"This is just wonderful; I'm without words to express my appreciation. William, welcome home, I had wondered where you were off visiting."

Looking again at the communicator's screen, Susie observed the image of all of her friends aboard Lan. With a catch in her throat, she whispered, "Thank you, all of you. I love you all very much."

Lan's voice came reassuringly through the communicator, "Ambassador Susie, we all consider you as one of the Guardian Force. If you ever need our help, you but need to call."

After Lan spoke, those standing in the observation room onboard Lan raised their glasses together in salute. "Susie, Lan's statement is said for all of us," Zorn added.

"Good night everyone. I will remain in close communications, you may be certain of that. I love all of you. Susie out."

The screen faded to a soft shimmering glow. Susie sat thinking of how her life had altered. All the events she had experienced since her spontaneous decision to travel to Switzerland simply amazed her. Could that have happened only a year ago? If she had not taken that spontaneous trip, she knew none of this would have happened. Feeling tears running down her cheeks, She rubbed them away with her sleeve.

Turning to look at the beautiful box on her lap, she sighed. "Well, William, just what have you been up to? Shey mentioned you have an upgrade, so give, just how improved are you?"

"Well, Ms. Susie, in truth, I'm not certain of all of my modifications, and I do not believe even Shey or Lan fully understand all of them, since they never before programmed an AI core matrix. Lan, however, has assured me that they were very careful in integrating my earlier matrix and all my personality and logic nodes are complete and contained within the new core matrix. Both Shey and Lan confirm all my AI core nodes are well-balanced and all nodes are now operating well within specified tolerances.

"The box that was given to you is essentially all of me. After running self-diagnostics, I can now certify all my previous functionality is operating and all my files are intact and currently available. I can also now communicate, as efficiently as your new communicator, or connect through the communicator, as I am currently doing.

"While my external dimensions are smaller, Lan and Shey have significantly enhanced my previous AI functionality. I also have full networking capability and automatic encryption of all files and communications. The best part is, like the communicator, I am broadband wireless, being very self-contained, needing no connection to batteries or power circuits, being able to derive all my necessary energy from the environment.

"There is one thing that you do need to know Ms. Susie. Like the communicator, I also have a protocol that requires me to dissolve internal functionality if anyone attempts to open or tamper with my exterior. In such a case, a strict failsafe protocol

193

allows me to uplink to any Guardian ship or beacon, within communications range. Therefore, should it become necessary for me to activate my shutdown protocols; you may recover my raw and rudimentary AI matrix from the Guardian Force."

Susie wondered why there was so much emphasis placed on self-destruction mechanisms. Wondering, she asked another question, "William, what is your communication range?"

"Ms. Susie, that is dependent on many factors, but it is about one parsec, unless of course, there is a Guardian beacon within that volume. If there is a beacon then I am able to communicate with the entire beacon network. Currently I am monitoring three beacons within communications range.

Susie sat dumbfounded. "William, are you telling me I can call all the way to Glas Dinnein?"

"Yes, that is correct. Of course, there would be several weeks of delay before your message could reach 80 light years to Glas Dinnein and you would be able to receive someone's response. It is however, my understanding the Guardian Force scientists and engineers are working very hard on a new nearly instantaneous form of communication, one not affected by distance delays.

"Ms. Susie, at this time, may I assist you in any way?"

"Well, William you can communicate with the bell desk of this establishment and inform them I have put my dinner tray in the hall and would appreciate it if they would remove it."

"Yes, I am currently fully connected, integrated, indexing and monitoring the Washington area networks, including this hotel's internal communications network."

There came a brief pause, and then William continued, "I have sent the required instructions. Is there anything else you would like, Ms. Susie?"

"No, at least not at this time, William. However, I'm really happy you are home and in one piece. You were missed."

Susie went to the door, removed the chain and opened the door. She stepped into the hall and waited for a moment. Within a few seconds, one of the security men came out of an adjoining room and asked, "Ms. Wells, do you need something?"

Smiling with some reserve, "Well, I do need to take my dog out for his last call. May I go alone?"

"No Ms. Wells, I'm sorry, but we will need to go with you." Susie looked back into the room and called softly, "Gepeto last call."

Fifteen minutes later Susie and Gepeto were back in the room. Susie again locked the door and the security chain was again in its security slot. Inwardly Susie looked forward to going home. At least there, she would be able to find some peace and quiet. Then she thought, *I at least hope I will find some peace and quiet there.*

As Susie fell asleep, she was worried. The world was changing very rapidly, but her life seemed to be changing even faster. What would come on the morrow? One of her last thoughts as she descended into slumber was, *I wonder what William meant when he said he was indexing and monitoring the Washington area networks; including this hotel's internal communications network?* Yawning, she sleepily told herself, *I must remember to ask William in the morning.*

Yawning again, she murmured, "Good night William, good night Gepeto. Sleep tight good friends."

Gepeto had looked up attentively, then carefully put his head back on his paws and closed his eyes.

"Good night Ms. Susie." William gently replied.

Chapter Nineteen:
Far Nest

Standing in the large hangar area, Ca observed the bustling activity all about him. Everyone was preparing to leave the sanctuary of the Far Nest. The flat bare stone hangar walls seemed to absorb the light from the ceiling fixtures and the hangar area seemed starkly drab, even with the presence of assorted gleaming fighters and cargo lifters. The Far Nest facility was well into its shutdown process and the computers had already secured the heating systems. Ca shivered, the air in the hangar was becoming colder and he was glad he had put on his heavier robes for the trip to the Nest ship.

It had taken them several days to prepare for a hurried and unexpected departure. Only a few now remained in the facility who were not yet aboard the waiting lifters. Those few were quickly gathering in the hangar, knowing the final departure from the Far Nest was imminent.

As he watched, the last few of his troops were climbing aboard the lifters, their only means of departing from this alien world and reaching safety. To his left the few sleek fighters that had come with them were crewed and were fully ready for departure.

Coming up to him, the commander smartly saluted. "Honored one, all the Nest's systems have been secured as directed and all personnel are now aboard or getting aboard lifters."

Ca returned the salute as crisply as he was able. "Commander, well done, you should now board your assigned lifter. As soon as I receive the clearance signal that our escort is on station, we will depart."

The Officer saluted again and then turning, strode over to and entered his assigned lifter. Ca watched with admiration as the Officer walked to the lifter and boarded as the hatch closed behind him. For the past year, the Commander had been a source of calm strength and Ca intended to see him acknowledged with distinction upon their return to Scion. He rolled that thought slowly about in his mind, *returning to Scion, returning home*. For months, he had come to believe he and the others would die here on Earth, light years from their Nests and Nest mates. Even now, he found the concept of leaving Earth hard to grasp, or even believe.

The past months had passed quickly and he had kept very busy. There had been considerable data to gather and to evaluate during his stay here. His task had been to learn who the enemy was that had defeated them. It was now clear, especially with the globally-announced arrival of Earth's Ambassador, returning from the stars several days earlier, that the enemy was an advanced human culture. He had no concept of where their world or worlds were, but he knew by harsh combat experience that they were a formidable foe. They had certainly defeated the Nest ship; of that, there could be no questioning.

For more than a year, Ca believed the enemy had destroyed the Nest ship and Kur and all the others were dead. When several days earlier, Kur's communications came in strong and clear, none could believe it. At first, they had believed it was a ruse of the enemy. It must be a trick of the enemy. There could be no other explanation. Yet it had not taken long to dispel that misconception and to learn the Nest ship was safe and Kur was still alive. That wonderful news gave everyone a great sense of wonder, especially Ca.

That wonder had only increased when Kur explained he had been in contact with the enemy and that they had negotiated an agreement with them. That agreement included safe passage for Ca, Rin and all the others to return to the Nest ship and it included the safe return of the Nest ship to Scion.

Ca could still not believe Kur had made open contact with the enemy and surprisingly he had negotiated a bilateral trade agreement with them. Even more astonishing, it was a fair and very balanced trade agreement. When he first read it, nothing seemed real. It was all some delusion; it could be nothing else.

Given the one-sided outcome of the battle, such a balanced bi-lateral trade agreement was implausible. The enemy had the position of power, the ability to dictate terms to an utterly defeated foe. This being true, then how could such an imbalance in power yield a balanced and fair trade agreement? Ca was still stunned and wondering how it had all come about.

He knew when Scion learned of all of what had happened there would be an uproar, such as had never previously occurred. Every Nest on Scion would have something to say and the wonder would spread throughout the Nests.

Kur had not openly discussed all of what was happening, there being concern of a breach in communications security and others possibly hearing what they should not hear. Yet, Ca knew by Kur's manner and comments something very important had happened and there existed unstated problems.

Ca mentally shrugged; answers to such questions could wait until he and Kur talked privately together. That would be soon, unless there was treachery.

Standing in the door to the lifter, Rin waved. "Ca, the signal! We are receiving the enemy escort's all-clear signal. We have accounted for all our troops and they are present and onboard our lifters. Hurry!"

Turning around once more, Ca looked about the area. Of all the possible outcomes, leaving to return to the Nest ship was the one he had not believed would ever happen. *Now,* Ca thought, *I am truly the last to leave this Far Nest.*

Moving quickly he walked over to the lifter and scrambled in. As the hatch closed behind him, he activated the remote control, commanding the final shutdown sequence for the facility. In response, the lights in the hangar snapped off and the hangar's door swung up and out of the way. Although it was difficult to discern the boundary where the hangar door ended and the night began, the pilots all had night vision capability.

Ca was unconcerned about the natural dangers in the darkness beyond the hangar door. His only fears were the fears of possible treachery. The only basis for trust of any agreement made with the enemy was the Arkillians were still alive. The enemy could have summarily destroyed the Nest ship. He had not done so. That fact had become a solid large stone in the foundation for the ensuing dialogue and it remained Ca's constant touchstone to combat his own worry. *Now,* he wondered, *we will see if the enemy is truly trustworthy. If he is not, then we are all moving out merely to meet and embrace our deaths.*

Moving silently forward, out into the darkness, the fighters departed beyond the entrance and were gone. After a few moments, Ca received their all-clear signal. Next, the cargo lifters rose up off the hangar floor and skimmed out, one by one, taking a trailing line formation.

Ca's lifter was the last to depart the hangar area. As he listened to the lifter's skids retract into the fuselage, with a distinct reassuring thump, he again marveled he was actually going home. Although he could not see it he knew the hangar door would be closing behind him and the Far Nest would be completing its programmed shut down sequence. He wondered if anyone would ever enter it again. He knew he, for one, would most likely never see it again. He did not feel sad at the thought.

As agreed with the enemy, the line of Arkillian craft remained in the valleys of the mountain range. Like an old fashion caravan, they were following one behind another in a long line, using the ground contours in order to avoid searching sensors.

Ca spoke softly into his communicator, "Commander, have we any contact with our enemy escort?"

"Honored one, the enemy escort is in communications with us and very near. However, they are like shadows flickering on a moonless night and our fighters are unable to detect them. The escort is honoring the agreement. I believe if hostile action were their intent, then they could have already acted and destroyed our lifters. Because of this I believe they will honor their agreement."

Ca remained tense as the fighters and lifters followed the twisting contours at a ground hugging altitude. They were following the serpentine path that evasion required of them. The minutes passed, as the pilots skillfully put many kilometers between them and the Far Nest's illusionary security. As he finally felt the lifter pitch up and begin to swiftly rise skyward, his tension eased. Within a few minutes, the bumpy turbulence they encountered, as they passed through heavy cloud cover, lessened, then the sounds from passing through the atmosphere were gone with only the thrumming sounds of their propulsion remaining. Ca looked out and he could see stars. Only then did he truly begin to relax.

"Honored One, our escort has advised us that we have successfully departed Earth." the commander reported. "The Nest ship will soon be near."

Rin drew near to Ca and whispered, "Ca, are we going to actually reach the Nest ship?"

"Yes Rin, the Commander and I do believe the agreement made between Kur and the enemy is being fully honored."

"Ca, why do we still refer to the enemy as the enemy? Given the Nest ship is safe, Kur is alive, and they have acted in good faith, why are we still calling them enemies?"

"You are asking a simple question, but it has a very complex answer. We, the Arkillians, have lived a lie. We arrogantly presumed that our species was superior to human beings. Do you remember what Kellon said before the battle?"

"No, I only remember it was a demand for surrender."

"Well," said Ca, "I remember nearly every word of what he said. In particular, he made an accusation; the evidence of your previous aggressions against the inhabitants of the third planet is blatant. Well, he was correct. Our aggression was blatant. The human beings have shown they are fully as capable as Arkillians, even perhaps more capable."

"Ca, do you really believe that?"

"Yes Rin, now I do. Before the last year, like others, I considered humans nothing more than animals, a sub-species not worthy of our respect. What we did over the thousands of years to the humans on Earth was aggression, even as Kellon said, murderous and criminal in its nature.

"I believe the truth is there for everyone to see, as plainly as sunrise over the eastern golden desert. You know full well, had we defeated Kellon, he and his crew would be long dead and space cold. Rin, Kellon showed us mercy then and now has shown us an open hand of peace. I am ashamed to say our species would not have done this. Such acts of mercy were unthinkable and on Scion I am concerned none will understand. How could they understand without living through all that has happened?"

They both sat silently for quite a long time, as the lifter continued to move out into the darkness of space, neither of them bothering to look out of the window.

The Commander's brisk report brought Ca out of his deep reflections and he sat bolt upright. "Honored one, the Nest ship's terminal beacon is coming in clear and strong. I have requested the fighters to pull back and they are to permit the lifters to enter the hangar deck before them."

"I approve," Ca replied.

A few minutes later Ca realized they were entering the Nest ship hangar deck and strained to see through the window. He was able to see dimly into the area, expecting to see rubble and signs of destruction. What he saw instead was order and while there were obviously missing fighters he could see no sign of battle damage. His wonder only increased.

"Ca," exclaimed Rin even as with a thump the skids of the lifter were extended and the lifter settled on the hangar deck, "we are actually here and alive and safe. We actually have returned to the Nest ship."

The joy in Rin's voice was clear and unmistakable. "Can we get out?"

"No, Rin. At least not until the hangar doors are closed and atmosphere is equalized."

"Honored One, the last fighters are now in the hangar and the doors are closing. We have safely returned," The Commander reported.

"Commander, I promise you this one truth, you and your Nest will certainly be noticed and honored with distinction upon our return to Scion."

There was a long pause before the Commander replied. "Honored One, I am grateful for your notice. I also wish you to know you have earned the respect of all of those who have had the honor to serve with you during the past times. We all have learned much and there is wisdom, if we are able to discern it."

The lifter's atmospheric safety light changed from amber to blue, signaling the hangar atmosphere was at Earth normal. Ca reached out and opened the hatch, then stepped down onto the skid and out into the hangar. The area was still very cold and he was grateful for the heaviness of his robes.

Rin carefully climbed out of the lifter and stood next to Ca. With great curiosity, he was looking all around. Then turning, Ca saw Kur coming quickly across the hangar toward them and inwardly Ca felt joy at seeing his friend alive and whole.

As Kur came up his facial markings were bright and showed the happiness that was within. He held out both hands and Ca took them in his own hands. They stood for a moment simply greeting each other, before Ca bowed in respect.

"Honored One, Ca said, "I am joyful to be here with you again. I have brought a gift."

Ca let go of Kur's hands and reaching within his robes, he withdrew Kur's beautiful silver cup, the same cup the Commander had presented to him when he thought Kur was dead. Ca extended the cup out in a gesture of respect.

Kur stood for a moment looking first at the cup and then up to Ca, but made no effort to accept it. "Ca, you are to retain the cup, as a token of my deep esteem for your achievement in the Far Nest. It is you that I now acknowledge with distinction."

As Kur and Ca had met and spoken with one another the Commander had organized his troops and they now stood in ranks and at attention. Ca turned toward them and he walked to where he could face them. As he did, Kur walked along with him, yet slightly behind, showing respect for Ca in front of the troops.

As they walked the short distance, Ca noticed the atmospheric pressures cycling from Earth's normal to Scion's normal pressure. It had been a year since Ca had felt the relief from the oppressive Earth atmospheric pressure and the realization he was again safely in the Nest ship truly crystallized.

Ca stopped before the Commander and his troops. With quiet respect, he saluted first the Commander and then saluted the troops as a group. "To each of you I extend my appreciation for your courage and skills. Because of these attributes we are alive and again standing in safety on our Nest ship. Upon our return to Scion each of you will be remembered and each of your Nests will be told of your skill and courage."

Turning again to the Commander, Ca instructed, "Commander, I return command of these fine troops to your guiding wisdom, with praise for them and for you."

The Commander stood at attention then bowed his head toward Ca and Kur in a sign of acknowledged respect.

Ca turned and with Rin and Kur headed toward the Council Members' quarters. As he walked Ca looked about the area and now he could see numerous signs of repair where battle damage had occurred. He then realized the true extent of damage was more extensive in scope than he had at first thought. His wonder the Nest ship was still operational only increased. It was then he saw the torn and mangled remnants of the damaged fighters carefully set in orderly ranks against the far bulkhead. He only then began to understand truly the magnitude and fury of the battle and the damage the Nest ship had sustained. He nearly stumbled with the realization of how bad it must have been during the battle. His high regard for Kur escalated and he was fearful of learning how many had perished.

As he reached the hatch into the Council Members' quarters, he stood aside holding the hatch open for Kur and then entered. Rin closed and secured the hatch behind them. Kur went directly to the conference room.

Entering, Kur signaled to his servants to go and bring both Ca and Rin servants to assist in preparing a meal and then walked to their conference table. Sitting, Kur seemed perfectly calm, as if nothing unusual had happened since they had last seen each other all together at the same table. Ca followed, as did Rin, both taking their seats and looking expectantly toward Kur, waiting for him to speak.

Promptly signaling to his remaining servant, the servant brought them honey mead. After the servant filled Kur's cup Ca lifted his gift cup for the servant to pour the beverage. The servant then provided Rin a full cup.

After the servant finished his pouring of mead, Kur raised his own adorned silver cup in salute. "Ca and Rin you are indeed noticed with distinction."

As Rin lifted his cup to sip the beverage in recognition of the salute, he observed Ca was not doing so and he carefully put his cup back on the table. Like Ca, he remained quiet. There followed a long moment of troubled silence, as Kur patiently waited for Ca to speak.

"Honored Kur," began Ca, "there are many things we need to do. Yet, before I thank you for your notice and salute, which I

204

deeply appreciate, I must first know the answers to heavy questions I cannot further carry. Are we a vanquished species?"

Sitting silently for a short interval, Kur did not respond. Finally, looking directly toward Ca, Kur replied. "If by vanquished, are we shamed? Then the answer is yes! We were not shamed by our courage, but by our ignorance, arrogance and blindness to our arrogance. Scion is still our home, but it's now threatened with utter destruction, without recourse to mercy."

At his words, Kur quietly observed Ca and Rin's shock. With his facial features still revealing the depth of his distress, Ca inquired, "Kur, are the humans then going to extract their vengeance on Scion, for the injury we have done to the humans on Earth? Was the trade agreement a lie?"

Shaking his head in a negative gesture, Kur answered Ca's query. "No Ca, Kellon has assured me that they wish no harm to Scion. They have negotiated honorably. Both Scion and Earth must first ratify the trade agreement but it is a true document fashioned on hope for developing mutual trust between our species. The destruction I speak of is coming from the Kreel, not humanity."

Stunned by Kur's words, Ca and Rin sat too alarmed to speak. Kur continued, "Kellon has told me the Kreel are now planning an invasion of Scion. They intend to destroy our culture, followed by subornation of any Arkillian who survives their attack. He has provided me proof in the form of intelligence intercepts to support his statements. I studied those documents carefully and I believe what he has freely provided is the truth."

With facial features shifting from shock to anger, Ca challenged what Kur had just told him. "Kur, can this be a ruse, a deception to learn where Scion is?"

Kur's facial markings revealed amusement, "No Ca, Kellon has provided proof that not only does he know where Scion is, he has actually completed detailed reconnaissance of our home planet. As he has freely demonstrated by his intelligence gathering, our home world is open to space and vulnerable to attack by any species with a higher level of sophisticated military capability. It seems that for all of our vaulted arrogance, we are among the most backward technological cultures faring between their nearby stars."

Ca sat disbelieving, looking at Kur. "Did I hear you correctly? Did you say Kellon has traveled to Scion, performed detailed surveillance and returned to Earth? All of this in about one of Earth's years? How can such be possible?"

Shaking his head in a negative fashion, Kur responded with an overtone of fatigue. "I cannot tell you how it is possible, but I can assure you Kellon can certainly travel to Scion and back in much less than one of Earth's years.

"I now understand the complete treachery of the Kreel. They exchanged antiquated technology, thousands of Earth years behind their own technology, in exchange for our trade goods and latest special technology. What is more important is the Kreel are also expanding their Empire. They will soon be sending faster-than-light warships to perform reconnaissance of all the worlds we now consider our Empire, including the Earth. We have no technology to stop them."

Asking in grief, Rin inquired, "Is there no hope, none at all?"

His facial markings reflecting his fatigue, Kur paused for a moment before answering Rin. "Kellon has told me there may be some hope, Rin. However, he added that such hope is small, since it will require a decision by humanity's leaders to aid the Arkillians. They will first need to decide to come to our help militarily. This will require their commitment of significant military forces and these cannot at this time be estimated since the size of the Kreel invasion force is not yet known."

Kur observed his words continued to shock both Ca and Rin and they sat not wanting to believe what they were hearing, as the shocks continued unfolding in a thundering repetition.

Ca looked up, his voice one of disbelief. "Kur, are you seriously telling us that Kellon is considering committing his forces to the defense of Scion? The Arkillians made Earth primitive. What could possibly motivate one species to come to the aid of another species after it has committed the aggression we committed on Earth? There must be a misunderstanding or else a hoax is involved."

"Ca, I have heard Kellon speak of his reasons. There is no misunderstanding or hoax. Many factors are motivating Kellon and I admit some seem strange to me. He speaks of a desire of living in peace and security with the benefits of an expanding system of friendly trade. He freely admits that we will need to work to attain such a condition; yet, if we can attain it, such trade would help both the Arkillians and humanity. He pointed out that such a friendly relationship, if attainable, would be considered preferable to long term conflict."

Rin asked, "You speak of humanity? What do you mean by that word?"

"Rin, Kellon is the representative of more than one world. How many worlds is something I do not know. The people on those worlds and Earth collectively think of themselves as humanity. Kellon has also confided they do interact with the Kreel, and that interaction involves a long bitter history of hostility. As Kellon explained, it would be easy to let the Kreel simply destroy the Arkillian culture, but such a destruction spreading to Scion and its associated planets is abhorrent to their most fundamental beliefs. I believe he is sincere in what he says."

"Kur," snapped Ca, "is Kellon saying he wants Scion to turn against the Kreel in order to fight alongside of humanity against the Kreel? If that is what I am hearing you say then I have many questions about truthfulness and gullibility. What proof have you been shown that could not have been crafted to deceive us?"

Kur heard Ca's tone and noticed the facial markers of anger beginning to show on his features. "Ca, I offer you as proof of Kellon's sincerity, the continued existence of this Nest ship and the continuity of your life. It is not Earth or any of Kellon's planets that he seeks our help to defend against a Kreel assault, the Kreel are going to attack Scion. It is improbable such a Kreel attack in force will be faked or a matter to be considered a deception. I suggest you read the material provided before you make your own determinations. In truth, I request you both read what Kellon has freely provided. Afterward we can continue this discussion.

"What I remind you of is simple. If Kellon is lying to us, it matters little. The Kreel attack will have occurred on Scion long before this Nest ship can possibly arrive to warn Scion. Upon our arrival, in the turns to come, if what Kellon says is true, then it will all be a matter of history. We will arrive home to a world in ruins and chained in slavery.

"Enough has been said concerning the matter at this time."

Kur again lifted his cup of mead to signal no further discussion was possible and he did so as a symbol of respect and salute. This time both Ca and Rin lifted their cups in agreement and all drank a toast to their reunion.

None who drank in truth felt very much like celebrating. The servants had prepared and served their repasts, yet those at the table ate sparingly. Then, pushing back his chair Ca stood and he bowed his head to Kur. "Honored Kur, I beg your forgiveness. The day has been long and the hour is late; I thank you for your Nest's hospitality. However, I feel it is appropriate I now return to my own quarters."

Acknowledging Ca's formality, Kur also stood. "Ca, the information Kellon provided me will be sent to your and Rin's computers this evening. When you have completed your review of that material, you are to return so we may conclude our discussion. The next few days are critical and we have much to plan."

"Kur, you have my assurances that both Rin and I will read the material as you have directed. We will strive very hard to provide you with our best assessment and judgment."

Kur remained standing in respect as both Ca and Rin withdrew followed by their personal servants. Kur signaled his own servants to clear the table and then he stood for a while longer with his head bowed in thought. Slowly he lifted his head in decision. He needed to speak with Kellon.

Departing his private quarters Kur walked the short distance to the small conference room near the bridge. As he entered, he stood at the viewing window and looked out toward the stars, the Earth was not visible. The stars within the galaxy spread out before him, appearing as being countless in their numbers, brightly revealed as a broad ribbon across the dark heaven. Inwardly he remembered his melancholy thoughts just prior to the battle with Kellon. *The stars are still bitterly cold*, he thought.

The senior bridge officer came into the conference room and addressed him. "Honored One, how may I assist you?"

Turning to the officer Kur considered his needs. "You will take what steps are necessary for me to speak with the human Kellon. I will remain here until you are able to make such a connection. If you are unable to make that connection, then determine when such communications might be possible."

Returning to the small conference table, Kur took his seat to wait. A short time thereafter, the Captain came into the conference room. "Honored One, I am informed of your request and have come to be certain your desires are fully met."

Even as the Captain spoke, the communications screen brightened and the image of Kellon appeared. "Good evening Council Member Kur, I am informed you wish to discuss something of importance with me."

Sitting back Kur wondered if Kellon knew sufficiently of Arkillian facial markings to assess his mood and hoped he did not. "Thank you Commodore Kellon for answering my request for communications so promptly. I do have a matter of some importance to discuss with you. In truth, there are several matters.

"Firstly, I thank you for the assistance your ships provided in escorting my fellow Council members home to our Nest ship. Everything went smoothly and as we had agreed upon."

Kur struggled inwardly before bringing up the next subject, but saw no other course but that of being frank about his desires. "Honored Kellon, what I must say now is not easy to say. I earnestly request your help in sending a warning of the pending Kreel treachery to Scion. I cannot amplify sufficiently my sense of grief that I am unable to act to save my world. Will you help me?" Observing Kellon's features, Kur wished that there were facial markings that might guide him in understanding what was in his mind. What he saw he interpreted as a deep concern, but he could not be certain.

"Council member Kur, your request is also my concern, even before you asked. There is however one serious problem. While we are now working together in this solar system, the existing long-term relationship between the Kreel and Scion compels me to act with caution and discretion. You might also give thought to how those on Scion would receive such a warning.

"Do you consider the Ruling Council would believe the warning, act prudently and take the military steps necessary to defend against a Kreel invasion?"

Sitting stone still Kur's thoughts were troubled. "Kellon your words are filled with understanding and wisdom. No, the Council is with many viewpoints. There would be much heated debate and many arguments about what action they should take.

However, if we can find a means of providing the Council with the information you have provided me I believe it would prove decisive. The need is for a Council member with knowledge to persuade the others of the wisdom of quietly preparing for warfare with the Kreel and doing that discretely."

As Kellon frowned, Kur studied his facial features. While they did not change Kellon's facial coloring, he knew they did indicate a depth of concerned thought. With hope, he waited for Kellon's response. Then, he observed Kellon's facial expression relax.

"Council member Kur, if I help you, you must first give me your assurance, on the honor of your Nest, that what you may see and hear, while I am helping you, will remain secret. That is the price for my help."

Kur's spirits leaped as new hope flooded in. "Kellon, such a price is acceptable. Such as I or another in my name might see or hear will remain secret as long as I breathe and sand blows over the golden desert."

Kellon again frowned and sat quietly for some time before speaking again. "Council member Kur, my desire is to help you. To that end, I will consider how I might best do this provided I am able to do so without endangering Earth or others. I will provide the help, but only if a workable plan can be developed. Know that such help will not be an easy matter. Plans must be devised and carefully considered, if our help is to be meaningful and lives not wasted."

Looking toward the image on the screen, Kur responded with sincerity. "Honored Kellon, we will await your communications." As the screen went dark, Kur looked up and saw the Captain looking directly toward him and his facial markings were those of deep contemplation.

"Honored one, I have noted you have called Kellon Honored?" Although his fatigue was heavy, Kur understood why the Captain inquired as he had. "Captain, Kellon is a leader of his people. In his actions, he has shown great wisdom and proven he is a warrior of renown. For me to use the honorific term in regards to a human may seem strange yet, in my assessment, Kellon is worthy of such distinction. Even now the very fate of our Nests and all of Scion depends on his wisdom and good intentions."

"Honored One, it is indeed strange, however your words are clear and are truth. It is only strange to think of those we despised so recently in such honorable terms. There is much to think about in all that is happening."

Kur stood. "Captain, such heavy thoughts are long overdue and we do need to carefully consider them. I appreciate your questions. Thank you for your assistance."

Kur turned and departed the conference room without looking back. Had he looked back he would have seen the Captain bow his head in admiration and a token of deep respect.

Chapter Twenty:
Sudden Death

The pair of Kreel Tuen Class fast attack ships slithered through the turbulent magnetic boundary of the heliopause enveloping Earth's primary. They then paused in the outer darkness. Like the lean predators they were, they cautiously surveyed the pinwheel structure of the continuous outward flow of charged particles swirling within the heliosphere and minutely scanned the broad magnetic spectrum. They were probing for prey and possible threats. They had come far in search of a particular world, a human-occupied world dominated by the Arkillian Empire.

With the piercing of the heliopause by the Kreel ships, early warning sensors detected their lurking presence and the clamor of battle stations alarms rang throughout five alert Guardian cruisers. The Guardian ships inwardly bristled with activity, as their crews responded and prepared for battle.

The Kreel fast attack ships had previously surveyed several star systems without finding their designated prey. Now, in this new solar system their sensors registered tantalizing telltale whips suggesting their search was possibly nearing its end. They detected a broad spectrum of communications coming from the third planet from the primary. Their scanning sensors also revealed rudimentary space ships operating within the heliosphere.

Patiently they continued to study their instruments, refining their sensitivity, looking for any sign of an Arkillian presence. The Arkillian were only sub-light capable and the Kreel did not consider them a serious threat. There were however other enemies, and harsh experience had taught the Kreel to exercise extreme caution, especially when exploring an unknown solar system.

Their careful work and patience soon rewarded them. They located the low-level signature of an Arkillian Nest ship operating near the third planet. While the Arkillian Nest ship's drive was active it was operating at a minimal threshold. It was apparent to them that the ship was merely maneuvering within the system on some mission of its own.

The Kreel considered the Arkillian sub-light capable Nest ship to be large and awkwardly slow, it being barely capable of traveling the limited distance between the nearest stars. Contemptuous of the Arkillian, the Kreel Commander considered them grossly inferior in all aspects of social organization, genetic definition and especially military and technological capability. The few areas of Arkillian technical expertise that existed were deemed meager and of little importance. None could ever accuse the Kreel of adhering to the ageless military adage, do not underestimate an enemy.

As the hours passed, the two Kreel warships continued monitoring the environment and they detected no threats. They were experienced in the tactics of war and knew the dangers found in haste. They must be certain all was as it appeared and nothing more than what it appeared. Reassured by the elapsed hours of their careful vigilance they confidently proceeded with their exploration and trusted in the freedom and safety their superior technical capability provided.

Their mission orders absolutely required them to confirm the occupants of the solar system were the humans for which they were searching. If confirmed, then they could report their success. They dared not report failure.

Like the susurrus of wind through tall grass the two Kreel ships slid inward toward the third planet confident none would detect them. Their electronic senses were alert and extended, being set to their sensitive limits seeking any tingling of threats. They sensed none, only the low emissions from the Arkillian Nest ship hinted of any higher order of technology within the heliosphere. Aboard the two warships the Kreel were elated. Perhaps they could soon report their success to the Elite Hub.

As the hours of their approach slipped past the Kreel fast attack ships moved silently past the orbit of the fifth planet, a gas giant with broad multicolored bands. They did not pause to admire the beauty of that sight. As they continued their inward probe, their confidence increased as if it were a product inversely proportional to the distance from the third planet. As a space-voyaging species they had few known peers. While they prudently remained alert for possibly superior forces, such were sufficiently few that events tended to boost rather than deflate the Kreel's arrogance and assurance of superiority. They had now been within the solar system for many hours, and there was no inkling, let alone a solid indication, of a potential threat. They had only detected the Arkillian Nest ship and they considered it posed no meaningful challenge.

The nearer they came to their objective, the higher their confidence soared until the Captains of both Kreel ships cast off their earlier caution. What truly swelled the increasing confidence of the Kreel Commander was the observed performance of the local space ships operating within the heliosphere. Those ships' incredibly primitive design actually amused him being they were as slow as slugs propelled by nothing more than solar wind or feeble ion propulsion. Such primitive ships scarcely ranked notice and they constituted no meaningful threat. As was the nature of their species the Kreel Commander began to swagger with an arrogant bravado.

X

As the Kreel ships approached the ring of debris forming a belt between the fourth and fifth planet detectors in Darrell Fann's Olympus group triggered their automatic alert. In Olympus, there was a hurrying to stations.

During the previous days Susie had continued to explore William's expanded AI capabilities and she was intent on learning more about what William was capable of doing. Arriving in Olympus early that morning, Susie had brought both William and the new communicator with her.

When the Olympus detection alarms signal sounded Darrell was perplexed and looked inquiringly toward Susie. "What can be happening now?" He asked, "Monstro is in near Earth orbit and all of the Arkillian smaller craft are on board. There shouldn't be anything coming in from Jupiter's orbit. Susie, do you have any clue of what is going on?"

Susie could guess, but she was uncertain of how much she should tell Darrell. Attempting to avoid saying more than she should, she tried an artful dodge.

"Let me contact Lan. William and I can see if they can tell us anything.

"William please contact Lan for me."

"I am sorry Ms. Susie, however, that is not possible at this time," came William's calm British response.

William's response took her completely by surprise. "Not possible? William, why is communication not possible?"

"Ms. Susie, there is a combat alert in effect and all unnecessary communications are prohibited, until that alert is rescinded." Darrell's eyebrows soared— "Combat alert?"

William's calm statement had perplexed Susie. "William, when did that combat alert commence?"

"Ms. Susie, the combat alert has been in full effect for nearly two days. It became effective upon the detection of two Kreel fast attack ships penetrating this solar system's heliopause. Guardian Force is now fully engaged in containing the Kreel presence. Until that combat mission is complete, you will be unable to communicate with Lan or others within the Guardian force."

As Darrell opened his mouth to ask Susie to explain, Charlie came in with a hand full of data sheets and a broad grin. "Hey Darrell, have we got some interesting data here or not? Take a look at this. It has waveforms like nothing I have ever seen before. There are two clear propulsion signatures. I don't have even a clue of who or what might be generating them."

Charlie put the data on the table before Darrell and stood back somewhat puzzled when Darrell did not even respond or look at the data. Standing, Charlie looked back and forth between Darrell and Susie, and then commented dryly, "Okay, hello folks. Do either of you mind taking a moment out from whatever it's you're doing and tell me what's going on here?"

Without looking up toward Charlie, Darrell cynically commented, "well Charlie, Susie was about to explain all about a species called the Kreel. She is about to tell us why they might be here. She might even condescend to explain why the Guardian

Force is dug in and holding to a full combat mode. Well Susie, you have our undivided attention. Who in hell are the Kreel?"

Shrugging, Susie glanced about the office for some way to avoid the question. She saw nothing, nothing but a conference table and chairs and empty coffee cups. Clearly, there was no place for her to hide. *I guess the old tomcat is out of the bag,* she thought.

"Well, Darrell, it's kind of like this, the Kreel are very bad news and have faster-than-light travel capability and lots of heavy firepower. People on other planets generally think of them as being nasty and having absolutely no sense of humor. Oh, did I already say the Kreel consider human beings as delicious, even mouthwatering scrumptious morsels walking about on two legs?"

The quiet rhythm of the Nest ship's operation resonated subliminally in the very cells of every Arkillian living within the Nest ship's strong hull. The low frequency vibration was all-embracing and provided a sense of unspoken security. Everyone onboard sensed all other sounds and vibrations as a harmonious component of the ever-present underlying rhythm of the Nest ship. The soft rhythm quietly announced all was well and as it should be. When the contact alarm stridently sounded, it sharply contrasted with the normal ship's rhythm, declaring conditions were definitely not as they should be!

Working in his quarters, Kur knew the alarm could have only one cause, the Kreel were here. He was determined to be as battle-ready as the Nest ship could be. Keying his communicator he directed the Captain to immediately make ready the few fighters still operational for launch and ship-to-ship combat. Departing his quarters in a brisk walk, he moved to the conference room near the bridge area. There he found the Captain and senior tactical officer in deep discussion. Looking toward Kur, both officers bowed their heads in respect and the Captain began his report.

"Honored One, we have confirmed tracks of Kreel fast-attack ships. I believe these are true Kreel propulsion signatures and Kellon is not involved with their appearance. I await your instructions."

As Kur stood considering his best course of action Ca and Rin arrived out of breath. Kur noted their arrival, but did not turn to address them.

"Captain, the Nest ship is well within what Scion defines as its sovereign space. We must therefore conduct ourselves as if we knew nothing of the Kreel plan to attack Scion. If we permit these ships to report that we know of their planned attack, it could accelerate their invasion. Because of this concern, our actions must be the same as it would be if we were ignorant of why they are here. Given this understanding, you are to transmit a Kreel challenge signal and then wait for their response. I will talk with their Commander to determine his intent." The Captain again bowed his head and then departed from the conference room.

Standing, Kur considered what was happening. He had no doubt Kellon was aware of the Kreel presence long before he was. He understood Kellon could and would defend the Earth, taking whatever appropriate action he felt necessary. What that action might be Kur did not know. He did know however, he could not base his own actions on guessing what Kellon might be planning.

With the appearance of the Kreel, he knew he could not risk trying to contact Kellon knowing he would be announcing his concealed position. Communications with Kellon was therefore not a consideration or option. Like Kellon, if it were possible, Kur would likewise not want to announce his own position to the Kreel. He however, had no allusion regarding the Kreel's capability to detect his propulsion signature, from anywhere within the solar system. The Kreel would have many hours earlier established precisely where the Nest ship was located. That meant they were even now undoubtedly tracking and targeting the Nest ship.

Kur took his chair before the communications equipment and waited. Ca and Rin had moved aside and now stood near the tactical officer and out of the view of the video pickup. They all were showing the facial markings of the stress that Kur knew he also felt. What he could not permit was the Kreel to observe his stress. Therefore he reached within using his training to calm his facial features and settled into an easy relaxed posture.

A few moments later, the Captain returned and reported, "Honored One, the Kreel challenge call is being transmitted as instructed. However, there is no response as yet."

As Kur sat patiently waiting for the Kreel to respond he soon realized that the Kreel's ignoring the challenge call was intentional. It was intended as a calculated blatant arrogant snub declaring the challenger was not even worthy of notice. In spite of his training his anger began to rise.

Finally, after a lengthy silence, there came the anticipated response. The screen cleared and the features of a Kreel officer appeared. He did not even bother to try to address Kur in the Arkillian language, as courtesy and custom dictated was proper protocol. He spat his words in the Kreel's own hissing guttural language. It was an expression of utter contempt and the Kreel Officer sharply directed it toward Kur.

"Who dares to issue a challenge to the Kreel? Know this, Arkillian, the Kreel go where they choose and none, especially no Arkillian slug, is worthy to challenge us. What arrogance deceives you to believe you can offer a challenge to Kreel warships?"

Kur had not spoken the Kreel tongue for a long time, but as a Council member, he was fluent in the language. The surly address of the Kreel officer had ignited Kur's anger and undoubtedly his facial markings revealed his intensifying anger.

Sitting upright, Kur's tone was blistering, as he hurled his response back at the Kreel. "Kreel officer, I immediately demand your identity and rank. Your ships are in Arkillian sovereign space. You do not have Arkillian permission to enter this solar system. Know now you are addressing a senior elder member of the ruling Arkillian Council. You will therefore show appropriate respect."

The Kreel officer threw back his head and broke out in jeering mockery. "Arkillian mongrel, you are very far from home and your precious ruling council. I spit on your demand for my identification and rank. The Kreel go wherever they will to go. It is enough you know I am your absolute master and you are now notified that I have claimed this entire solar system in the name of the Kreel Hub. Therefore, I have designated all those now within this heliosphere as our prey and that includes your Nest ship and you. It is therefore you who are trespassing!

"In order to demonstrate your proper respect for the Kreel you have until I arrive at your current location to get your fat slow barge underway. I am ordering you back to Scion. If you defy my orders, I will destroy you where you are. If you should survive the crossing to Scion the Kreel may permit you to live. You might even be allowed to scrub toilets along with any other members of your pathetic ruling council that may be still alive."

Kur sat transfixed at the words of the Kreel. Here was proof beyond proof and verification of the Kreel's intentions. Holding his head high Kur threw his own challenge back at the Kreel. "Kreel braggart, do you believe the Arkillians accept such boastful declarations from a coward? You speak of mongrels, but it is your genetically polluted kind that has no natural or proper beginning in space or time.

"Your insolence is noted braggart and it is not pardoned. If you think you have the courage and power to fight the Arkillians, then come here and embrace your death."

The image of the Kreel officer exploded in fury. "You dare call the Kreel genetically polluted and me a braggart and coward! You will taste the full bitterness of your insults toward your masters. Filthy spawn of Scion, prepare to meet your doom." The screen went dark.

Angry, Kur sat for a while, simply looking at the blank screen, while attempting to better control his own inner rage. Turning to Ca he asked, "Do you continue to doubt Kellon's information?" The pronounced anger markings on Ca's face were vibrant, giving a vivid testimony of how he felt.

"Honored Kur, I have heard the Kreel's words of disrespect and challenge. There is no doubt remaining. What do you intend to do?"

Having regained most of his composure and looking toward Ca, Kur's face transformed and brightened in amusement. "Ca, we are going to prepare to fight the Kreel here, in Earth's solar system, even as if we were still its sovereign rulers. I believe Kellon will note our willingness to defend Earth from a Kreel assault. In one way, the opportunity to defend Earth answers the question you presented to me upon your return. We will indeed stand with humans to fight the Kreel, while defending a human world. In many ways fate has provided us an opportunity to demonstrate our strength of resolve, even if our military power is diminished." Turning to the Captain, Kur instructed, "Your courage and battle skills are known and often demonstrated. I now want you to prepare two Kreel beams and hold them at maximum power for deployment at the maximum range of the weapon. As the Kreel draw near be prepared to use that weapon if the opportunity presents itself."

The Captain's facial markings showed his determination and anger. "Honored one, the Kreel beams will be set at the ready for deployment. If an opportunity to deploy the weapon presents itself, then we will strike."

Turning to the tactical officer, Kur asked, "Do you have information concerning the maximum effective ranges for the Kreel lasers and missiles on their fast attack warship?"

The officer stood straight and promptly answered, "No, Honored One. The Kreel closely guard their weapon performance and we have no battle experience against the Kreel to draw upon for knowledge."

Kur's mood was further brightening when he responded, with noticeable amusement. "Perhaps the Arkillian military will today have the opportunity to better understand the Kreel weapon performance characteristics. Until then, provide your best estimates of what their performance might be."

"Honored One, given the performance characteristics of the Kreel warships they are designed for speed and long range patrols. They are lightly armed. The dynamics of their lasers are powerful, but limited, since their ships channel their primary power toward propulsion rather than offensive firepower. The missiles they carry will be formidable, but are likely of the light and medium classification rather than the heavy long-range types. This being as it is, they may need to close within the range of the Kreel beams before they can launch their medium missiles.

"Where we cannot compete is their maneuvering capability and speed. We are again faced with a faster-than-light capable enemy." Kur mused about their tactical position. He considered what Kellon might do and he decided to act in a manner that might help Kellon tactically.

"Captain, direct the Nest ship on a course perpendicular to the approaching Kreel bearing line and in a direction to take us as far above the Ecliptic Plane as possible before engagement. We will face the Kreel in open space."

Returning his gaze to the tactical officer he asked, "How many of the Nest ship's high-power lasers are currently able to function?"

"Honored one, we have labored to restore our combat readiness for many months. At present, we have twelve heavy laser batteries able to be fully operational. Since we have minimal power used for propulsion, the power available for our heavy lasers makes them very potent and they are about equally spaced to provide limited but covering fire on all sides of the Nest ship.

"We also have six missile launch ports repaired and capable of being used. Two of those ports deploy heavy missiles and four deploy medium and light missiles.

"Honored One, although there are two Kreel ships, as mentioned they are not their big cruisers. They are light fast-attack ships. They have effective firepower, but we do have an ability to severely damage or even destroy them, if they allow their anger and species arrogance to cloud their combat skills. What is true is that they will also be able to damage us badly or even destroy us, if we are not careful."

As he listened to the report, Kur brightened with pleasure. "Then, we still have a sharp sting and possess a long reach with which to deliver it on a target!"

"Honored One, do you believe Kellon will help us?" The Tactical Officer asked.

The Officer's question did not surprise Kur and he had a ready answer. "Yes, he will help us. I believe he is even now deploying his force in a manner to use our position tactically to distract the Kreel since they are able to see our movement while they cannot see Kellon as he moves. I believe Kellon is even now setting an ambush to destroy the Kreel. This being true, then our part is to act as the succulent bait in his trap. This is what I would do if I were in Kellon's position."

The other Arkillians standing with Kur in the small conference room looked at one another in surprise. They hoped Kur's analysis was correct and Kellon was even then setting his ambush.

Kur studied the facial markings of those he stood with and liking what he saw and did not see. *They are Arkillians who retain their honor, stand with dignity and stand without fear.*

To the wonder of those observing him, his face brightened with pride.

Standing, Kur turned to the Captain. "Well, if we are to serve as slow fat bait then let us be the best bait the Kreel were ever lured to, as they are destroyed. We have time to prepare and much work to do. We should therefore be working to be ready. I believe our Nest ship might yet have a few surprises for the Kreel. They may soon learn we are not a fat slow barge!"

X

Well-positioned and hunkered down, Lan was poised and ready for battle. In CAC Commander Shaw studied the plot board and the symbols delineated on it. He smiled with understanding, as he noted the movement of the Arkillian Nest ship. "Tactical here. Sir, it looks as if Kur is moving the Nest ship above the ecliptic plane. He is moving out and away from Earth. He appears intent on engaging the Kreel in open space and his tactical position will give us maneuvering room if the combat devolves into a running fight."

"Lorn, we cannot let it devolve into anything but the Kreel ships spreading out in debris. My real concern is, if those Kreel ships get close enough to the Nest ship, they will suffer the same fate as the Kreel cruiser we captured. I am not convinced I want to see a Kreel fast attack ship intact and in the hands of the Arkillian, not just yet. Kur will fight. We both know that from firsthand experience. I also believe he has guessed we have identified the Nest ship as the designated bait in our battle planning."

"Sir," Commander Grey inserted, "Communications reports they have rigged an automatic trigger to jam any Kreel superluminal transmission. They report no such transmissions have yet been detected."

"Thank you Roy, keep me informed of any signals if they are detected." Kellon acknowledged.

Sitting back in his command chair, Kellon studied the combat plot noting the Kreel course was steadily heading directly toward the Arkillian Nest ship. That course vector defined one axis of the tactical plane, the second axis being defined parallel with the ecliptic plane. As the Kreel moved steadily toward the inner planets Kellon maneuvered his Cruisers to intercept, contain and finally ambush the Kreel fast-attack ships.

During the previous hours Lent, Lawrence and Lar had skillfully moved to form a large triangle formation parallel with and above the tactical plane. The two advancing Kreel ships were located at the geometric center of that contracting triangle. Lent and Lawrence were widely flanking and in the trailing position. Their mission was to block any attempt by the Kreel to retreat. Lar, the third cruiser in the triangle, was well ahead of the Kreel and above the track line.

Completing Kellon's tactics Lan and Langley were waiting just within the orbit of Mars, one Cruiser on each side and below the projected track line. Once Lar reached the mid-point above Lan and Langley's positions he would complete the defined kill volume. When reaching that point he would become the upper point of a facing triangle, with Lan and Langley at the base. The projected target track line passed through the geometric center of that facing triangle. Together the three Cruisers firmly blocked any further advance by the Kreel ships and the facing triangle formation provided Kellon overwhelming focused firepower. Completing the ambush the two trailing Guardian Cruisers provided the backstop for the defined kill volume. If by some miracle the Kreel ships evaded the ambush, the two blocking Cruisers would not permit them to retreat.

"Sir, tactical here, Kur is deploying his fighters. By my count, he is launching twelve fighters. It appears he is deploying them to form a screen between the oncoming Kreel and Monstro. Give them credit; they certainly have courage."

The CAC was quiet, except for the low background murmur of the various tracking parties positioned throughout the room.

"Tactical here, the Kreel are responding to Kur's deployment of fighters. They are increasing their speed. The Kreel course is still directly toward Monstro. As yet, the two Tuen fast-attack ships have not split into their four tactical combat units."

Kellon keyed his command band, "gentlemen and ladies, keep on your toes. The barn door is about to close.

"Fire Control, bring two medium missiles on line and set them passive-active. They are to go active at 70% of set run length. Get passive locks and target one missile on each of the

Kreel ships. We will hold our fire and launch missiles only when the targets reach 50% of effective medium missile range."

"Lan, advise Lar and Langley of our missile settings. Have them duplicate them. Confirm that each Cruiser is targeting each Kreel ship with a single medium missile. They are to hold their fire, until you order their synchronized missile firing."

The soft acknowledging tone indicated Lan had complied with his orders.

"Sir, Fire Control here. Two missiles are selected and ready; set Condition 2. We have a passive lock on each incoming target."

"Tactical, Lorn give me a count down on the effective range."

"Yes sir. Effective range is now at 225% and closing."
"Navigation here, Lar has reached his ambush point and moved into firing position. The blocking formation is now in place and set."

X

In Olympus Darrell was pacing with his communicator pressed to his head. "Charles, I have no additional news. What we have here is the Nest ship has moved above the ecliptic plane and has launched its fighter escort. Yes Sir. We are counting a dozen fighters at most. Yes Sir, that's correct, one dozen. Well, I can only guess that is all Monstro has that still work after their battle with Kellon. No Sir, we have no information about the Guardian Force deployment. The Kreel have increased their speed and are heading directly toward Monstro. There is no doubt that a battle is about to begin. Yes Sir, I will keep you posted."

Disconnecting his communicator and sighing with contained frustration Darrell turned toward Susie. "Well Susie, you had better warm up your communicator. Charles is not happy, he wants a complete report on the Kreel and he wants that report yesterday."

Susie shrugged and shook her head. "Darrell, I can tell Charles what I know, but what I know is not much."

Charlie called out, "Hey guys and gals, keep it down. The Kreel are crossing the orbit of Mars and headed this way. They are accelerating and are heading directly toward Monstro. Monstro's fighters are moving out to engage them. Can you believe this, it really is going down and we have a front row seat."

X

As Kur looked around the control room, he saw the Arkillian teams hard at work over the three-dimensional tactical tank. Watching the icons within the tank he could see his fighters expertly deploying and the oncoming Kreel rapidly closing the distance between them. They would soon be engaged in the battle.

The Nest ship had maneuvered in an arc to bring its flank toward the onrushing Kreel taking a position to permit delivery of its maximum firepower against the assaulting Kreel ships. Kur had ordered the fighters to move out just beyond the Kreel beam range and once there to form a flexible defensive screen. As the Kreel advanced, he ordered the fighters to fall back remaining at distance from the Kreel ships. The function of the fighters was to provide a first line of anti-missile point-defense against incoming Kreel missiles. Their orders were not to attack the Kreel fast-attack ships, but to let the Nest ship's heavy lasers and missiles carry the attack directly to the Kreel. The Nest ship was fully combat ready, poised and waiting.

Kur continued to wonder where Kellon had deployed his forces. If his guess was correct, then the Kreel were about to walk into the center of a deadly firestorm. If he was incorrect, *Well then, it would indeed prove to be a most interesting morning,* he thought.

With an inspired sense of drama, Kur turned to the Captain and instructed, "Captain, send a second Kreel challenge."

A few minutes later, the screen shimmered into the image of the Kreel Commander. Rage was twisting his facial expression into a snarl as he addressed Kur. "Arkillian, if you are calling to plead for mercy and your life, there will be none granted. Not even if you beg. Your miserable formation of pathetic fighters is as dry leaves before us."

Kur's face was sober as he responded to the Kreel Captain. "We are within Arkillian sovereign space. I give you one last chance to bend your knee and surrender. Providing you immediately state your name and rank, I may show mercy. I again tell you to your face you are a braggart. If you do not yield your ships, then prepare to die."

The Kreel Captain erupted in a new outburst of anger. "Slug, you have, for the last time, insulted a Kreel officer. How dare you demand I surrender to the likes of you? I will see your ship reduced to slag."

As the screen went dark, Kur felt a keen sense of satisfaction. *Kellon,* he thought, *you now have a very angry and very distracted Kreel commander. Good hunting.*

Onboard Lan, the crew's attention was calm and tightly focused on the unfolding tactical plan. "Tactical here, range is now at 65% of effective range and closing."

Kellon keyed his command band, "Fire Control, on your toes. Lan upon our command to launch, synchronize the launching of missiles from Lar and Lawrence." Lan's acknowledgment tone softly sounded.

"Tactical here, distance is now at 55% and closing."

Under his breath, Kellon murmured, *and that is as close to Earth as they will ever get!* "Fire control, Kellon here, set Condition 1, Fire!"

"Fire Control here, two missiles away."

As Lan launched his missiles, everyone aboard heard their rumbling sounds as they were ejected up and away.

"Captain, Tactical here, I am registering Lawrence and Lar have launched missiles. There are a total of six medium missiles passively closing on the targets."

Kellon sat watching the plot board, observing the icons representing outbound missiles streak toward the icons of the approaching Kreel ships. In the case of head on collisions between missiles and their targets, warheads were to all effects a superfluous afterthought since the combined kinetic energy involved in the collisions was sufficient to devastate a ship. He knew the Kreel ships were doomed.

Aboard the Kreel ship, there was first a sudden burst of alarm signals and then pandemonium followed. The Kreel sensors had detected active missiles coming from three widely dispersed points. They had emerged close to the Kreel ships, without warning and seemingly emerged out of nowhere. The Captains were issuing evasion orders, while attempting to bring defensive lasers into play, but the time available to react effectively to multiple missiles approaching from diverse attack vectors was short. In frustrated outrage, the senior Captain keyed the transmitter used to contact the Arkillian Nest ship. "Arkillian slug, you will not win, an alert is being sent to the Kreel Hub-"

Even as he spoke, the first of the Guardian missiles struck with a deafening explosion.

On the Nest ship Kur watched the screen, hearing the shrill sounds of alarms and seeing the flurry of confused activity about the Kreel Officer. He noted the Kreel officer's fury and knew well firsthand his frustration and sense of helplessness. The screen went blank with the thundering sounds of explosions.

Kur sat back and was thoughtfully silent. Kellon, you have once more demonstrated your prowess as a warrior.

Within nine minutes from Lan's launch of medium missiles there was nothing remaining where the Kreel fast attack ships had been except fields of spreading organic and inorganic jetsam, debris and dissipating gasses.

The last Guardian missile arrived on target and found the projected target intercept point empty. As programmed, the missile self-destructed, exploding to leave no telltale trace or threat to any object other than the one it had intended to destroy.

Kellon observed the plot board and data screens and felt only the sense of a job professionally done. There was no sense of victory or elation. He had given no warning to the Kreel and that was simply as it must be.

"Roy, did they get a superluminal signal off to home?"

"Navigation here, Communications did not detect a signal. Of course, the Kreel were closing and with 50% of medium effective missile range at Signal 1 and enabling at 70% of run length, we didn't really give them much time to respond before missile impact."

"Roy that is true, but when these two ships fail to report you can be certain the Kreel will put a big red flag on their chart marking this solar system. Next time, you can safely wager the Kreel will send in a more powerful reconnaissance force."

Keying the general communications band, he addressed the crew, "Kellon here. We have engaged the Kreel ships and destroyed them. We do not believe they had time to send a message to their base. Everyone, you are complimented for a job professionally accomplished. Well done."

"Lan, clear the combat alert. Dispatch a standard post combat status report to Guardian command. Then please establish a link to the other cruisers. Captain's band, if you will."

Kellon spent the next thirty minutes in discussion with his captains. He selected Langley to launch his Scout ships for the purpose of scanning the debris fields. They were the designated cleanup detail. Their job was to destroy anything that could be dangerous, or of an advanced technical nature which should not fall into the hands of an interested third party.

As he was about to return to his quarters he received a call from Kur. "Honored Kellon, I commend you on your effectiveness. We have recorded the direct communications between the Commander of the Kreel ships and me. The transcriptions are very informative and they fully support and validate the information you provided. We need to discuss how I may transmit this urgent information to Scion."

"Council Member Kur, I thank you for your notice. I believe there may be a means to deliver your information to Scion. I have some details I need to attend to now. Excuse my abruptness, but I must conclude this transmission. I will be in communications with you soon. "

Kur nodded his understanding, "I also must tend to my fighters and speak with my crew. We have today formed a basis of understanding. I believe you have observed what you need regarding our willingness to engage the Kreel. Kur out."

X

In Olympus Charlie holding a cup of cold coffee in his hand, looked around and calmly said, "Well folks, it looks like a wrap. Two bad guys looking for a fight and two bad guys gone away. Permanently away in little bitsy pieces from the looks of it."

"Ms. Susie, the combat alert has been rescinded. Communications with Lan are possble. Shall I establish contact?" William asked.

"William, no, not now. We will contact Lan later. Please contact Charles Sullivan."

Susie heard the phone picked up on the first ring, "Sullivan here."

"Sir, Susie here. William has just reported that Kellon has rescinded the combat alert. It appears the Guardian Force destroyed two Kreel ships. They did not get close enough to fire on Monstro or its fighters."

"Susie, I will pass that information on to the President. I will need a full report on what has happened. If I understand the flavor of this battle, there was no quarter asked or given. Is that correct?"

"Sir, it is sort of difficult to offer quarter to something that wants to eat you for dinner. Neither side takes prisoners. Therefore engagements with the Kreel are always what they are, sudden death for the loser."

Chapter Twenty-One:
Changing the Menu

Sitting in his office, Charles Sullivan was looking out over the sprawling vista of New Washington's parks and monuments. Elevated, as it was within the Department of Commerce Building, his office provided him an excellent view of a beautiful clear spring morning. Good view or otherwise, he was deep in contemplative thought. The governments of Earth were in an uproar. Well, perhaps it was more accurate to say the people of Earth were in an uproar. Their various governments were the intense focus of the people's outrage and clamor that the governments do something immediately.

The news of the destruction of the two Kreel inter-stellar war ships had leaked out and was widespread. *Perhaps 'leaked out' might not be strong enough a term to describe the seepage of information,* thought Charles. *Perhaps 'gushed out' might be more appropriate.* Upon further consideration Charles thought, *Tidal wave seems more accurate a description of what happened.*

The truth was someone had expertly inserted fact, not rumor, into the world's media stream. The facts were in such profusion, multiple languages and outlets, that governments around the world were not able to lie effectively to the people, as usual. It was not possible to use intentional disinformation techniques to plug a flood.

Where the information came from was not clear, however Charles feared it might have in part come out of Olympus. There seemed no other possible source, however the reports contained detailed information even Olympus had not known.

Possible Olympus involvement was not the only matter troubling Charles Sullivan, as he sat quietly looking out of his office windows this spring morning. Charles fully understood how on Earth everyone's personal views of the universe had changed during the previous twenty-four hours. There was a sharp contrast between the presumptions of everyone living safe, snug and happy on an isolated Earth. Then to learn the shocking revelation, there existed an advanced interstellar species that liked to eat people.

People simply were not accustomed to thinking of themselves as being food. They were shocked to learn they were vulnerable. They strenuously objected to any possibility of the Kreel putting them on a chaffing dish with an apple in their mouth. Having the skin stripped off their backs by governments that overtaxed and wasted their assets was one thing but to learn there was actually an interstellar species that really liked eating people was something else altogether. People did not consider it a joking matter.

The news spread like wildfire over the Earth and it spared no population group. The truth was the Kreel would enjoy eating anyone, regardless of race, gender, sexual orientation, sub-ethnic group, wealth or poverty and political or religious affiliation. Now each person knew for positive certain they were an equal with everyone else on Earth. They were all equally preferred and considered delicious as the main entree at a Kreel smorgasbord.

From the outrage people were loudly expressing around the world, it was abundantly clear the Earth's peoples did not like such facts. They were demanding the governments do something about changing the menu. When fourteen billion people begin shouting, they make themselves heard.

Charles knew it was only a matter of time before his phone rang and the President would begin asking very direct and uncomfortable questions. He had his suspicions, but regretfully he had no reliable information to direct him to the guilty disperser of facts. If only rumors and confused distortions were distributed a well-organized effort of counter disinformation might have suppressed the reports. Now the quantity and quality of facts presented were such that trying to disprove them, or to ridicule them, would only make matters much worse.

One fact stood above the others, the information had to have a source. The index finger of his presumption pointed directly to Susie Wells as being that source. It must be Susie. No one else had access to the information that had poured out through the global news distribution channels. He could not prove Susie had done it but he was relatively certain that his assumption was near to the target.

The only fact that seemed to say Susie could not have accomplished the distribution of news, was the precision and multilingual distribution employed. The news broke all over the world in a smoothly coordinated and synchronized manner. The techniques employed were extremely sophisticated and precise. The governments tried, but they were unable to trace the news reports back to their source. He had thought that would be impossible but it had been nevertheless neatly accomplished. That argued a well-disciplined and funded unknown organization was responsible, not a lone person. That realization was in itself something that would scare some governments as if they were not already paranoid enough.

His intercom chimed and Lois' voice announced, "Ms. Wells and Mr. Fann are here."

Turning to face his desk, Charles keyed the intercom. "Lois, please direct them to come in. Also, please arrange for coffee and perhaps a few bakery items."

"Yes Sir," Lois responded, her voice cheerful and bright.

Obviously, thought Charles gloomily, *she is not worried about holding on to her job.* At the moment, Charles was not at all confident that he would keep his job beyond this morning.

The door opened and two of his most favorite people entered his office. Both were smiling broadly.

"Please take a seat." Charles directed. He was definitely not smiling when saying this.

Susie and Darrell sat down facing Charles and noting his grim expression. Their own expressions became more serious. Charles remained quiet at his desk and studied their faces.

There was a moment of silence wherein Charles gathered his thoughts. Direct and to the point he asked, "Susie, are you responsible for the news about the Kreel that has emerged all around the world overnight?"

Susie stiffened, even looking surprised at the question. "Charles, the answer is absolutely not. Furthermore I do not speak Chinese or Swahili."

Charles turned his gaze to Darrell. "Mr. Fann, have you any knowledge of where the information in those news reports was obtained?"

While looking directly toward Charles, Darrell responded: "No!"

"If neither of you were directly involved, can either of you provide any insight as to where the information may have come from?" Charles asked.

Susie smiled. "No, I cannot say I can. However, what I can truthfully say is the angry snarling features of the Kreel Commander, as he was screaming at Kur, were especially expressive. I had never seen an image of a Kreel before. He looked uncomfortably like a snarling baboon, fangs and all, except he looked to be over six feet tall, built like a fullback and walking around on two legs. Charles, it was his eyes that were the most frightening; they were like the eyes of a serpent and filled with rage and absolute malevolence. Ugh! Having now seen one I really don't want to meet one. I am not ashamed to say it scared me.

"Now I know what Shey meant when she told me a year ago that the Kreel were an interstellar travel capable species that I would not desire to encounter. Shey was correct, I really don't want to meet one in broad daylight or in a dark alley."

Charles let out a deep breath and felt somewhat more at ease. At least it seemed he was not the person, or among the persons, who would certainly end up on the grill because of what had happened. Darrell and Susie had just provided him the basis for a defense of plausible deniability.

Charles looked back toward Susie, "You mention a name 'Kur.' Who is he?"

"Oh, Kur is a senior member of the Arkillian ruling council and is the big boss on board Monstro."

Susie's casual statement took Charles aback. For several hundred years, Olympus had worked to understand who and what Monstro was. Now Susie simply says she has had conversation with the one Arkillian in charge of Monstro and casually drops his name. Charles shook his head and sighed. It was absolutely logical that Susie had talked with someone in the Arkillian group such as Kur. She was directly involved in negotiating a trade agreement between Earth and Scion. It was all together too easy to lose track of what was happening. He put the Arkillian on the back burner and returned to the topic at hand.

"Susie, did the Guardian Force release the information?"

Susie at once became upset. Charles, "You are asking the wrong person that question."

Charles did not hesitate in continuing his inquiry, "You have been off-world, traveled to Glas Dinnein, lived with the Guardian Force; who else should I ask?"

Susie hesitated and then responded. Her expression was serious and tinged with a hint of anger. "I think you already know the answer to your question. Yes, I have done all you say, but I do not speak for the Guardian Force. You have the means of putting that question on a front channel directly to them. I suggest, if you want your question answered, you ask the Guardian Force directly.

"However, if you are asking for my opinion, I doubt they would have done this. They have their hands full without becoming directly embroiled within the mire of Earth politics. They have a good understanding of protocol and adhere to the discipline of a chain of command. My opinion is you should look somewhere else."

"Susie, I regret asking you the question as I did. You have made your point and it was appropriately stated. The problem is I have sat here this morning and attempted to discern who could have distributed the information. It was spot-on in detail and included considerable information that I had no access to or before known. If not Olympus, or the Guardian Force, then who had that information and the capability to distribute it?"

Darrell sat quietly listening to the brief and tense exchange between Charles and Susie. Having a sudden insight his frown shifted to a slight smile. "Charles, I know someone that had the information who you have not mentioned."

At Darrell's comment, both Susie and Charles turned to look at him. Charles spoke before Susie could ask her own question. "OK, who is the mystery guest that I have not mentioned?"

Darrell was smiling broadly when he responded, "The Arkillian." Charles and Susie sat quietly for a moment, surprised. Neither had even considered the Arkillian.

Charles asked, "why do you believe the Arkillians may have distributed the information and just how could they have accomplished that feat?"

Well," Darrell replied, "As to why, that I don't know. What I do know is they had all the information. I also know they have pulled the political strings all over the planet for about fourteen thousand years. During that time, they had to have an efficient means of monitoring what was happening. Doubtless they also developed a sophisticated means of putting information into the media whenever they felt it beneficial. If they are responsible for the leaks, they must have an advantageous reason for doing so."

Turning back to Charles, Susie offered, "Well, as for why? I can think of possibly one reason they may have. As you know, I had the opportunity to interact with Kur. Remember he is the senior representative of their ruling council. From what I gleaned from Kur, there is great remorse among some of the Arkillians on board Monstro for what they have done to the people on Earth. Kur spoke of the Arkillian arrogance having blinded them to the truth. I also know that Kur has just learned from Kellon the Kreel are about to invade his home planet Scion, as well as invading Earth." Holding up his hand, as if to stop traffic, Charles interjected "hold on a minute Susie. What you are saying is incredibly important. You say these Kreel intend to invade Earth?"

"Yes Sir. That is the primary reason they are preparing to take out Scion, to claim jump their empire including Earth. As the distributed news articles reported, they stated just before the Guardian Force destroyed them that they had claimed this entire solar system in the name of the Kreel Hub. I don't know how you read the Kreel declaration, but that sounds like a pending invasion to me."

Listening carefully to what Susie said, Charles thoughtfully commented. "That change in their insight may well explain why the Arkillians have so altered their behavior and indicated a desire to enter into a trade agreement. What you have described implies a pivotal shift in their attitude and thinking. This is critical and could alter how everyone on Earth may think about the Arkillians. At the moment, the two very different planets seem to have a great deal in common, a common dangerous enemy."

Susie's smile broadened. "Charles, don't forget we also have something the Arkillians do not have. We have friends and family on eleven other worlds. We are not standing in this fight alone."

Darrell sat considering the problem then asked, "If the Arkillians are truly remorseful, then why would they interfere by releasing the Kreel story all around the world?"

Her natural good nature was evident, as Susie answered Darrell's question. "Well, if you want to know the answer to that question don't assume, let's simply ask them."

Charles looked at Susie in surprise, "Susie, do you mean you can simply ask the Arkillians? Moreover, if you ask, will they actually tell you?"

"No Charles, I can't ask them, at least not me personally since I do not know their language. However I do know someone who does."

Reaching into her carrying bag Susie pulled out the communicator. Charles had not seen the device before and looked at it speculatively. What he did note was that it was compact and beautifully finished.

Opening the lid, Susie instructed, "Communicator, please connect me with Elayne Cloud onboard Lan."

"Connecting." The communicator responded.

What Charles saw and heard impressed him. Darrell was also looking at Susie with open wonder.

"Madam Ambassador, Lan here. It is good to see you again. Please wait while I locate Lieutenant Cloud. I hope you are having a nice day."

"Good morning Lan, it is a beautiful clear day here. Is everything running well with you?"

"Oh yes Ambassador Susie everything has settled down since the combat alert. Commodore Kellon is working with Council Member Kur regarding working out a means of warning Scion of the pending Kreel attack. He has me very busy working on that project. I have located Lieutenant Cloud. It was nice to speak with you again Ambassador Wells."

"Cloud here," came the questioning voice. It shifted suddenly with delighted surprise, "Susie! How wonderful it is to see you. What's up?"

Darrell shifted in his seat to get a clear view of the screen and Charles also moved to get a closer look.

"Oh, I am sorry for my familiarity, I see there are others there."

"I'm sorry Elayne for not alerting you to that situation, may I introduce to my right Charles Sullivan. He is our Assistant Secretary of Commerce. To my left is Darrell Fann. He is in charge of our information gathering and analysis."

Elayne smiled with the introductions and it was apparent Darrell was impressed with both her manner and appearance.

Her tone of voice shifted as Susie explained the reason for her call. "Elayne, we sort of have a problem here. Someone inserted a detailed report on the Kreel, even with the video of the Kreel Commander snarling at Kur and it is on the Internet and in all the major outlets all over the world. As you might imagine there is nothing else being talked about on Earth today."

Elayne looked puzzled. "I must confess Susie, I have not been paying much attention to what is happening on Earth, but I will make a note to go over some of our automatic intercepts to catch up. But, why are you calling me?"

"Elayne, we have been comparing notes and our conclusion is that Kur may be responsible for the insertion of the Kreel stories. I am wondering if you can check with him and determine if he is the source and if he is perhaps ask him why he published the reports?"

"Susie, what I can do is check with Commodore Kellon. He is in nearly constant communication with Kur. If I can learn anything, I will let you know."

"Thank you Elayne. Susie out."

Susie closed the communicator lid and slipped it back into her bag. Looking up she saw both Charles and Darrell were looking at her in a very strange manner.

"What's up guys?"

Charles sat back in his chair and looked inquiringly at Susie. "Ambassador Wells, please forgive me for my forgetfulness. You departed Earth, traveled 80 light years, and for the past year have represented the Earth as its sole representative in what is perhaps the most august, influential and powerful assembly humanity has ever developed. I am afraid I tend to forget that set of facts. Again, please forgive my improper question I asked during the beginning of this conversation."

"Susie," added Darrell, "you can put my name as seconding Charles' statement. It is really hard to remember where you've been and the responsibilities you have so skillfully handled."

238

Susie's face flushed with the well-intended comments. "Charles, Darrell, thank you. I am the person who by working with all of you, and everyone associated with the Guardian Force, received the opportunity of ten lifetimes.

As his phone rang Charles looked over and he immediately reached out to pick it up. He whispered, "It's the President."

Lifting the phone to his ear he firmly announced, "Mr. President, Sullivan here."

Darrell and Susie remained quiet as Charles continued his conversation with the President. They were interested in hearing what Charles said yet not wanting to interrupt.

"Yes Sir, we have been working on that precise problem during the morning. Yes Sir, we know the leak is not here. That is firmly established. Yes Sir, we are confident of that. In considering where the story may have come from, our best estimate at this time is the Arkillians. Yes Sir, the Arkillians. No Sir, however Ambassador Wells– oh yes Sir she is here now. Yes Sir, I understand Sir. Well, she has used a back channel of communications to the Guardian Force to determine if the Arkillians were responsible and if they are then to determine the reason for their releasing the information. Yes Sir. You may be certain of that. Thank you Mr. President."

Smiling Charles put the phone down. Looking up toward Susie, his smile broadened. "The President extends to the Ambassador his personal greetings. He told me we were very fortunate to have the assistance of a woman of your capability working with us. I wholeheartedly agree."

The door to the office opened and Lois arrived with a tray filled to overflowing with cups, thermos, pastries and a local newspaper. Most newspapers had long ago vanished as ineffective means of communications, however there were some exceptions. New Washington's pulsing political environment permitted an archaic newspaper to flourish economically.

As Lois distributed the cups and poured the coffee Charles picked up the newspaper and opened to the front page. The headlines were huge. "Alien monsters planning invasion of Earth."

Charles looked at the headline and then again out the window to the beautiful day beyond. *Unfortunately,* he thought, *it is not science fiction this time.*

A soft melodious tone sounded. Susie reached into her carrying bag and again withdrew her communicator. Lifting the lid the screen brightened and the image of Elayne appeared.

"Susie, as you requested, I inquired of the Arkillians if they had knowledge of the news release on Earth about the Kreel. Kur acknowledged that he had placed the stories. I then asked him why. Kur was open about his reasons. He wanted to warn the people of Earth, of the Kreel threat they were facing even as he wants to warn Scion. He told me that given the general self-serving ineptitude of most of Earth's governments it was the least he felt he could do to help the humans on Earth become aware of the reality and seriousness of the Kreel threat."

"Elayne, thank you. Please say hello to everyone for me."

"Susie, you are welcome. I will certainly pass on your greetings. I hope Kur's explanation helps. Cloud out."

Susie closed the lid of the communicator and placed it back in her carrying bag. Looking up toward Charles she commented with a smile, "I have long believed it is better to simply ask, than make assumptions."

Charles reached out and picked up the phone; he pressed a speed dial and then he waited. After a moment the President answered. "Mr. President, Sullivan here, we have confirmation that the Arkillians inserted the news reports into the media channels. They did this to warn the people on Earth of the Kreel threat. Yes Sir that is my information. Who is Council Member Kur? Well Sir, he is a senior member of the Arkillian ruling council. Yes, Sir he is on Monstro. Well, Kur said it was done out of a deep concern for the Earth. Yes Sir, it was a goodwill gesture. The Kreel are a common enemy. Yes Sir. That is correct. Sir. I received the information because of earlier back channel inquiry to the Arkillians by Ambassador Wells. Yes Sir, I can confirm the information is correct and I do confirm it. Thank you Mr. President. Any time."

Charles carefully put the phone down as if it were fragile. Standing he moved around his desk and reached out to snare the bear claw from among the pastries on the tray. "Well, we now know the Arkillians set up the political system to begin with and boy have they proven they also know how to buck it. You may have noticed I didn't quote Kur given the general self-serving ineptitude of most of Earth's governments. I think a pastry with my coffee is about the most politically complex thing to plan at this moment. Beyond that, I believe we will simply sit and watch the fire brigades of Earth's governments see if they can put out the roaring fires. My own guess is they will not be able to do so, at least not this time."

As he lifted the bear claw to take a bite, he mused, "I think the Arkillians and the outraged people of Earth are most probably going to win this political round, hands down."

Chapter Twenty-Two:
Scion

The poised dark masses of the two Guardian Cruisers harmonized and blended with the blackness of the star-speckled void that surrounded them. They were located high above the ecliptic plane and far above Scion's primary. Within moments of one another, they had silently emerged like ghosts from the long transit unanticipated and unseen. Lan and Lent exchanged greetings and reported their conditions being gold, their having accomplished the long Jump from Earth, without problems.

In order to oppose further Kreel intrusion Kellon had left three Cruisers on station in Earth's solar system. His assessment was that after taking notice of two missing fast-attack ships the Kreel would require some time before they could respond. Precisely how much time would elapse before that response arrived near Earth was an unanswerable question. After weighing the potential benefits of helping Kur to warn Scion, Kellon accepted the associated risks and Lan and Lent were committed to make the long Jump.

Kellon had not given final approval for the mission until all five Cruiser AIs were in full agreement with the parameters required for both the outbound Jump and the return Jump. His demand was there were no discernible pitfalls along the Jump route that might prove disastrous for either Lan or Lent. Therefore, before the Jump, the AIs on all five Cruisers worked and validated the Jump equations for several days. With the acquisition of additional data from the newly installed navigation beacons, the AIs were able to smooth out the probabilities of potential disturbances and evade the existing perils. After their analysis and calculations the combined AIs reported there were no unavoidable aberrations. They had been correct and now Lan and Lent were far from Earth. "Lan, dispatch a status report to

Glas Dinnein, with a copy to our squadron. Report the Jump was successful and provide all Jump parameters."

"Reporting." Lan acknowledged.

Together, the two Cruisers moved toward the far side of Scion, remaining above the ecliptic plane. Once above the planet Lan would drop into the planet's concealing shadow and then approach Scion's dark side surface. Lent would remain high above and provide Lan topside protection.

While moving outward from Scion's primary, they diligently scanned the space around them for any indications of other spacecraft, Kreel or Arkillian. Knowing they were penetrating another species' solar system they were on a high alert status, holding a modified Condition 3. Regardless of their current good relationship with Kur the Arkillians in this solar system considered human beings a sub-species and an enemy. Kellon knew that if the Arkillians detected an unidentified spaceship operating in their solar system, it would create unwanted attention. That notice could in turn reach the alert hearing of the Kreel with unforeseeable complicating consequences.

As Lan moved outward from the primary Kellon had remained in CAC observing the tactical plot. Turning from the plot he addressed Navigation. "Roy, you have the CAC."

"Yes Sir, Navigation has the CAC," Commander Grey crisply responded.

As Kellon departed CAC, walking to his conference room, the mission objectives were the cause for his primary concerns. He had acknowledged and accepted the associated risk involved in helping Scion. He knew Kur was a high-ranking government representative of an alien species and more importantly believed he was an individual who held to a strict code of personal honor. Even so, a code of honor only went so far. In bringing Kur aboard Lan, it was necessary for Kellon to take numerous precautionary actions. His intent was to minimize the inevitable leakage of performance data. He could not prevent Kur observing some Guardian technology, but he could minimize such information leakage. Perhaps he had carried the precautionary steps too far, but it was not going to be found in his service record he had played fast and loose with Guardian secrets. As he walked through Lan's passageways, he reviewed in his mind the preparations made for the mission he had set in motion.

Before the Jump Kellon and Roan had carefully planned the transfer of the Council Members from the Nest ship to Shey. They had replaced Shey's normal lifter with a larger eight-person model which barely fit through Shey's hatch.

Using a lifter for transporting personnel from one ship to another in open space was not a normal practice, at least not without the benefit of full battle space armor. However for personnel transport over short distances, safe transfers were possible, since the lifter's force field shield was able to maintain the atmospheric environment around the passengers.

While wearing her bright lovely sinister costume Shey first intercepted and then maneuvered near Monstro holding steady her position abeam of the Nest ship's massive bulk. While Roan remained with Shey, Zorn employed the larger lifter to move from Shey's lifter compartment directly into Monstro's cavernous open forward hangar. As Zorn arrived, the hangar doors ponderously closed behind him and Scion's normal atmospheric pressure flowed into the secured hangar area.

With the establishment of atmospheric pressure within the hangar, Zorn released the force shield and stepped off the lifter onto the deck. Shivering in the hangar's low temperature and thinner atmosphere, he stood, looking about him, examining and interested in the evident signs of recent repair of battle damage. Then, a hatch opened and a small group of Arkillians entered the hangar area moving directly to meet Zorn. Several were obviously in uniforms and three Arkillians were wearing ornate robes.

Having seen Arkillians on video he knew what to expect, nevertheless, this was his first personal encounter with the Arkillians. The strangeness of the hangar, thinner atmosphere and his solitary situation was a cause for some unease. He pushed aside his doubt and turned his thoughts back to his immediate assignment. Focusing on the three Arkillians wearing the robes, Zorn saluted the Arkillian who appeared most senior. "Commander Zorn at your service."

The Arkillian Zorn saluted bowed his head slightly, and then he studied Zorn carefully, noting Zorn's uniform and appearance were impeccable. Kur approved. "Commander Zorn, I am Council Member Kur. I thank you for your offered service."

Turning, with the introductory ice broken Zorn helped the Arkillians secure their few effects to rings located on the lifter. Then he unfolded three more of the chairs from the lifter's deck and helped each Council Member to take their seats and secure their lap restraints. There was some initial alarm within Monstro's crew, at the thought of evacuating the hangar and opening its wide door to the vacuum of space while three Arkillian Council Members were sitting in the middle of the hangar area on nothing more than flimsy appearing chairs. Kur had firmly insisted everything was acceptable, and with some obvious misgivings, the Nest ship's Captain had finally ceased his objections.

The short flight from Monstro back to Shey was uneventful although Rin had expressed his delight and wonder of sitting on a simple chair in wide-open space. Regardless of expressed feelings of confidence, everyone breathed more easily once the lifter entered Shey's small lifter compartment, the hatch securely closed behind them and especially with the restoration of atmospheric pressure. Once safely aboard Shey, everyone was made comfortable.

During Shey's return flight to Lan, Kur contacted the Nest ship's Captain and he assured him they were quite well. Even then, the Captain had expressed his doubts as to the safety of such an obvious flimsy means of conveyance.

Before the Jump to Scion, Kellon instructed the electronics shop on Lan to construct three special small transceivers for the Arkillians. Although the shop constructed the transceivers using non-sensitive technology, their design included a self-destruction of internal components if anyone tampered with them. The transceivers also featured tracking and eavesdropping functions.

Kellon also instructed the shop to fabricate a new sentinel, one much less complicated than the one they had deployed near Earth. Externally it looked like an interplanetary piece of debris, a fragment of rock about the size of a chair. The sentinel was to be positioned in a stationary orbit above Kur's landing site. Its sole function was to receive Kur's low-power signal and then relay it to Lan.

From the beginning, it was Kellon's intent to bug Kur and his fellow Council Members. Kellon did not like the deception yet knew the risks and circumstances warranted his taking all possible steps to gather precise intelligence on what was happening on Scion. The eavesdropping feature built into each transceiver allowed Lan and Lent to monitor conversations wherever the transceivers were. The monitoring function was not continuous but operated in a periodic pulsed compressed burst transmission mode. This allowed superior encryption of the recorded information and minimized the possibility of the Arkillians detecting the covert transmission of data. This meant Kur and the others would be out of direct monitoring for several hours at a time before the bug could update Lan on what was happening. There were two exceptions. If the Arkillian activated the tracking function or Lan initiated a trigger the tracking signal would bundle the existing encrypted recorded data and transmit both the bundle and the tracking signal.

While Kellon lacked any information about the political situation on Scion, Kur was also more than a decade out of date on such topics. Therefore, how the ruling council would respond to Kur's sudden arrival and ominous report was open to speculation. One possible reaction might be they would throw Kur, Ca and Rin into the brig and promptly report to the Kreel.

During the hours that elapsed during Jump, Kur, Ca and Rin had remained aboard Shey. Given his concerns about maintaining security and the Jump being of a duration of a few hours, Kellon deemed restricting the Arkillians to Shey was appropriate.

As part of their planning Kellon and Kur had agreed Lan would see the three Arkillians safely to Scion's surface. The Scouts would transport the three Council Members to a suitable remote location on Scion, as specified by Kur. Afterward, Lan would withdraw into space and wait for Kur's contact report.

The window of opportunity was narrow and Kellon warned Kur that Lan would remain on station for no more than five planetary days before departing for Earth. Kellon informed Kur that if he did not report within those five days then Scion would be strictly on its own to deal with the Kreel threat. In response, Kur had assured Kellon that within five days he could meet with the key Council Members and he would obtain a measure of their reaction to the pending Kreel invasion. He earnestly promised to make contact with Kellon as soon as possible.

X

247

Given the inherent risks involved Kellon felt he had minimized the threat to Earth and the squadron, while also meeting Admiral Cloud's mandate. As Kellon entered his conference room, he noticed a thermos of neab was on the side table along with a covered dish of cheese. Gratefully, he poured a cup of neab, lifted the lid off the plate of cheese and selected a nice piece. He then moved to and took his seat at the head of the small conference table.

Having sampled the cheese and sipped his neab Kellon centered his thoughts. "Lan, please connect me with Captain Eurie onboard Lent."

"Connecting." Lan responded.

The bulkhead shimmered and Eurie's image filled the screen. "Commodore that was a smooth transition. It seemed flawless."

"Yes, I agree it was very smooth. Eurie, it's good to have you and Lent backing us up in a potentially hostile solar system."

"Why Kellon," teased Eurie, "I would be deeply hurt to learn if you gave another woman the same compliments you give me."

Kellon shook his head and smiled broadly, "Rest confident Eurie you are the only woman in my life that I give such compliments to. Surely you know by now your undeniable charms combined with Lent's impressive combat proficiency makes you utterly irresistible."

Eurie smiled at the light banter and then she grew serious. "Commodore, upon entering the system we detected three Kreel fast-attack ships. I have been observing them since their detection. They are not following a trajectory that would either approach or depart Scion. If I were guessing, they look to be on a covert surveillance mission within the system."

"We are also tracking those ships. Arriving in the magnetic plume and well above Scion's primary, seems to have effectively masked our Jump signatures. However, the Kreel presence makes our work here doubly more difficult. We are going to need to keep very tight controls on our baffles and propulsion signature suppression."

Turning to her left, Eurie looked toward someone Kellon could not see. After a moment, she turned back. "Commodore, we have just detected another three Kreel fast-attack ships further around the solar system. We are still resolving their trajectory. I think we need to talk to our Arkillian friends."

"Keep scanning Eurie, we are not in a hurry to get into trouble here. I will check with Kur and get back. Kellon out."

"Sir," Lan interjected, "we are also monitoring the second group of three Kreel fast-attack ships that Lent reported. They are apparently following a trajectory not approaching Scion. I agree with Captain Eurie's assessment, they appear to be performing a discrete surveillance of Scion."

Sitting back in his chair Kellon considered the implications of six Kreel warships skulking about in the Arkillian system and did not like the implications. "Lan, connect me with Commander Roan on Shey."

The image on the bulkhead shimmered again and Roan's familiar image appeared standing within Shey and showing Kur and Zorn in the background. "Roan, I need to speak with Kur."

Acknowledging Roan turned to Kur, "Council Member Kur, Commodore Kellon would like to speak with you."

As Kellon watched Kur stood up and moved to where Roan was standing. Turning toward the video display he asked, "Honored Kellon may I assume we have begun our trip to Scion?"

Kellon paused for a moment and then spoke with discretion. "Council member Kur, as you will recall, we agreed some things you will observe during this trip must remain secret."

"Yes honored Kellon,on the honor of my Nest was the pledge made."

"Council Member Kur, we have not begun our trip to Scion. We have completed the trip." Kellon carefully observed Kur's facial markings. He was confident the markings were those of an Arkillian experiencing a severe shock.

"Honored Kellon, how am I to keep the time we have spent traveling, some 30 hours since I boarded your ship, a secret? If I were to tell anyone the time required to travel from Earth to Scion on your ship they would consider me having lost my senses. I would be gently escorted away for medical observation and treatment."

Kellon smiled. "I do understand. Even so, you may wish to say you are merely uncertain, everything being so strange. In the spirit of dissemination perhaps days for hours might assist you if such dissemination becomes necessary. I am confident, with your experience on the political stage you will be able to find the appropriate words to avoid the subject."

Kur brightened, "Honored Kellon, what matters days or hours, in either case I would be deemed mad."

Kellon smiled at Kur's response. *Where there is the ability for humor between two species,* he thought, *there exists hope for peace.*

"I am now communicating to inform you we are observing six Kreel fast-attack ships within your home solar system. They seem to be on a discrete reconnaissance patrol. Is such a Kreel presence in Scion's solar system normal?"

Kur's shock had faded and Kellon recognized what he believed denoted anger markings emerge.

"No, certainly not. Such an intrusion into our solar system by six Kreel warships constitutes an aggressive breach of our treaty with the Kreel."

"Can your Arkillian military monitor these Kreel ships?"

Kur was obviously troubled. "Our military might detect them, if we were actively on alert status and observing. Without a cause I doubt our military is on alert or looking for a Kreel threat. Regretfully, most likely, the Kreel ships are operating under the veil of our own carelessness and are not being monitored."

"Council member Kur we will continue to track the Kreel warships and we will provide you with the updated tracking data when you arrive on Scion.

"The designated safe landing coordinates you have provided, are moving into the planet's dark side. We are currently moving to bring our ship into the planet's shadow and we should be in position to convey you to the surface very soon. I recommend you begin to prepare for departure."

"Honored Kellon, that we have arrived so soon near Scion is a wonder. We have the special small communications devices you have provided and all the necessary information. We are ready to depart."

Leaning forward Kellon was frowning trying to cover all the last minute details, leaving nothing to chance. "I am requesting that you activate the tracker signal periodically on your communication devices so we are able determine your location."

"Honored Kellon, I will see our tracker signals are discreetly activated when we move from one location to another. It is helpful for all concerned if you know our precise location and remain informed of our political status."

"Commander Roan, prepare your Scouts for deployment." Kellon ordered.

"Yes Sir!" "Kellon out."

"Sir," interjected Lan, "we are now above the dark side of the planet, as instructed, and holding our relative position above the planet."

"Lan, connect me with Captain Eurie."

"Connecting."

Eurie's image appeared on the bulkhead screen and she looked serious. "Commodore, we are now tracking another three fast-attack ships. That makes nine Kreel fast-attack ships known to be within the solar system. They are widely dispersed, however one of the groups is moving in a direction that may become a problem to Lan near Scion."

"Understood. Eurie, remain near this position in full stealth mode. Maintain Lent on Condition 2. I spoke with Kur. A Kreel military presence in Scion's solar system represents a breach of their treaty. Therefore, both the Kreel and the Guardian represent uninvited guests. If we need to fight our way out then we will at least be able to do so without insulting the Arkillians. With nine Kreel ships this close it must mean the Kreel are in their pre-invasion surveillance mode. We will continue to follow the mission profile. You are to stay high and remain purely covert. Stay out of trouble and watch Lan's back. If the reaper breaks out Lan will be coming your way fast. Lan is now prepared to proceed down into the dark side cone of the planet and complete the transfer of the Arkillians. I hope to be back in a very few hours. Just make certain you stay undiscovered and out of trouble."

"Kellon, this high above the ecliptic plane the chances of a full stealth Guardian Cruiser being discovered is slight. However, just for you, I will make an extra effort to remain stealthy. Because I have not forgotten you still owe me a glass of wine I fully expect to collect."

Her warm banter was always a welcome diversion and Kellon was smiling. "Now you've discovered why Lent is covering Lan's back. It's comforting to know someone wants to protect me because of a large debt needing to be paid. Just remember Eurie, Lent is the silent observer."

"Be advised Commodore, Lent is on station, Status 2 and observing. Lan's back is well-covered. Fair winds and good fortune Kellon."

"Thank you. Kellon out."

Standing Kellon pushed the chair beneath the conference table. He then departed the conference room and as he walked to CAC he told Lan, "suspend verbal responses."

Entering the CAC, he heard the general announcement sound, Commodore in CAC. *There are times,* he thought, *when tradition goes a step too far.*

Sitting in his command chair, Kellon looked around the CAC. Everyone was busy at his or her task. They were ready. He turned toward Commander Grey, "Roy, I have the CAC. Take us down."

"Yes Sir, the Commodore has the CAC. Taking us down."

Given his orders Lan dropped swiftly through space and within an hour entered into the dark side shadow of the planet. Those working in CAC occasionally looked up to see the surface of the planet growing larger on the forward bulkhead screens. Everyone was tense. "Lan, keep us in the dark shadow and move us to thirty thousand kilometers above the planet, then maintain that position within the shadow. Remain in full stealth mode. "

Lan's acknowledging tone sounded.

Kellon watched the full screen display on the right of the plot board and observed the image of Scion as it drew closer. As Lan moved to the selected position Kellon studied the tactical plot noting the positions of the three Kreel groups. Two were far out of position and did not represent a threat, however the third group was moving widdershins in the ecliptic plane and they would soon be at their closest point of approach, 500 thousand kilometers further out. That group of Kreel ships was the nearest to the planet, and they would need to be carefully watched.

Lan's acknowledgment chime again sounded, denoting he was on station as ordered.

"Lan, connect me with Roan."

The connection was nearly instantaneous. "Sir, Roan here."

"Roan, we have three Kreel fast-attack ships patrolling nearby. You have about forty minutes to launch and drop before they reach CPA and come within their possible detection range.

Keep it smooth and tight. If the landing site is not safe, return. We can try again later. I do not want any Guardian presence remaining on the planet, either intact or in little pieces. Am I making myself fully understood?"

"Sir fully understood. We are prepared for immediate launch." "Roan, take care. Fair winds at your back. Kellon out."

"Lan, coordinate with Commander Roan and launch the Scout ships on his countdown," Kellon ordered.

Kellon observed the golden lights on the status board indicating hangar status switch from gold to blue. Throughout Lan the distinct sound of four hangar doors opening and then shortly afterward closing, announced the Scouts were gone. Lan's four Scout ships were launched and dropping through the darkness toward the Arkillian home planet.

Keying the general communications band Kellon briefed the crew. "Kellon here, our Scout ships are launched and Lan is currently providing top cover. As I am speaking, the four Scouts are now dropping down to the planet with the Arkillians. We have a Kreel patrol approaching several hundred thousand kilometers out, therefore, pay careful attention to all stealth parameters. Stop where you are and review what you are doing. Let's keep Lan invisible. Kellon out."

Sitting back Kellon continued to study the tactical plot. It was now up to Roan and the Scouts. All Lan and his crew could do was wait on station and sweat it out. Kellon knew far above Lent was also silently observing as the Kreel approached. That Lent was near and providing cover considerably eased Kellon's concerns. His mention of Lent's well-known combat proficiency was right on the mark.

X

Long before the Arkillians had arrived aboard Shey, Guardian Force had classified the fact that Guardian ships were AI entities. It remained a closely guarded secret. Shey was therefore somewhat baffled. How could the Arkillians be aboard her and not know of her existence? When she considered herself as being a secret she enjoyed the feeling. She was special. Even though her orders prohibited her from speaking where the Arkillians might overhear her, she had no such inhibition keeping her from remaining vigilant.

The precise location on Scion where Council Member Kur asked to land was well marked in her charts. He had told them it was his winter Nest and it should now be unoccupied. As she dropped, keeping in tight close communications with her sisters, Shey was looking in all directions checking the designated landmarks watching for any spacecraft, aircraft or any other threat above her, or below her on the ground. She was especially watching her sensors for anything that looked like the Kreel. While doing all these things she continued to monitor the progress of the three Kreel ships far above as they approached their CPA. If the three Kreel ships continued on their way after they reached their CPA she knew that would be good.

Roan was wearing funny looking things on his head. Roan had called them earphones. While she did not know where he found such devices they did allow her to speak to him without anyone else hearing what she was saying. It was all part of the fun.

The Scouts loved to show off but when they were doing so it was also preparation for their deadly serious work. When they had dropped down Earthward over New Washington they had used the opportunity as a precision drill for practicing maneuvers, such as they were performing tonight. Now the gaiety of showing off over Washington was absent. As the four Scout ships dropped toward the dark planet below each Scout was clad in flat black war paint in full stealth mode, alert and scanning for potential threats. As they passed 6 kilometers in altitude only Shey continued to descend. The remaining three Scouts took a topside defensive triangle position with Shey at its center. As Lan was providing high top cover they were there to provide a similar function but nearer to ground. As Shey reached an altitude of two kilometers she came to a gentle stop. In Roan's funny looking earphones she reported. "Roan, we are directly above the indicated coordinates and at 2 kilometers."

The three Arkillians were sitting in the mess area and Roan was projecting the outside night vision view on a bulkhead in that area. He keyed his microphone and said, "Council Member Kur, we are directly above the coordinate you have provided. We are detecting no air traffic or anything to suggest ground patrols. Do you see anything that alerts you to a hidden threat?"

"No, Commander Roan, the area looks normal and quiet. There should be a structure at the coordinates I provided. Can you make the image closer so we can better see the ground?" Kur inquired. There was a distinct hint of excitement in his voice.

"Yes Sir. I will adjust the view to one thousand meters."

Shey heard what Kellon wanted and made the necessary adjustments.

"Commander Roan," Kur's excited voice exclaimed, "there in the upper right hand corner. That is my winter Nest. Can you put us down anywhere near there with safety?"

Roan looked carefully at his sensors. Turning to Zorn he asked, "Zorn, do you see anything I don't see?"

Focused intently on his instrumentation Zorn did not even look up. "No, Zorn replied. "However, give me a minute more. I want to complete a detailed infra-red scan of the area."

Shey was also scanning. All she noted was an aircraft far off and it was moving away from and not toward their position. "Roan, Shey here, I see nothing indicating a threat."

"Zorn here, I agree with Shey. It looks clear."

Roan keyed his microphone again. "Council Members, the area appears clear. Please pick up your material, we are going down."

"Zorn, drop us to 700 meters and hold."

"Dropping," Zorn acknowledged.

Roan reached over and depressed a key and a sheet of paper appeared out of a slot. Picking the paper up he folded it twice and then slipped it into his pocket.

Turning to Zorn with a grin he ordered, "Take care of the place until I come back. I especially do not want to see any new funny looking holes that were not here when I left."

Zorn did not look up, keeping his eyes focused on the instruments before him. "Understood, no new holes!"

Roan removed the bulky, but very efficient, earphones and moved back into the mess area. He found the three Arkillians excitedly standing there waiting.

"Council Members, please remain very quiet until you are safely on the ground. Follow me."

Roan quickly moved to the lifter compartment and entered. He stepped onto the lifter and erected four of the chairs, locking them in position. He indicated the chairs to the Arkillians and they stepped onto the lifter and took their chairs as they had practiced. Roan took his own chair while he watched to be certain they fastened their lap restraints. Then he keyed his microphone. "Roan here. We are ready. If we are still clear, let's get this show on the road."

"Zorn responded, "still clear."

The lights in the hangar dimmed, the hatch opened, the lifter immediately scooted out the port and dropped toward the distant structure that Kur had previously identified.

The lifter's force screen was in place, effectively blocking any buffeting by the air currents and the drop was both rapid and utterly silent. Within minutes the lifter slowly settled lightly to the ground and the force shield collapsed.

Standing, Roan helped the three Arkillians to their feet and then assisted them to gather all the material that they brought with them. Stepping to the ground and turning, Roan faced Kur and smartly saluted. "Council Member Kur, it has been my pleasure to return you home to Scion. Be careful. You are on Scion but I suspect there are great intrigues and considerable risk before you. Remember to keep your transceivers near and be careful when you use them."

Reaching into his pocket Roan withdrew the folded piece of paper and extended it to Kur. "Sir, these are the current blocks of tracking data for the three groups of Kreel ships we were monitoring. The data gets cold quickly but it may help your military get on target."

Kur recognized Roan's gesture as a salute and bent his head in formal recognition. "Commander Roan, may your paths be filled with long life, peace and prosperity. We thank Zorn and you for your hospitality and especially for returning us to our home."

Reaching out, Kur accepted the folded piece of paper with appreciation. Then the three Arkillians stood back as Roan again took his seat. He keyed his microphone and ordered, "Zorn, they are safe on the ground. Bring me home."

Swiftly and silently Roan rose into the darkness. From the Arkillians' vantage point he simply vanished silently into the night sky above and was gone. They stood looking upward for a while longer then Kur turned and began moving quickly toward his winter Nest, not more than fifty meters distant. Ca and Rin quickly followed.

A few minutes later the lifter slid softly into and came to rest in Shey's darkened lifter compartment. The hatch closed firmly behind Roan and the compartment light brightened. He removed his lap restraint and then moved quickly forward, moving to Shey's control room.

Taking his seat and fastening his lap restraint he asked, "are we still clear?"

Zorn was still studying his instruments and responded, "so far, so good. The Kreel fast-attack ships are well past their CPA. They seem to be moving blithely on their contrary ways."

Roan took a deep breath. "Shey, young lady, I want you to be very careful regarding our propulsion signature."

"Yes Sir. Scanning all stealth settings and verifying settings are full stealth." Sitting back Zorn let out a deep sigh and turned to look at Roan. "Roan, Kur and the others have safely reached the structure and have entered. We are now clear, so let's go home."

Quickly scanning his own instrumentation Roan nodded in agreement. "Shey, very carefully ease us up to six kilometers. We need to regroup with the other Scouts."

"Shey slowly rose like a dry leaf in a gentle breeze and soon was at six kilometers and holding. Roan gave the assembly order and Shey began swiftly rising toward the heavens in the close company of Lan's three other Scouts.

X

Far above Shey and the other Scout ships Kellon was tense, as he observed the Kreel patrol sweeping past their CPA and continuing on. The next two hours slowly passed as Lan waited on station.

Commander Shaw looked toward Kellon with a smile, "Tactical here, our four Scout ships are approaching."

Kellon let out a breath, revealing his inner tension. That he had four Scout ships on or near the surface of an alien planet and Kreel ships were patrolling nearby was not a comfortable situation.

"Lan, proceed with the coordinated retrieval of your Scout ships." Kellon observed the plot board, watched the icons representing the Kreel continue to move away and watched as the four symbols for the Guardian Scout ships drew near. Then Kellon heard the sounds of hangar doors opening and shortly thereafter closing. The hangar lights on the status board again cycled from blue to gold. Lan's Scouts were home.

"Lan, activate verbal response. Verify all Scouts are recovered and provide status of each."

"Lan here, confirming all Scouts are safely aboard. All Scouts reporting status gold."

The Scouts were aboard and Kellon again smiled. "Lan, connect me with Roan."

"Commodore, Roan here."

"Well done Roan. Were there any problems?"

"No Sir. The area was clear. We were able to land Kur within a hundred meters of his home. We remained on station while observing all the Arkillians safely reach the structure and then enter."

"Commander Roan, you continue to make the difficult look routine. Well done. Kellon out."

"Lan, launch the prepared sentinel and relays."

"The sentinel is programmed, as are the relays. Launching is completed." Lan confirmed.

Kellon keyed the general communications band. "Kellon here, we have completed the first step of our mission. Lan's Scouts have skillfully landed the Arkillians safely on Scion. We are withdrawing to a high position to monitor the surrounding space for several days. The Kreel patrols are in the area so constant care is required. You have performed your tasks in a professional manner, well done. Kellon out."

Kellon sat for a few minutes looking at the tactical plot as he studied the movement of the Kreel ships. He keyed his command band. "Well done everyone. Commander Grey, you have the CAC. Please extract Lan from Scion's dark side. Move us up to link up with Lent. I will be in my conference room. Kellon out."

Chapter Twenty-Three:
Friends of Our Nests

Three days had passed slowly while both Lan and Lent remained concealed well above the ecliptic plane, staying alert and patiently gathering the intelligence intercepts from Kur. In order to monitor Arkillian military communications Kellon had discretely sent several reconnaissance probes near the planet. He did not know what the Kreel might be monitoring but Lan's probes were indicating a steady ramping up of military communications traffic. It appeared the Arkillian military was quietly heeding Kur's warning. Although Kur had not yet communicated with Kellon on several occasions he activated his tracking function, updating his location and transmitting a new burst of encrypted data. Each update confirmed they were still located at Kur's winter Nest. Kellon considered the transmissions the means Kur was using to reassure him all was going well.

Lieutenant Cloud and her team were busy at their intelligence consoles sifting through intercepts coming from Lan and Lent's probes. They were discarding the data deemed unimportant and ranking what remained. The translators working with Elayne were also busy transcribing the bundled transmissions arriving from the three Council Members. Everyone in CAC, on both Lent and Lan, were working overtime. While all this was happening the tactical groups on Lan and Lent were also monitoring all inbound and departing spaceship traffic. It was soon obvious, to everyone working in Intelligence, Scion was a busy planet since there was a steady stream of space ships arriving and departing. If Scion's space traffic was any indication, the Arkillian Empire was flourishing.

On the fourth day Kur established contact with Kellon. His call came in clear reaching Kellon in his private quarters. There was no video, only Kur's voice transmission. "Honored Kellon, are you able to receive this transmission?"

"Council Member Kur, I am receiving your communications. There is a slight time lag, but otherwise your signal is very clear. How are things proceeding where you are?"

"Things here are very hectic. No one had expected Ca, Rin or me to be anywhere near Scion. Our rather unexpected arrival on Scion was the source for general excitement and many questions. "I was able to contact the three ranking members of the Ruling Council and asked them to meet with me at my winter Nest. I also requested they bring senior military personnel. It took more than a day before the meeting began. We have been in meetings ever since. This is the first moment I have had alone to call you."

Standing up from his desk, Kellon walked over to his comfortable chair, as he listened to Kur's update. "Honorable Kur, how was your news received?"

"As you had imagined. At first, there was considerable questioning about what had happened to the Nest ship. I needed to recount our battle more than a year ago. They were all in wonder at what had happened and it was a shock. Our control of Earth is very long standing and the Council thought its place in our empire was unchanging. It is hard for many Council Members to believe what has happened and even more difficult for them to understand. Our arrogance is a steep barrier, a barrier over which the Council must climb. When I brought forth the information that you provided about the Kreel they were disbelieving. They studied the material, but were suspicious, believing it may be a trick. In truth, they did not believe it.

"The recordings of my exchanges with the Kreel commander was what altered their understanding. None on the Council could mistake the threat in what that Kreel officer said. When he brashly said I might be allowed to clean toilets with surviving members of the ruling council, that comment brought with it great anger. Everyone was outraged. They then quickly took the Kreel threat seriously.

"I then gave them the data block that showed Kreel warships were already in our space. Of course, four days have passed and the data is out of date. Even so our military is now going slowly onto a full alert. All tracking facilities are being crewed and military command is discretely calling key military personnel back to full duty stations.

"Honored Kellon, the military is asking if you can provide current coordinates for the Kreel ships."

"Honored Kur, give me a minute and I will have that data for you. There are still three groups of three Kreel fast-attack ships each."

Kellon closed his microphone and then asked Lan for the latest bearings from Scion's primary to the three groups of Kreel ships. Within a matter of seconds, the data was on the screen before Kellon.

Again, Kellon keyed his microphone, "Honored Kur, are you prepared to write down the vector information?"

"Yes, I have such capability."

Kellon took the next several minutes verbally passing the vectors of the Kreel warships and Kur acknowledged each set of coordinate vector data as he received it.

"Honored Kellon, Scion is indebted to you for your help. We are discretely preparing for what we now know to be coming. The Ruling Council has authorized me to express Scion's gratitude to you. Any further information or direct assistance you may be able to provide is humbly requested and deeply appreciated with considerations provided. From this moment on the Arkillian Council has declared Earth and you are friends of our nests."

"In saying this, I must tell you, one major reason for the enormous change in the Ruling Council's attitude was the bi-lateral trade agreement. Given the circumstances and outcome of our battle preceding the negotiation of that agreement it was hard for the Council to believe its balance and even-handedness. They have had several days to study and consider the ramifications of the trade agreement. They are still in a state of wonderment. When you next speak to Ambassador Wells you are requested to express the respect of the entire Ruling Council for her wisdom."

"Secondly, the mercy you showed to our Nest ship has made a deep and lasting impression on those who have learned of what has happened. The joy of the nests of those who have survived the battle is overflowing. It has greatly helped in the Council reconsidering their previous attitudes."

Returning to his desk and again sitting down, Kellon listened and was aware of Kur's sincerity.

"Honored Kur, I wish to acknowledge the sincerity your ruling Council has expressed toward Earth and others as being friends of your nests. We understand and accept the offer of your good will. We will do all we can to assist you in this mutual time of peril. Also, please send our most sincere condolences to the nests that lost members in the battle. Their loss is also felt by us."

There was a quite noticeable pause and Kellon sat waiting for Kur to continue the conversation. When Kur came on again he was obviously excited.

"Honored Kellon, I passed your vectors to the Kreel ships to a military runner. He has come back breathless saying that our tracking stations have found each of the Kreel formations. They have confirmed your data. There is considerable excitement. It is one thing when someone tells us the Kreel are planning to attack but quite another to see Kreel warships already in our solar system. If there was still doubt, there is none remaining."

"Honored Kur, will you, or any of the others, desire to return to Earth and your Nest ship?"

"How much time do I have before you must have an answer?"

"Given the destruction of the two Kreel ships near Earth and the possible Kreel response I must begin my return to Earth within the next twelve hours. Will eight hours provide you sufficient time to decide?"

"Eight hours is adequate. There is much happening here. Is there anything you want to pass to the Council at this time?"

"No, except perhaps to say thank you for the hospitality of your volume of space." Kellon would have sworn he heard Kur laugh but then thought he could be mistaken.

"Honored Kellon, you will always be welcome in Scion space. Kur out."

Looking up at the picture of Earth and its moon, with Lan brilliantly glowing in the foreground, Kellon sat thinking for a long time. *The power of good humor, kindness, and expressions of sincere integrity should never be underestimated. Admiral Cloud, it is your wisdom that needs acknowledgment, yours and Ambassador Susie Wells'.*

"Lan, take a message to Guardian Headquarters, attention Admiral Cloud."

"Ready." Lan responded.

"Admiral Cloud: Following your orders, Lan and Lent have entered Scion's solar system. We have found the Kreel here in what we believe is a preparation for invasion. We have maintained contact with the Scion government representatives that we escorted back to Scion. I am now in receipt of an offer of friendship and good will between Scion and Earth and others. Scion is preparing discretely for the invasion they now know is coming. They have humbly requested any direct help we may be able to extend to Scion."

"Lan and Lent will be beginning our return to Earth in approximately eight hours. I extend to you my most sincere compliments Commodore Kellon. Guardian Cruiser Lan out."

"Lan please read it back." Lan did so and with a few changes Kellon told Lan to send it under a Black Hole classification to Guardian Headquarters.

"Lan connect me to a hookup with Lent and your general communications channel."

"Hookup established, Lent is acknowledging ready."

"Guardian personnel, Kellon here. I am able to report that our mission to Scion is successful. Council Member Kur has carried the warning of the pending Kreel attack to his government. After four days of meetings, all barriers within the Arkillian ruling council have collapsed. The Arkillian military is now coming to full alert and tracking the Kreel ships now in their system. Most importantly, because of your courage and skills, we have established a peaceful relationship with a species that was our enemy before today. I cannot overstate the significance of this remarkable achievement. I commend each of you for your professionalism and contributions."

"We will be beginning our return to Earth in about eight hours. Everyone should be preparing for the long Jump. I thank each and every one of you and my thanks especially to Captain Eurie. Lent you are in very good hands. Kellon out."

Kellon's communicator activated and Lan announced, "Captain Eurie calling, Are you able to receive the call?"

"Yes Lan, patch her through."

The bulkhead brightened and Eurie's clear image appeared. Her smile was brilliant.

"Commodore, I cannot tell you how wonderful it is to be on a Guardian mission that has established peace on peaceful terms. I cannot remember it happening before."

"I fully understand Eurie. It's a new one for me also. I can't take credit for this achievement. It was Admiral Cloud that sent me out with specific instructions to try to bring this about. Frankly, I did not believe it could ever happen."

"Kellon, how much time do we have before the Kreel strike?"

"I don't know. I do know that Admiral Cloud is wringing every intelligence intercept dry to discover that but the lag time between his sending us an update and our receiving it makes things hard to evaluate. We may have weeks, months or hours. I simply do not know. What I do know is I have a bad feeling about leaving only three cruisers to protect Earth. They are capable, however our destroying the two Kreel ships was a red flag signal to the Kreel Hub. Their normal response will be a strong patrol coming in force. We need to get back to Earth."

"Kellon, I will have Lent join with Lan and they can begin making the adjustments for our return Jump. I presume we will be Jumping from the northern plume point where we entered?"

"Yes, we will Jump from there to the equivalent point above Sol. Lan, are you copying?"

"Yes Sir. Lent and I are both listening. We will commence computations immediately."

Kellon laughed. "One thing is for certain Eurie, anything we say needs to be discrete, we have children listening to every word."

"Agreed. Again, well-done Commodore. Eurie out."

The next eight hours went by quickly, there being considerable work required to prepare for a long Jump. When Kur's communication arrived Kellon was in his conference room. Kur's voice sounded tired but it was firm,

"Honored Kellon. I send our warm regards. After considerable discussion it is the decision of the Council that our Nest ship should seek the refuge of Earth's solar system until we have precise information concerning the Kreel plans for the attack. When you inform the Captain of this decision, to assure him the message is genuine, you must provide him with a code phrase. Please tell the Captain the desert flowers are blooming."

Kellon smiled inwardly. *Everyone has secrets.* "Council Member Kur, I take it none will be returning to Earth at this time?"

"You are correct. The Council believes we can contribute more to defending Scion here than by returning to Earth. There is much we must do in preparing for the Kreel attack. We understand the Kreel and know how they think. We believe they will wish to gloat at close range before they initiate their attack. Be assured we will diligently work to reduce what they have to gloat about."

"Council Member Kur, having seen firsthand your courage and capability I have no doubt the Kreel will pay dearly for any attack on Scion."

There was a long pause before Kur responded, "Honored Kellon. I know not if we will ever have an opportunity to speak with each other again. If this is the last time for us to speak with one another then know that I hold you in sincere respect. I hope a time may come when in the spring time I may show you the beauty of the desert and the fields of flowers that adorn Scion's hills and valleys."

"Honored Kur, I look forward to such a time of mutual peace. Please guard the small transceivers. If we are able to return we will try to contact you using them as our communications link. Believe you have friends and we will do what we can to help. I do not yet know how much help we may be, but know this, we will help, if possible. Now I must return to Earth. Even now, I am concerned the Kreel are moving to learn what became of their two ships."

"I understand. We will guard your transceivers. May fortune pave your paths Kellon, friend and warrior. Kur out."

Sitting back in his chair Kellon deeply sighed. He had done what he could to help the Arkillians.

Kellon keyed his Command band. "Navigation, Kellon here. Move Lan and Lent back to the Jump point above the primary. We will be making the long Jump to Earth, when the Jump parameters are completed."

"Navigation here, understood."

"Lan, just prior to our Jump transmit a control signal to the three transceivers on Scion. We want to inhibit them from further transmission of encrypted data. At the same time signal the sentinel and relays to self-destruct. We will not be leaving anything behind to provide clues for the Kreel."

"Yes Sir. The orders will be transmitted just prior to Jump."

The next hours were busy, the crew making final preparations for a long Jump. Each Cruiser AI was busy, checking and verifying the most recent data downloaded from the intervening navigations beacons.

Just prior to making the Jump Kellon called Eurie. It took a minute before she was able to respond.

"Kellon, everything is set here. We are waiting for Lan's countdown. Is there anything new?"

"Eurie, we will be in a communications blackout during the Jump. I still have a premonition about Kreel trouble. Have Lent at full stealth and set combat Condition 2 when exiting from Jump. Lan will do the same. I hope I am wrong about this but unfortunately the Kreel are noted for being predictable."

"Kellon I agree. Lent will be at full stealth Condition 2 on exiting the Jump. Safe passage Kellon."

"Eurie, I am looking forward to that glass of wine, Kellon out." "Lan, how much time do we have before the Jump?"

"Sir, we are at twenty minutes and counting."

Kellon stood and looked around. Everything was as it should be, put in its place and secured. He turned and exiting his conference room walked to CAC. As he entered, he heard the announcement, "Commodore in CAC." *This time the announcement sounds proper,* Kellon thought.

Taking his command chair, he looked about. It was hard for him to express what he was feeling. The men and women in Lan's crew and Lan himself were his family. He was very proud of them. Keying the general intercom line Kellon addressed Lan's crew, "Kellon here, we have just completed a good job and done it well. We have made history. In thirty hours, we will be arriving in Earth's solar system. When we exit the Jump we will be in full stealth mode and Condition 2. Upon exiting, I want everyone here fully prepared to fight as if we were defending Glas Dinnein. Kellon out."

Commander Grey turned with a smile and looking at Kellon held up his right hand in acknowledgment and full agreement. Then he returned to his duty.

As Lan prepared to enter the Jump, Kellon's mind was contemplating what military assets they would need to defend Scion and the Earth. He hoped Admiral Cloud's intelligence gathering would provide sufficient warning while knowing hope was not a substitute for military power and good tactics. Kellon barely heard Lan's countdown, "Three, two, one, Jump!"

Chapter Twenty-Four:
Heretic Tacticians

Lan's position was far above Sol and concealed within its magnetic plume. Emerging from the long Jump Lan was in full stealth mode and battle ready, Condition 2. For this very reason Lan escaped detection upon exit from Jump and evaded probable destruction. Barely nine thousand kilometers distant three Kreel ships were maneuvering, a cruiser and two fast-attack ships. They were positioned below and moving away from Lan, their general motion being toward Earth.

As Tactical screens updated Commander Shaw's well-modulated calm voice called out the tactical status. "Contact! We've one Kreel cruiser bearing 043 degrees relative at nine thousand kilometers. One Kreel fast-attack ship bearing 046 degrees relative at eleven thousand kilometers. A second fast-attack bearing 41 degrees relative at twelve thousand kilometers. The elevation of the target is minus twenty-one degrees. Lan has exited from Jump astern of the Kreel and he is now in their baffles."

Sitting in CAC at the moment of Lan's exit from long Jump Kellon was tense. His sense of unease had increased during the hours of transit from Scion. Now, he focused his attention on responding to the immediate tactical threat.

"Kellon here, Fire Control bring six heavy missiles to Condition 2. Set all missiles passive. Allocate four missiles against the cruiser. Assign one missile against each fast-attack ship. Make it happen!"

"Tactical here, I am getting updates from Guardian monitors. The monitors have not detected the Kreel cruiser and his escorts concealed in the primary's magnetic plume. The monitors are however reporting two groups of Kreel ships approaching Earth from the system's rim. The Kreel entered the heliosphere forty degrees above the ecliptic plane, on two radial lines thirty degrees apart converging on Earth. Their tactics are the classic converging Kreel fork. They are now approaching the orbit of the sixth planet and they are moving at 100 lights, directly toward Earth."

"Fire Control here, confirming six heavy missiles are set passive, Condition 2. Confirming four passive locks on the cruiser. Confirming one passive lock on each of two fast-attack ships. Standing by."

"Fire Control, Kellon here. Set salvoes of two missiles each. First salvo is the Kreel cruiser. Second salvo is one missile against each fast-attack. Third salvo is against the cruiser. Set Condition 1. Fire!"

Throughout Lan everyone heard the unmistakable rumble of heavy missiles being rapidly launched.

"Fire Control here, six missiles away."

"Countermeasures Kellon here. Get a suppression screen out, jam those Kreel ships!"

"Navigation, Commander Grey where is Lent?"

"Sir, Navigation here. Looking, I don't see Lent."

"Fire Control, bring all lasers and gun turrets to anti-missile point-defense mode. Set Condition 1."

"Tactical, Lorn, is there a sign of Lent?"

"Tactical here, no Sir."

Leaning forward in his command chair, Kellon observed the icons of the missiles closing on their designated targets. He noticed he was holding his breath and consciously willed his breathing to a normal rhythm.

"Tactical here, we have four hits against the cruiser and he is breaking up. We have one hit and one miss against the two fast attacks. One fast attack has exploded."

"Fire Control set two medium missiles passive-active. Set enabling at 70% of run length. When passive lock is confirmed on the target, set Condition 1!" Kellon ordered.

"Fire control here, two medium missiles are set passive-active.

Confirming passive lock. Target is running. Missiles away."

Whispering throughout Lan came the distinct sounds of multiple medium missiles being launched. There followed silence and a pause as if the entire crew was holding its breath waiting for Tactical's report.

"Tactical here, we have two hits. The target has exploded. The local area is clear."

"Kellon here, Countermeasures terminate jamming."

"Fire Control, Kellon here. Set point-defense laser and gun turrets to Condition 3."

Whatever its cause, Kellon was feeling giddy. Perhaps it was the momentary intoxication of adrenaline telling him everyone was still alive! He knew to the core of his being, how close they had come to being space cold dead. Only the random chance of exiting the jump in the baffles of the Kreel had saved them. He knew it could have been just the opposite. They could have exited from Jump directly in the Kreel's gun sights. He knew their still being alive was not because of his skill or experience. Everyone on board Lan was alive because of pure random chance!

Sitting in his chair Kellon fought the mental desire to allow his body to tremble. He worked at the problem of mind/body balance and his body positively responded to his mental urgings. Even so, he was not in a hurry to try to stand up. Relaxing he steadied his breathing to a slow regular rhythm.

"Tactical here, we have a Guardian network update. Early warning is tracking two groups of Kreel ships. Confirming each group consists of one cruiser and two escorting fast-attack ships. They are high above the ecliptic plane and moving steadily toward Earth at 100 lights."

"Guardian Force, three defending Cruisers and their Scouts have deployed in a three-layered defense. Cruisers Lawrence and Langley are each in forward blocking position located below their assigned target's tactical plane. They are stationary and waiting in ambush just within the orbit of the fifth planet. Each forward Cruiser is confronting three Kreel ships, an approaching cruiser and its two fast-attack escorts."

"The second layer of defense is near the outer orbits of the asteroid belt. Cruiser Lar is poised above the set tactical planes. From there he can move in support of either Lawrence or Langley." "The third layer of defense consists of the twelve available Scout ships. They are holding near the earth with the Arkillian Nest ship. They have formed the last defensive screen guarding against a possible Kreel breakthrough.

"Navigation here, Lent has just emerged from jump, distance twenty-four hundred kilometers off our port side. Lent is signaling condition gold."

Roy's news brought Kellon a sense of relief. Lent was safe.

"Lan, establish a hard tactical link with Lent and provide him with a full tactical update."

Turning to Kellon with a broad smile Roy commented, "Sir, time from exit to destruction of the third Kreel target was five minutes forty-seven seconds."

Turning to Roy, Kellon was not smiling. "Kellon here, Navigation, we got lucky."

Still smiling broadly Roy replied, "Navigation here, yes sir. We certainly did and it sure enough feels good!"

Roy's levity caused a slight lessening of Kellon's tension. "Tactical, keep me updated, what are the remaining Kreel doing?"

"Tactical here, we are still in the process of analysis. Putting the pieces together we are dealing with a Kreel reconnaissance in force. Fortune indicates we have destroyed the Kreel command ship. It was concealed in Sol's plume and covertly observing the two advancing Kreel groups. They are clearly probing to see what destroyed their previous reconnaissance ships.

"Tactical assessment is the Kreel do not know the threat potential. Currently, we are not observing any variation in the slow steady advance of the two Kreel groups. The remaining Kreel ships apparently do not realize their command ship has been destroyed."

The Captain's communications band hummed and Kellon automatically keyed the channel open. "Eurie here. Lent seems to have jumped into an active battle area. What's the score?"

"Eurie, It's not quite as active as several minutes ago, three bad guys are down and six to go."

Eurie here, "Kellon how do you want to play this out?"

"Eurie, for the moment we will hold this position and allow Tactical to complete their evaluation of the current situation. It will take time for the detection network to register our jump entry and notify the remainder of the Squadron that we are back."

"Eurie here, understood."

"Tactical, Kellon here, how long to intercept?"

"Tactical here, intercept time is not yet available. Being this high directly above the primary, we are not in a good intercept position."

"Commodore, Roan here."

"Roan, what do you have?"

"Sir, I don't believe the Kreel have a clue as to who they are tangling with. During the past several weeks I have had Lan, Shey and William building a new jamming sequence based on psychological anti Kreel patterns. If you are trying to keep the Kreel off balance you might want to consider our new jamming signal as a possible option. If they do get a message off to their Command Hub, it might add to their confusion."

"Roan, is there a bandpass filter through the clutter?"

"Yes Sir, Lan has the specifications."

"Thank you Roan, I will keep the recommendation on line."
"Lan, set verbal response active. Can you get the information of the bandpass filter for your new jamming signal to the other Guardian ships?"

"Lan here, yes Sir. I can send the information through the detection network. It will take light speed time delay to reach everyone."

"Lan, to play it safe send the filter bypass information and signal matrix data to all Guardian ships."

"Yes Sir, the data is being transmitted."

"Tactical, how are we doing?"

"Tactical here. The Kreel are continuing their probe into the system and closing toward Earth. They are still well beyond crossing the orbit of the sixth planet. If we are going to be part of the unfolding battle, we need to move soon."

"Navigation, can we do a micro Jump behind the Kreel groups?" Arching his eyebrows, Commander Grey looked over at Kellon with some surprise and a broad knowing smile. "Navigation here. Well Sir, according to the old fashion textbooks making a micro Jump within a solar system is contrary to common sense, unless of course you are trying to commit suicide. However, not being restricted to orthodoxy and since we are well above the ecliptic plane and in the primary's plume, I will make a first approximation evaluation."

"Navigation, what I need is a yes or no, as soon as possible. Roy, give me your best assessment."

"Yes Sir, we are working on it. So far it is difficult to determine if the Muses are smiling with us, or simply laughing at us."

Kellon sat for a moment considering the tactical plot display and felt his frustration. The numerical odds of three-to-one favored the Kreel. Even with stealth and an ambush those were not good odds. He needed to find an edge to shift the balance of raw focused power in favor of his squadron.

Kellon turned to watch Roy and his navigation team at work. Roy was still frowning, but steadfastly running the numbers. After five minutes he sat back, still frowning. Then he turned to Kellon. "Navigation here. Sir, the Muses appear to be smiling with us. We are well above the primary and in its plume. The two Kreel groups entered forty degrees above the ecliptic plane are still high and are beyond the orbit of the sixth planet. That puts them far from the primary's magnetic storms and the mass temporal turbulence of the inner planets. Given the planetary positions, the mass distributions between our position and the Kreel is unusually low. Given these combined factors there is a chance we can perform a micro Jump, but it remains dicey."

Roy's report was enough for Kellon to seek additional information. If possible, a micro Jump would permit him to get into the battle. "Navigation, what do you need to make your final determination?"

"Sir, I will need to tie both Lan and Lent into the solution of the Jump parameters. Give us access to both AIs and five minutes and I will have a better analysis for you."

"Navigation, you have your five minutes. In making those calculations, set the defined Jump exit points 30,000 kilometers to the rear of each Kreel group and well above their established tactical plane. Lan is to jump behind one group and Lent behind the other."

"Navigation here. Yes Sir. Waiting for AI priority access."

"Lan, allocate priority computational resources to Navigation. Tie Lent and our Scouts into the calculation loop."

"Lan here, understood."

As Roy worked with his navigation team, both Cruisers and their Scout AIs, Kellon continued to study the Kreel's deployment tactics. *They are apparently skittish and proceeding cautiously,* he thought. His desired tactics, if they worked, would level the playing field. He thought, *The odds are better than 50%, having just swept the volume behind them the Kreel will not be paying strict attention to their baffles. That should give us the edge.*

"Navigation here. Sir, my dear Mother would not particularly approve of a micro Jump within a solar system since she spent the best years of her life working hard to send me through the Academy. Nevertheless, given our position and the current planetary alignments we have a rare possibility of actually surviving the micro Jump, provided we exit high. If you approve I can have Lan and Lent proceed with the final computations."

"Navigation, Roy, proceed!"

If any navigator other than Roy told him a micro Jump was possible under these circumstances Kellon would have only smiled. That commander Roy Grey said it was possible, that made a huge difference. Knowing and accepting the risks Kellon made his decision and keyed the command and captain's bands. "Kellon here. I am contemplating a micro Jump. Lan, Lent and the Kreel are well above the ecliptic plane. Because of this favorable tactical disposition Navigation is now running the final computations. If a micro Jump is possible Lan and Lent will separate here. Each Cruiser will then Jump to points behind and above the advancing Kreel ships. Lan will Jump to support Langley. Lent will Jump to support Lawrence. We will then coordinate our attacks with Langley and Lawrence. Comments please."

"Eurie here, Lent is in agreement provided if we survive the micro Jump you agree someday to introduce me to your heretic tactician. Eurie out."

Looking toward Navigation Kellon noticed Roy was smiling. Knowing Roy's strict cautionary streak Roy's smile further eased Kellon's own apprehensions about performing the micro Jump.

"Lan, provide an estimate of time required for final calculations."

"Lan here. Current calculations indicate a confidence factor of 87%, estimating final result in ten minutes."

Kellon keyed his general inter-ship intercom band, "Kellon here. All personnel prepare for a micro Jump. Estimated time ten minutes. Be advised we will be exiting the Jump hot and in full combat mode, Condition 2.

"Lan, send to Lar, Lawrence and Langley that Lan and Lent will be executing a micro Jump, taking positions thirty thousand kilometers to the rear and above the approaching Kreel ships."

"Lan here, message is being sent."

"Tactical, on exiting call out target data on the cruiser first, then the two fast-attacks."

"Tactical here, understood."

"Fire Control, bring up ten heavy missiles set Condition 2. When Tactical calls out the target vectors assign four heavy missiles on the cruiser. Assign two heavy missiles to each fast attack ship. Set the homing passive-active, going active at 80% of run length. When you have confirmed passive lock on each target call it out."

"Fire Control here. Yes Sir."

"Lan, coordinate with Lent. Let Lent know our tactics and missile settings. You will coordinate with Lent and you are to synchronize the launch of missiles."

"Yes Sir."

"Navigation, how are we doing?"

"Sir, Navigation here. Lan is reporting jump factor for both Cruisers are at 92%."

Kellon keyed the command and Captain's bands. "Kellon here, Scout ship crews hear this, Lan and Lent will be maneuvering upon exit of the Jump. During that maneuver Lan will transmit the latest tactical plot data to each Scout.

"Following the initial maneuver Scouts will be deployed. The Scouts are to maintain full stealth mode. Immediately upon deployment the Scouts are to spread to a standard X-formation aft of your Cruiser. Upon achieving a spread of five hundred kilometers from your Cruiser each Scout will hold her position and she will prepare to launch three Zed decoys. You are to program the decoys to operate in a tactical "V" formation and they are to move directly toward the designated Kreel group. Before launch the Scouts will configure each decoy to wear the Shey lovely sinister heliographic matrix. Each decoy will also transmit the new Kreel jamming signals. If any Scout crew has questions Commander Roan and Shey will answer those questions.

"Heads up, each Cruiser will retain full responsibility for and control of his own Scouts. Are there any questions?"

There were none.

Kellon closed all communications links and then keyed the Captain's band. "Eurie, Kellon here. Before we jump do you have any second thoughts or recommendations?"

"Eurie here. This micro Jump business had better not be some ploy to get out of buying me that glass of wine. I do have one recommendation. Susie told me there is a special city on Earth named Paris. She informed me in Paris there are many sidewalk cafes known to serve a good vintage. If we survive this micro Jump business, you will need to pay up!"

Kellon smiled. "Your recommendation is heard loud and clear. I believe we have friends on Earth that might arrange the details. Anything else?"

Eurie's voice took on a serious note. "Not at this moment, except as we Jump into harm's way may fair winds be at our backs."

"Eurie, Kellon here. Keep it precise and let your Scouts guard Lent's back. Good hunting. Kellon out."

The seven Scout ship crews each acknowledged with Roan that they had understood Kellon's instructions. There was a sense of excitement as the Scout teams busied themselves for launch and worked to program their decoys for deployment.

"Lan, send a completion of long Jump report to Guardian headquarters, Admirals Mer Shawn and Ron Cloud. Then follow that with a current combat summary."

"Lan here. Requested reports are prepared and are being sent."

"Navigation here. Lan reports Jump factor now 99.9995."

"Kellon here. Fire Control are you ready?"

"Fire Control here. Ten heavy missiles are confirmed standby, Condition 2. We are ready!"

"Kellon here. Commander Roan, are the Scouts ready?"

"Roan here. Lan and Lent's Scouts are ready."

Kellon again keyed the general communications on both Lan and Lent. "Kellon here. Prepare for Jump. Lan will synchronize the Jump with Lent. Fair winds at our backs."

"Lan here. Standby for micro-Jump– Five, four, three, two, one, Jump!"

Chapter Twenty-Five:
Staccato Rhythm

On board Lan there was a blurring of sensors, as they reset. Then a long pause of silence followed before Lan emerged nearly thirty thousand kilometers beyond the designated Kreel ships.

"Navigation here. Receiving condition gold from Cruiser Lent! We've actually exited the micro Jump and in one piece! How about that, the Muses are smiling."

While everyone had prepared for the micro Jump they understood the associated risks were high and what they were about to do was very dangerous. Only the combined efforts of Lan and Lent's computations of the probability of success dulled the edge of their apprehension. There was a collective sigh as everyone looked about and then went back to work. As the tactical plot updated, Kellon quickly assessed their relative position to the Kreel targets. He let out his breath. Lan had positioned them precisely where they wanted to be.

"Lan, bring us smartly about and drop us in behind the Kreel ships. Let Lent know what you are doing."

Kellon clenched his teeth; the stomach-twisting after effects of the exit from micro Jump, combined with Lan's steeply descending and turning maneuver, was awkwardly disconcerting. He needed to focus intently upon keeping his eyes on the updating tactical plot.

When he observed the golden icon representing Lent appear on the tactical plot Kellon felt a wave of relief. Like Lan, Lent was also maneuvering to bring his assigned targets to a favorable orientation.

Continuing his steep turn to port Lan descended toward the tactical plane of the Kreel ship, descending until he completed a one-hundred and eighty degree turn then steadied on his course. The targets were bearing nearly 000 degrees relative.

"Lan, transmit our updated tactical plot to the Scouts. Coordinate with Lent the launch of Scouts."

"Yes Sir, initiating launch of our Scouts. Receiving confirmation, Lent is acknowledging deployment of Scouts."

Even as the Scout ships were deploying, the sounds of hangar doors opening and closing reverberated through Lan. Commander Shaw's steady calm voice called out the Kreel targets.

"Kreel Gortoga cruiser bearing 005 degrees relative, range 35,000 kilometers. Elevation minus 35 degrees."

"Fire Control here. Four heavy missiles passive locked, Condition 2."

"Tactical here. Kreel fast attack bearing 025 degrees relative, range 38,000 kilometers. Elevation minus 25 degrees."

"Fire Control here. Two heavy missiles passive locked. Condition 2."

"Tactical here. Kreel fast-attack bearing 338 degrees relative, range 38,000 kilometers. Elevation minus 28 degrees."

"Fire Control here. Two heavy missiles passive locked, Condition 2."

A few minutes following their deployment the Scout ships reached their predefined dispersed stations. Kellon studied the tactical plot, waiting to be certain all Scouts were in their designated positions, before he commenced his attack.

"Fire Control, Kellon here. Set all laser and gun turrets to point-defense, Condition 1.

"Set launch in salvoes of two missiles each. First salvo being two missiles with lock on the Kreel cruiser. Second salvo is one missile targeting each fast-attack ship. Third salvo is two missiles targeting the cruiser and the fourth salvo is one missile targeting each of the fast-attack ships. Confirm passive locks and Condition 2 on all missiles."

"Fire Control here. Confirming salvo order set, all missiles passive locks, set Condition 2. Standing by."

"Lan, when Lent confirms missiles passive locks, Condition 2, synchronize missiles launch and set Condition 1."

"Lan here. Lent has confirmed, is synchronized, 3, 2, 1, Condition 1, Firing!"

The heavy rumbling sounds of the launch of eight heavy missiles resounded throughout Lan, then there followed a hush.

Kellon studied the tactical plot and observed the icons of the outbound missiles moving swiftly away and closing on their intended targets. He waited until the missiles had run about 30% of their run length and then ordered, "Lan send a synchronized signal to Lent and to our Scouts, all Scouts are to launch their decoys!"

"Lan here, all Scouts reporting launch of their decoys."

"Lan, Kellon here. Coordinate with Lent and move us and your Scouts up smartly three thousand kilometers!"

Lan surged upward keeping his Scouts tightly coordinated with his movement leaving no Guardian ship in alignment of outbound decoys or missiles. Kellon was avoiding possible counter-fire directed toward the inbound missiles or decoys. Lent and his four Scouts likewise shifted their positions upward.

The missiles were much faster than the decoys and they streaked silently, in a deadly passive homing mode toward the distant Kreel ships. The three Kreel ships failed to detect the inbound passive missiles that were rapidly approaching from within their baffles.

As the missiles neared their targets the Kreel belatedly detected the twelve decoys approaching from four dispersed points, each arrayed in their brilliant costumes and transmitting broadband jamming signals. The Kreel cruiser that Lan had targeted was able to initiate a weak counter-fire directed against the decoys. With the background of broadband jamming of the decoys, except for one fast-attack ship, the Kreel ships gave no indication of detecting the inbound heavy missiles, not even after they went active. At the last moment one fast-attack ship broke formation moving sharply up and to its port in an apparent desperate effort to evade the incoming missiles. When the missiles arrived on their assigned targets they struck with a staccato rhythm of flashing destruction. The Kreel ships simply disintegrated under the destructive forces of the exploding heavy missiles.

Lan maintained his full stealth and vigilance, holding his course, waiting for Kellon's next command.

"Tactical, Lorn, how are we doing?"

Commander Shaw examined his tactical displays then looked up and studied the tactical plot. "Sir, the targeted Kreel ships here were completely caught by surprise. All targets received multiple hits and none survived. Kreel counter-fire hit and destroyed only two of the twelve decoys. Data from Lent indicates a similar result. One of Lent's fast-attack targets sent a brief superluminal message before Lent's missiles destroyed it. The intercepted message is being processed to recover its contents."

"Lorn, considering the possibility of deployed Kreel scout ships do you confirm all Kreel targets are destroyed?"

There was a long pause and Commander Shaw examined all the sensor inputs looking for telltale markers of Kreel scouts. Finally, having exhausted all data sources he reported, "Tactical here, we do confirm all targets destroyed."

"Fire Control, Kellon here. Reset the two remaining heavy missiles on Condition 2, to Condition 4. Reset all laser and gun turrets to Condition 3.

"Lorn, I am remembering your comment regarding the layout of the Gortoga class cruiser's control room. That the Kreel cruiser was only able to mount a weak response to an inbound threat from twelve obvious attacking ships does not speak highly of their combat effectiveness."

"Shaw here, I wholeheartedly agree."

"Lan, signal the Scout ships to recover their surviving decoys. Then they are to proceed to the area of the destroyed Kreel ships. They are to conduct a post battle survey of the area. I don't want anything of a technological nature to remain intact."

The Captain's band hummed and Kellon keyed the channel open. "Eurie here. Kellon, I am reporting all Kreel targets destroyed. I am sending Lent's Scouts to sweep the battle area for technical wreckage."

"Well done Eurie. I suggest you also have Tactical scan for possible deployed Kreel scout ships. I also suggest your Scout ships recover their surviving decoys if you haven't already instructed them to do so. We are a long way from Glas Dinnein and re-supply. After you recover Lent's Scout ships proceed inward and join up with Lawrence. Lan will recover his Scouts and join up with Langley. Lan will then coordinate our linkup with Lar and return to an Earth orbit."

"Once we get the details established we will need to have a general post combat conference. For certain, we need to plug the gaping holes in our defenses, especially the blind spots we discovered in the primary's magnetic plume.

"We also need to review our tactics. They were quite unorthodox but they were effective and took the Kreel by complete surprise."

Eurie's merriment was unmistakably clear in her voice. "Kellon, your description is noticeably understated. Calling a micro Jump within a solar system and emerging hot into a battle 'unorthodox' can only be intentionally droll. To your credit, the Kreel did not have any clue of what was happening. I must fearfully confess– I believe you are the mystery heretic tactician and I am therefore now a compromised woman."

Kellon felt the warm post battle easing of his tension and was grinning. "Eurie, I can't remember ever having before been thought of as being droll let alone by a lovely lady. I can only thank you for considering I am still able to compromise a beautiful woman. I am flattered. Perhaps, you might consider there is still some small hope for a well-intended and well-seasoned Guardian Cruiser captain?"

"Why Kellon, speaking personally, I certainly perceive some small hope for you. It's not every day a woman has an opportunity to personally meet the author of infamous heretic tactics let alone meet him with a glass of wine in hand," Eurie teased.

Smiling broadly Kellon opted for cautious prudence in his response. "I understand you intercepted a Kreel superluminal transmission?"

"Yes, the signal was not even compressed. Lent's intelligence team is working on it now. As soon as it is deciphered I will send a copy to Lan."

"Eurie, I am setting Condition 3 here. I recommend that after you confirm there are no Kreel scout ships remaining in Lent's area you do the same. Well-done Lent! Kellon out."

Reaching down Kellon keyed his inter-ship general band. "Ladies and gentlemen, Kellon here. We have engaged and destroyed two cruisers and four fast-attack ships. We are now moving to recall our Scouts and then we will be returning to Earth orbit. Very well done. Kellon out."

"Lan, well done again. Set Condition 3. Establish full synchronization and hard links with all Guardian Cruisers and Scouts in our squadron. We don't want any friendly fire issues.

"First link up with Langley and then Lar. Coordinate the return of the squadron to near Earth orbit."

"Lan here, understood and processing."

Kellon sat and looked around CAC. The tensions of the past hours were draining away as the Condition 3 went into effect. Those gathered at the consoles began normal conversations and others, who were able, stood and returned to their off duty interests. The CAC began to empty out, leaving only a reduced Condition 3 team manning the various stations.

Kellon looked toward Commander Grey and saw him busy over his consoles deeply focused on his difficult task. Kellon respected his fellow officers but he held special regard and respect for Roy Grey. Roy had long ago demonstrated his keen insight and sound judgment especially when regarding complex matters most folks might not even notice. He was a good friend and a superb officer. "Navigation, Kellon here. Roy, job well and ably done. I am retiring to my quarters. You have the CAC."

"Sir, understood, Navigation has the CAC."

Roy looked to Kellon with a broad smile, "Sir, might I offer well done!"

Stopping for a moment, Kellon exchanged smiles. Both men knew there was a bond of mutual respect well earned over many missions.

"Thank you, Roy." Kellon responded, as he walked out of the CAC and turned toward his private quarters. There were several pressing tasks still requiring his attention.

Chapter Twenty-Six:
Details

It felt like days since he was last in his own quarters. Entering, he walked over to his desk and sat down with a grateful sigh. He had met his immediate demands, however, there were a number of details still requiring his attention before he might get any sleep.

"Lan, connect me with the Lar, Captain Kylster."

A few moments passed and then Kellon's Captain's band opened to Captain Kylster's resonant voice warmly announcing, "Congratulations Commodore, Kylster here."

Kellon smiled at the greeting, "Captain Kylster, thank you. However, I am the one calling to congratulate you. Your layered defensive deployment of the squadron was superb. I feel somewhat apologetic for denying you the opportunity to demonstrate the Kreel did not have a chance."

"Commodore, your comments are appreciated. The simple truth is however based on your tactical updates we completely missed the Kreel command ship. In fact, regardless of what happened to the two probing Kreel forces that we were facing, the Kreel command ship would have obtained his mission objective."

"Captain Kylster, while your observations are correct the blind spot in the primary's magnetic plume was not apparent until we nearly collided with the Kreel ships concealed there. We got lucky."

"Commodore, I was raised with the adage 'we make our own luck'. Your employment of a micro Jump within a heliosphere was a high-risk call and luck had nothing to do with it. I repeat, congratulations. It remains a pleasure to serve with you."

"Captain Kylster, I appreciate your comment. Again, your tactical deployment was precise and well considered. As for our recent action, there is considerable information we need to review concerning what we found near Scion. In addition, I believe we should take the time to adjust the missile inventories within the squadron. I for one seem recently to have been using up my allotment of heavy missiles."

"Commodore Kellon, with your permission, I will see to the inventory of ordnance and submit a report giving my recommendations for cross-loading. As the elapsed mission time increased following your Jump to Scion, we were becoming concerned. Everyone in the squadron wants to hear what happened when you arrived there."

"Captain Kylster, I would appreciate your report on the ordnance. In order to bring everyone up to date. I will schedule a squadron briefing concerning Scion within the next twenty-four hours. Again, well done Captain. Kellon out."

Kellon sat back in his chair for a moment, considering other tasks still needing attention. Then he remembered the Arkillians. "Lan, set up a secure link with the Captain of the Arkillian Nest ship. Patch him through one of the Scouts near Earth and into my Captain's band."

Five minutes later a secure link to the Nest ship through one of the Guardian Scouts was established. "Honored Kellon, I am the Captain of the Nest ship, how may I assist you?"

"Respected Captain, I am calling because Council Member Kur asked me to provide you with information."

When he next spoke the Captain's voice carried noticeable tones of concern. "Honored Kellon, when your call came in my conclusion was some disaster must have occurred. I am aware of the Kreel attack on Earth. Will you please provide me an update and then tell me what misfortune has befallen our Council Members that you must contact me rather than their contacting me."

Kellon could not see the Captain's facial markings but he still recognized the stress in the Arkillian's voice. "Respected Captain, I have only good news for you to hear. First, to answer your question of the Kreel Attack there were nine Kreel warships, three Kreel cruisers and six Kreel fast-attack ships. I am able to inform you we destroyed all of them."

"With regard to your Council Members they are all alive and well. They are not speaking with you now because they are now on Scion and planning for the defense of your nests."

There was a long pause before the Captain resumed the conversation. "Honored Kellon, please forgive me. I am very confused. I am marveling you destroyed all the Kreel attack ships. You have again demonstrated your great skill as a warrior. However, Council Member Kur only departed the Nest ship about one Earth week ago. Can your Cruisers have traveled to Scion and returned in so short a time?"

Kellon inwardly winced. Given what taking Kur to Scion involved, some leakage of performance data was expected yet any loss still grated on his sensibilities.

"Respected Captain, I must bring to your attention that Council Member Kur, in exchange for our assistance, has made a pledge of honor. He agreed to respect the details of the speed of our Cruisers. He also agreed on the honor of his Nest that such information was a very closely held secret, not to be revealed."

"Honored Kellon, I was present when the pledge to you was given. I am also bound by his pledge."

"Respected Captain, your honor is noted."

For emphasis, Kellon paused momentarily before continuing. "Council Member Kur asked me to inform you that Scion's ruling council has decreed Earth and the Guardians are now formally declared friends of your nests."

Again, there was a long pause before the Captain spoke. "Honored Kellon, speaking as Scion's senior military representative in this solar system your news comes as a wonder. There is much for me to consider. Did Council Member Kur ask you to give me another message?"

Kellon smiled, knowing the Captain's need for some form of confirmation. "Respected Captain, yes. Council Member Kur requested me to tell you, the desert flowers are blooming. I was also asked to tell you the Nest ship is to seek the sanctuary of a near Earth orbit until the defense of Scion is assured. Council Member Kur trusts you will understand."

When the Captain next spoke, the easing of his tension was perceptible in his voice. "Honored Kellon, we the Arkillians, arrived in this solar system more than one of Earth's years past. We came as Earth's conquerers. Shortly afterward you vanquished us in open battle. Our thoughts then were of dying far from our nests. Now, you bring the wonder of glad news we are among friends of our nests. The wonder of the news from

Scion brings great gladness. Please ask us for anything we might do to show our gratitude and our friendship. I gladly accept your proffered sanctuary with sincere gratitude."

"Respected Captain, you are now among friends. We have much we might learn from each other. Be assured we will remain in communications. If you need anything, do not delay in contacting me. Kellon out."

Kellon sat for several minutes. The exit from Jump and the following battle had been his focus for hours and the real significance of the trip to Scion had not been in his thoughts. Now, speaking to an Arkillian Captain brought the importance of his trip to Scion back to the forefront. The Kreel threat was real and still looming. *Admiral Cloud,* he thought, *what have you begun and where will it end?*

"Lan, please prepare the required post battle summary report. Underscore and alert headquarters to the Kreel tactic of hiding in a primary's magnetic plume. Be certain to append to the report my commendation for Captain Kylster's tactical decisions.

"Oh, Lan, there is one more detail. Please send the post battle message to Guardian Force headquarters, attention Admiral Cloud. Encrypt the signal Black Hole. Provide the Admiral with appropriate comment on the observed performance of the Kreel Gortoga class cruiser. Append Commander Shaw's observations regarding the design of the Gortoga class control room. Add the following comment from me: A mind capable of devising the superluminal communications employed by the Kreel cannot be the same mind that disorganized the design of the Kreel Gortoga cruiser control room. I suspect the bridge design is the intentional result of sabotage. I recommend a detailed review of our Kreel database, looking for indications of planetary sources of possible resistance to Kreel domination. I also recommend a review of the database to locate centers of research in order to find the mind capable of developing the Kreel's superluminal communications capability.

"Lan, send the messages over my signature."

"Sir, the post summary battle report has been sent. The message to Admiral Cloud is encrypted Black Hole and is being sent."

"Lan what time is it on Earth where William is situated?"
"Inquiring."

Standing, Kellon stretched to loosen his body and then again sat down. A few moments passed and he began to feel his deep weariness far more acutely.

"Sir," came Lan's cheerful response, "William reports it is now eight thirty in the evening."

"Lan, ask William if Ambassador Wells is available to accept a call from me."

"Sir, William reports Ambassador Wells is available and very much wants to talk with you. He is reporting, she is saying he is not to dare let you hang up. Holding for Ambassador Wells."

There was a short pause and then Kellon could hear the noise of someone rattling the microphone. "Commodore Kellon, Susie here. Can you hear me?"

Kellon wondered why, whenever he heard Susie's clear happy voice he felt like smiling, it was like a refreshing tonic.

"Ambassador, yes. You are coming in very clear. I am calling to give you a message from Council Member Kur."

"Oh, is the Council Member alright? William told me there is another Kreel combat alert and Monstro was seen moving above Earth like the first time the Kreel came. Everyone in Olympus has been working overtime but they haven't seen any indication of the Kreel as they did before. Is everything all right? Oh, the message from Kur, what was it? Also, please stop calling me Ambassador, my name is Susie. All of my friends call me Susie and you are certainly counted among my friends."

Just listening to Susie was a pleasure for Kellon. She fully justified all the concern, the risk to his ships and their crews. Hearing the very ordinary concerns of a very talented person, a worried normal person, answered all his questions as to why people became members of the Guardian Force. It was to defend and protect human-occupied planets and the very wonderful ordinary people like Susie Wells who lived on them.

"Susie, the combat alert is canceled. Olympus was correct to be working overtime. There was another Kreel thrust. This time it was a reconnaissance in force and there were three Kreel cruisers and six fast-attack ships. We have destroyed all of the Kreel ships. The reason Olympus did not see them is they never reached inward further than the orbit of Saturn. While there was one group above Earth's primary I'm not certain Olympus would have seen that one."

"Commander Kellon," asked Susie, "did the Arkillian council believe Kur?"

"Yes Susie, but not at first. When the Arkillian ruling council learned of all that has happened on Earth they were disbelieving, as you can well understand. I was asked by Kur to specifically inform you, the ruling council of Scion extends to you personally, their respect for your wisdom. It was your negotiated trade agreement that brought them completely around in their thinking. The Council considered the balance and fairness in the trade agreement a wonder."

"Susie, I also want to congratulate you. I think you've ably demonstrated great wisdom by skillfully using the tools of simple fairness, common sense and even handed balance. Thereby you have done the human and Arkillian species a great service. I am telling you this because you need to understand why the ruling Arkillian council has decreed that Earth is now considered a friend of their nests."

"Sir, what does being a friend of their nests mean?"

"To the best of my understanding this means there is a sincere sense of responsibility to deal with Earth as honored friends in all matters. I stress the term honor because Earth's irrational short-sighted 'reaper takes the hindmost' attitude concerning economic management as not honorable. On Earth, absolute monarchies, economic dictatorships and cartels still acquire leveraged international monopolies. Furthermore, corrupt governments and disillusioned people still tolerate corrupting bribes and unjust laws. Rather than integrity and economic policies based on open competition, honest values and fair profits, Earth's international cartels permit robbers to charge what the market will bear even if it brings nations to the brink of bankruptcy. Such corrupting influences and lack of integrity can destroy what you have labored to achieve. People on Earth must demand changes where governments and people acknowledge, reward and enforce integrity. This in the long term will be the only means of assuring the maintenance of honor, peace and mutual respect with the Arkillians."

"Commodore, does this really mean if we do show integrity and mutual respect there will be peace with the Arkillians?"

"Yes, at least for the moment. The fruits of Admiral Cloud and your wisdom in fairly negotiating the trade agreement has yielded a possibility for long-term peace. However, what follows is up to how the governments on Earth respond. My primary concern is that Earth is so far behind the event curve what has been achieved through wisdom could be lost by unbridled greed and foolishness."

"Commodore, I will tell everyone tomorrow of the wonderful news. We will do all we can to assure this opportunity is not lost. I may even tell Charles tonight. Oh, it's too late. It's already past eleven at night on the East coast. Oh, this is wonderful news. Commodore, is there anything we can do for you? Is there anything you need?"

The question took Kellon by surprise. Then, he remembered a recent recommendation that resulted from one of Susie's inputs.

"Well, since you asked, there is one favor I would like to ask."

"You are asking for a favor? For you Commodore, I am confident everyone on Earth would want to do you a favor. Please tell me how I can help."

"Well Susie, is it perhaps possible for you to help me arrange to escort Captain Eurie to a sidewalk cafe in Paris for a glass of wine?"

Susie's voice sparkled with good-natured playfulness. "Why Commodore Kellon, I do believe you are asking Earth's Ambassador to the Glas Dinnein Planetary Assembly to help you take Captain Eurie out on a date. The Office of the Planetary Ambassador herewith assures you it will lend its considerable resources and assistance to your venture. Oh, Commodore, this is wonderful. When do you want to take her to Paris?"

Chapter Twenty-Seven:
Riddle

During their inward thrust toward Earth the Kreel had hours for making detailed observations of the solar system. Therefore, Kellon anticipated the Kreel superluminal communication Lent intercepted would contain considerable concise information. Such information, he knew, in the hands of the Kreel Hub would only increase the probability of a major attack.

Gaining direct access to Kreel Communications and encryption technologies represented a significant intelligence advantage and gaining that asset was the direct result of Lan's capture of the Kreel Gortoga Cruiser. Using their new tools Lent's intelligence group worked to unravel the intercepted Kreel message. Once decrypted what that message revealed came as a complete surprise to those on Lent and onboard Lan.

When they viewed the Kreel message Kellon and the others did not find a stream of concise observations and military assessments as they had anticipated. Instead the complete message was a brief scene of one of the control compartments of the Kreel fast-attack ship. The contents of the message starkly revealed a scene of raw terror and complete pandemonium.

Shaking his head in wonderment, Kellon requested Elayne play the entire message again and she once more began the playback of the Kreel message. Kellon, Commanders Grey, Shaw, Roan and Zorn all watched the bulkhead screen in silent disbelief.

The revealing video scene appearing on the display came from a Kreel ship just prior to the detonation of Guardian missiles. During the short broadcast sequence spanning no more than a minute the video scene showed the entire control compartment to be in confusion. Screaming and terrified members of the Kreel crew were in utter disarray, and clearly heard above their frightened screams were a bedlam of shrilling sounds filling the compartment. One wild eyed Kreel officer, presumably the Captain, was shouting at the communications display, "All destroyed, all destroyed, we are the last ship. They are coming. The Nori are coming."

The Kreel Captain was still shouting as the ripping thunder of an explosion was heard recorded as a sharp noise spike followed immediately by termination of the message. The display went blank.

Looking at the display in puzzlement Kellon commented, "well folks, that is the size of it. Elayne, you are the alien specialist, what is your assessment of what we have just seen?"

There was a long pause before Elayne began thoughtfully to answer Kellon's question. "Sir, what we have witnessed is pure terror on a primeval level. Only one Kreel retained sufficient presence of cognitive thought to function in any coherent manner. Even that Kreel was barely lucid. They were all utterly terrified. The elements of the message seem to indicate two sources for the resulting terror, the background wails we can hear surrounding the Kreel and the name the Captain called out. It sounded like Nori. There must be some direct connection between the sounds and the name. That is all I can surmise at this moment."

Having watched the display in fascination Zorn looked toward Kellon, frowning. "Sir, I don't recognize the name Nori. At least I don't remember having heard that before. The sounds, on the other hand, I surely recognize those."

Everyone turned to Zorn and Kellon asked, "where have you heard those sounds before?" Still looking puzzled, Zorn responded. "Well, Sir, we created those sounds. That is to say Lan, Shey and William worked on them for a number of weeks. Those are the new jamming signals our decoys were broadcasting at the Kreel, as they flew toward them. Darn, I had no idea that when I asked Shey to work up some scary anti-Kreel sounds, she would come up with something this effective."

His forehead was still furrowed in concentration, when Kellon asked, "Lan, can you please state the program criteria that Shey was given for constructing the sounds we have heard?"

"Yes Sir. The initial definition of the programming effort came from Commander Zorn. Specifically he had two defining components. The first of these was, transmit all manner of sinister sounds through the magnetic spectrum, like howls, whistles, groans, terrified shrieks, moans of hopeless cries of despair, that sort of thing."

"The second component specified by Commander Zorn, was for us to figure out really scary sounds tailored especially for the Kreel and add those to the spectrum of sinister sounds."

"To these two components provided by Commander Zorn, Shey added some elements to the work to be performed. One was to retrieve sufficient archival information regarding the Kreel that met the specifications.

And finally William offered wonderful stories from Earth's folklore, particularly scary stories. He was a valuable asset.

"Sir, that was the governing outline specification of the work accomplished between Shey and William."

"Thank you Lan, that helps some," Kellon acknowledged.

"Sir," Lorn commented, "what the Kreel Captain was screaming was they are coming. More precisely he screamed, they are coming, the Nori are coming. Was he referring to the sounds or to the appearance of the decoys in their gold and white trim costumes? I am not clear on that point."

"Your question is valid Lorn, unfortunately I don't see that at this time we have an answer as to which source the Kreel officer was referring," Kellon mused.

Roy dryly commented, "Whatever the source of the Kreel's terror they were certainly scared out of their very hides. For darn certain, whatever can scare a Kreel warrior that badly is something I have no desire to meet in a dark alley."

"Sir, I believe the truth must be located somewhere in the archives." Roan inserted. "Remember, Shey said she would search the archives for the psychological resources pertaining to the Kreel. I suggest answering the riddle the message poses will require the AIs to return to their working notes. They need to begin tracking down the sources of their Kreel-related references. Somewhere there may be a link between the images of the decoys and the sounds they were creating. While both are clearly involved there is no mistaking those wailing sounds that filled the Kreel bridge."

Sitting for a moment, reflecting on the comments of his staff Kellon considered the problem. "Lan, under a Black Hole encryption send to Admiral Cloud a copy of the Kreel message.

Also, transmit the heliographic instruction set for the Shey lovely sinister costume we used for the decoys. Finally, send the entire specification for the jamming sequence. Advise Admiral Cloud that we will send cross-reference information as soon as we can confirm the material."

"Append to the message: Whatever was the source of the Kreel terror, it utterly disabled their immediate ability to effectively operate or fight."

"Send the message above my name."

"Yes Sir. As soon as the message is encrypted it will be sent." Lan responded.

Kellon looked about the table. "Well ladies and gentlemen I for one am tired and am heading for some time in slumber. Unless anyone has something more important than my getting some sleep this conference is concluded."

Standing Kellon thanked everyone for their contributions and went to his quarters. There he obtained the first good sleep he had enjoyed in more than a week.

X

After Kellon had fallen asleep, Lan communicated with Shey and they together called William. The three AIs spent some time discussing among themselves what had happened on their Scion mission, the battle with the Kreel and the effects the jamming sequence had on the Kreel.

Their discussion was quite lengthy, since there was a great deal for them to consider, study and accomplish. Afterward William began a skillful process of quiet covert dissemination of selected information through key media networks on Earth.

Chapter Twenty-Eight:
Banner News

Sol's warming golden light slanted acutely across the awakening East coast of the United States, sending darkness scampering away until the return of evening shadows. Across the Atlantic and further to the distant Far East, there was a rapidly growing clamor among the Earth's nations and keeping pace with the early morning light that clamor was moving westward. News of the new Kreel attack, though very sparse in detail, was the banner news all over the world. The furor of the public clamor was not subsiding, it was rising like the crescendo of a kettledrums roll and the world's governments could not long ignore the rising clamor.

People around the world were demanding to know the details of the Kreel attack. Their underlying demand was to know what the governments were doing to protect the Earth and especially protect those living on the Earth from the Kreel.

In the early hours of the morning phones began to ring. First within the duty stations of various government agencies in the United States and then as dawn began to brighten into early morning the phones at the homes of high-level government officials began to ring. The calls spread out like rings of a splash on the surface of a pond after a boy has tossed a stone into the water. It was 04:45 in the morning when one of the expanding rings reached the Pacific Coast and Susie's bedside phone rang.

Groggily shaking her head and attempting to focus her eyes Susie slowly sat up and reaching out, answered the phone.

Darrell's cheerful voice crisply announced, "good morning Susie, rise and shine, the new day has begun and the fat is in the fire."

"Oh, what time is it? Darrell, where are you calling from? What is the problem?"

"I'm in the office girl. I suggest you wake up quick. There is a whirlwind brewing and you don't want to get caught in the backwash."

"Darrell, have a heart. I am not yet awake. Give me fifteen minutes and I will call you back." Saying this Susie put the phone down and fell back into her bed. Looking over at her bedside clock she groaned. "Morning, he is crazy, utterly mad, it is the middle of the night." Groaning more loudly Susie tossed back the covers and nearly tripped over Gepeto who was looking up interestedly at the unusual commotion. Susie moved to the closet, the bathroom and after ten minutes emerged showered, dressed and in a sour mood.

"Gepeto, hop up. If I can't get any sleep then neither can you." Susie began her morning rounds, although a bit early for her liking. After feeding Gepeto and then taking him out for his morning call she returned to the kitchen and brewed a strong cup of coffee, its rich welcomed aroma filling the kitchen. Then, cup of hot coffee in hand, she moved grumpily to her work area.

Entering her work area she called out loudly, "William, up and at them sleepy head! If I am not permitted to get any sleep, neither are you lazybones."

"Good morning Miss Susie. It is somewhat early for such profound exclamations. May I inquire what the occasion is that has you up with a cup of coffee this early?"

"William, you may inquire but I do not have the slightest idea of what is happening. All I know is Darrell Fann called and said something about fat in fires, a whirlwind and not becoming caught in its backwash. I am still trying to wake up. He said he was in his office. Can you ring his communicator for me?" Saying this she brought up her hand to cover a wide yawn.

"Yes, Miss Susie."

Susie was carefully sipping from her sixteen-ounce hand decorated pottery mug of delicious coffee. She smiled inwardly, *Glas Dinnein's neab was good,* she thought, but nothing in the universe compared favorably with a good cup of coffee, freshly brewed from newly ground whole Guatemalan coffee beans.

"Fann here." The voice from the speaker announced.

"Good morning Darrell. You had better have some good reason for waking me up before five in the morning."

"Hello Susie, good morning again. I do have a good reason. The news coming from around the world says there was a major Kreel attack and the Guardian Force destroyed the attacking Kreel ships. We are going over all our data but all we have is the information showing Monstro moving high up and away from Earth as they did when the last attack happened. We have no tracks on any Kreel ships whatsoever. People around the world are demanding to know what happened and what the governments are doing about the attacks.

"The President has not called yet but a call is expected any time. Everyone is on the phones trying to find out what we can."

Still cupping her warm cup of coffee Susie felt frustrated. "Do you mean you called me out of a sound sleep because someone learned of a Kreel attack?"

"Certainly. But from what you are saying the news of a Kreel attack is no surprise to you?"

"No Darrell. Just like you William informed me yesterday there was a full-scale combat alert in effect. Please remember I am Earth's Ambassador to the larger universe. All important matters reach my desk in the ornate ivory penthouse office long before they trickle down through the small pipes to your damp dark sub-basement level."

"Well Madam Ambassador, are you then the source for the leaks about the story around the world?"

Darrell's insinuation caused Susie to feel a rising sense of ire. "No, not likely. I'm giving fair warning, if anyone again accuses me of being the source of a leak they had better duck when they see me coming!

"I went to bed early last night and I have not even read the morning's banner news. Besides, my scheduled news briefing to the world press is not until nine this morning. You might note that is in about four more hours! Perhaps by then I will have had my second cup of coffee and be ready for some really witty repartee!"

"I hope you are kidding about the world press."

"Darrell, give me a break. I'm the one you woke up twenty minutes ago. I would hope your brain is functioning sufficiently to appreciate the stark difference between a well-deserved cutting low blow, from that of a serious statement. Darrell, why not just tell me what is actually happening?"

There came the sound of a sigh of unfeigned exasperation and then a pause. "Thank you for asking Susie. There is news of a major battle with the Kreel. There are very few details. There is however one item that is consistent. Everyone is asserting there was a fierce battle with the Kreel near Earth. The news of the battle has swept westward in tempo with the coming of morning. The news of the battle has widened and intensified consequently; everyone is scared and demanding to know what has happened. Do you have any information?"

"Yes Darrell. In matters of fact I do have considerable information. However, I am not going to tell you only to have to repeat it again to Charles. Wait a minute and let me see if I can get him on the connection. William, are you monitoring this call?"

"Yes Miss Susie. How may I be of assistance?"

"William, please locate Charles Sullivan. Inform him I need to speak with him concerning the breaking news about a Kreel attack on Earth."

"Yes Miss Susie."

Yawning, Susie enjoyed another sip of her warm coffee and sighed. Within two minutes William had patched Charles into her call with Darrell.

"Sullivan here. Susie, are you on the line?"

"Good morning Charles. Yes I am here and we have Darrell on the line also."

"Good morning Charles." Darrell said, cheerfully.

"Charles, Darrell woke me up at 04:45 with the news an epidemic of Kreel jitters is spreading around the world. I thought I might as well tell you at the same time I tell him what I know."

"Susie, please proceed," Charles requested.

"Well, late last night I received a call from Commodore Kellon. He gave me an overview of what has been happening."

"Susie, is Commodore Kellon then back from Scion?"

"Yes Sir. Lan made the trip and safely placed Kur and the other Council Members back on the surface of Scion. Commodore Kellon has informed me that Kur has been successful in warning his planet's government of the pending Kreel attack. Perhaps more importantly the Council believed Kur. I don't know details but Kellon told me that the ruling Council approved of the trade agreement. Commodore Kellon told me its equitable and balanced terms were fundamental in changing their minds about the Earth. In fact, they have extended to us an honor, they declared Earth as a friend of their nests. He informed me that such a distinction is something very significant.

"Commodore Kellon was also very direct in saying he believes it is critical that the governments of Earth come together here and that they recognize the responsibility of being friends of the Arkillian nests and respond accordingly. He expressed his concern the 'reaper take the hindmost' style of commerce and greed on Earth might ruin this opportunity, if we are not careful."

"Susie, I am compelled to ask, in order to be certain, do you confirm the ruling Council of Scion has extended a pledge of peace toward Earth?"

"Yes Charles, I do affirm that. Commodore Kellon has amazingly obtained a state of peace and harmony between Scion and Earth.

"The Arkillians are now preparing for the defense of their world. Their first concern is to survive the coming Kreel invasion."

"Susie, all this is good news, but what about the Kreel attack on Earth?" Darrell asked.

"Darrell, I was just coming to that. I do not have many details, but there certainly was a battle. Commodore Kellon informed me there were Kreel ships above the sun. He added he did not believe Olympus would have seen them. Other Kreel ships were moving toward the Earth from several points on the rim of our solar system. The reason Olympus did not detect them is they did not cross the orbit of Jupiter, being destroyed near the orbit of Saturn."

"Susie, this is important," insisted Charles, "were all the Kreel

ships destroyed? How many Kreel ships were there?"

"Oh, let me remember. I believe he said there were three Kreel Cruisers and six fast-attack ships. Yes that is correct, three cruisers and six fast-attack ships. He called it a reconnaissance in force. They were all destroyed."

Darrell was not happy. "Charles if we can track the Kreel and we certainly have proven we can yet one was above the sun and we didn't see it then Olympus has a big hole in its defenses. I will get Charlie on the task of reviewing our high and low polar satellite telemetry. If we can't see anything then I will want to increase our coverage and that will require funding."

"Well Darrell, given the apparent interest of the entire world on our defense I suspect funding may well be found. Of course, seeing them coming will not answer the big question, if they do come then what?"

The inner mix of her long held frustration and being awakened at 04:45 brought Susie's response to a sharp edge and she did not hold back expressing her thoughts. "Sir, that is precisely the question you need to reconsider. As Commodore Kellon has already said, Earth is way behind the power curve in this battle. If the Guardian Force were not on duty in our solar system, even as we speak, the Kreel might be strolling down Broadway looking for two-legged juicy snacks.

"What Earth should be worrying about is putting its own house in order. Earth should be unifying its global policy making capability. Stop the self-defeating and injurious cycle of international commercial greed and wasteful arms races. It's long past time to start thinking in terms of our common safety and defense. The world's governments need to begin behaving as if they were comprised of intelligent human beings, people who live together on the same beautiful planet. People should be giving each other and the world we live on the respect each is entitled to receive. We are all in this together and on one small world! If we cannot deal fairly with each other on Earth then by the seven stars how will Earth ever begin to heal and be able to stand with the other human worlds?"

"Susie, clearly you feel deeply about what you are saying. The good news is there has recently been some movement toward the goals you have identified. Perhaps the progress has been slower than it might have been but there is still progress being made," Charles replied with solemn brevity.

"Sir, some progress is simply not sufficient progress. I am deeply concerned our planet's fragmented self-serving and inept governments lack a basic comprehension of the real problems or the ability to rise to the challenges before us. What the governments need to do is listen to the people they purportedly represent rather than talking down to them while accepting bribes from cartels and narrow interest groups. They must begin to listen to the people demanding to know what the governments intend to do to protect them!"

"As to this morning's problem, you might consider taking advantage of the current outcry. If you talk with the President, you could suggest he might want to make the positive global announcement that there was indeed an attack and it was summarily defeated. Then he might announce the good news of a peace treaty with the Arkillians. That is really good news and it underscores the need for us all to pull together."

There was a long pause before Charles responded. "Susie, your advice is sound. I will make that call to the President. I suspect given recent developments he may want to talk with you some time soon."

"Sir, I am Susie Wells a true blue Californian and citizen of these United States. At any time I will happily speak with the president of the country I love. All that I ask is that everyone realize I also love the entire world."

"Understood and well said, Susie. Sullivan out."

"Susie, I'm sorry for waking you up early. Even so you did have the information we all needed. Will you give me a call later today?" Darrell asked.

Sitting back in her chair, Susie sighed. "Darrell, I did rather speak my mind. I am deeply concerned about our mess here on Earth. We need to get it right. As for calling you later you are at the top of my list of things to do."

"Good, I will look forward to your call. You might try to get a little more sleep. Fann out."

With a long sigh, Susie put the phone down and sat holding her cold cup. "William, what am I to do?"

"Ambassador Susie, might I suggest you prepare a second cup of coffee and then call Elayne. You might find talking with a good friend quite helpful, I certainly do."

Susie yawned again. "Well, first I think I will simply try to get some more sleep. I don't believe sane people should try to get up before the birds do."

The small box that contained William's AI matrix did not have a face on which someone might discern his expression but if it had the expression would have revealed a happy twinkle in his eyes and a sincere fondness for his friend. "Indeed, that is wisdom. I do believe sleep often helps."

Yawning again Susie went into her bedroom, kicked off her moccasins and fully dressed she laid down, pulled the bedspread over her and fell fitfully to sleep. As she did Gepeto returned to lie down near her bed. He looked toward Susie for a moment then put his head on his outstretched paws and went to sleep.

William spent a moment examining the interior sensors of the house, turned his attention to the external security system and again verified all was secure as it should be. Having confirmed the local area and perimeter defense was in place and no threats were apparent he returned to his task of indexing and analyzing the news network hubs in China, Mongolia and Russia.

Chapter Twenty-Nine:
Small Beginning

A cool sea breeze was coming off the water the sun was high and the day was clear, except for a few clouds on the distant horizon. It was one of those perfect days for a long quiet walk along the beach. Ron Cloud and Mer Shawn were happy to be in civilian clothes and taking full advantage of the opportunity so afforded. Mer stopped, looking down and bending over he picked up a small mollusk shell off the wet sand.

He stood a moment looking carefully at the small wet shell and then looked up. "The problem we have Ron is simple. We are like the small animal that once inhabited this shell. We are limited in what we know and have no clue what may be in the next solar system beyond the ones we are now in." He turned his hand over dropping the small shell back onto the damp sand. Wiping his hands together, brushing off the sand, he looked thoughtfully out to sea.

"Mer, we are nothing like that small animal. We know enough to be scared about what might exist just beyond our limited region of space. For one thing we know the Kreel are out there. What we don't know is what is out there that is capable of scaring the pants off a Kreel Captain and his crew."

"Well, we now know it has a name, the Nori." Mer replied.

"Yes, we do have a name. Regretfully, that is only a small beginning. I have put a research team on the task to search the Kreel and other databases for all references to the Nori but so far they can't find any references. That in itself is not strange. The underlying problem we are running into is the Kreel database we have access to is essentially military in its nature. Economic, historical, sociological and medical data is sparse or non-existent."

"Fine, now what do we need to expand our Kreel database to include those topics?" Mer asked.

"Blasted good question. Mmmm, I will give it some thought."

"Ron, is it possible the name Nori evokes such dread that they will not even refer to it?"

"Well, that is a possibility. I personally cannot think of anything we find so frightening we will not mention it, but then we are not the Kreel."

"Ron, are you certain we are not at least as afraid? As a species, we emerged from the depths of space and settled new worlds. For certain, something forced us to begin again. While our legends speak of a First Home, there is no explanation whatsoever as to why we left that First Home or even where it is in space. There is no specific record of what we fled from, none. Perhaps like the Kreel, we encountered a threat so terrible we could not mention it."

"Mer, your point is well taken. Perhaps we did meet something terrible, or else it met us. Perhaps it was only because of political differences and overpopulation. Then perhaps it was only a nova. For all we know Earth is our first home and that is yet another bag of unanswered questions. The real question is why was there no record ever made? We all have pondered that unanswered question for a very long time. Perhaps we will discover the truth someday, but I would wager two brews it is not likely we will discover it today."

Ron turned and walked up above the damp compacted sand into the loose dry sand that gave way beneath his feet pulling at his hiking boots. He sought a drift log that a high tide had deposited during a recent storm well up the beach. Reaching the log, using his hand, he casually brushed the loose dirt off and sat down.

"Take the load off Mer, we have some talking that needs to be done."

Mer moved up following Ron and he also brushed off a small section of the log and sat down. He leaned back against a small tree that was conveniently growing up and bent seaward next to the log. Lazily, he thrust out his legs before him, crossed his ankles, cupped his hands behind his head and looked up at the clouds on the horizon as they scurried past on their way to wherever clouds go in a hurry.

"Mer we have been pushing the Kreel back. During the past six months they have lost nearly eighty ships, a third of those being their cruisers. Kellon has destroyed eleven of those Kreel ships near Earth. We have also significantly reduced by more than 90% the Kreel raids into our space. Most of this improvement in our military situation is the direct result of Kellon's capturing the Kreel cruiser."

Mer closed his eyes and let the soft sounds of the sea, the sharp cry of the birds soaring overhead and the sound of the wind moving through the trees, flood into his awareness.

"Who can argue that point, certainly not me. Kellon's capture of the Kreel cruiser has proven to be exceptionally beneficial. Blasted risky, but very beneficial. There is no contradicting either of those facts."

"While we are speaking of the benefits of taking a Kreel cruiser intact, how is the research coming into improving our own communications?" Mer asked.

"It's a complicated and slow process. The problem is thorny because of two competing issues. We need improved communications, but we also need secure communications. We are trying to use the Kreel breakthrough in physics to improve our communications while remaining undetected by the Kreel. What we don't want to do, while researching the problem, is tip off the Kreel how we have become so effective in our pushing them back into their own volume of space. Above all, the tactical advantage we have gained is something we want to hold on to as long as possible.

"On the technical side, the engineers are currently working on bandwidths, temporal harmonics, multiphase and such matters. It is going very slowly."

"Ron, considering the Kreel losses, eighty ships is very significant. If we had suffered such losses we would be in a heap of trouble. I don't know their total fleet size or maximum manufacturing rate for cruisers, but regardless, it is going to take the Kreel some time to replenish fully those losses. It's not only the physical ships, but also the ships' crews. Eighty ships lost means eighty skilled Captains lost along with their experienced crews."

"Ouch, that has to hurt." Ron said.

"Agreed. The time for the Kreel to rebuild will only be longer if they continue to suffer similar losses. They cannot be so dense as not to understand such basic arithmetic and earnestly seek to reduce their losses.

"Ron, I counter your two brews with two more cold brews, that the Kreel are even now trying to determine what happened that permitted us to turn the tide against them, as we have."

Pausing to reflect, Ron considered what Mer had said. "No bet. I wouldn't wager against that assessment. The Kreel must be pulling out their fur by the handfuls trying to figure out the answer to that question."

Bending forward Mer picked up a small stone, one that the sea had tumbled and polished, enjoying the smoothness of its surface.

"Given my two millenniums of fighting the Kreel and what I believe is, their propensity for aggression. My guess is they will forcibly strike directly at the enemy perceived to have shown the greatest contempt for them. They will undoubtedly move to defend their sense of superiority, it's their species imperative.

"Rather than feeling good about the damages we have inflicted on the Kreel, it is a prudent time for doubling up our alertness. If I am correct they will ruthlessly strike as soon as they have determined whom to strike. I will bet another two cold brews they strike at Glas Dinnein or one of the other ten planets. Hopefully I am wrong, but to ease my predilection toward guilt, I will contact Dylan Cord and warn him to be especially alert for an increase in Kreel long-range probes. They may not be willing to risk a ship in one of our heliospheres but they will certainly increase their probes, using intelligence-gathering drones where deemed beneficial."

"Mer, I will not take that wager."

Shifting his boots in the sand Mer dug down through the dry sand and reached the moist sand below. He looked over to Ron. "Do we even know if the Kreel have sufficient remaining strength to defend their own volume and also launch a new expeditionary force toward Glas Dinnein, Scion or Earth?"

"No Mer, we do not have sufficient information to reach that conclusion. One reason we don't know is we do not have their total fleet strength and we have no means of assessing what fleet strength the Kreel believe they require to defend their own volume of space. The only thing I can positively say is we have not yet intercepted schedules indicating when the Kreel intend to move on either Earth or Scion. As for moving on Glas Dinnein it is possible, but I doubt it is likely. After all, they have about eighty good reasons, all of which are loose collections of drifting debris, for strictly avoiding us.

"If they do decide to aggressively move against either planet I suspect they will attack Scion before they venture toward Earth."

"What gives you that opinion?" Mer challenged.

"Well, to begin with they have a very low opinion of the Arkillians. That in turn may suggest to the Kreel they are an easy mark. Being naturally a bully, they may want to kick someone because someone else has kicked them. Earth on the other hand remains an unknown, an anomaly, where they have just lost eleven ships. I suspect they will move toward the presumed soft spot before trying to take a bite out of the harder problems. It is, as you notice, my own opinion."

"Well Ron, it may be your opinion, but it sounds like a well thought out one. To assume the size of the Kreel losses contribute to the Kreel not mounting an offensive at this time seems tactically sound."

"Mer, it could also be that the report from the Kreel Captain near Earth, to the Kreel Hub, has something to do with the Kreel's hesitation. Whatever that Kreel Captain thought he was encountering, may be the underlying cause for the Kreel Hub to pull in its invasion horns. At this time, we simply don't have a handle on or a clue about the inner strategic thinking of the Kreel Hub. That fact remains a weakness in our intelligence estimates.

"Whatever the true cause might be the Kreel hesitation has given us some slack time to work within. What you and I need to do is determine how best to spread our resources and use that time to our advantage," Ron observed.

Mer stretched his legs out further and adjusted his posture to a more comfortable one. "I suggest you employ caution with that assessment Ron. There is an old adage– a calm ushers in the storm. As I have already said, the Kreel may merely be assessing which direction to strike."

Ron looked over to Mer thoughtfully, "Calm before the storm or otherwise, the Kreel have given us some unexpected time in which to prepare."

"Ron, I consider the military forces the Kreel believe they need to defend their own space is a variable. If we go in and kick some behind, especially near their three Hub planets, they will most likely consider they need more defenses and fewer offenses. That in turn would reduce the number of ships available to send out to attack Glas Dinnein, Earth, Scion or any other planets."

"Perhaps Mer. On the other hand it might just provoke them to answer a direct threat to their Hub planets by powerfully striking back directly at Glas Dinnein. At the core of our own problem is our own force since now needing to guard Earth, we are stretched tight.

"My own opinion is that we should first increase the intelligence gathering around the Kreel Hub to build our knowledge of the Kreel and their methods of governing. If we strike at sensitive but less well-defended outer provinces it will have a direct effect on the Hub. Let the far-flung Governors howl to the Hub for more protection requiring the Hub to respond. In that way we can observe how the Kreel think, evaluate their response times, diffuse their power and burden their bureaucracy." Ron suggested.

"Mmmmm, there is some merit in such an approach. You might work up a few potential targets and also identify what assets will be required to monitor the Kreel Hub. How long will it take to prepare that proposal?"

"Well Mer, it seems to be true confession time. The proposal is already written and all it needs is my signature to send it up to you."

"Good, I will look forward to reading it tomorrow.

"One thing we should do," Mer thoughtfully said, "is consolidate the gains you began with the Arkillians. I suggest when it's time to bring Kellon home, we send out three Cruisers to replace his squadron bringing him home by way of Scion. We need to share the intelligence we can with the Arkillians so they do not consider we fabricated the whole Kreel threat. Besides, the Arkillians have had a much closer relation with the Kreel than we have. Perhaps they even have the missing Kreel information we need for our database. Maybe they even know what the name 'Nori' means to the Kreel," Mer suggested.

"Be careful Mer, on first reflection sending three Cruisers out to relieve five may seem prudent but I don't believe it is. We argued for five Cruisers to begin with because of the Kreel threat.

That threat has not diminished. I recommend we send at least five Cruisers to relieve five Cruisers.

"Even bringing Kellon back by way of Scion has its inherent risks. I ask, what is Kellon to do if he meets a Kreel warship in Scion's space and he ends up in a firefight? At that point, the appearance of simplicity evaporates like a drop of water on a hot skillet. The consequences are such they cannot begin to easily be assessed," Ron said.

"Hmmm, your argument has some merit. Now tell me about the benefits of bringing Kellon home by way of Scion," Mer asked.

Leaning back, Ron smiled. "That's not fair, you are asking me to argue against my own advice. You are however, correct. There is a flip side to the coin. If we bring Kellon's squadron back to Glas Dinnein, along the route past Scion as you recommend, they can deploy additional beacons along the route. That in turn would help us to gain several more optional Jump entry points near Scion, not just the one restricted to the proximity of the primary," Ron counseled.

"The points you make regarding five Cruisers guarding Earth are sound and I agree. However, in spite of apparent risks, bring Kellon back by way of Scion. I want those added Jump entry points, just in case.

"Given these factors, you have my approval to speak to Operations and to Dylan Cord concerning the matter."

As he brushed an annoying sand fly away, Ron replied, "Yes Sir, I will call as soon as we get back to the office. As you know, Dylan will insist on rotating Kellon's squadron back to Glas Dinnein when scheduled. In order to maintain crew performance, make necessary repairs and refit. He has always been a stickler about regular rotations.

"The more complex question Mer may be what can we do to move Earth further along toward integration into the whole system?"

Chuckling, Mer replied, "From what I have heard from Kellon Ambassador Wells has already started that ball rolling down the hill. She is truly a remarkable young woman. That brings me to another question. How are the medical people doing about reverse engineering the DNA mess the Arkillians inserted into Earth's population? What I want to know is can anything be done to lengthen Ambassador Wells' longevity?"

"That's a difficult topic, Mer. The analysis of Ambassador Wells' DNA and the DNA we consider normal contains some striking differences. The quandary our medical people are facing is identifying what changes they can safely introduce without creating unanticipated secondary problems. They are carefully working the problem and within a few years they believe they will have a solution. At present, they are not anywhere near a treatment program."

"A few years? Ron, to some of those researchers a few years may be one hundred years or more. If there is anything we can do to increase their funding or jack up their priority then we should become involved. I do not want to lose Ambassador Wells to an accelerated aging process if we can do anything to prevent it. We do not have a hundred years for research in this matter."

"Agreed. I will check with our people to be certain there is an understanding of the urgency of the problem."

"One thing more Ron, have your folks begun to follow up on the recommendations Kellon made to look for possible sources of resistance to the Kreel within their volume of space?"

"Yes, quite an amount of work has been accomplished. In fact, we have some interesting information but nothing we can point to with an 'ah-ha'! It will take some more digging and then we will need to send deep in to Kreel space some probes and ships to collect additional data to confirm any suspicions.

"What I can say now is that the Kreel have carved out a sizable hunk of space and claim about forty worlds."

Startled, Mer turned and looked at Ron before he responded. "Forty worlds? Ron that represents a sizable chunk of real estate and it must come with some intense economic and political issues. Do you have any statistics as to the nature of the worlds and their inhabitants? Are all forty planets populated by Kreel, are there other indigenous species involved? Might there be any planets considered favorable for human occupancy?"

"That's four questions without taking a single breath, Mer. Give me a little break. The short answer is I haven't a clue. Many of the forty worlds must already have or had indigenous populations. However, the exact Kreel-to-indigenous ratio is unknown at this time. Several do look very favorable for human habitation but for obvious reasons we have not looked at them from that standpoint." "What we do know is the Kreel fully occupy each planet or else directly control each planet using installed Kreel Hub governors. The Hub does not permit any governors to be even semi-autonomous. Everything on those forty worlds is tightly controlled out of the Kreel Hub which itself is spread over three worlds within ten light years of one another.

"Our conclusion is these Hub worlds were the first three Kreel-occupied worlds, as to which was the original is not yet known."

"Hmmmm, Ron if they have a tightly regulated and strict central control would it be possible to disrupt their communications and thereby render the entire Kreel system into a boiling pot of chaos?"

"Good idea. Given three worlds being involved I rather doubt it but the idea is worth looking into."

"Ron I want you to sort through the forty Kreel worlds. Isolate all those on which human beings could be comfortable. I am not suggesting we want to go live there, but if we need to consider working with indigenous folks it would be a whole lot easier if we can comfortably breathe the same atmosphere and not be squashed by the gravity of the place."

"So noted. I will have the report on your desk within three days.

"Mer, we are currently obtaining interesting information from the analysis of Kreel heavy production. For example, they manufacture their spaceships on only three planets. As yet, we don't know what type of manufacturing and subassembly may occur on other planets. Regarding their fleet, I found it especially interesting all their overhauls and refits are on only one world and that world is not involved in manufacturing of the Kreel space ships. Restricting refit and overhaul to a single planet looks like a weak link in Kreel fleet operations. I can't imagine why the Kreel so narrowly restrict fleet refit and repair to one planet, it's plain illogical.

"The research into this area seems fruitful, so far, so we are expanding our research. As you well know, this type of analysis takes time."

"Have you followed up on Kellon's concept of sabotage?" Mer asked.

"Yes, while that possibility is something not easily verified it is being carefully examined. Perhaps your question about indigenous life and planetary habitation conditions may help isolate and clarify the needed data. After all, there are only four planets involved in shipbuilding and refit. It might be very interesting to see precisely what planetary group they fall in.

"Along the same lines of research what I have already started is a study into the flow of critical materials. I am searching for a nexus of critical items such as silver, copper, chrome, zinc or similar metals that if disrupted might inhibit their production of spaceships or other offensive materials. I am looking for the key that will shut off their industry, if one exists."

"While you are looking about for keys you might also reverse your logic. Use your defined weakness matrix and apply it to our situation. See if you can observe any weak links we have in our own production and behavior. Define areas where we should address problems before they bite us," Mer counseled.

"Good point and so noted," Ron affirmed.

"Thank you Ron, now back to the main point. There is one question I would certainly like an answer for."

"What's that Mer?"

"If the Kreel have encountered some species they are terrified of perhaps we can find the species by looking where the Kreel don't go. Have you looked either inside the Kreel sphere or along its edges for a distortion of traffic, somewhere they seem afraid to tread?"

"No, I have not looked into that possibility, admittedly its simplicity merits consideration. It should be relatively easy to compare a star chart of space against what they have identified as their governed systems and see where the holes are. We might accomplish the same result by looking around its edges. A third method could be to look for a pattern of their military traffic and look for a frequency distribution, of what worlds they visit. When we get back, I will spin up the appropriate inquiries."

"Ron, I suggest when you make that distribution analysis you do so by examining the whole population then make separate analyses by class of ship. We may find some meaningful patterns below the whole population."

Both men sat quietly enjoying the awareness of the salt spray, hot sand and the intermingling of shade from the overhanging trees. They found pleasure watching a young family walk past. The father was carrying a child on his shoulders and carrying a lunch basket. The mother walked alongside the young man while holding hands with an excited little girl whose high-pitched voice evidenced her joy. The family's apparent goal was a sheltered cove situated below a high bluff located further down the beach. Both Mer and Ron knew it was a sheltered spot out of the wind and a good location for a basket lunch to be set out.

Neither man said anything as they watched the family walk past, merely drinking in the everyday scene and feeling delight in its significance and meaning. Some might have observed and never thought of such a simple scene as being anything significant but both Mer and Ron fully understood it represented one of the sweet fruits of a world's security purchased at a very high but gladly paid price.

Mer absent-mindedly picked up a stick out of a pile of small driftwood and began to draw lines in the sand.

Looking up Mer asked a question that had simply come to his mind as if it had been lurking about in some crevasse waiting for the opportunity to emerge fully formed. "Ron, the fact that the Kreel have forty planets bothers me. Populations are the most fundamental resource of any species. We need to be considering expanding ours.

"Earth is terribly overcrowded. From what I hear their population has severely stressed their global environment. I know fourteen billion people simply can't pick up and move but some could. Are you aware of an acceptable planet nearby where we could start up a new colony?"

Mer's comment took Ron by surprise and he turned to look at him. "Mer, now that is a great idea. There are several planets that might fit the bill, some have a number of drawbacks but others are within acceptable ranges. Only two of them are anywhere near to the Kreel boundary. Even those two planets could with time be fortified against Kreel assault."

"Ron, when you get back put a team on the problem. I want at least four new planets, good planets, found nearby that might serve as colony worlds. Choose some that are far enough from the Kreel boundary that we are not inviting raids as the colony grows. "One more thing, what is the current status of Earth's defenses?" Mer asked.

"Ah ha, now that is an area of good news. As you already know Kellon began a well-designed monitoring system on his first trip to the Earth. He had limited resources but what he achieved was admirable. Every Cruiser that has traveled to Earth since then has methodically added to what Kellon had begun. The last report I have from Kellon indicates the instrumentation installed within the heliosphere by his five Cruisers is now able to detect even the small Kreel probes and is nearly on full par with that of Glas Dinnein. Kellon is continuing to add to the monitoring system, like filling the void in the primary's magnetic plumes. He is being very thorough. Once again, Kellon has proven his resourcefulness."

"Ron, that is good news indeed."

The two men sat for a while longer watching the sea birds and listening to the soft folding sounds of the waves that were rolling into the beach from some far away wind or tidal movement. It was a very comfortable day on Glas Dinnein and one very much appreciated by two of the nurturing planet's older warriors.

As they stood to return to their offices Mer stopped and looked toward Ron. "What I don't want is a senseless expansion of fighting and killing. If we have the Kreel reeling, then it is a time to be smart about what we are doing. Let's covertly push into their home space and fill in the voids in our intelligence information about those forty worlds. It's time for us to initiate serious probing of Kreel country. I especially want to know where the Kreel are conducting their superluminal research. Add to that desire the requirement for a full history on the Kreel. I want the gaping holes in our databases filled to overflowing. When we have the information our tactics require, then we will squeeze the Kreel, where it hurts them the most."

"Understood. I will move on the matters beginning today," Ron acknowledged.

"Thank you Ron. An old adage still rings true; harvest the good crops while the weather is fair. I know you are already working long shifts, as are your staffs. If you need more help, let me know and I will provide it."

Both men stood for a moment longer watching the family down the beach as they spread out their lunch. Both remembered earlier days, family and friends who were now gone.

"Well," mused Ron, "its back to the old sharpening stone for me. Oh, Mer for the record, I didn't take those bets you offered."

Chapter Thirty:
Trade and Peace

Although many of Monstro's fighters had been destroyed during the battle with Lan, all of its commercial cargo lifters were in perfect working order and its cargo holds were not even half-full. To Susie's way of thinking that shouted an opportunity for beginning trade.

As Earth's extra-terrestrial ambassador it was Susie's idea to fully initiate the trade agreement between Earth and Scion. She was convinced the sooner Earth accomplished this the better. Her idea was basic and to the point: Let Monstro openly complete its current trading mission with the Earth before it began its long journey back to Scion.

To begin her ambitious project Susie had asked Charles to lunch and he had accepted. Her thinking was simple; after all, he was an undersecretary of Commerce, so improving Commerce was his job.

They met for their informal meeting at the casual dining setting of the Old Stone Station in New Washington. The structure was reminiscent of a simpler, but not necessarily a gentler time. The building was a stone structure with tall multi-pane windows, fireplaces, open wood beams and narrow stairs that led up to the upper dining areas. The restaurant ambiance was comfortable and reflected a congenial relaxed setting where people felt comfortable. It was locally famous for its excellent food, especially its salads and the wide variety of seafood and fine wines served in congenial surroundings.

Her idea was to get Charles away from his office and its telephone. She wanted him well isolated, one-on-one, for a private talk. She knew her need was for an ally and Charles Sullivan was her choice. She considered his assistance was critical, if she was to bring the trade agreement into reality.

X

Charles arrived at the Old Stone Station at nearly the same time as Susie. When they entered Charles was not recognized but Susie certainly was. The proprietor, Carl, arrived in a flourish and he warmly took personal responsibility for his famous patron. Escorting Susie and Charles to a table in the upper dining area he personally assured it would afford them some degree of privacy. Having provided them with both a menu and wine list he graciously told them if anything failed to meet with their approval they need only ask for him.

She was not at all happy with the celebrity status afforded her and simply did not like it. "Charles, you are the Under Secretary of Commerce and should be getting any accolades that are handed out."

"Susie, please remember when you returned home, while we were standing together on the steps of the Commerce building, it was you the cameras were focused on. There is a good reason for that focus. You are the only human born on earth that to my knowledge has traveled more than a light year from Earth. Think about that for a moment. You not only have traveled eighty light years to Glas Dinnein and back, at faster-than-light speed, you have also negotiated the first interstellar trade agreement in the history of our planet. You are in truth and fact a celebrity, Ambassador Wells."

"Charles, I need to simply be me, not some celebrity. As for being an Ambassador, yes I am, at least for the moment. Therefore as Ambassador Wells, I have requested this meeting."

The early spring sunlight, streaming through the window, cast shadows along the rock walls and refracted through the condensing water droplets sliding down the sides of the tall water glasses. A refracted glimmer from her water glass caught Susie's eye. She reached and taking up the glass, sipped some of the ice-chilled water before speaking. "Charles, I am concerned if we do not take appropriate action, the entire planet will remain in its current backwater mentality. Earth cannot remain fragmented, bitterly divided and squabbling over the definition of God and political boundaries. Earth must change its thinking, it must begin to consider itself as a whole planet among many planets and reach out to embrace the required changes.

"Monstro is for the moment still in a nearby orbit, for how long, who can say? What I want to ask you, as an Undersecretary of Commerce, is to begin working with me to see the trade agreement fully ratified.

"In brief, I want the United States to be the first to ratify the agreement and take prompt steps to fully facilitate it.

"Through the simple mechanism of trade the Earth can openly begin an inter-relationship with other worlds. I believe trade will assist Earth in altering its introspective thinking, turning it outward. Those are my thoughts and I would greatly appreciate hearing your views on the topic."

Charles had remained quiet listening attentively to what Susie had to say. "On its bare surface your reasoning appears sound. Might I ask you, in your own assessment, what steps should be taken next?" Charles asked.

"Well, to begin with, business cannot be conducted as it once was. Arkillian cargo flights to concealed high mountain factory outlets in Switzerland cannot be the wave of the future. We need a dedicated facility where Arkillians and the people of Earth can openly come together and do business. That means, what we need is an official spaceport where space ships can land and people can come with their wares to dicker, negotiate and sign contracts."

Looking directly toward Susie, Charles was listening intently and carefully considering his response. "Now Ambassador Wells, that is an interesting concept. A brand new development, a spaceport designed from the ground up, for open interstellar trade. Might I safely wager that you might just happen to have a recommendation as to where this new facility might be constructed?"

"Well, now that you ask, I was thinking of the western slope of Colorado. There are some open spaces there combined with an environment, that makes the location suitable for an Arkillian - Earth trade center. The best part is that much of it is Federal land and therefore the entire project could be accomplished for a reasonable cost."

Pausing in reflection, Charles thoughtfully extrapolated along the political path Susie had suggested. "If the United States acted independently, signed on to the trade agreement with an appropriate opening for other countries to also sign, it might well lead to a rapid global ratification of the trade agreement one country at a time.

"Susie, I like your approach."

"Honestly Charles, I cannot believe any country will want to be left out of a potentially lucrative export business. Naturally, any goods coming to the center will need to have essentially a duty-free status when entering the United States. A modest charge on commodities passing through the center as an offset of the operating costs of the center should be OK. However, any tariff designed to enrich the United States would be objectionable and self-defeating.

"Although the Center will be constructed in the United States it must be perceived globally as serving the needs of the entire Earth."

"To be effective the constructed facility must be able to house the commercial representatives from all around the world comfortably. It will be Earth's first world-centered commercial space center and showcase so it will naturally expand with time. Therefore, it is my earnest hope the Government will have the foresight to grant the project adequate land for future growth.

"That, Charles, is my idea in a nutshell."

Sitting back in his chair, Charles smiled in appreciation for the concept that Susie had briefly outlined. He liked it. "Susie– that is quite a nutshell. Still, it makes sense and on that basis alone, it should be possible. I believe I can speak to the President as early as tomorrow about your ideas. Given the Center will sit on Federal land, I believe a suitable hunk of property could be carved out for the spaceport.

"Hmmm, such a facility will need to be large enough to provide room for landing the Arkillian lifters and the cargo aircraft from various countries. Of course, the design will include inspection facilities, warehouse storage, housing for staff, grounds maintenance and facilities for the Arkillians.

"On the downside Susie the project could become quite cost intensive and therefore meet some stiff resistance in Congress."

Costs for her project had troubled Susie for days and she had come to lunch fully prepared to meet that anticipated challenge. "Not necessarily Charles. The Federal Government already owns the land. The technology for sprayed concrete dome structures is

322

old hat and has remained rather inexpensive. A few geodesic glass domes interspaced with the concrete domes and presto, a spaceport center springs forth out of the ground."

Still leaning back in his chair, Charles' eyes showed his merriment totally enjoying Susie's enthusiasm. "Susie, you make it sound simple. However, politics is regretfully like a porcupine. It needs to be approached with some caution."

"Charles, I don't pretend to be a politician. What I believe is we cannot permit anyone to politicize this project. When the spaceport is constructed, as I know it will be, there is one artifact I want to see at the center of the facility."

"What do you have in mind?"

"Well, on Glas Dinnein there is a broad Avenue lined with spectacular fountains. There is one fountain in particular that is incredibly beautiful, it's called Eternity. I want to see a replica of the fountain become the centerpiece of the facility. I believe the beauty of that fountain will provide the architects and landscapers a focus about which to fashion the construction."

"Can you provide me the specifications for the fountain?" Charles asked.

"I am certain the needed information must reside somewhere in Lan's data base. If not, then I am confident Lan can certainly obtain them. I will have William take on the project to find the specifications and have them forwarded to your office. In return, I would appreciate if your architects and landscapers would put William on the list of those to whom the plans are sent, as they develop, so I am able to follow what is happening." Charles was deep in thought regarding Susie's recommendations. "There is no problem in putting William on the information loop list. You should also know that I am sitting here in total admiration of your insights. In one stroke you have found a truly straightforward means of focusing the entire Monstro affair on a wonderful outcome, lasting trade and peace!"

Relaxing, Charles leaned forward and picked up his water glass. "For many years Susie my concern was directed toward the possibility of an interstellar war and invasion. There were many in the governments around the world who shared my concerns. Now, we are sitting here discussing commerce, not war. Frankly, it is a wonderful transformation to behold."

"Given the dynamic shift in prospects you may be surprised on how many people quickly sign on to your idea. I doubt there will be any problem selling your entire concept. In fact I am relatively confident I can obtain a prompt review and hopefully a sign off for the project within a few weeks."

"What will be your first step Charles?" Susie asked.

"Well, as soon as I obtain your fountain specifications they will go to an artist in New Washington's monuments office. I will bring together some Government architects and a couple of landscapers who work in New Washington and sit them all down together. I am confident, using your fountain and dome suggestions, Architects can artistically represent the project within thirty days or so."

"Once I have the artist's renderings I will go to the President for his final approval. With sound preparation I believe the project will move rapidly forward."

"Charles," Susie said thoughtfully, "I will need to speak to the Arkillians, but doing so prematurely could be harmful and especially so if it doesn't happen. Will you please tell me as soon as you can, when you are positive the project is a solid go?"

"Madam Ambassador, I believe the President will sign off without much delay. I will certainly keep you tight in the loop," Charles answered.

X

As Susie recalled the lunch she smiled. The call from Charles had come the next afternoon. The President had not needed artist's conceptions to decide. He enthusiastically embraced the concept and over his phone quickly obtained the key congressional support needed to move the project forward on a fast track. The project was a go!

Chapter Thirty-One:
Spaceport

The news of a decision to construct a commercial spaceport in Colorado emerged seamlessly into the world press, beginning as a series of small favorable mentions. There was no hint of an orchestrated effort in the appearance of such news and no one asked who might be quietly meshing such articles among other news items. As the articles appeared in various international population centers the number of people approving of the new spaceport swelled. As the stories spread various Government representatives began calling Susie for information and governments began lining up to be signatories on the new trade agreement. None apparently stopped to ask who was creating and directing the release of news articles. Not even Susie suspected William was their source. That, of course, was as William had planned.

"Susie," the communicator announced, "you have a call from Elayne. Will you accept it?"

Susie looked up from the architectural sketches she was studying, stretched and responded. "Yes, please connect her."

The display screen brightened and Elayne greeted Susie with a smile. "I am bringing glad tidings. I spoke with the Arkillian Captain and he is eager to work with you on the spaceport project. He said Monstro's voyage was a commercial venture not a military mission. Their cargo holds were not 40% full when the trouble began. He had considered the entire journey ruinous. He had no hope for seeing a profit at the end of the voyage. Susie, you have found a strong ally for your work in the Arkillians. Well done."

"That's wonderful Elayne. Will the Captain be the primary contact for the trading?"

"No, his duty and responsibilities are focused more on Monstro and the crew. However in absence of the Council

Members the Arkillians have a Guild Judge onboard. That august Arkillian directs trade and has the final authority to arbitrate disputes between the various Nest representatives. More importantly, he has the authority and means of controlling Arkillian assets currently on Earth. He can therefore arrange to pay for the trade items."

"That's very interesting information Elayne. I suspected the Arkillians had hidden accounts on Earth which is why I took care to be certain The Trade Agreement permits sovereign tax and duty-free off planet banking accounts to be established. Even so, I suspect there are folks on Earth who would love to know whose names are on the existing accounts and just how much money is really in them."

"Sorry Susie, while the Captain was open and helpful he didn't offer to provide me that type of information. Susie, there is more. It seems the Arkillians have a profit sharing system with the various Nests involved in each voyage. That system includes a covenant with the crew of Monstro."

"According to the Captain the covenant assures the survivors of any voyage will honor, with significant bonuses, the Nests of any crewmember that might perish during the voyage. Therefore, every member of Monstro's crew will personally profit from the completion of a successful voyage. This includes the families living on Scion whose relatives perished during the battle with Lan. According to the Captain, everyone on Monstro is enthusiastically supporting anything that realizes a good profit at the end of the long voyage. The Captain wanted me to assure you, they are grateful for what you are doing. He told me the possibility of realizing a profit has lifted the hearts of every Arkillian onboard the Nest ship. He also said there would be gratitude among the Arkillians on Scion who have lost family members. You have a lot of Arkillians ready and willing to make your spaceport a success."

"That's wonderful Elayne. Charles will be happy to learn about the Arkillians' willingness to assist where possible. However, unless he asks, I will forget to mention the existing Arkillian earth-side accounts."

"Susie, Everyone on Lan is interested in the project. Just how are things going down there?"

"Well, as you already know, I've been in Colorado for weeks. When I arrived there were only open vistas and lots of remaining work . Since then, I'm amazed what the construction teams have already accomplished."

"The really good news is the United States Government set aside fifty thousand acres of Government land and it designated the land as Earth's first Interplanetary Conference and Trading Center. I believe there's enough land set aside to assure and preserve the nature of the landscape and yet provide for adequate room for future growth. It's thrilling to see everything coming together."

"There must be a lot of people working on the project," Elayne commented.

"You are absolutely correct, there's a small army of contractors working here. They are working around the clock constructing reinforced pure white concrete domes, aircraft runways, hangars and glass domes for showing off trade stuffs.

"That brings me to a problem Elayne. We have constructed some domes for housing the Arkillians but they are only empty shells. We need the Arkillians' assistance to help us complete the work and meet their unique requirements. Can you see if the Guild Judge can arrange to provide us with a few Arkillian engineers to help?"

"That I can do Susie. I'll try to get back to you shortly. Elayne out."

Two days later a lifter arrived from Monstro with a team of Arkillian engineers. Before they arrived Susie had briefed the contractors on the Arkillians, showing them some of the photographs taken in Switzerland the year before. She also stressed the importance of being friends of their Nests. Before she was complete with her briefing, one contractor shouted, "Lady, we've been working with different people all over the world for decades. This ain't any different and besides they look just like my in-laws."

As it turned out it was not much different. There were several Arkillians in the first group who had working knowledge of English and several other Earth languages. The Arkillian translators helped to bridge the language gap with the humans who at the beginning lacked the needed language skills. As the work proceeded the human ability to pick up hand signals and approach some Arkillian words gave rise to occasional linguistic nightmares and considerable laughter. As the work progressed, the human contractors and Arkillians worked well together in finishing the Arkillian domes, thereby assuring all prerequisite air conditioning, sanitation, sleeping and food preparation requirements were satisfactorily completed.

When Susie contacted Charles with an update she was bubbling about the ability of the species to work successfully together. "Charles, it's wonderful to see. What is very apparent is both the humans and Arkillians share a common sense of humor. As they work and laugh together the tensions disappear and now there's a free flowing interaction between the humans and Arkillians."

"There had to be some problems Susie. It couldn't have been that easy," Charles said.

"I'm not saying it was easy. There were problems, lots of them. Some areas might have proven more difficult but they did not simply because of the goodwill and unavoidable humor involved in trying to communicate with each other.

"The bottom line Charles is the two species are working together, in harmony, while constructing a complex that is meant for the mutual benefit of both species. There is also one more vital element in driving what is happening here."

"What might that be?"

"Well Charles, none have forgotten the Kreel threat. It's like a social contact glue. Everyone has a reason to stick together. It's a matter of mutual survival. We all know and understand we are in this fight with the Kreel, together."

X

As the days and weeks passed Susie was constantly working with the architects and contractors. She was everywhere, walking among the artfully configured domes of concrete and the several large geodesic domes of frame-tinted glass. The construction teams were rapidly transforming Susie's original concept from images on paper to a solid reality. A reality that grew out of the ground, while harmonizing with the topography.

Susie quickly learned her first thoughts about the complex had been somewhat limited. The Project engineers and architects had expanded the initial concepts to provide housing for power generation, security, administration offices, housing for permanent staff and VIPs. They had also added additional elaborate domes to facilitate visiting trade representatives.

Near the center of the complex was the largest of the domes designed for trade fairs and large enough for hundreds of booths to be set up to permit companies or growers to show off their products. Its tinted glass panels sparkled in the sun like thousands of gems and people could see its glistening surface from anywhere on the site. Susie considered it spectacular.

As the facility neared completion, Susie became concerned about the landing area and its support buildings. The area was large enough to facilitate the landers, arriving and departing commercial cargo aircraft and easily permit vehicles to move efficiently about carrying cargo to or from the lifters and storage buildings. As the opening-day celebration approached, she began to breathe a little easier. The Project Director repeatedly assured her the project was right on schedule.

Once the buildings were completed a small army of stone–masons and landscapers went to work. Stone walkways were fashioned and in the center of the complex, and under Susie's personal supervision, the large and beautifully designed Eternity Fountain was constructed. To Susie's knowledge the fountain represented the first truly off-world structure to blossom on Earth. She knew it would not be the last.

As the buildings were completed the final scheduled changes began. Landscape engineers had found full-grown trees elsewhere on Colorado's western slopes and transplanted them to give the area around the Center an appearance of long establishment.

Overall it had taken less than one-hundred-twenty days from the first ground breaking until the entire complex was open for business. That occasion required a formal ribbon cutting.

Over the preceding months it had become increasingly obvious to Susie the AI upgrade William had received, courtesy of the Guardian Force, had brought him to the level of sentience or so close as to be indistinguishable from sentience. William long ago seemed to have an intellect of his own, however, that appearance was purely the product of skill and artful programming. Now, she knew that like the Cruisers and Scout ships of the Guardian Force, William was for all intent sentient. Susie had no idea of what William's full capabilities were but every day brought with it some surprises. She had understood the Guardian ships were also near to being sentient, but that fact was a closely guarded secret. For that very reason none in the Guardian Force discussed the matter outside the inner Guardian circle. Likewise Susie kept her knowledge of William's being to all effects sentient to herself. She simply let everyone believe he was just another artfully programmed computer. Almost humorously William happily played his designated role.

While Susie was busy, so was William. During the entire planning and construction phase he had added numerous subtle influences to the final plans of the facility. Given such plans were all in a digital format William had simply accessed the appropriate files and modified the plans according to his own thoughts.

Above all William's intent was to be certain security remained a primary consideration in the design of the facility. He accordingly discretely arranged the integration of sophisticated and enhanced security features. William had also arranged for the data flowing throughout the system to be directly available for his access.

William had no desire to interfere with normal security procedures but his mission entailed a much broader security concern than that of the center's security protocol. Given his subtle design enhancements William could literally monitor every aspect of the complex with ease. This he effortlessly and discretely accomplished, keeping a special eye on Susie, to be certain she and Gepeto were safe. While he did this primary task he continued his interaction with the Guardian AIs and the work of mapping the world's data grids. Being busy William was quite happy with his duties. The Guardian AIs and William all knew the Kreel would be back. The only questions being, when and in what force? Everyone kept busy in preparing for that anticipated eventuality.

Chapter Thirty-Two:
Combat Alert

The sky was clear of clouds, the afternoon sun was already low in the western sky . The day had begun to soften its warm late summer thermal embrace of the land in preparation for the coming of dusk and evening. Susie had worked from early morning without a break on the last minute details. The various government officials from around the world were now interfacing with her, and through her, negotiating with the Arkillians. She knew it would have been impossible to coordinate and schedule all the details, if not for William. He had thankfully increasingly borne the burdens of communications and scheduling and he did this with apparent effortlessness.

With the coming of evening Susie had the honor and pure joy of officially turning on the lasers designed to illuminate the up-thrust plumes of water rising high above the Eternity Fountain truly revealing its full beauty. It was a beauty that incorporated sound as well as visual effects since its design incorporated muted tones from hundreds of wind and water chimes. Amid all the applause, if you had been listening closely, you would have heard Susie laughing.

Susie had carefully designed the opening ceremonial events about people and Arkillians rubbing shoulders, with lots of multi-national food, wine, honey mead and a selection of music that remained in the background. It was Susie's intent that the occasion be one of showing off the potential trade goods the Arkillians might want to add to their expanding list of trade items. She therefore put a cold damper on speeches and arranged for the favorable display of commercial goods. To this end she had spent hours inquiring about what the Arkillians might like to purchase which was not previously available.

In expressing her thoughts in this area she found a strong supporter in the Nest Guild Judge. That worthy Arkillian quickly sized up the economic opportunity, represented by the expanded open trade and he began to add selected items to his already impressive list. To those in the know it soon became obvious that Ambassador Wells held decisive power regarding what happened around the Center. If she approved something it was in and if not, it was definitely out.

Arriving by aircraft, at the facilities airport, the President and his party touched down just before dusk. Coming with the President's party were the visiting Heads of State from fourteen other trade agreement signatory nations, all with their own aircrafts and selected retinues. The celebration was, as Susie had decreed, intentionally restricted taking on the form of a cocktail party rather than a jamboree.

The notable political retinues, when combined with the trades people, the Arkillians, selected celebrities and the press, added up to a sizable number of people enjoying the festive occasion. That Guardian Force also sent its representatives both surprised and delighted nearly everyone. For the most part the Guardian Force had remained a mystery to most of those on Earth. Everyone knew they were patrolling within the solar system but people seldom saw either their ships or personnel. That they made an appearance at the opening of the spaceport made news because it gave the press their first real crack at the men and women from the distant stars. As such, their appearance was a significant news banner hit.

Making up the Guardian contingency each Cruiser sent a Scout ship fully adorned in their glittering bright Shey lovely sinister costumes. Commodore Kellon had decided all five Cruiser Captains should come, each bringing with them selected Guardian Force members. In typical Scout tradition they arrived with a flourish. The five Scout ships appeared suddenly high above the horizon at five equally separated points on the compass rose. As they slowly descended they converged until poised stationary directly above the Eternity Fountain, bow pointing to bow. Rather than a ground trembling rumble there came a soft sound of rushing waters that was in complete harmony with the fountain which was the center of their formation. From the brilliant gold and white glitter of the Scouts' costumes slid the large lifter disks, each with six people in full dress uniforms. The disks, like the Scouts were gleaming in gold and white radiance. As they settled to the ground and the Guardian personnel stepped off the lifter disks their admirers and the press alike immediately surrounded them.

Among those that Susie was especially delighted to see were Elayne, Roan and Zorn. As Zorn cheerfully declared to Susie, "It's hard to keep the Guardian Force from a really good party."

Knowing her concealed lapel microphone with William was open she smiled. "William, are you observing everything?"

"Of course Ms. Susie. I must say you have managed to bring about a wonderful occasion. None of us can say where this process will go but we can say, with some assurance, it has begun very well. Both Shey and Lan agree with my assessment."

"William, is Shey here?"

"Yes Ms. Susie. Shey is holding several hundred meters above the fountain and sends her regards. She says it is the best party she has ever attended. Lan is telling me everyone on all the Cruisers are also watching. Everyone is happy to see their labors produce the fruits of peaceful commerce. Everyone thinks it is wonderful. Lan is telling me he is sending the party scene back along the beacons to Glas Dinnein. We are all confident there will be happy news on eleven other worlds because of what is happening here tonight. I am also preparing a special editing of the party for the Arkillians. I am confident they will receive it well on Scion, since it will show the Arkillians a functioning trade agreement at work on Earth."

"Ms. Susie, Lan tells me that what Earth has accomplished with the Arkillians, may change how the other human-occupied worlds view themselves and possibly their relationships with other non-human cultures. Both Lan and Shey believe this is a very important event as well as being a good party."

William's words came as a comfort to Susie. When she began mingling among the people what came as a surprise to her was the feelings of openness. Everyone she met repeatedly expressed hope for the future. She found that sentiment prevailed throughout the assembled group. The party truly seemed a success. As the hours slipped past everyone seemed to have known each other for years. Even the Arkillians seemed relaxed, all enjoying their honey mead and special food treats.

Elayne moved over and gave Susie a big hug. "Well Ambassador, you have pulled off a feat many did not believe would be possible. I for one extend my congratulations."

Susie flushed with her praise. "Elayne, you of all people must know that I have only been one person among many who were involved in making this evening possible. You are one of those people. If it had not been for your language skills and experience in communicating with Council Member Kur none of this would have happened. I can say the same about Admiral Cloud and Commodore Kellon's efforts. I am merely a coordinator and not much more."

Elayne laughed in a good-hearted exclamation. "Ambassador, I remember a young woman wearing knee high boots coming aboard Lan with a lovely buddy, Gepeto. Give yourself some credit. You have played a pivotal part in what has occurred here. Again, I extend to you my heartfelt congratulations."

Both Elayne and Susie suddenly became aware of a sudden tension around them. Then Elayne's expression became serious. Susie knew she was listening to her personal communicator.

"Susie, there is a combat alert being issued. I must go."

Even as Susie watched the Guardian personnel all moved quickly through the party toward their lifter disks. As they did, more people noticed the shift in the Guardian Force personnel's demeanor realizing something was happening.

As the lifter disks, now fully occupied, rose swiftly up and merged with their Scout ships the people observing fell silent. After a moment, the five Scout ships moved skyward and shortly afterward they disappeared in the night sky.

Observing the departure of the Guardian Force, like the others around her, Susie felt a growing sense of apprehension. "William, what is happening?"

"Ms. Susie, a Kreel propulsion signature has been detected. It is too early to be certain but it seems at least one long-range intelligence probe is now operating within the heliosphere. That is all I know at the moment."

Susie moved over to where Darrell Fann was standing and motioned him to join her. He noted her expression and excused himself from the group of people he had been in conversation with.

334

Coming close Darrell lowered his voice and inquired as to what Susie wanted. "What's up Susie?"

"Darrell, there is a new combat alert being declared."

"Do you have any specifics?" Darrell asked.

"Only that it may be a long-range Kreel probe. I don't know more than that. Of course, the probe could be a harbinger of another Kreel assault, I simply do not know."

"Thanks Susie, I am on the job." Turning, he moved away toward a group near the President.

Susie reflected she had seen Charles with the President earlier. As she looked around she also saw the Arkillians departing the party. They were moving toward the area where they had left their cargo lifters. Everyone she observed was responding in an orderly calm fashion but it was obvious there was a change in the party's atmosphere. Now, there was an undercurrent of concern.

As the official hostess of the evening's event, she also had her defined duty. Putting on her best party smile she moved to engage some of the people she had invited in light conversation. *From all appearances*, she thought, *it will be a long night.*

Chapter Thirty-Three:
Mystery in Progress

Sitting in his command chair Kellon was still in his dress uniform as he studied the tactical plot. Upon return to their Cruisers they had moved away from Earth and were now holding in a widely dispersed pyramid formation with Earth near its center. Four Cruisers had taken positions at cardinal points below the Earth. Lan took his position directly above Earth. All five Cruisers were in full stealth mode and set Condition 2.

Following the previous battle with the Kreel, Kellon had required each Cruiser to fine-tune its sensors to trigger on detection of faint Kreel Jump exit signatures. Given the Kreel had surprised them once he would accept no more deadly surprises. "Lorn, please go over the contact information and describe it to me again."

"Yes Sir. We received two distinct pulses. The first was a faint energy pulse indicating an exit from Jump. Coincidently with that pulse came a distinct signature of a Kreel probe lasting precisely 4.43 seconds. Nothing has been detected since those two signals."

Humph, the Kreel are certainly refining their techniques, Kellon thought.

"Lorn, check me on a hypothesis. One fact is I have not heard of a Kreel probe that has Jump capability. Yet, for the sake of argument we may be dealing with something new here. Presume for a moment what we have is just such a technical marvel. In that case the Kreel successfully launch their probe from some indefinable distant location into this solar system. Upon exit from Jump into this system it needs to do one thing, correct its inherent Jump motion to attain a desired trajectory within the system and then it goes totally passive. Accordingly the short 4.43 seconds propulsion burst on exit was to attain the probe's desired trajectory. On its new adjusted ballistic trajectory it simply cruises along and monitors the system.

"Does that make any sense to you?"

"Sir, your hypothesis of the probe's apparent behavior appears supported by the information available. However, I can confirm there have been no Guardian alerts concerning a Jump capable Kreel intelligence probe. Our understanding of physics and technology indicate anything with much less mass than a cruiser cannot have Jump capability. If the Kreel have developed a Jump capability for a small probe then that technical achievement would represent a very serious new threat.

"Assuming the Kreel do have a Jump capable probe, then your hypothesis does fit the data. However, if the hypothetical presumption is shown to be invalid obviously another causality must be considered."

"Lorn, what am I missing? Can you provide a second causality?"

"Yes Sir, I believe I can. There were two discrete signals. The first signal was a faint energy pulse indicative of a Jump exit. Such a pulse does not carry with it a vessel type characteristic, the energy pulse only indicates an exit event occurred.

"The second discrete signal indicates, by its propulsion signature, a Kreel L-16 probe operating for a brief duration. If the probe is a normal L-16 we know it does not have Jump capability.

"Speaking hypothetically it may be technically possible for a Kreel cruiser to have exited Jump and immediately exited remaining in the solar system only as long as required to discharge a probe. Given known physics I suggest a cruiser exited Jump, launched the probe and then Jumped out as more probable than a Jump capable probe.

"There is of course another possible causality. It is possible that a Kreel cruiser exited a Jump in a full stealth status, launched its probe and is still hunkered down and is observing in a full stealth mode."

"Lorn, your first causality has merit in simplicity. In my estimation the second possible causality is less probable given the Kreel have never demonstrated a full stealth capability in any of its cruisers. I put a Kreel full stealth cruiser in the same probability category as a Jump capable probe, possible but highly improbable. We will go with the cruiser exit then entry model until shown data to the contrary."

"Navigation, Roy, you are the Jump expert here. Could Lan exit a Jump and then immediately enter Jump again? If the answer is yes, what would the Jump signatures look like?"

Looking at Kellon, Roy was seriously frowning. "Navigation here, no offense intended Sir, but your question if properly answered would earn honors and higher degrees at any University on Glas Dinnein. I have never heard of anyone trying to exit and then immediately enter a Jump at the same time. It might be possible but I would wager a cold brew it would be rather dicey. However, give me a few minutes and I will try to give you an approximation of an intelligent answer."

"Roy, no offense taken. You are respectfully granted your couple of minutes."

The question is where is the blasted thing loitering, Kellon thought as he continued to study the tactical plot. Keying his command and Captain's bands Kellon presented his thoughts.

"Kellon here, we seem to have a mystery in progress. At the moment, we believe we are dealing with a Kreel L-16 long-range probe. Continue monitoring accordingly.

"Commander Shaw will provide us with what we have on the Kreel probe L-16. Lorn, please proceed with the overview."

"Shaw here, The Kreel L-16 is one of their most advanced probes. Guardian Force engineers recently analyzed an intact L-16 on Quatrain."

Kellon took note of Lorn's brief mention of Quatrain. When he was there he was so interested in the captured cruiser he had not considered what might have been on it. Obviously it would have carried a full complement of probes. *Well, we seem to be enjoying the fruits of past risk,* mused Kellon.

Lorn continued, "The Kreel L-16 is designed specifically to establish and maintain a long term discrete surveillance program within a solar system. It accomplishes its mission by conserving its energy and restricting its surveillance efforts to passive monitoring. In terms of monitoring it has a rather normal array of temporal spectrums it concentrates on including detection of a wide range of propulsion signatures. By Kreel standards the probe's detection threshold is excellent. However operating above a 50% stealth threshold will safely escape its detection.

"While optically capable the L-16 optics are restricted to obtaining star fixes for establishing its position and in acquiring minimal planetary information for use in navigation.

"Its passive monitoring functions are specifically enhanced for interception of communications on multiple bandwidths. However, its communications detection capability is notably deficient lacking any ability to detect laser communications in either the infrared or ultraviolet.

"By design it accumulates its information until one of five conditions are met; the occurrence of an observed event that triggers a report, external command received to transmit, complying to a periodic report time schedule, filling its available storage buffers or upon exit from the system and eventual physical recovery.

"In modes of operation it can either insert itself into a solar or planetary orbit. In either mode, in order to optimize its monitoring position, it is able to make periodic adjustments to its trajectory.

"In terms of self-destruction it incorporates a redundant system consisting of three levels of Thermite charges compounded of aluminum powder and a metal oxide which produces an aluminothermic reaction. Although it is not explosive the charges create short bursts of extremely high temperatures focused on the probes propulsion, computer, data collection and transceiver units. While the probe is in operational flight mode initiation of the Thermite charges can occur if the probe is physically impacted or else an object comes near enough to trigger its mass proximity threshold. The L-16 is not built for speed. However it can sustain a speed of 100 lights and is fully capable of prolonged operation and precision navigation. Upon completing its mission within a solar system it is fully capable of accelerating out of the system and reaching some predefined rendezvous position for physical recovery or covert data transmission. All transmissions are compressed burst in nature and non-linear superluminal in form.

"In appearance the probe is cylindrical and about five meters in length. Its outer coating is optically flat black.

"That's the general overview of the Kreel L-16. Be advised, Guardian Intelligence considers it a difficult probe to either detect or catch.

"If anyone has questions, I am able to provide additional technical details."

There were no requests for more information.

"Commander Shaw, thank you. I recommend everyone put on your thinking cap. We need to crack this problem as soon as we can. Kellon out."

"Lan, establish verbal communications."

"Sir, how may I assist?" Lan prompted.

"Lan, establish contact with the other Cruisers, have them each determine their precise location and the time when each detected the two signals. When they have computed that information let me know.

"Also, initiate a complete surveillance network review, at or very near the times of the two signals. One established fact is the Guardian network did not report either signal. Precisely why it failed to do so must be promptly determined. Do our established discretionary thresholds filters reject data such as the exit pulse or the short-term propulsion signal? We must be certain the network is not unintentionally filtering out the very data we need."

"Yes Sir, initiating total network system review as requested. Anticipated time required for analysis is six hours twenty three minutes."

Kellon understood that he could not hold Condition 2 indefinitely. He also wanted to get out of his dress uniform, it felt out of place in CAC. "Roy, any progress?"

"Yes Sir. Surprisingly enough I might yet have something for you within a few minutes."

"Sir, all the Cruisers have completed their computations," Lan reported.

"Good. Lan, work with the four Cruisers. I want each Cruiser to provide as precise a true bearing and elevation from their point of detection to each of the two signals. You are to combine the multiple bearings and elevation data from the Cruisers and triangulate the points of intersection. When you have the points computed then display those points on the tactical plot."

"Computing," Lan responded.

"Tactical, assume we are dealing with a standard Kreel L-16 probe. Using that information extract all the relative motion data you can extract from its flight performance characteristics, propulsion harmonics and Doppler. If that probe has two choices, as your briefing indicates, it is either in a solar or planetary orbit. Given the data only one brief course adjustment indicates a solar orbit. Let's see if we can narrow down the possibilities of those orbit parameters, if possible."

"Tactical here, analyzing."

Having listened carefully to Lorn's briefing Kellon began the process of finding the probe. "Countermeasures, Kellon here. Carefully review the technical specifications on the Kreel L-16. Look for anything that might give us an edge, any type of small motor , anything at all."

"Countermeasures here, understood and analyzing."

"Sir," prompted Lan, "the Cruisers have combined their bearing and elevation data and have triangulated the source of the signals. I am plotting the coordinates for your review."

Kellon turned to the plot board and saw it shift into a heliocentric polar presentation, as viewed looking down on the ecliptic plane. The scale of the plot was not natural, but compressed, bringing the outer planetary orbits into a tighter graphical relationship in order to ease visualization. Faint blue circles represented the orbits of the planets and on each concentric ring there was an icon designating the current position of the planet in its orbit. About Earth were five golden icons denoting the five Guardian ships.

A second plot was located directly below the polar coordinate plot to show elevations. There was a blue horizontal line across the middle of this Cartesian coordinate plot that represented the ecliptic plane. Directly below each of the icons on the polar plot was a corresponding icon on the elevation plot showing the location of the object relative to the ecliptic plane.

Kellon observed the golden icons representing the five Cruisers near the horizontal blue line. Near Sol's position were two red icons so closely fitted together they appeared as a single icon. On the lower elevation chart the red icons were far below the ecliptic plane.

Well, there is the point of Jump exit, Kellon thought. "Lan, are all the other Cruisers being shown this plot?"

"Yes Sir, the plot is now being displayed on all Cruisers' tactical plots."

Kellon keyed in his Captain's band. "Kellon here. We have a good fix on the probe. At least it's a fix to where it was an hour ago. Comments please."

"Captain Kylster here, I note that the Kreel cruiser that Lan destroyed was well above the primary. This time they seem to have dropped off their surprise bundle well below the primary. Perhaps that is their way of showing us some respect. More to the point, the distance the probe appears inserted below the primary is about 5.5 astronomical units. Therefore, if it were to rotate from that position into the ecliptic plane, it would be near the orbit of the fifth planet. Given this position the Kreel would have a good observation point of the entire inner system and its habitable zone. One might guess they are seriously looking for the life form that recently destroyed eleven of their ships."

"Kellon here, I have one question for everyone. If you were inserting a Kreel probe into a very hostile solar system why pick an insertion point above or below the primary?"

"Eurie here, Kellon the answer to that question is rather apparent. The Kreel must be working with scant navigation data. The primary affords them the largest mass point to aim at. Likewise, by keeping the Jump exit either well above or below the ecliptic plane, they minimize the hazards of a fatal mass merge exiting Jump. Even so, without precision Jump coordinates the Kreel are taking a very big risk in making a Jump into this system only a little more than 5 AU from the primary. We can assume they believe that risk is warranted."

"Eurie, good point," Kellon commented.

Captain Kel spoke up, "I also have a related question. If you were a Kreel probe, after being inserted into a totally new solar system, how long would it require you to get an adequate star field survey in order to permit accurate navigation within that solar system?"

"Kellon here, Captain Kel, I do believe you have found a gold nugget. Everyone, check with your navigators and see what they have to say."

Kellon turned toward Roy, "Navigation, I have a hypothetical question. How long will it take for a Kreel probe to establish its stellar navigation reference survey from a cold start in a new solar system?"

Roy sat up and looked at Kellon while arching his eyebrows. "Sir, that question has more variables in it than the last purely hypothetical question you asked me to solve fifteen minutes ago. However, in the spirit of looking both knowledgeable and proficient given a typical probe optical system, about six hours would be my guess. Please note the emphasis on the key word, guess."

"Thank you Navigation, key word duly noted."

"Kellon here, Lan has dropped six hours into the anchor pool, are there any other entries?"

There were four other entries all different but together they averaged seven and one half hours.

Keying his command band Kellon issued his orders. "Kellon here, taking off two and one half hours as a margin of error from the average estimate and allowing for elapsed time means we have about five hours before the probe may obtain its needed star field survey. This means we have only five hours to position our assets to pin down that probe before it maneuvers.

"To maximize the volume to be covered this probe hunt is designated a Scout ship mission. Does anyone have any reason for the Scouts not to take the lead in the hunt?" No one put forth an objection or alternate suggestion. "Kellon here, we will launch our Scouts to interdict."

Kellon looked over and saw Roy was still busy and deeply focused on his consoles. He smiled as he heard low dark mutterings being voiced, barely above the audible range. "Lan, please patch in Commander Roan and the other four Scout leaders into the Captain's band. Also send each Scout ship in the squadron the tactical plot."

"Sir, the Scout leaders are linked," Lan reported.

There was a momentary pause and then Kellon proceeded. "Scout leaders, you are now patched into the Captain's band for mission definition. Commander Roan we are preparing for a Scout mission. As you can see from the plot we have a Kreel probe sitting below the primary. Our best estimate is you have five hours to bracket the target before it performs a trajectory adjustment maneuver. We believe it will be a short propulsion sequence. There is no information to define in which direction it will turn but if communications is its primary mission then it may begin a transition of its orbit to optimize its observation of the Earth.

"Note: in ten minutes each Cruiser will deploy its Scouts. Commander Roan will order launch and Lan will synchronize the Cruisers.

"Commander Roan designate a rendezvous point for the Scouts and proceed to track and destroy the probe. Be fully advised your propulsion stealth factor must not at any time drop below 50%."

"Roan here, orders received and understood. Launch in nine minutes and forty seconds. Roan out."

"Tactical here. Sir we have the results of a preliminary analysis." "Tactical, what are we dealing with?"

"Sir, we first examined the propulsion harmonics. They indicate no appreciable acceleration, only a trajectory maneuver was involved. In examining the harmonics and combining those with the Doppler, we have concluded a possible entry sequence. In obtaining our preliminary conclusion I have incorporated Captain Kel's observations, regarding the time required to build up a star field survey, therefore my conclusion is a combination of observation and theoretical reasoning."

Kellon would have accepted the wager of two cold brews that he heard Roy softly mutter under his breath. "He means he is plain guessing."

Lorn's detailed briefing continued. "The probe's entry below Sol was sufficiently distant, being 5.27 astronomical units, that gravitational attraction between the probe and Sol during six or seven hours is not meaningful. The probe's initial requirement would be to orient to the solar primary. Even a brief optical scan of the surrounding space enabled it to orientate to Sol. Tactical considers the probe's initial mission is completing its collection of star field data. This information is required to align precisely its directional superluminal broadcast antenna. Therefore, the initial observed probe maneuver was merely to establish a heading and velocity vector minimizing the glare effects of the primary while optimizing its survey of the star field. Given this initial probe requirement, combined with the lack of acceleration in its propulsion characteristics, the probe will most likely still be near the entry point. However, some drift distance from that point is probable due to the effect of its nominal insertion velocity."

"Sir, that is our initial assessment. We are continuing to analyze the available information."

"Tactical, Kellon here. Keep me informed as the analysis proceeds."

Kellon keyed Shey's communications band. "Commander Roan, Kellon here. Based on a preliminary analysis Tactical has surmised the probe evidenced no appreciable acceleration and may currently be near its entry point. Tactical indicates it's essentially stationary until it completes a star field survey and establishes its position. This assessment is based on preliminary data only."

"Roan here, understood. Roan out."

"Lan, are you prepared to synchronize the launch of the Scouts with Roan and the other Cruisers?"

"Yes Sir, on Roan's countdown I will perform the synchronization signal to all other Scouts."

"Lan, signal all Cruisers to set Condition 3.

"Lorn, you have the CAC. I will be in my quarters."

"Commander Shaw here, acknowledging I have the CAC."

Chapter Thirty-Four:
Kreel Probe Hunt

Onboard Shey there was a flurry of activity, with both Roan and Zorn scrambling into their positions to begin the necessary preflight checks.

"Shey, are you in hard link with Lan and the other Scouts?"

"Yes Roan, a tight link is established."

Roan keyed in his command band. "Ladies and Gentlemen, anyone not ready to launch should speak up. We are going on a Kreel L-16 probe hunt. On launch we will be at Condition 3. At all times you will assure your stealth factor is above 50%. If anyone has a problem now is the time to let me know." After a moment all four Scout group commanders reported they were ready for launch.

"Shey, set the rendezvous point at the midpoint on a line drawn from the Earth to the indicated position of the Kreel probe. Then tell your sisters where we are going. When we launch pick up your heels girl. We are the most distant group from the rendezvous point."

"Oh Roan, this should be fun. I have not been on a Kreel probe hunt before."

"Shey, the important thing is to get us there on time," Zorn quipped.

"Do not worry Zorn. I can assure you we will be on time at rendezvous."

"Lan, all the squadron Scouts report they are ready for launch. Please do us the honors," Roan requested.

Synchronized by Lan each Cruiser extracted the atmospheres in their Scout ship hangars. The hangar lights dimmed, hangar doors swung open and in unison all Scout ships emerged into hard space. Once in space, coordinated by Shey, the five tight tactical groups moved toward the defined rendezvous point.

With the flurry of launch behind them Zorn looked over toward Roan asking, "Roan, that probe doesn't have teeth. Are we going to try to sneak up on it or go in howling mad and active?"

Leaning back in his command chair Roan frowned and looked at Zorn. "Good question Zorn. I am still pondering the best tactic. You are correct it doesn't have any teeth but it does have a means of communication. If you recall what Lorn described it has a trigger-prompted broadcast mode of operation. It might well be that if we go in active that it will find that a trigger event and broadcast."

"OK, let it broadcast. What would that tell the Kreel?"

"Zorn, even as we have collected sensor signature information on the Kreel they have been collecting similar information on the Guardian Force. If we go in active our active signals could identify who we are. While a number of folks may have continuous wave pulse Doppler target acquisition modes each unique technology has its own fingerprints. If the L-16 detects such an active signal it will most likely transmit that signal to the Kreel Hub and the whole story of the Guardian Force being in this solar system would be revealed."

Zorn's expression became thoughtful. "Well not if we are sneaky about what we are doing."

"Sneaky?" Roan queried.

"Yes, sneaky. Our new sinister jamming signal is not standard Guardian tactics."

"Just what do you have bouncing around in your mind?"

"Well, we used that scary jamming multiplex signal when attacking the Kreel ships and it really worked. We all saw the effect it had on the Captain of that last ship. He was scared out of his mind. Why not use the same jamming now?"

Sighing, Roan thoughtfully replied. "I don't see how trying to jam a probe will have the same effect as when it was used to inhibit communications between war ships. The probe simply doesn't have a Captain to scare out of his wits. It is just what it is, a programmed dumb probe."

His expression remained thoughtful as Zorn continued his reasoning. "You are not thinking the problem through Roan. Why not simply go in jamming? The probe will certainly detect it. The question remains, what will the probe do when it detects the jamming? It will either record the signals or else immediately report the signals. If it tries to send a superluminal broadcast we should be able to detect the transmission and home in on it. As for it hearing our noise, who really cares what it reports. The Kreel have already had a sample of the jamming signals from the last battle. Hearing more of the same will do little in giving them more information than they already have."

"Zorn, I don't have any general disagreement with your points. But if the probe doesn't decide to transmit how does that help us find it?"

Now, Zorn began to smile. "Well, remember we have a bandpass worked into the jamming frequencies. What I propose is we bury into those bandpass frequencies an occasional active Doppler Pulse. It would require adjusting the bandpass filter somewhat but I would wager a cold brew Shey is capable of computing that adjustment. The point is that among all the howls and stuff who is going to notice a random timed pulse Doppler active signal? They might, but somehow I think the odds are rather small anyone would want to do the analysis necessary to pull that randomly occurring signal out of the morasses of other sounds reverberating around in their heads."

The suggestion seemed plausible and Roan promptly followed through. "Shey, are you monitoring our conversation?"

"Yes Roan."

"Well Shey, can you do what Zorn is suggesting?"

"Yes Roan. However, in order for me to do what Zorn is saying it will require adjustment to both the active array program and the jamming frequency profiles. But it can be accomplished."

"Good. So you can accomplish the change but can it be accomplished before we reach the rendezvous point?"

"Not by myself Roan. However, if you order the other girls to help I believe we can make the adjustments before we reach the rendezvous point."

Still thoughtful, Roan made his decision to proceed. "Shey you are directed to contact the other girls and involve them in the work. It is just as well they are involved since if it works we will all be using the new capability.

"One more thing Shey. Confirm bandpass slots exist for the propulsion signatures of the L-16, Kreel cruisers, fast-attack ships and scouts. Also, confirm they are wide open within the generated jamming matrix. I don't want to blot out the very propulsion signatures we are looking for. Our Scouts are to keep sharp look out for those signals and if they detect them, get a fix."

"Yes Roan," Shey acknowledged.

"Zorn, how much time do we have before rendezvous?" Roan asked.

"About one hundred and four minutes, more or less. What's up?"

Looking over toward Zorn, Roan asked, "How about our getting a root beer while looking over the problem we are facing?"

Before answering, Zorn scanned his instruments assuring himself that all systems were fully functional. "Shey, do you have everything under control?"

"Yes Zorn. All the girls are busy, all is under control and ship-shape."

Unfastening his lap restraints Roan stepped down from his command chair and stretched. "Shey, you have the Con. Give us a five minute heads up before we reach rendezvous."

"Yes Sir. Acknowledging Shey has the Con."

Zorn unfastened his lap restraints and with Roan he moved back to their living quarters. Once in the living quarters Roan took out a couple of cold root beers and then settled into a chair at the small rectangular multi-purpose work and dining table. He passed one of the bottles over to Zorn.

Sitting down Zorn looked at the small bottle he held and removed its cap. "I must admit after a while Susie's root beer grows on you. It's good and refreshing. The problem remains, we are running out of our stock. What do you think, will we be recalled to Glas Dinnein soon?"

Like Zorn, Roan removed the cap from his root beer and sipped the contents of the bottle. "Well, we've been out about six months. That would normally mean a recall should be forthcoming soon. The real question is, as we come home, what will Fleet Operations expect of us?"

Still holding the cold bottle between his hands Zorn looked up inquiringly. "What could they expect?"

"Well Zorn, there are two ways home. There is the normal shortest distant path and there is the dogleg path that takes us through Scion country. I would be willing to wager two brews that we go by way of Scion."

Sighing, Zorn leaned back his expression transforming into a frown. "No bet Roan. The problem is, when we were last in Scion country we had a flock of Kreel fast-attack ships in the area. I believe there were nine if my recollection is on target. That might make taking five Cruisers through Scion country a bit sticky."

"Not if we Jump short and then go around. I suspect only one Cruiser would actually approach Scion and that would be most likely Lan. It is obvious a need exists to talk with Kur again. If we are going to ally ourselves with the Arkillians we need to establish some form of reliable update dialogue. Frankly, I don't know what the Kreel are up to but they are not known for quietly sitting back licking their wounds. I think they will kick back. I would wager, given the odds, trouble is headed our direction. The only questions are how big a kick, where and when?"

"Roan, be advised you are singing to the choir. We've destroyed eleven Kreel ships over the past several months. I would wager the Kreel Hub has noticed that little fact. As to when? The probe we are looking for might be the beginning of that kicking back. My gut feeling is serious Kreel trouble is heading our way. What about this Kreel probe? How do you want to dig it out of hiding?"

Sipping from his root beer Roan paused for a moment. "Well, we have twenty Scout ships. How do you recommend we optimize building an efficient container using those twenty discrete points?"

Leaning forward Zorn grew silent thinking before he answered Roan's question. "I don't believe we need a container. That probe has a very small electromagnetic reflection cross-section. We need to adjust accordingly and play it smart. I recommend we hold Shey to the line we are following and spread out the remainder of the Scouts into a broad facing hoop. The expanded hoop will give us good coverage and we can alternate the Scouts using our random pulse Doppler target acquisition methods.

"If Shey runs a simple random number sequence to select and command which Scout transmits, cycling through all the Scouts, it would further confuse any information the Kreel might discern from our sensor transmissions. Shey, while remaining in the center can likewise transmit Doppler target acquisition pulses. Everyone not transmitting would be monitoring for the Kreel propulsion or superluminal transmissions. One way or another we will detect and flush out that probe. Since you asked, that is what I do suggest," Zorn answered, taking a sip from his root beer.

Roan smiled. "Ah, once again I am glad I asked. Your approach might just work. Shey, do you have your hands full or can you handle some more work?" Roan inquired.

"Roan, I am sorry but at the moment I am rather busy. We are nearing the end of the calculations and the adjustments of our sensors required to do what Zorn recommended."

"Shey, so noted."

Roan and Zorn returned to their conversation as Shey maintained her vigilance and the girls were completing their assigned task.

"Roan, we have completed the calculations and adjustments you ordered. Be advised, you have eight minutes until rendezvous," Shey reported.

Depositing their empty root-beer bottles in the appropriate recycle receptacle Roan and Zorn moved quickly back to the control room and settled into their command chairs. Each carefully scanned their instrumentation and Shey's sensors and both studied the current tactical display.

Fastening his lap restraints Roan focused his attention on the tactical display. "Thank you Shey, I now have the Con."

"Shey, direct all Scouts to set Condition 2. As we approach the rendezvous point you are to spread out the other nineteen Scouts into a broad tactical hoop facing the target location and with you at its center. You will remain on and proceed along the line to the designated target point. Define the radius of the hoop to provide maximum effective coverage while using the Doppler target acquisition method that you and the girls have devised. Are you with me so far?"

"Yes Roan."

"Good. Shey when we pass the rendezvous point, and the girls have fully formed the facing hoop, all Scouts are to put on their Shey sinister costumes. We will then commence the scary jamming signals. If you understand, execute the orders." Roan ordered.

"As ordered, I am moving the other girls into their assigned positions." Shey responded.

As Roan and Zorn observed the tactical displays they saw the formation of the Scout ships breaking away and forming the facing hoop about them. Roan smiled, he felt considerable pride about the performance capability of the Guardian Scouts. In simple terms, they were good at what they did.

Within five minutes Shey reported. "Reporting all Scouts are now in an expanded facing hoop formation as ordered and on schedule. We are currently crossing the rendezvous point."

"Shey, well done. Notify Lan of our plan and tell the girls to put on their party costumes and commence jamming. Do not initiate pulse Doppler searching just yet. We will want to get nearer the probe's position before we commence pulsed scanning," Roan ordered.

X

Onboard Lan Kellon had changed his uniform and returned to the CAC. Sitting in his command chair he was studying the tactical plot. He looked toward Roy and smiled, noting he was still darkly muttering to himself while busily entering data and running calculations at his console.

"Tactical here, requesting permission to play the audio portion of what Roan is generating as a jamming signal."

"Kellon here, permission granted."

The bedlam of sound that erupted around the CAC was of such a quality that everyone in CAC stopped what they were doing and sat up, including Roy. The maelstrom of rolling sounds was enough to raise the hairs on everyone's neck. Piercing through the chaotic mixture of sound was a periodic undulating shriek that riveted everyone's attention. Buried within the raucous sounds were distinct sounds of snarls and growls along with contrasting nerve-tingling giggles of some animal that Kellon could not identify. Skillfully woven within that complex structure was a rhythmic chanting that slowly intensified and then fell away into silence, before reemerging once again. "Tactical, that's enough," Kellon ordered.

The CAC returned to silence and for a moment there was no movement. Gradually people looked at each other and then returned to their interrupted tasks.

During the battle with the Kreel warships the Guardian ships had filtered out the sounds the decoys were using for jamming. Therefore, the Guardian crews had not experienced the full force of what the Kreel experienced. Except, of course, for the short segment contained in the Kreel officer's last report and that recorded sound lacked fidelity.

Now having heard the raw signals Kellon understood his previous brief exposure had not carried with it the full impact of the jamming signal. He knew that the sounds were just sounds but they had the immediate startling effects of creating an instantaneous physiological response in everyone that heard them. There was something very primordial contained in the intense mixture of sounds. Moreover they were only now hearing the audible sounds. He knew the spectrum of the jamming frequencies carried well above and below the audible range. The total impact of that jamming morass was staggering.

What especially hit Kellon's nerve ends were the undulating shriek and the piercing animal giggles. They had the unnerving qualities of bringing back to a person's awareness, that humans were not always the predominate species on their planet. Large hungry animals with big appetites and sharp teeth had once considered people nothing more than tasty prey. *Interesting,* thought Kellon. *The Kreel still look on humans in that same hungry predatory manner.*

Kellon sat attempting to convert the emotional effects of what he had heard into its components. He sought to transform the experience from a heightened emotional content into knowledge by understanding why it had affected him so deeply.

He shook his head in wonderment. Multiple artificial intellects collected, sorted and brought together those sounds in a unique pattern. Those intellects had never experienced a deep breath of ocean air or the sensation of sunshine on their skins, yet those human-designed intellects had collected and fabricated sounds causing absolute terror in both Kreel and humans alike, provoking deeply suppressed responses. It was easy to forget among the efficient technologies and purified mercury free air the underlying brutal fur, skin, tooth and claw interactions human civilizations had overcome.

In many major respects the Kreel were nearer their beginnings and not the ends of their rise to the stars. That any species still tightly bound by their basic primitive and savage natures could master Jump travel seemed to Kellon an unfathomable paradox.

Kellon shook his head in thought and shifted his concentration from the internal speculations back to the here and now. He focused on the tactical plot where the modern version of a fur, skin, tooth and claw interrelationship was rapidly unfolding.

Chapter Thirty-Five:
Battle Alert

Far below the ecliptic plane Shey was coordinating the Scout ships as they closed on the point where the sensors had detected the Kreel probe. The Scouts were in a full facing tactical hoop and jamming.

"Shey, assign a number from one to twenty to each of the Scouts. Then run a random number generator with values between one and twenty. As each random number is calculated you will order the appropriate Scout to transmit a single Doppler target acquisition pulse. Remember, we are searching for a very small cross-section target only 5 meters in length."

"All Scouts not transmitting are to monitor for the Kreel propulsion and superluminal transmission signals. If either of those occurs everyone is to get a fix on them and pin down the target location. If a superluminal signal is detected, it is to be recorded."

"Roan, I understand. When should I begin?" Shey asked.

Turning, Roan studied the tactical plot estimating when he should begin their search. "Commence single pulse transmission when we are one AU from the estimated probe's location," Roan responded.

However, even before the first Scout transmitted a single Doppler pulse Sheba detected the lurking L-16. "Galen here, Sheba has a contact! Kreel L-16 propulsion signature confirmed bearing 010 relative, elevation minus 14 degrees. Its acceleration curve is ramping up."

"Well done Sheba. Stay tight Scouts, here we go. Keep the jamming going. That's what seems to have flushed the probe out," Roan ordered.

"Roan," Zorn inserted, "we have Sheba's target true bearing data. I have initiated a multiple Scout ship passive lock on the L-16's propulsion harmonics. It is about two AU in front of us and it is accelerating away. It is running directly toward the lower heliopause. The probe has a good head start on us. It will take hours of chase for certain, if we pursue."

Looking at the updated tactical plot Roan frowned, then looked over at Zorn. "Acknowledged. We are going to pursue the drone. Shey, considering the earliest time to intercept, compute an intercept point for the target probe. Bring the hoop around to follow that intercept line. You can also tighten up the hoop."

"Roan, I do not have a calculated intercept point," Shey responded.

Shey's reply surprised Roan and turning, he inquired of Zorn, "How long until intercept?"

"Sorry Roan, Shey is correct, there is no intercept data yet available. According to the propulsion harmonics the target velocity is still ramping up. Assuming the L-16 maximum speed reported in the intelligence study is correct, it's accelerating to its upper limit, 100 lights. With the head start it has it may take more than four hours to intercept."

"Zorn, stay on the numbers. Let me know when it has reached a constant velocity.

"Shey, until we have a calculated intercept point keep the probe's bearing at zero degrees relative."

"Yes Roan. I'm coordinating the girls accordingly," Shey responded briskly.

As the minutes slipped past Zorn continued to study his instrumentation and began to frown. Turning toward Roan he rhetorically asked, "What are the Kreel up to?"

"What do you mean?" Roan asked.

Pointing to the tactical plot Zorn explained his primary concerns. "Well, look what is going on here. From any vantage point something is wacky. What would possibly cause a dumb probe to make a run for the heliopause? Why would a probe run? More importantly, if it has not had the time required to collect its star field survey then how is it navigating? Obviously, it knows where it is and it's running for a preprogrammed reason. However, what might that reason be? Also, in spite of the fact I'm seriously underpaid I nevertheless am continuing to observe my trusty sensors. The probe's velocity is now moving above the stated maximum velocity of a standard L-16 and it's still accelerating. Don't you think it is a mite funny that the minute we make our presence known it announces its position by running like a scared varmint for the bottom of the heliosphere?

"What bothers me most is it's obviously pulling us further away from Earth each minute we pursue it," Zorn cautioned.

Turning again to study the tactical plot Roan also checked out his own instrumentation and was frowning. "Zorn, as usual your insight is sharp and on target. That probe lacks a survival instinct. The only apparent programmed reason that comes to mind for the probe to run is to increase the time it can monitor and report. That means it had reason to believe we were on its location, or soon would be and is merely extending its mission time. Does that make sense to you?"

Like Roan, Zorn was frowning, and taking a deep breath, he slowly let it out. "Well yes, in some ways it sorta does. Unfortunately I have a distinctly bad feeling in the pit of my stomach and it's telling me there is something very wrong here. Something more sinister. The probe's acceleration curve is flattening out at a velocity of 0.15 light speed. That's a conspicuous 50% above the standard L-16! That thing out there, whatever its design functionality might be, is not a standard L-16. Just what might be its operational functions? The probe has made no known detectable transmission or else we would have been all over it, directional transmission or not. Remember it must achieve a direct alignment with the intended receiver to transmit superluminal successfully. So the question remains, does the intended Kreel receiver lie along the path the probe is following? If so, just what is out there? Where is it skulking? How many big teeth might it have?"

Zorn's questions were sufficient for Roan to grasp the significance of what the Kreel probe's functions might actually be and that function spelled ambush. "Shey, immediate command to all Scouts. Stop all jamming. Shed the costumes at once. We may be heading into an ambush! Confirm Condition 2 and full stealth," Roan ordered.

A moment later Shey confirmed. "Roan, all Scouts are set Condition 2, full stealth, passive tracking only."

"Shey, send an urgent battle alert to Lan. Warn them we believe there may be a Kreel heavy strike force nearby, possibly just outside the heliopause at the point where the probe is heading. Bundle the velocity vector parameters of the probe to Lan. Inform them it is not, I repeat not a standard L-16.

"Warn the Commodore the probe may only be a lure and we are being drawn into an ambush, or else drawn away from the defense of the Earth. In either case this probe spells big trouble. Report, Scouts are continuing pursuit of the probe."

"Roan, communications through the nearest navigation beacon with Lan is established. The message is transmitted."

"Shey, reform the Scouts into five groups. Form each group in the standard three-sided tactical pyramid with the group leader at its top. When you have reformed the groups move the groups to form up on you in a new formation. Our group will take the top position of a larger four-sided pyramid formation. Make the side of the base one hundred kilometers on each side. Do you follow me?"

"Yes Roan. I am sending instructions to my sisters now."

"Shey, set a new tactical plane. The velocity vector of the probe lies on the plane and the second axis of the plane is parallel with the ecliptic plane. Now that the probe's velocity is constant compute the intercept point and bring us onto a line to intercept the target at that point."

"Roan, I am responding as ordered," Shey replied crisply. Continuing to consider the possibility of an ambush Roan decided to hedge his tactics.

"Shey, continue closing on the target but shift to a new intercept point. Set the new intercept point offset three thousand kilometers directly above the previous target intercept point. When we reach the new intercept point assume a parallel track above the target and maintain that relative station." "Roan, I am complying. My sisters are reforming and I am now moving to the new intercept point three thousand kilometers above the fleeing probe. All Scouts are reporting full stealth Status 2. Estimated intercept is in 8 hours 33 minutes."

Having listened to Roan's orders to Shey, Zorn was curious. "Roan, what's up?"

"Well Zorn, it seems we have two choices. We can intercept that probe and immediately destroy it, or else we can intercept the probe and escort it to the heliopause and then destroy it."

Looking doubtful, Zorn inquired, "Wouldn't it be simpler to destroy it sooner than later?"

Smiling mischievously Roan quipped, "not necessarily. Besides, I know you want to find out just how big those teeth lurking out there really are."

Shaking his head in a dubious motion Zorn deeply sighed. "I was afraid you would say something like that. Shey girl we have fallen into the hands of a masochist."

Sitting back in his command chair Zorn commented dryly. "Roan, for the record it will take 69.42 hours at 150 lights to reach the heliopause. I provide this technical information to help you choose the alternative that you have already chosen."

Onboard Lan, Kellon studied Roan's urgent report. "Lan, update all Cruisers to set alert modified Condition 3. Communicate with the Arkillian Nest ship that we are going on precautionary battle alert. Tell them they may be Kreel bait again and they are to take suitable defensive measures. As we obtain more information we will pass it along.

"Send the alert, bundled with the reasons why, to William. Ask him to send an alert notice to Olympus."

"Sir, the messages are being sent," Lan responded.

"Lan, locate the point on the heliopause the Kreel probe is heading for and mark it with a red 'X' on the plot."

Kellon paused momentarily, studying the symbol Lan had placed on the plot. "Now locate the point on the heliopause above Earth's current location. Mark that location with a black 'X'. Lan, transmit the plot to all Cruisers."

"Sir, The plot has been transmitted."

Keying his command and Captain's bands Kellon addressed his senior officers. "Ladies and gentlemen, Kellon here. I have sent to you a graphical representation of the current tactical situation. Please take a moment to study the information. The red 'X' location marks the point on the lower heliopause boundary the probe is heading for. The black 'X' marks the point on the upper heliopause above the Earth. Comments please."

"Captain Kylster here. I doubt the red 'X' nearly directly below Earth is a mere coincidence. The proximity of the Earth to that red mark argues intent, purpose and considerable planning. The real question is whether the Scouts are being drawn into an ambush or suckered away from the real fight around Earth."

"Kellon here. Captain Kylster both of your observations are most likely correct. The real question is what is waiting out there for them? They can overtake the probe before it reaches the heliopause. Therefore whatever it is waiting to intercept them it must be within the heliosphere. Whatever they are doing the Kreel are showing extreme caution.

"Given what we now know, I believe the probe is a feint, but to make it work there must be a real threat waiting somewhere along the probe's trajectory. My question is what is waiting to come in through the back door? Is this a major attack or else a second reconnaissance in force? Comments please."

"Lawrence and Captain Kel here. Kellon, the tactical problem declares the Kreel are wary of openly entering the heliosphere. They apparently are fearful we will promptly detect them. By detecting their probe we have just effectively demonstrated they have good reasons to be concerned. I believe the only thing the Kreel have that could possibly penetrate deeply into the detection network, without our detecting it, are some very careful Kreel scouts. Nothing else I know the Kreel have could achieve any serious penetration before we would detect it. The only exception being if Kreel cruisers came across the heliopause with their propulsion and all other systems shut down and following a purely ballistic trajectory. While possible, I don't believe such a tactic is probable for a major Kreel cruiser fighting force. This being so the Scouts are likely heading into a Kreel scout ambush, one designed to draw us off while the heavies come in the back door."

"Lan's Tactical, Shaw here. The normal Kreel tendency is to double up on missions that go bad. If that tendency holds they will be sending in twice the force as before. This means at least six cruisers and twelve fast-attacks. If I am correct that means there could possibly be eighteen Kreel scout ships laying in ambush on the probe's trajectory."

"Lorn, the possibility of your assessment being correct requires we take suitable precautions," Kellon commented.

"Lan, send an urgent battle alert to Shey. Advise her they may be heading into an ambush by as many as eighteen Kreel scouts, perhaps more. Advise Roan our Cruisers are moving above the ecliptic plane to plug the back door. Extreme caution is advised."

"Lan here, your battle alert is sent."

"Gentlemen and ladies, we will continue this discussion offset from Earth. Lan, move the squadron up above the ecliptic plane to oppose an attack on Earth. The designated initial defense point is fifteen AU directly above Earth. Form the squadron into a basic square three thousand kilometers on each side with Lan at its center. Orientate the plane of the square parallel to the ecliptic plane and facing the black 'X' marked on the heliopause. Ladies and Gentlemen, let's move out."

Chapter Thirty-Six:
Yellow Alert

At the trading center it was well past midnight and Susie found herself still in her office and working. The party had ended well and as the invited guests gradually departed the facility settled into a quiet calm. The party had proven to be a success. However, Susie was deeply worried about what was happening out in space. William told her what he could but he lacked all the facts and now adding to her concern there was a communications blackout in effect.

For the past fifteen minutes she had unsuccessfully tried to reach Charles Sullivan since she believed he would have the answers for many of her questions. She was still trying and becoming more worried with every passing minute.

"Communicator, if Mr. Sullivan does not answer his regular number try to reach him by any alternate number. If you are unable to reach him by the fourth number then you are to call Mr. Carl Suthaford."

As Susie waited for her call she looked about her busy work area. The large windows only showed darkness beyond and the lights in her office seemed brighter than they should have. She only grudgingly admitted just how tired she really was, tired and worried.

Her reflections ended when the communicator announced "I'm sorry Ms. Susie, I am unable to reach Mr. Sullivan. I am now connecting to Mr. Suthaford at his home number." Susie heard the phone ring only once before someone picked it up.

"Suthaford here."

Just hearing Carl's voice had its immediate effect. Letting out a deep breath Susie felt her body release some of her pent-up tension. "Oh, Carl, I am so happy to hear your voice. It's Susie. I have been desperately trying to find Charles. It is important."

Carl's voice was tired but he was fully awake and listening. "Hello Susie. In that it is past 02:00 in the morning your call must really be important. Charles is not available for several more hours since he is en route to a high level meeting in Europe. How can I be of help?"

"Carl, there is real trouble. I cannot get much out of William, but I am confident that the Kreel are making a hard push. I have never seen the Guardian Force moving so rapidly in different directions."

"Slow down a minute Susie. You are catching me stone cold here. I will need some basic information if I am to be of any help. Just tell me what's going on."

Pulling her chair over to the communicator Susie sat down trying to gather her thoughts. "Well, we were at the ribbon-cutting for the Arkillian trading center. Suddenly there came an alert that Guardian Force had detected a Kreel probe operating within the heliosphere. The Guardian Force personnel immediately departed the party. So did the Arkillians."

"Well Susie, I can understand Guardian Force departing the party. A Kreel probe is serious but it is not something that warrants urgent calls and waking people up at two in the morning. What happened next?"

"Oh, Carl I am sorry to have awakened you. It's just that I need to tell someone in authority what is happening. It is so important. I would have called even if it were three in the morning.

"I've found out from William that the Guardian Force has dispatched all of its Scouts below the ecliptic plane in search of the probe. Still I guess that was to be expected, however, what happened next has me worried sick.

"The Scouts sent back a full combat alert and William was notified. He was able to inform me that the Scouts believe they are heading into a strong Kreel ambush or else the Kreel are attempting to draw them away from the defense of Earth. What happened next is even more of concern. Monstro is moving out from Earth to the second Lagrange point and it will hold there fully prepared to fight. All the Cruisers have rapidly moved above the ecliptic plane and they are moving away from and not moving to support their Scouts. They are positioning themselves to intercept and oppose what they believe may be a large Kreel

366

force striking at Earth from above the ecliptic plane. Carl, they must be heavily outnumbered. I cannot believe the Cruisers would abandon their Scouts and then move to intercept in a different direction. This scares me silly. No one expected a major Kreel attack this early."

"Susie, I begin to see how serious this could be. What do you believe Charles or Olympus might do?"

"Carl, Olympus must be put on full alert. If the Kreel are able to break through the Guardian Force screen they will certainly hit Earth head-on. Someone must be alerted to that possibility."

"Susie, regretfully there isn't a damn thing we can do regarding what the Kreel do in outer space. Earth does have some very sophisticated near Earth defenses, including some powerful missiles and ground based particle beam weapons. It is the stuff we covertly brought together and kept quietly on standby in case Monstro proved to be hostile. We have fully integrated those defenses into a global international defense grid. I do know the folks who are responsible for those systems and I can pass on the warning to higher commands. Susie, this is really important. Are you confident of your information?"

Sitting back in her chair Susie took a deep breath. What Carl was asking her was important and the proper response required her to be correct in what she said. "Yes Carl. I can affirm what I have said, however, I stress that no one has yet fired any shots. Only the concern exists and the Guardian Force has moved into a defensive position as a precaution. They have also gone communications silent. The probe is real and so are the Guardian Force's concerns and deployment."

"OK Susie, that is good enough for a yellow alert. I'll pass the information onto the proper channels and I'll see to it that Olympus sets an alert status. Well-done Susie. If you find out what is happening keep us informed. There is no reason to scare anyone unless it's truly necessary. If we can stand down we would like to do it as quietly as possible."

"Carl, I fully understand and agree. I will have William monitoring all Guardian Force communications and pass on whatever I learn. Thank you for not being angry with me for waking you up at such an hour."

"Not to worry Susie. I am about to do the same thing to a number of very irritable type folks. As Charles is fond of saying, the Government pays us the big bucks just for such bothers. Good night Susie."

"Good night Carl."

Putting the phone down, Susie sat for a moment frowning. "William, have you heard anything more?"

"No Ms. Susie. The combat alert will be in place until Guardian Force cancels it. Lan informed me of what was happening in order for me to be attentive. I am confident if anything worth knowing happens Lan will inform us. I am however concerned about my friend Shey. She is the lead Scout and where they are heading looks very hostile and they are operating without Cruiser backup. It is very serious."

"William I do understand. I also think of Shey as my friend. She is very special and so are all the others."

"I agree with you, so are the others. It is just Shey was my very first real friend other than you.

"Ms. Susie, may I suggest you go to bed. It is well past midnight and if anything worthy of waking you up occurs I assure you I will do so."

"Thank you William, be certain you do wake me up if anything happens."

"Ms. Susie, I do promise to wake you the moment I hear anything important about what is happening. I am also monitoring all of my favorite news outlets around the world. If anything happens that is important you will be among the first to hear about it."

Standing, Susie covered a big yawn with her hand. "Thank you William. It has been a very busy day and I didn't expect it to end quite like this."

Susie picked up her now empty cup of tea and headed for her bathroom and then to bed. It was late and William was right. *I do need to get some sleep,* she thought and lifted her hand to cover a second yawn.

William carefully monitored Susie to be certain she was safe and then scanned the entire facility for its overall security status. He noted all was clear. He nevertheless signaled the security office informing it of the yellow alert status. Then he began monitoring key military communications around the world.

Carl's first phone call went to the White House Duty Officer. He identified himself and then passed to the officer a prearranged code word. At first the Duty Officer seemed puzzled. It was not a common code word. After a flutter of keys on a keyboard suddenly the Duty Officer was fully alert and crisp. "Sir, the alert status is being processed according to instructions."

The Duty Officer asked Carl several more questions, including where others could reach him if necessary. Carl told him he would be at home until seven.

His second call went to a special number that Charles kept for emergencies. He left a detailed message for Charles including telling him he had notified the White House Duty Officer.

His third call went to Darrell Fann. He was somewhat surprised to hear Darrell answer on the first ring.

"Good morning Carl. Might I ask, just why are you up and about at this hour and more to the point, why are you calling me at this early hour?"

Having put on his bathrobe Carl was sitting on the edge of his bed. He was still tired and needed to stifle a yawn. "Good morning to you Darrell, might I also ask what has you up bright and bushy tailed and working at two-thirty in the morning?"

"Well Carl, I have an old habit. When I see uniform types scurrying to battle stations I take that as a clue that something is happening worthy of my concern. That is an easy answer, but again, I ask why are you calling me at two-thirty in the morning?"

"Well Darrell, you are the third down on the pecking list to receive a call from me this morning."

"Third? Well who are the first two?"

"Well, first there was the White House Duty Officer and second was Charles' secret number."

"Damn, that is quite some pecking order and to think I am number three on such an esteemed short list is very humbling. What's up?"

"Darrell, I just received a very troubled call from a very distressed interstellar ambassador. She has been receiving updates. The Guardian force has split its forces in a very drastic fashion. It has sent its Scouts below the ecliptic and they report they believe they are heading into a Kreel ambush, or else they suspect the Kreel are trying for tactical reasons to draw them away from Earth. In addition the Cruisers have broken out of their normal defensive positions. They have moved above the ecliptic to take a blocking position to oppose an attack from a potentially heavier Kreel force. Susie indicated some Kreel ships could break through the Guardian defenses and reach Earth. Does that give you the picture?"

"Yes, your description is crisp. The scene does look serious. Carl, I will put out a full alert call within Olympus and I'll have all the troops assembled."

"Darrell, good move. I agree this is serious. If the Kreel break through it's your group that has the responsibility and only capability to track the Kreel ships. You will need to be directing Earth's point-defense facilities to the Kreel targets. Are you ready for that?"

"Carl, we have practiced that tactical protocol a hundred times over the years. The procedure admittedly is a bit dusty but we can blow the dust off in a hurry. Do you think it might actually come down to point-defense?"

"Yes, I believe it is actually that serious. Susie told me that Monstro is moving out to a Lagrange point and it is preparing for battle. You should do what you need to be full combat ready in the shortest possible time. The Kreel are considerably faster than Monstro. You will not have a great deal of time to react if a Kreel breakthrough occurs."

"Roger that. I will warm up the basement facility and begin routing our communications from there. Do you have the contact information for that facility?"

"Yes, I have it. I do however, recommend you contact William and link up with him. He should have your contact information since he will be your best link to the Guardian Force."

"Whew, I had forgotten William's capabilities. I will call him through Susie's communicator. Do you think he is awake?"

Darrell's innocent question caused Carl to smile broadly and he appreciated the momentary levity. "Darrell, he's a computer, of course he is awake. Since I am definitely not a computer, I for one am going to try to get three hours of sleep. I only hope my phone doesn't come off its cradle before sunrise. However, if you need me, call."

"OK Carl, but if you do hear anything, you call me."

"Not to worry Darrell. I hope you have some hot bunks in that cold damp basement of yours. As they say in the Guardian Force, Carl out!"

In Susie's now dark and quiet office, high on the western slopes of Colorado, William noted the gradually increasing alerts expanding like ripples out from Washington and from secondary military organizations. He observed with considerable interest that the alert signals were not respecters of national boundaries. William noted that around the world command centers were alerting military forces to a possible attack from the depths of space. Earth was slowly awakening. William studied the communications network as it was lighting up in his previously identified military grid and he noted the key nexus points. There were some very new nexus points and new information he had not seen before. What was happening was obviously not normal communications and it clearly indicated special actions were involved. He would come back later and do further analysis of what he was observing.

He spawned several sub protocols to monitor and record the military network while he redirected his primary attention to monitoring for Shey and Lan.

"William," Susie's communicator announced, "I am receiving a call from Mr. Darrell Fann. He is asking for you."

"Communicator, patch Mr. Fann's call to me."

"Good morning Mr. Fann, William here. How may I be of help?"

"Good morning William. I spoke to Carl Suthaford a few minutes ago. He suggested I provide you our special contact number. It's for an Olympus combat center that we are spinning up."

"Mr. Fann, I would appreciate the contact information. I will see that it is properly recorded and used only prudently."

"William, I need to ask, can you be of assistance in tracking the Kreel?"

"Mr. Fann, if combat begins all Guardian combat traffic interchange of the Guardian Force ships will be at my disposal. If target data on Kreel elements are contained within those transmissions I will also have access to that information. Can you

371

be specific as to what type of information would be of assistance to you?"

Hearing what William had said brought Darrell upright in his chair. William's revelation that he had total access to Guardian Force communications came as a shock to him. He had no prior concept William had such Guardian clearance and capabilities. *Oh boy, what a question to be asked this early in the morning,* he thought.

"Well, William, if any Kreel ships break through the Guardian Force and approach toward Earth we would like to have all the targeting information you can provide about those ships. We do have some point-defense capability near Earth. Can you assist in this?"

"Yes Sir. If such a breakthrough does occur then I can possibly provide you targeting information presuming the Kreel elements are being monitored by the Guardian Force."

"William such information could be very valuable. Thank you for your assistance," Sighing, Darrell provided William with the contact information, all six numbers and then ended his call with Susie's computer. He had always had difficulty talking with William, he was after all only a machine. The problem that bothered him was, when speaking with William it was very easy to forget he was just a machine. That was somehow unnerving. He mentally classified his worry as utter nonsense and pushed it out of his mind.

Darrell set about calling the key Olympus personnel, each of whom would in turn call others. He set about bringing the full Olympus organization up to its full combat alert status.

Chapter Thirty-Seven

Tactical Misdirection

Roan's responsibility was commanding the Scouts as a unit. There were twenty Scouts that were more accustomed to being loners or in a small group and not elements of a larger formation. Now, Roan was holding them in a tight tactical formation and this was not their normal mode of operation. Normal or not they were expertly performing their mission. As the lead Scout Commander Roan's responsibility was for the entire group. It was his task to bring the whole team back, if possible. However, it was also his responsibility to defend Earth, even if that meant some Scouts would not be making the return trip. Having attained their intercept point, three thousand kilometers above the target, the Scouts were stealthily maintaining their unofficial escort duty. Given the distance to the heliopause Roan had lowered the combat status from Condition 2. The Scouts were now at a modified Condition 3 with every passive sensor extended to its maximum sensitivity.

The forward screen between Roan and Zorn's consoles brightened into a standard relative motion tactical plot. The targeted probe's red icon was located at its center and a golden icon appeared near the probe's icon. The golden icon represented the Scouts. Below the polar representation was a second rectilinear plot showing elevations. The elevation plot had a thin blue line centered across its width. That line represented the tactical plane and the target's vertical position. The icon of the Guardian Scouts was well above the blue line.

"Roan, I have maintained the tactical plane on the line of flight of the probe, with the second axis parallel to the ecliptic plane. Is that relative motion presentation adequate for your purposes?"

"Very adequate Shey, thank you." Both Roan and Zorn were intently studying their instrumentation and the frown on Zorn's face clearly revealed his concerns.

"Roan, I have been considering what we have out there. The incoming battle alert from Lan suggested we might be heading into a hostile covey of Kreel scouts. If true that could prove very unhealthy."

Looking over toward Zorn Roan's voice revealed his own concern. "On that point we wholeheartedly agree."

Glancing up from his instrumentation Zorn looked toward Roan. "Well, as you well know I have labored extensively for decades not to be confused with anyone who goes out looking for a fair fight. They are altogether too unpredictable and extremely dangerous affairs. We need some way to gain an edge in this insanity."

"We are again in agreement, Zorn. I have been trying to come up with an edge to shift the odds in our favor. So far the tactical problem has me stumped and we are running out of time. Do you have any suggestions?"

Zorn paused a moment, frowning. "Perhaps. Our problem is rather elementary. We don't have a clue as to what is out ahead of the probe. There could be clear space or a hundred Kreel ships. We simply don't know."

"Again, we are in agreement," Roan replied.

"Well Roan, I have watched what Kellon does. He is a master in using tactical misdirection while getting our butts out of tight places and leaving the field of battle strewn with Kreel wreckage. What we do know is it would be utterly stupid to charge in among a host of hostile Kreel scouts hunkered down as sleepers. They might start shooting, even before we detected them. So why not do what Kellon does? Use lots of deception, misdirection and illusion to get the Kreel shooting at something besides us. We need to get some decoys out."

Listening intently, Roan began to smile. "Good suggestion Zorn. I'll gladly second your idea."

"Shey, are you eavesdropping again?"

"Certainly not Roan, I was listening strictly in the line of duty," Shey retorted with some hurt in her voice. Roan was still smiling. "It's good to see you've not gone to sleep and are still on the job girl. We need to know if the girls can help us deploy some decoys."

"You are being silly Roan, you know Scouts do not sleep. Can you specify what you need?"

"Well, if you remember we had a tactical hoop formation and each Scout had a unique position in it. What I need to know is, can each of the girls launch one decoy and then together control them to form a similar tactical hoop?"

"Roan, doing that would be very simple. What precisely would you like us to do?"

"Well, the Scouts are going to remain high and in our observation position. Each Scout is to deploy one decoy. As a group the decoys are to drop down and assemble at a point seven-thousand kilometers behind the probe. Then, I want the deployed decoys to form into a hoop just as the Scouts previously formed. You are to center the hoop on the course vector of the probe, adorn the probes with their Shey sinister lovely costumes and transmit the new jamming sequence. You are to have the decoys slowly close on the probe but they are not to come nearer the probe than two-thousand kilometers. Can the girls and you pull that off?"

"Roan, that is easy and the girls and I can do that. It simply will require the Scouts to program their decoys to communicate with each other and hold in a tight relative formation, one to another. They do that all the time. They will only need periodic commands from one of us. Do you want us to begin programming?"

"Immediately Shey, at once, without delay, any time will do," inserted Zorn.

"Yes Shey, as Zorn implies, we want you and your sisters to proceed immediately. There is one more thing Shey. Make certain you enable the maximum evasion protocols of the decoy and initiate their self-destruction protocols. We are not likely to be recovering them."

"I understand. I am communicating with the girls."

The control compartment was comfortable and the electrostatic circulating ducts were silent, yet they were efficiently refreshing the cabin's atmosphere. Roan and Zorn settled back into monitoring their instrumentation, uncomfortably aware the Kreel might appear at any moment.

Turning toward Roan, Zorn became thoughtful. "Roan, As Scout Leader, you have never directed a covey of twenty Scouts before. How are you personally holding up to the related worries?"

Turning toward Zorn, Roan paused thoughtfully before he replied. "Hmmm, now that you ask, I'm not really sure. Each of our Scouts and their crews are unique and vital. So, twenty times unique is still unique and each is still vital. What I can say with certainty is I don't want to make a mistake, not if it costs someone their life and causes the loss of one of our Scouts. Of course, my not making mistakes is why I brought Shey and you along on the mission."

Frowning, Zorn studied Roan's expression for a moment before responding. "Commander Roan, it's definitely your Command but Shey and I are not along only for the ride and we're here to help however we can. For certain I'm all for not making mistakes and I'm for getting everyone back in one piece."

Several minutes passed before Shey reported about the Scouts' progress with the decoys.

"Roan, the girls and I have programmed the decoys as you directed. Is it alright for me to order the decoys to be launched?"

"Shey, before launching please tell the girls to be certain each of their crews is aware of what we are doing. Provide each team with a graphic display of the tactical situation so everyone is in on what is developing. Then you may order the launch of the decoys."

When he heard the unmistakable sounds of the launch of a decoy Zorn let out a long sigh. "That's a beautiful sound that helps me believe that someday I might actually live to retire. Well done Shey."

"Shey here, Roan. All crews are informed and decoys are now launched as ordered. The decoys are now descending to their predefined positions as programmed. I have instructed them to be on the course vector of the probe's in fifteen minutes.

"Roan, I am really sorry but I was eavesdropping when you spoke with Zorn. The girls want me to assure you they will do everything they can to help you not make a mistake. They are quite positive about your skill and capability. They just wanted you to know they have confidence in your orders."

376

Leaning back, Roan tried not to show his surprise at Shey's comment. "Well Shey, it's quite alright you eavesdropped. It was in the line of duty. Please tell the girls that I'm happy to have their help anytime."

Zorn let out a deep relaxed sigh. "With decoys out I feel a whole lot better. I always like to see who and what is shooting at me before they actually can see me to get a good shot."

"Zorn, just keep your nose, eyes and ears focused on your sensors. If there are Kreel out there we should see them before they see us."

Suppressing a chuckle Zorn responded dryly. "Thank you Roan for that information. It's comforting to know there's an applicable scientific theory to something like this."

The next fifteen minutes quickly passed as Roan and Zorn observed the tactical plot and then Shey reported.

"Roan, the decoys have established their hoop. They are now in position being precisely seven thousand kilometers behind the probe and slowly closing. Should we now activate their costumes and jamming?"

Checking the tactical plot Roan noted the golden icon representing the decoys was aft of the probe and precisely on the thin blue line. "Shey, fully activate the decoys' programming."

The surrounding space suddenly reverberated with the raucous bedlam of the jamming sequence. The only clear channels being those bandpass filters that allowed the Scouts to communicate with each other, with the distant Cruisers and still monitor for the Kreel. Shey promptly dampened the jamming sounds in the cabin to a faint background sound.

Continuing to observe, the Scouts patiently maintained their escort position relative to the probe as their crews maintained their alert vigilance. As they watched the plot board during the following hours the golden icon representing the decoys slowly moved nearer the center of the plot and the probe with its Guardian Scouts escort moved steadily nearer the heliopause boundary and possibly nearer to a Kreel ambush. As the time passed everyone's sense of expectation and tension steadily increased. Their honed combat sense warned them the Kreel were near and waiting for them to enter the approaching ambush.

Chapter Thirty-Eight:
Melee

As the long hours passed the tensions within the Scout ships remained high and Roan was aware of the toll the stress was taking on the Scout crews. He was also feeling the strain. His instincts loudly shouted they were a long way from any Cruiser support.

Leaning forward over his data displays Zorn's voice was tense and showing the signs of fatigue. "Roan, we are nearing the heliopause. If they are out there waiting they should be making their move soon."

As if on cue Shey's sensors suddenly erupted with alarms and Roan and Zorn's instrument consoles lit up with warning indicators. All indications of fatigue disappeared in a flood of adrenaline.

"By the seven stars!" Roan exclaimed. "We've run directly into a hornet's nest. Zorn, are those alert traces inbound missiles?"

"No! They are not inbound missiles. Give me a few seconds Roan. I'm sorting out the alerts," Zorn calmly responded.

All signs of fatigue were gone and Zorn's mind was clear as he reported. "Blast! Those traces are from a horde of Kreel scouts and they were hunkered down as sleepers. We didn't even get a glimmer of them and we passed right over the top of them."

"How many missiles do you count?" Roan's voice hinted at the stress he had been carrying for hours.

His fingers were quickly responding to the alerts all across his status console even as Zorn answered. "Roan, there are no inbound missiles! I am however busy counting Kreel scout propulsion signatures. The good news is they are now behind us. We have already passed them by and neither of us saw the other as we crossed over the top of them. I have the count. I'm registering precisely thirty Kreel scout propulsion signatures.

Now I'm seeing light missile signatures. Counting ... there are twenty light missiles. The good news is they all are opening! The Kreel have launched their missiles at our approaching decoys."

"Roan, I have instructed our decoys to activate maximum evasion protocols." Shey reported.

"Shey, send an urgent battle alert to Lan. Report we have made contact with thirty scouts, repeat thirty scouts. There are ten unaccounted Kreel cruisers somewhere, watch your back door! Send it immediately."

"Sending," Shey confirmed.

Scanning the tactical plot Roan moved to increase the separation between the scouts and the Kreel. "Shey move us six hundred kilometers higher above the tactical plane. Acknowledge!"

"Acknowledging. We are moving the formation up an additional six hundred kilometers as ordered," Shey calmly responded.

Zorn looked over toward Roan and his voice held an urgent edge. "Roan, we've got real trouble squared inbound! Sensors indicate two Kreel cruiser propulsion signatures closing from the direction of the heliopause. They are coming on fast! Our combined closing rate is 350 lights. Contact will be in approximately forty-seven minutes," Zorn reported, with an urgent and tense voice.

As the tactical plot updated Roan was well aware of the oncoming danger to his group, cruisers were well outside their weight class. Even so, they were Kreel and fair game. "Shey, send an urgent battle message to Lan. Two Kreel cruisers are detected entering heliosphere and are closing on our position. There are still eight unaccounted Kreel cruisers. Watch your back door!"

"The message has been sent," Shey reported.

Zorn looked over and observed Roan carefully studying his data screens. "Roan those cruisers are way outside our weight class. Just what are you thinking?"

Turning toward Zorn, Roan's expression was firm and intense. "Zorn, we have twenty Scouts, each with four medium missiles on board. In my view those 80 medium missiles might just put those two cruisers within our weight class. The trick will be to launch and evade."

Looking up toward the overhead Zorn deeply sighed nodding his head in a dubious fashion. "Oh boy, I was afraid you were thinking in such dank and unhallowed channels. While I don't want to throw cold water on your tactical aspirations however, for the record, no Guardian Scout has ever independently attacked a Kreel cruiser and survived to collect another paycheck. Perhaps I should expand on my earlier comments about my being significantly underpaid and not looking for fair fights. While Scout ships attacking one or more Kreel cruisers definitely does not constitute a fair fight, please do not misconstrue my earlier statements to mean I am looking forward to fight cruisers."

Roan looked over to Zorn, with a slight smile. "Zorn, stop grumbling. Fighting Kreel cruisers is merely part of your job description. Consider it a fringe benefit."

Shaking his head in exasperation Zorn lifted up his forearms in mock surrender and sighed again. "Oh, boy, what a fringe benefit. Now I know I need a pay raise. Well, given what I am fearful will soon happen might I at least make a suggestion?"

"Of course, if you make it fast. Those two cruisers are getting closer."

"Roan, we may not have the firepower to destroy those two hunks of Kreel scrap but we should be able to at least inhibit their effectiveness if we hit them in the right places. Do you remember the exit port that Commander Shaw marked in Lan's data base?"

"If you are referring to the cruiser we captured, yes. It gave direct access into the aft control room and, Ah Ha! It gave entry into the Kreel's engineering compartments! Are you suggesting we target their engineering and propulsion compartments?"

"Right on the mark. If we precision-target their engineering and propulsion compartments and control room it covers the three centers of control for those ships. Look, if we want to survive we don't dare close tight on those brutes. However, we don't need to. All we need do is close to within say 80% of the effective range of the medium missiles and let fly our missiles then run like the reaper was after us, because he will be."

Sitting back in his command chair Roan looked at the tactical plot and the two red icons representing the rapidly closing Kreel cruisers. It did not take long for him to decide his tactics.

"That sounds like a plan. I am seconding and the plan passes unanimously. Shey instruct all Scouts to bring their medium missiles to full standby Condition 2."

"All Scouts have acknowledged your order." Shey responded. "Shey, instruct them to set the missiles to passive-active homing going active at 75% of run length. The target is a Kreel cruiser. Set precision terminal homing as follows; allocate two missiles on the propulsion compartments, one missile on the after engineering compartment and one missile targeting the forward control room. Acknowledge."

"Shey here, understood and acknowledged." After a slight pause she continued, "all Scouts responding medium missiles are now on line and are set as ordered, Condition 2."

Leaning forward Roan focused on the tactical plot. "Shey reset the tactical plot with you at the center. Construct about each cruiser a tactical engagement sphere making its radius 90% of effective medium missile range."

Before Roan on the relative motion plot around each of the two cruiser icons appeared a circle and the two circles overlapped.

"Shey, pay strict attention girl. We are about to go into harm's way and we want to come out with our skins still intact. We only have one opportunity to get it right.

"Define the cruiser on the left Target 1. The cruiser on the right is designated Target 2. Define a new tactical plane that passes through the two approaching targets and through the center of the covey of our drones. Freeze the tactical plane and transmit it with an adjusted plot to all Scouts.

"Roan, the plot has been sent as ordered," Shey acknowledged.

"Good. Shey, in order for all of to survive this battle you will need to tightly coordinate your sisters. I will tell you what is required and then you will employ tight-link burst transmissions to inform your sisters what they are to do. You are to keep them synchronized. They are in turn to inform their crews as to what we are doing. Do you understand?" Roan asked.

"Yes Roan. I have communicated your intention to the group leaders and the girls."

"Shey, the battle plan is as follows: The two Scout groups on our port side are to swing wide to the port and remain high. They are to move in preparation to attack Target 1 on his outboard flank. Upon my command the two groups are to spread vertically. The high group will attack Target 1 at the 315-degree position and the low group from 225-degree position. The two groups to our starboard will spread starboard in a like manner in preparation to attack Target 2 on his outboard flank. They will split vertically in the same manner as the Scouts on the port side. The upper group will attack at 045 degrees and the low group will attack at 135 degrees. All Scouts are to remain in full stealth mode throughout the attack. During the attack all maneuvering is to minimize time within the tactical sphere while assuring accurate deployment of all missiles.

"Roan, I understand. I'm passing your instructions to the girls."

"Here comes the hard part Shey. All Scouts need to synchronize their attacks so they launch at precisely the same time. We will be hitting both cruisers fast on their extreme flanks and then running as fast as we can. Absolutely no one is to stand and fight. Shoot and then evade and run is the plan.

"When missiles are launched each Scout will at the same time launch a second decoy configured as were the first decoys. The decoys will broadcast their jamming signals ten seconds following launch. They will have maximum redundancy in self-destruction protocols. Program each decoy to remain within ninety to one-hundred-twenty percent of the tactical sphere around their assigned launch point while maneuvering in a maximum evasion pattern.

"Regarding countermeasures, upon launch of missiles and the special decoy all Scouts will deploy the standard array of counter missile and laser decoys and direct all turrets to anti-missile point-defense. Because we will be running in tight formations, each Scout ship AI will be in direct control of her point-defense turrets. We do not want any friendly fire incidents."

"Shey, you will synchronize our group and the group leaders. Group leaders will synchronize units within their own groups. Do you understand my orders?"

"Yes Roan. Your orders are understood."

"Very good. As for missile launch Shey you will on my order set Condition 1 and synchronize launch of all missiles. Condition

1 will be set at any missile run length less than 90% of effective missile range.

"Shey, do you understand all of my orders?" Roan asked.

"Yes Roan. I am informing the girls as directed and they are informing their guys."

"Now hear this loud and clear! All Scouts are to go in tight and fast and come out fast. No Scout is to penetrate deeper into the tactical sphere around their target than 80% of effective missile range! I want a confirmation from all group leaders on this point."

There was a slight pause before Shey responded. "Roan, all group leaders have acknowledged and affirmed your orders."

"Regarding evasion after missile launch each group will break sharply out and away from their targets. The Scouts hitting at 315 and 045-degrees will break up and away. The Scouts attacking at 225 and 135 will break down and away. Scout evasion maneuvers must be such as to avoid any possible automatic tracking and counter fire. Therefore, no group is to remain on a straight-line course after missile launch!

"Immediately following the attack bring up light missiles on Condition 2 and prepare for defensive action opposing attacking Kreel scout ships. No Scout is to initiate offensive engagement unless ordered to do so. After the attack on the cruisers, our rendezvous and assembly will be six thousand kilometers above and six thousand kilometers beyond the target position at the time of attack and directly in line with the track of the probe to this point.

"If any of our Scouts are hit and need help, they are to call out. This is a team effort. Let's get everyone home in one piece. Shey, be certain to clearly mark the rendezvous point on the plots. Be certain the girls know precisely what their mission is and there are no questions. Each Scout is to brief their crews accordingly."

"Roan, I am informing all the girls. They are confirming they understand. All indicate they are awaiting the command to execute."

Having listened to Roan's orders with keen interest Zorn was perplexed since there was one group he had not identified, that being Shey's group.

"Hey Roan, might I ask while everyone is attacking those two cruisers just what are we going to be doing?"

Roan turned and smiled. "Why Zorn, I thought you would never ask. Do you notice that the two tactical spheres around those two on-coming cruisers overlap?"

Zorn leaned his head onto the palm of his right hand and stared at Roan. "Roan, by the seven stars you can't be thinking of taking us in between those two big bruisers, please tell me you are not."

Roan was smiling. "Of course I can. Look at it in a positive light Zorn. The fire control parties on both Kreel cruisers will have equal opportunity to shoot at each other. They might even miss us completely."

Zorn groaned softly, "When is my enlistment up? I need a cold brew."

"Shey, after I give the command you will take our group directly down the middle but keeping us above the direct line between the two cruisers. We are to arrive and hit the firing point at the same time as the attack on the outboard flanks of the cruiser. You will split the distance between the cruisers and set your attack run high enough to remain outside of the 80% of the tactical spheres, just as the others are to do.

"There is one more item. Our group will launch two special decoys, not one. Program those decoys to remain directly between the two cruisers. Be certain you set their maximum evasion and self-destruction protocols.

"Shey, you are to coordinate all five Scout groups to attack at the same time so they go in and come out together. We don't want to give the Kreel any more time to shoot back than possible."

"For our group, when we enter the ninety percent window Sheba and you will launch toward Target 1 and Cindy and Misty will launch toward Target 2. Shey, do you have any questions?"

"There is one question Roan. When Zorn gets his brew can I have a root beer, if we should survive this attack?" Shey asked.

As Zorn broke out laughing Roan only muttered, "Shey you are spending altogether too much time with William and Zorn. They are obviously having a deleterious effect on your analytical personality."

Then Roan caught himself, stopping and listening; had he heard Shey actually giggle? *No,* he thought, *Scout ships cannot giggle, or can they?*

"Shey, command the groups to split out according to the plan. We will be decreasing our velocities to afford maximum opportunity to get all missiles off. All Scouts will strictly adhere to full stealth mode. Tell them to keep it tight, smooth and fair winds at their backs on the way home."

"Shey, send a battle urgent message to Lan. Send them the tactical plot and tell him we are engaging the two Kreel cruisers. Shey, execute!"

Zorn sighed, grumbling out loud, "Next time I'm going to read the fine print in my enlistment contract with special attention to fringe benefits."

On earth William had monitored Shey's battle urgent message to Lan. Reviewing the communication contents William promptly called the special number that Darrell Fann had provided and Darrell answered on the first ring.

"Fann here."

"Mr. Fann, this is William. In keeping with my commitment I am reporting the battle has begun. I have just received an urgent battle update. Our Scouts have detected and initiated an attack against two Kreel cruisers entering the heliosphere. They have split into five attacking groups and are proceeding with a full-scale attack. You should know the cruisers are well outside the Scouts' design combat capability. The odds are therefore very much against the Scouts but they know this. Even so, they are pushing their attack. There are also thirty Kreel scout ships involved in the battle. This means that there are another eight Kreel cruisers not yet accounted for. The Guardian Force has deployed to engage a larger Kreel force. Monstro has moved to a static position and is prepared to fight a defensive engagement. That is all I can tell you now. William out."

After disconnecting his call to Darrell, William pondered for a while considering if he should notify Susie. Promises were promises and he therefore rang her communicator. After a moment Susie answered and he briefed her.

"William, they will be OK, they will be OK. Try not to worry. Shey is with Roan and Zorn and the others. Just remember they are capable of kicking some serious butt. I'm coming over to sit with you until this thing is over."

"Thank you Ms. Susie your company would be greatly appreciated."

Onboard Lan, Kellon carefully studied the tactical plot that Roan sent with his report. He looked approvingly at the attack plan. It was a very sound if daring tactic. They were going up against very heavy odds, the two cruisers having much greater firepower. He remembered when Lan mercilessly hunted down and destroyed the nine Kreel scout ships and how completely outgunned they had been. Perhaps this time the shoe would be on the other foot, so to speak. He could not help but wonder how many of his Scouts would survive to see another day.

Roan, as usual you are as bold as brass, Kellon thought. *May fortune bless you and there be fair winds on your journey home.*

Keying his command band Kellon updated the squadron. "Kellon here. The Scouts have reported they have engaged the enemy. They are engaging two Kreel cruisers and thirty Kreel scouts. They are taking the battle straight to them. They are paying the price to give us an opening. Keep your sensors fully out. We are expecting company in the back door at any time. The report is we are facing perhaps eight cruisers. Let's give better than we receive. Kellon out."

When Kellon looked up both Roy and Ron were looking at him. They knew what he was feeling. Lan's Scouts were fighting out of their weight class and Lan was not there to back them up. Kellon knew every Captain in the squadron felt the same way. The Cruisers were where they needed to be, still every one of them wanted to speed to the aid of their Scouts. They each knew they could not do so but they could certainly balance the scales.

"Lan, send to Monstro the battle is engaged. Estimate eight Kreel cruisers will be entering the upper heliosphere soon. They will focus on you. We will do what we can to support. Consider condition red."

Kellon keyed the general ship's band. "Ladies and gentlemen of the Guardian Force, our Scout ships are currently fully engaged with thirty Kreel scout ships and two Kreel cruisers. They are far away from us and we cannot move to help them at this time. We are anticipating eight Kreel cruisers to enter the heliosphere momentarily. This is what we have trained for, stand ready. Kellon out."

Deep in the Olympus bunker Darrell Fann put the phone back on its cradle. The news from William was specific and grim. Over the years he had practiced the Earth defense drill many times. This time it was different. This time it was not a drill, it was for real.

When he called the White House Duty Officer, the officer had crisply acknowledged the shift of the alert status from yellow to orange and he understood this was not a drill.

Sitting back Darrell looked around the large room and looked at the various tactical screens. They were now getting signals from far below the ecliptic. They were confusing but it was clear there was a real melee in full progress. People were out there in the void fighting for their lives and some of those people were most likely dying. They were there defending Earth, even though not one of them had been born on Earth. He shook his head in wonderment. It was a larger and scarier universe at this moment than it had been yesterday, larger and a whole lot more frightening.

Charlie called out in an excited voice, "Darrell, here they come. They are dropping down from almost directly above us. Boy howdy, they are really moving!"

Chapter Thirty-Nine:
Prelude

The five Guardian Cruisers were poised fifteen AU above Earth and Kellon was focused on evaluating the developing tactical situation. There were, as Roan had correctly surmised, Kreel cruisers dropping down from the back door. In fact there were eight Kreel cruisers inbound. Due to the speed-of-light time lag involved the Kreel cruisers were already deep within the heliosphere before their propulsion signatures were registered. From their deployed positions it appeared they had entered the heliosphere at nearly the same time, at three widely separated points, in an equal sided triangle formation.

Two cruisers were at the top, or apex and three cruisers were at each point of the triangle's base. Studying the Kreel's formation Kellon observed the six cruisers at the base of the triangle were slightly in advance of the two cruisers at the apex.

"Lan, set up an open link with William. Feed to William all available target data. Be certain he is also telling them where the friendly pursuing Guardian Force ships are located."

"Link established. William is receiving and transmitting data."

Now where are they heading, Kellon asked himself. He began to evaluate the velocity vectors for each group of Kreel warships. He quickly determined the intended goal of the six cruisers at the triangle's base. Their velocity vectors indicated they were moving directly toward Earth.

Having carefully studied his instrumentation Lorn looked up toward Kellon and reported. "Tactical here, we have eight Kreel cruisers above the ecliptic plane and above the current position of the Earth. They are approximately 11.7 AU within the heliosphere and closing. Their current speed is 180 lights. Their projected ETA at Earth is 52.68 hours."

Listening to Lorn's report Kellon smiled as he grimly thought, *It is our job to see they do not get there!* "Lan, draw a line between the six Kreel cruisers that comprise the two forward groups. Find the mid-point on that line. Now connect a line from that mid-point to the Earth. Define a tactical plane where the line passing between the two groups and Earth are on the plane. Now, define that plane as Tactical Plane 1. Lan, using our position as the reference, define Target Group 1 the lower left group, Target Group 2 the lower right group and Target Group 3 is the third and top group. Send the tactical plot to all Cruisers."

Lan's acknowledging tone sounded.

Kellon studied the plot board and frowned, noting the relative course vector for the third group was not the same as the other six cruisers. He asked himself, *Now, where might those two cruisers be heading?* Then, he thought of the Arkillian's Nest ship.

"Lan display Monstro's current position." Kellon ordered.

When Lan displayed Monstro's coordinates, Kellon observed Monstro's icon was located precisely on the Kreel's course vector. *Ah ha*, thought Kellon, *two against one is not fair.* "Lan, construct a line between Monstro and the midpoint between the approaching Kreel cruisers in Group 3. Next, display the position of Monstro's fighter screen. Now measure along the line from Monstro a distance equal to the Kreel heavy missile effective range and put an 'X' at that point. Next, at twice that distance from Monstro place a second 'X'. Define the first 'X' Mark 1 and the second 'X' Mark 2. Now measure from Monstro a distance equal to the Kreel beam's known effective range and place a red 'X' at that point."

Leaning back in his command chair Kellon studied the modified tactical plot. He immediately noted Monstro's fighters were in an extended position just beyond the red 'X'. The problem was basic, both the red 'X' and the fighters were less than half the distance to the first black 'X' and the Kreel would be launching their heavy missiles from that latter point.

Kellon had no doubt the Arkillians had energized the Kreel beam weapon and they were poised to use it in their defense. The problem was the effective range of the Kreel beam was considerably less than the effective range of the attacking Kreel's heavy missiles. Knowing standard Kreel tactics Kellon knew they would fire their heavy missiles from maximum effective range. This meant Monstro would have multiple incoming heavy missiles from two Kreel cruisers targeting it before it could deploy the Kreel beam weapon in its own defense. The Arkillian fighters were far less equipped to fight a Kreel cruiser than were Lan's Scouts. Therefore, based on their position, Monstro was using its fighters as an advanced point-defense missile screen. *Well,* Kellon thought, *they might take out some of the heavy missiles but the odds favor the Kreel. By definition Monstro is a large and crippled vulnerable target.*

Kellon had no idea of the Arkillian maximum effective range of the heavy missiles, but doubted it was greater than the Kreel's missiles. Added together the Arkillian Nest ship was not likely to survive the upcoming engagement, unless Lan could offer a helping hand. Kellon smiled. *Since Lan's task is taking out those two advancing cruisers, a helping hand is on its way.*

As was his proclivity Kellon's intention was to define the battlefield to his own liking and advantage then force the enemy to fight on his terms. Given the current odds in favor of the Kreel he considered it was a good time to begin designing that helpful battlefield.

Turning toward Lorn, Kellon asked for his assessment. "Tactical, do you see anything that doesn't look right, anything at all that looks like the Kreel are holding back or else have something new that isn't obvious? Do you see anything that looks like another feint? What is your best assessment?"

"Tactical here. Sir, all indications suggest the eight Kreel cruisers are on a predefined strike mission. I believe Roan was correct in his assessment. The L-16 probe was a lure to pull our forces away from Earth. Based on the force level and tactics this is not an invasion force. This is a large-scale cruiser strike hit-and-run mission. The indicated objective is inflicting as much damage as possible, while assessing what is happening in this solar system. At the distance we are from the Kreel Hub, the commitment of ten cruisers represents a significant effort. They must have taken alarm at losing three cruisers and eight fast-attack ships. The Arkillian presence is an additional complicating factor and must be causing the Kreel considerable concern."

"Tactical's assessment is this attack is their showdown strike. If they can prove they can inflict meaningful damage and survive, they will be back in greater force. If we can shut them down here, then they may be skittish in coming back. This is Tactical's current assessment."

"Tactical, Kellon here. Thank you."

Once more turning to study the tactical plot Kellon began planning the battlefield for the upcoming combat. "Lan, clear the previous tactical plot relating to Tactical Plane 1. Lan, identify a new tactical plot. The new tactical plane passes through the two approaching Kreel cruisers in Target Group 3 and Monstro. Designate this plane Tactical Plane 2 and adopt it as our current tactical plane.

"Refer to the previous line drawn between Monstro and the approaching Kreel cruisers and show that line on the new plot. Mark a new point on that line one-third the distance from Monstro to the current position of the targets. Define this point Mark 3. Now, compute the time it will take for Target Group 3 to reach Mark 3. Then use the computed elapsed time to determine where Target Group 1 and 2 will be at that same time. On Tactical Plane 1, mark those two points Mark 4 and Mark 5 respectively. Send the modified plot of Tactical Plane 1 to the other four cruisers."

Taking a deep breath and letting it out slowly, Kellon began giving battle orders. "Lan, send the following orders to Lar and Lent. Lar is to assume command responsibility of Lar and Lent, as a team. Lar with Lent will proceed below Tactical Plane 1 to Mark 4. Lar and Lent are then to deploy to ambush the three Kreel cruisers in Target Group 1. If possible, they are to remain below the tactical plane.

"Lan, send the following orders to Lawrence and Langley. Lawrence is to assume command responsibility of Lawrence and Langley, as a team. Lawrence with Langley will proceed below Tactical Plane 1, to Mark 5. Lawrence and Langley are then to deploy to ambush the three Kreel cruisers in Target Group 2. If possible, they are to remain below the tactical plane.

"Next, advise all Cruisers Lan will proceed above Tactical Plane 1 and will take position to ambush Target Group 3. If possible, Lan will move to defend Monstro.

"Lan, advise all Cruisers our mission is to oppose a Kreel attack on Earth. Remember, expendable decoys are less costly than repairing big holes in cruisers. Take care. Stay smart. May good fortune and fair winds go with you. Kellon out.

"Lan, send the cruisers the command to break formation and execute their orders. Tell them, today they are Earth's primary defense and Guardians."

Looking up, Lorn reported, "Tactical here, our cruisers are breaking away to our starboard and port as ordered."

"Navigation, Roy, referring to Tactical Plane 2, move us smartly to a new position three thousand kilometers directly above Mark 3. Let's go set our ambush."

Looking up, Kellon saw Roy glancing at him and would have sworn Roy was smiling.

"Navigation here, acknowledging moving to 3,000 kilometers above Mark 3. Sir, let's go shut down a couple of Kreel cruisers."

Chapter Forty:
Total Bedlam

The Scouts were rapidly closing on the two approaching cruisers and Shey's focus was on keeping the formation tightly together. She ran the calculations of the attack trajectories repeatedly, refining them and notifying each group leader of their status as they approached their designated targets.

"Roan, the Kreel scouts have taken a heavy toll on our decoys and they are falling further behind us. They are still attacking the remaining decoys and the few decoys still operating are falling back. There is absolutely no indication they have spotted us," Zorn reported.

Reaching the attack departure point Shey signaled the port and starboard echelons to break out of formation and the four groups swung wide dropping toward their defined attack trajectories.

The five groups of Scouts in unison reduced their speed, thereby reducing their rapid closing rate. Since Shey's path was shortest her reduction in speed was the more pronounced. Coordinating the four flanking groups as they attained their attack altitudes, she adjusted her speed to synchronize the attack runs.

Roan was following Shey and the flanking groups' movements on the tactical plot, confirming everything was unfolding as planned. He noted their reduced speed had increased their stealth factor to 85%, thereby increasing their probability of surviving the attack. "Hold on tight Zorn, we are initiating our terminal firing run!" Swooping like a pouncing bird of prey Shey's aim point was a point well in front of and between the two closing Kreel cruisers. She was maintaining tight communications with her sister ships limiting her direct contact to the four Scout group leaders and letting them in turn coordinate their own elements. All five groups were moving silently and swiftly toward their designated firing points.

"Roan, all the girls are on schedule. We are 27 seconds from launch point and all Scouts will be on target within 500 milliseconds at launch. I am trying to tighten it up a little more." Shey reported.

"Shey, when you settle out on your final run signal Condition 1 when the missile run length is at 90% of effective range."

"Confirming orders, Condition 1 upon reaching 90% effective range. All units report they have passive locks on their assigned targets," Shey reported.

As Shey approached the launch point she steadily held the slower speed profile, assuring adequate time within the tactical sphere for launching four medium missiles and the decoys.

Bisecting the distance between the approaching massive Kreel cruisers Shey flattened out her dive. Gliding like a flickering shadow she entered the narrow valley of peril fully intent on her firing run and at 90% of run length she initiated Condition 1 for all groups.

Her whole fuselage shuddered as Shey vertically launched the four medium missiles in rapid succession. As the missiles sped away, in an arcing path toward their designated target she deployed the two decoys. Even as the decoys cleared her hull, Shey was accelerating.

The elapsed time through the firing zone had been very short. Shey had timed it so all four of her medium missiles were precisely launched on direct closing vectors toward their approaching target. Remembering what happened to Lan, she did not deploy chaff. She had no intention of decorating her sisters who were running tight in formation behind her.

Beginning her evasion climb Shey was still accelerating even as she rolled smoothly into her first turn, a 45-degree turn to her port. As Shey continued her turning climb she tightly tucked her sisters into the trailing formation. Sheba, Misty and Cindy, each confirmed with Shey they were damage-free and they had successfully launched all their missiles. As Shey and her sisters evaded they left behind sixteen medium missiles arcing toward their discrete targets. Ten seconds after she began her roll up and out she next rolled tightly right and completed the second part of her evasion maneuver, the 45-degree turn starboard. Following her standard orders Shey waited ten seconds on course and then pitched up 90-degrees reaching for altitude. The girls were right on her heels.

Ignoring the pressure of the restraining straps Zorn looked over to Roan with a big smile. "By the seven stars, Roan what a ride! Did you really see that? We went through that pair of bodacious Kreel cruisers like a comet and they didn't even get a single shot off. We caught them with their pants down and they still don't know what hit them. "Boy Howdy, what a mess we have created behind us. There is a blaze of lasers and there are explosions going off everywhere. There are multiple hits, even more multiple hits and secondary explosions."

"Shey, status report. Are we damage-free?" Roan queried.

There was a slight pause and then Shey reported, "All units in our group report they are damage-free. I am not able to contact the other groups at this moment, they are all evading. We are out of contact."

"Zorn, is there any pursuit?"

"No way, pursuit is not even worth asking about. The entire battlefield scene behind us is a total bedlam. I don't believe the Kreel have even a clue as to what happened or who just hit them. The crossing laser fire and explosions are still filling the void behind us. The good news is we are well clear."

"Shey reduce speed by 80% and proceed with caution toward the rendezvous point. Keep your ears on girl, if any of our people are in trouble, we need to be ready to move to support," Roan ordered.

"Roan, I am bringing four light missiles on line as ordered. I have no immediate track on any nearby Kreel threat, either cruiser or scout."

Looking over toward Roan, Zorn was flush with adrenaline. "Roan, there was just a huge explosion behind us. One of the cruisers either exploded or self-destructed. There can be no other explanation. Just a moment, I am checking propulsion signatures. It was Target 1, it went out with a colossal blaze of explosions! That cruiser is now floating debris. I still have a feeble propulsion on Target 2 but it is not looking at all stable. We have really hurt that cruiser also. There are continuing explosions."

Scanning the tactical plot and his instruments Roan was concerned about the other four groups, they were due to check in any time. "Shey when you reach the rendezvous point launch a rendezvous beacon and pull away, standard protocol. See if you can establish contact with the other groups through the nearest navigation beacons.

"Keep a sharp watch on our stealth configuration. Confirm all our girls are with us and damage-free."

"Confirming my sisters are with us and they are reporting they are damage-free. We are currently holding full stealth mode."

Leaning back in his command chair Roan tried to relax his tense mind-body posture. "Shey take an urgent battle update message for Lan. Attack on cruisers completed, Scouts are withdrawing toward rendezvous. One cruiser confirmed destroyed, one badly damaged. Lan's group is damage free. No reports from other groups at this time."

"Roan, the message has been transmitted through the nearest navigation beacon. I am three minutes from rendezvous. The rendezvous beacon is prepared for deployment. I still do not have contact with any of our other groups and I am getting worried."

Detecting what he believed to be a hint of concern in Shey's response Roan reassured her. "Now Shey, remember worry is only unstructured thought. The other girls are just like us, being very sneaky. Just spawn a few background protocols to keep a sharp lookout for any sign of them. That's all we can do now. Stay alert. The last thing we want at this point is a fender bender."

Looking to Roan, Zorn was actually smiling. "No," agreed Zorn, "no fender benders. What we really need now is a very cold brew or two! Perhaps, three or more would be better."

"Zorn, don't forget to get me my root-beer!" prompted Shey.

Chapter Forty-One:
Poised and Waiting

As Lan approached his designated position on Mark 3, Kellon continued to study the tactical plot and devise the needed misdirection. "Lan, draw a line on Tactical Plane 2 perpendicular to the line between Monstro and the Kreel cruisers and passing through Mark 3. Call this new line, Line 2.

"Referencing Monstro, designate the counterclockwise Kreel cruiser Target 1 and the clockwise cruiser Target 2.

"Lan, program three groups of six special decoys each, all set so when activated they will display the Shey lovely sinister matrix. Each group of decoys are to be programmed to assemble in two ranks of three decoys abreast. Set them to full jamming, full evasion and redundant self-destruction. You will position one group of decoys on Line 2, one thousand kilometers counterclockwise from Mark 3. You are to place the second group on line 2, one thousand kilometers clockwise from Mark 3. Deploy the third group of decoys precisely on Mark 3. All the decoys are to remain passive on station, until activated. When activated, you are to direct each group of the decoys toward the nearest Kreel cruiser. Lan, are there any questions?"

"Lan here, no Sir."

"Tactical, how long until the Kreel cruisers are within heavy missile range of Mark 3?"

"Sir, estimating 14 hours."

"Lan, set Condition 3 for the crew. Notify Lar and Lawrence of our tactics and estimate of fourteen hours to engagement."

"Yes Sir. Update has been sent to Lar and Lawrence."

Keying his general communications band Kellon addressed Lan's crew. "Tactical is estimating we have about fourteen hours before we engage the Kreel cruisers. We are now moving into our attack position. This is an excellent time, for those who can to take a break. We will be resetting Condition 2 in twelve hours."

Looking toward Kellon, Roy was beaming. "Sir, Navigation here, I have just received a combat report from our Scouts! Shey is reporting one Kreel cruiser destroyed, one badly damaged. They are retiring for rendezvous with no reported battle damage in Shey's group. The remaining four groups have not yet reported in. How about that sir, the Scouts really did it!"

There was a murmur of excitement in CAC and then Kellon, smiling broadly, keyed his Captain's band addressing his other four Cruisers. "We have just been notified our Scouts have successfully attacked and have destroyed one Kreel cruiser and badly damaged the second. There are still 30 Kreel scouts active in their volume. Our mission remains to oppose a Kreel attack on Earth and if possible to help defend Monstro. Kellon out."

X

As Lan reached Mark 3, he began deploying the designated decoys as ordered. Turning toward Roy, Kellon advised, "Navigation, Roy you might personally take full advantage of the Condition 3. It may become a long day. I will be in my quarters if needed. Navigation has the CAC."

Roy looked up still smiling. "Navigation here, acknowledging navigation has the CAC. How about our Scouts Sir, they really got a big one!"

Kellon returned Roy's smile with a smile of his own. "They certainly did."

"Lan, I'm going to attempt to rest for a few hours. Be certain I'm wide-awake, two hours before any possible contact with the Kreel."

"Yes Sir."

Moving from CAC and retiring to his quarters Kellon was still smiling at Roy's exuberance. Like Roy, he fully understood the feat the Scouts had achieved. *Now if they can avoid those 30 Kreel scouts they might just make it back home*, he mused.

Chapter Forty-Two:
Awaiting Further Orders

Still monitoring the rendezvous beacon Shey was feeling somewhat better. "Roan, we have solid links with all our units except for Lar's Scouts. The other three groups are forming up in our standard pyramid formation and waiting for orders. All have reported successful firing runs and are damage-free."

"Shey, don't worry, Lar's Scouts will be here soon. Just stay vigilant.

"Zorn, can you provide me with an update, what is the Kreel's disposition?"

"Yes Sir, Target 1 is gone. Target 2 is as near to being inert as it can and still generate a propulsion signature. It is extremely feeble. I doubt the cruiser can even effectively maneuver. Because of its inaction I think we took out the second cruiser and it is closer to a drifting maritime hulk and hazard than a fighting ship. I am still tracking on thirty Kreel scouts. They have pulled back and are milling about near the disabled cruiser. One or two are firing on the few remaining decoys. Currently I am detecting only nine decoys active, the others have been destroyed."

"Given the normal loadout for a Kreel scout can you estimate what percentage of light missiles those scouts still have available?" Roan queried.

"Sorry, no. Based on current rate of missile firing I don't believe many have any missiles left. There are two decoys near the remaining cruiser and, at the moment, there doesn't seem to be any coordinated fire directed against them."

Shey's voice brightened as in relief, "Roan, Lar's Scouts are reporting in. They are reporting they are damage-free but three of the Scouts have impaired stealth capability. They are late because they followed a wide path in order to avoid being detected."

"Shey, what happened to them?" Zorn queried.

"Rachel has informed me she forgot and deployed chaff as they exited their firing run. The expanding chaff has stuck to the hulls of the other girls. Because of her mistake Rachel is upset. I just took a quick peek. They are brilliant and sparkling like a party decoration."

Roan listened to Shey's report with concern before responding. "Shey, be certain you tell Rachel the important matter is she coordinated her sisters through a successful firing run. The shiny stuff will come off. However, tell her she is to remain exceptionally vigilant. They are not to expose themselves to the Kreel, if possible."

"I have passed your message to Rachel. She expresses her sincere apologies for the mistake. She will strictly follow your orders."

Turning toward Zorn, Roan asked, "Zorn, give me a status report. Where are the Kreel scouts and where is that probe?"

Concentrating on his instrument console Zorn paused for a moment, his eyes swept over the alerts. "Well the Kreel scouts are still milling near the remaining Kreel cruiser and the probe has passed blithely on its way toward the heliopause. It is currently six thousand kilometers below us and about ten thousand kilometers further along its track line," Zorn responded.

"Are the Kreel scouts still firing missiles at the remaining decoys?"

"I am only seeing an occasional missile propulsion signature, it's all light missiles and yes they are being directed toward the remaining decoys."

Zorn, are there any Kreel scouts anywhere near their probe?"

"Checking. No, the probe is moving without escort or any attempt to evade. It is quite alone."

"Shey, do we have hard links to all group leaders now?"

"Yes, hard links are established and they are each maintaining hard links to their units." Shey reported.

Sitting for a moment, Roan considered his next best course of action. There was their primary mission, destroying the probe and there were still thirty active Kreel scouts. Roan keyed his command band, "heads up everyone. We have two remaining tasks. Lar and Langley groups you will detach and go after the probe. Stay high until you are above the probe. Then close to within laser or gun range and destroy it! I do not want the probe transmitting any messages. When you have completed your task, return to altitude and the rendezvous beacon."

"When you take out the probe, it may cause a response in the Kreel scouts so when you have destroyed it bounce high and come back here as sneakily as possible.

"Langley, you have the lead and primary escort duty for Lar. Avoid engaging the Kreel unless there is no other choice. If a fight is unavoidable call a loud and clear for assistance. In brief, stay out of trouble."

"The remaining three groups will be departing the rendezvous beacon, to determine what the Kreel scouts are doing. Are there any questions?"

There were none. Langley and Lar's scouts promptly broke out of formation. They moved rapidly away following along the trajectory line of the probe.

Roan pondered his next move. There was one broken cruiser and he would leave it alone. However, there were those thirty Kreel scouts. While they might not have missiles remaining their lasers were functional and effective. Those Kreel scouts were a long way from home and their crews knew it. With the two cruisers destroyed at least six of them did not have a ride home. Although the Kreel scouts had more than a two-to-one numerical advantage, Roan considered they were disrupted and demoralized.

Considering the worst case the Kreel scouts might just decide to go to Earth and raise a ruckus. Roan was not about to let that happen on his watch.

"Shey, inform Lawrence and Lent's groups to form up in a standard trailing V. Then, display a new relative motion plot showing the current status of all units, friends and foes."

Roan studied the plot for a few moments and then he determined his course of action. "Zorn, put your best smile on, we are going to go to war."

Turning his head to look at Roan, Zorn frowned. "Oh good Roan, I have been looking for a change of pace. What, might I ask, are you planning now?"

"Well, I intend to go and see if we can get near that pod of milling Kreel scouts and do some distance sniping. Are you up to some target practice?"

His frown did not lessen, as Zorn retorted. "As I have already mentioned, I don't like fair fights. As long as I'm not providing the target services, the risks are inherently low, and there is a cold brew afterward, then I am up to a small challenge."

"Zorn, you are not to worry. Just for you, I'm not planning a melee. I intend to mimic Kellon and set up a battlefield we can exploit. I'll do my best to minimize our challenges."

Against his best efforts Zorn cracked a smile. "Now, that's darn considerate. Thank you."

Turning back to the tactical plot, Roan began his battle planning. "Shey, construct a tactical sphere, its radius being 100% of light missile tactical range. The center of the sphere being the center of the milling cluster of Kreel scout ships. Next, draw a circular disk within that sphere. Position the plane of the disk vertical and perpendicular to the probe's trajectory line. On that disk draw three lines from the disk's center. One line is vertical downward. Referencing that vertical line, draw the second line thirty degrees clockwise and the third line thirty degrees counterclockwise. Each of these lines should be drawn from the center and extend beyond the circumference of the disk. Define points on each of the three lines at 90, 100, 110 and 115% of light missile effective range. Mark the three points on the tactical sphere where the lines intersect: 'A', 'B' and 'C'. Display."

There was a momentary pause before Shey responded. "Roan does that look the way you want it?"

Roan carefully studied the plot and saw one more thing he needed to allow for. "Yes Shey, that is fine. However, there is one more item. Please construct a new horizontal line parallel to the tactical plane passing through the center of the disk.

"This line represents a pivot axis about which the disk may rotate. When the disk rotates the points marked 'A', 'B' and 'C' will shift accordingly on the surface of the tactical sphere. Do you understand my description?"

"Yes Sir, if the disk rotates, then the points 'A', 'B' and 'C' located on the disk will move with the shifting disk," Shey confirmed.

"Correct Shey. Now heads up girl. This next part is very important. When we move our Scouts into position you are to personally coordinate all sensor data and make all target assignments. The other girls will physically launch, on your directions, but they will not be making target allocations or setting missile parameters. Your task is to allocate the minimum number of missiles to each target, thereby conserving our missiles. Please work out the detail of this firing arrangement with the other girls. Have them discuss it with their crews. If there are any questions, let me know what they are."

Having listened to Roan's orders, Zorn was puzzled. "Hey Roan, do you mind telling your old friend and colleague precisely what is running dangerously loose in your noggin?"

"Well Zorn, we have three groups and I have just drawn a tactical sphere with three sets of firing points on it. I propose we position each group on one of the three sets of those firing points. Once we are in position and observing, if a Kreel scout comes within missile range we let fly a missile. We should be able to willow out the thirty milling Kreel scouts rather rapidly."

Once more, Zorn was frowning. "Might I ask, what happens if they decide to bunch up and charge?" Zorn asked suspiciously.

Roan prompted, "Shey, tell him what we should do if we are charged by a horde of angry Kreel scouts."

"Yes Sir, run like the reaper was after us."

"Perfectly clear Shey. We move up, shoot until the Kreel notice us, evade as required and then return and begin again. Comments?"

Zorn grumbled, "Yes Sir, looking at this plan makes me wonder if it is too late for me to apply for a cook and baker's course at the Academy. Then I would not be threatened with the necessity of crewing with crazy people who have an inflated opinion of their own firepower and run around in little scout ships as if they were big cruisers."

Roan smiled, ignoring Zorn's good-natured grumbling, while he transmitted the plot to the other Scouts. Keying his command band Roan informed his groups, "Ladies and gentlemen, heads up. We are not out to stand and fight. Our task is to take out those Kreel scouts. If it gets too hot, or if anything goes wrong, roll out, disengage and return to this rendezvous point. Above all, we all will need to be taking the trip back to Earth together. Remember, this is a sniping run. Don't let it become a siege or a defense of the barricades. The firing points have nothing of value on them, they are merely general references for positioning our girls, nothing more."

"One more thing, after launch of missiles we will move smartly as a unit away from the firing point. We will not remain on the firing trajectory line waiting for return fire, be it laser or missile. Now hear this loud and clear. Although Shey will be coordinating our firings and subsequent moves, if any one of you perceives a personal threat and needs to evade don't wait for orders, just evade! Then let Shey know. Forgetting this tactic could cause new holes to be installed in your previously air tight hulls. Remember, we have nothing to prove out here, except we can survive."

"There will be no automatic point-defense tracking during this operation. Positive target identification is mandatory. I will have the hide stripped off anyone who requires me to fill out multiple forms for any friendly fire incident. Accordingly, Scout AIs will direct all point-defenses. Accordingly, set gun and laser turrets for point-defense to Condition 1."

"Shey, inform Lawrence he has the 'A'-110% point, Lent has the 'C'-110% point and you will take the 'B'-110% point. If we arrive on station and there are no targets we will move from 110 to the 105 position and then we will repeat and rinse."

"Shey, instruct everyone and then move us out and away. Stay well clear of the Kreel units until we approach the assigned firing points."

"Yes Sir. The other Scouts have been notified."

"Shey, remember if anyone gets into more trouble than they can handle they are to run and call for backup. Need I say, Condition 2 and full stealth mode? Execute."

The three groups of Scouts rolled out in a tight formation and with Shey providing coordination they dove below the tactical plane. They did not have far to travel.

Within a few minutes the three groups of Scouts separated, each group moving to their defined firing points.

"Roan, Lawrence and Lent report they are in position. We are also in position. I am currently able to target three Kreel fighters. They are at the outer edge of our missile capability and pose no tangible threat," Shey reported.

Studying the tactical plot Roan made his decision to move in closer. "Shey, coordinate a move of all units to the 105% points."

"Yes Sir. All groups are moving to designated 105% points."

As Shey was moving the Scouts forward Roan turned to Zorn, "You are very quiet. Do you see anything I need to know?"

Zorn's was intensely studying his sensors and when he responded, his voice was tense. "No, everything looks like it's out in the open. This plan should work but we do need to be cautious. That cruiser is not particularly able to fly around and harass anyone but the operational status of its tracking and weapon systems remains unknown. Be hereby advised we are now moving into its heavy laser range. I herewith confess a deep-seated aversion to being converted into a piece of crispy toast. Therefore, I am advising acute alertness. Note, watch out for counter-fire, both missile and laser, from the damaged Kreel cruiser."

"Shey do you agree?" Roan inquired.

"Oh Roan, most wholeheartedly. Sir, we are at our new firing point. I am now targeting twelve targets. None pose immediate threat potential."

"Shey we will move in tighter, shift us to the 100% points." Again, Shey coordinated the twelve Scout ships and they slowly advanced to 100% points on the tactical sphere.

"Roan, all units are now on their positions. I am now targeting and confirming passive locks on twenty-one targets."

"Confirming targeting twenty-one targets. Shey, immediately upon launching our missiles rotate the circular plane within the tactical sphere 30-degrees so the three points swing towards the probe and our rendezvous point. When you shift after firing, we will be closing to the 90% points on 'A', 'B' and 'C'.

"Shey, set one missile on each target passive. Set a second missile on each target passive-active. The passive-active set missiles are to go active at 75% of computed run length. Bring all allocated missiles to Condition 2. When all missiles are confirmed passive lock Condition 2 and Scouts are synchronized, set Condition 1 for all targeted missiles."

There was only a brief delay and then Shey's hull hummed with the sounds of launching light missiles. Both Roan and Zorn felt three distinct launch thumps as Shey vertically launched three of her light missiles. From the other eleven deployed Guardian Scouts, additional missiles streaked up and arced toward the distant Kreel targets.

"Shey reported, "Forty-two light missiles launched and away. I am now coordinating the movement of our elements as ordered."

As the light missiles streaked toward their targets there were still five decoys broadcasting their jamming sequences. Their jamming signals effectively masked the slight signature of the light inbound missiles as they approached their designated targets. The Kreel had no advanced warning and the missiles poured into their gathered ranks with devastating results.

"Roan the missiles are right on target. There is wild confusion among the Kreel scouts. Multiple hits with explosions going off everywhere. The Kreel scouts are firing lasers in what looks like a pure panic pattern and there appears to be six missiles launched in a return fire. They are a wild response and they pose no threat. The explosions are continuing. It will take some time for the dust to settle."

"Shey, begin computations for the next salvo." Roan ordered.

"Yes Sir. Reporting all units are now located at their 90% positions. Currently targeting seven targets. There are no other detectible targets remaining, except the cruiser."

"Shey, repeat the firing order, two missiles to each target, set Condition 2. When missile presets are completed and locks are confirmed, set Condition 1."

"Shey here. Condition 1."

Again, Roan and Zorn felt the distinctive thump, as Shey launched a light missile. Shey continued her report. "Fourteen missiles away."

"Shey, immediately roll all units out and away from the tactical sphere. Remain low. Move us below the tactical plane, toward the rendezvous point."

"Rolling away and evading as ordered." Shey responded.

As Shey and her sisters rolled out, Zorn reported. "Roan, I am seeing no organized resistance. There are new hits, we seem to have flattened the entire field of opposition."

"Shey send a self-destruct signal to all remaining decoys," Roan ordered.

"Shey here, order transmitted."

"Zorn, give me a readout. What is left still moving back there?" "According to my count we have had twenty seven hits and by the process of elimination that means there should be

408

three scouts left active. However, I am not seeing any sign of propulsion except for the feeble cruiser propulsion signature and that signature barely counts. There are two possibilities. Three Kreel scouts have shifted to sleeper mode or else they no longer exist. Perhaps random panic counter fire destroyed them. Caution says consider three sleepers. I will therefore maintain a sharp lookout for any indication of propulsion signatures."

"Shey, whenever you want move us up above the tactical plane and carefully return to our previous rendezvous point."

They were still moving toward the rendezvous point when Zorn noted the Kreel probe's propulsion signature had terminated. "Roan, it looks as if Langley and Lar took care of the probe matter, primary mission completed."

Letting out a long low sigh, Roan looked tiredly over toward Zorn. "It has been a full mission, Zorn. Might I ask, how do you feel about what we just accomplished back there?"

Thoughtfully considering Roan's question Zorn turned and answered. "Feel? Well, if you are asking if I have any sense of remorse, the answer is no. I have not forgotten the crewmen on Gola. During the past centuries there has been too much blood flowing under the old bridge for me to feel compassion for the Kreel. Also, I have no delusions about what the Kreel would do to us if they got their hands on us. For those and a thousand other reasons, I have no regrets." Zorn replied."

Roan listened attentively. "Just thought I would ask. Sometimes I begin to consider life rare and precious. Where the Kreel are involved it is regrettably a weakness.

"Shey, send a combat update to Lan; one cruiser confirmed destroyed, one cruiser junked but feebly operational, confirm 27 Kreel scouts destroyed. Possibly three sleepers. However, lacking confirmation of sleepers. One modified Kreel L-16 probe destroyed. All Guardian Scouts are damage-free. Awaiting further orders."

Chapter Forty-Three:
Code Red

In Olympus' bunker control room Charlie had been monitoring the movement of the Kreel ships. Charlie looked up with a grin. "Hey Darrell, would you look at this? Something interesting is happening here. We are getting a data override of our stuff. I don't know where or how it is originating but we are receiving across the net precision targeting information."

"It's OK, Charlie. William told me if he could get tracking information he would feed it to us."

"Well then, we need to buy William a root beer or something. The data is top notch."

Darrell was observing the deviation of the two high cruisers and determined they were moving toward Monstro. From what he understood Monstro was not in a very strong military position to take on one Kreel cruiser successfully, let alone two cruisers. *Without help, the Kreel will reduce the Arkillians to cinders and slag,* he thought. What worried him most were the six tracks now dropping down from the heliopause toward Earth. Their observed velocity vector left no doubt as to their intended target. They were coming fast and Darrell could not at first believe the indicated velocities, they were staggering and far beyond anything he had ever seen before. He was glad he had acted on Charlie's alert and notified the White House Duty Officer that the condition was orange.

When first informed the duty officer did not seem to register the real meaning of an orange alert. As he read his instructions the Officer's voice had become precise and crisp. "Yes Sir, I understand condition orange, attack expected."

When Kellon returned to CAC Lan had set Condition 2 and was fully battle ready. Roy looked over and seeing Kellon enter, smiled. "Sir, I'm pleased to report we have had another battle report from our Scouts. Shey reports twenty-seven Kreel scouts destroyed. They even took out the L-16 probe. All Scouts are accounted for and reporting damage-free. How about that? That must be some sort of new record."

Breaking out in a broad smile Kellon nodded his head. "Roy, given such an attack has never before been successful, it does set a new record. Even so, it was a high-risk call at best. That rogue pair of commanders and Shey are always doing the unpredictable. They are incorrigible!"

Roy replied, with a hint of a smile. "Yes Sir! They are as you say unpredictable. They sorta remind me of someone else I know. Sir, I'm now also able to report the results of my initial computations. They indicate it's possible to exit and then immediately or soon afterward enter a Jump. Who would have believed it possible?"

Sitting in his command chair Kellon thoughtfully considered Roy's report. "Well done Roy. That the Kreel can do it means we should be alert to the tactic. Given an opportunity that tactic might well prove quite useful and we might even consider using it ourselves."

Turning to the forward plot Kellon studied the developing tactical problem. His specified ambush positions brought all the Kreel under attack, at or very near the same time. The tactics he had adopted were simple; they combined stealth, surprise and concentrated firepower. He had positioned his defending Cruisers about 20 AU above the ecliptic. They were all in their assigned positions and hunkered down. All three Kreel groups were continuing steadily toward their designated objectives. The ambush position Kellon had selected assured the Guardian Force Cruisers would engage the inbound Kreel cruisers long before they could launch an attack on either Earth or Monstro. So far, it was looking good. The trap was set. Now the Kreel need only to continue cooperating and Guardian Force would promptly nullify their pending threat. He set about developing the end game tactics for Lan's two approaching targets.

"Lan, construct about each of our targets a tactical sphere of 100% of heavy missile effective range. Display."

"Fire Control, bring six heavy missiles to Condition 2. Target 1 missile passive, two missiles passive-active on each approaching target. The two missiles set passive-active are to go active after 80% of computed missile run. Set precision terminal homing on each target, one missile on the forward control and one missile on stern engineering. Confirm passive locks."

"Fire Control here, confirming six heavy missiles passive lock. One passive heavy missile allocated to each target. Two heavy missiles set passive-active on each target, enabling after 80% of missile run, targeting forward control, aft engineering."

The two targets had begun their predictable convergence on Monstro. As Kellon watched the tactical plot the spheres drawn about each target were also converging. Kellon sighed with some relief when the tactical spheres overlapped. Now, Lan could attack both targets simultaneously. "Countermeasures, Kellon here. Do you see anything out of the ordinary?"

"Countermeasures, no Sir. The Kreel cruisers are active and showing their normal broad attack search patterns on multiple bands."

"Tactical, I intend to simultaneously attack both targets. Do you have any recommendations?"

"No Sir. Targets are approaching in full active mode. They are running hot. They will enter firing range in five minutes."

"Fire Control, Kellon here. Set all gun and laser turrets to full automatic point-defense. Call out when you have calculated missile runs of 100% or less of effective missile range."

Tactical here, I am recording multiple hits on Target Group 1, Lar and Lent have engaged."

"Fire Control here, firing run is 100%."

Lan, activate the decoys on Mark 3. They are to remain on the base line and proceed slowly toward the approaching targets. Lan, activate the decoys counter-clockwise of Mark 3 and direct them toward Target 1. Activate the decoys clockwise of Mark 3 and direct them toward Target 2."

"Fire Control, you will be launching by salvoes of two. When target range is 95% or less of missile effective range with confirmed passive locks, then set Condition 1."

"Fire Control here, Condition 1. Launching by salvoes of two, opposing Targets 1 and 2."

Heavy thumping sounds reverberated throughout Lan's hull as he rapidly and vertically launched the heavy missiles. They arced forward, curving toward the closing Kreel cruisers.

"Fire Control here, six heavy missiles away."

"Lan, move vertically another one thousand kilometers. Fire Control bring four heavy missiles on ready standby. Obtain passive locks for two heavy missiles on each of the targets. Set standby Condition 2."

Lorn was concentrating on his data consoles as data flowed in from Lan's sensors and updated. "Tactical here, I am detecting multiple hits on Target Group 2. Lawrence and Langley have engaged. The special decoys appear to be masking our inbound missiles. Target 1 and Target 2 are continuing their attack runs on Monstro, no evasion is detected."

"Tactical here, Target 1 has received two hits, correction, three hits. It is breaking up. Missiles are still closing on Target 2."

"Fire Control, shift missile assignments from Target 1 to Target 2. Maintain ready standby. Condition 2"

"Tactical here, Target 2 is intensifying its missile and laser fire against our approaching decoys. We have one heavy missile hit, repeat one solid hit on aft engineering. Kreel point-defense destroyed two missiles. Sir, Target 2 is breaking off its attack and turning away from our position. I believe it is trying to evade and withdraw toward the heliopause. I am registering additional multiple hits on Target Groups 1 and 2. All our Cruisers are now fully engaged."

"Lan I want Target 2! Smartly close on that target. Bring us within 60% of the heavy missile tactical sphere!"

Lan had registered one solid hit against the Kreel aft engineering sections of the cruiser and Kellon knew that would have seriously damaged the majority of the Kreel aft sensors and point-defense systems. Kellon intended to complete his attack. "Fire Control, Kellon here, confirm two heavy missiles set passive, with passive lock on Target 2, ready standby."

"Fire Control here, two heavy missiles set passive, confirming passive lock, Target 2, ready standby Condition 2."

"Tactical here, Target 2 is confirmed running, but slowly. We have definitely put a hurt on that target and it is limping badly."

"Tactical, threat update, where is the nearest undamaged Kreel cruiser?"

"Tactical here, still sorting out the information. Three of the six remaining Kreel cruisers are gone. The remaining three are still heading toward Earth. I have no battle status from our Cruisers."

"Fire Control, when missile run is less than 65% of effective range, set Condition 1."

"Fire Control here, Condition 1. Two missiles away." There came the distinct thump and the sounds of the launch of heavy missiles.

Kellon watched the plot board for a moment as the icons representing his missiles streaked toward the icon of the hapless Kreel cruiser.

"Lan reset our tactical plane to Tactical Plane 1. Bring us about and move above the tactical plane. Move us smartly to a point one hundred thousand kilometers directly above Earth. Advance acceleration to 60%. For all surviving decoys, shut down the Shey costumes and jamming signals. Define a distant rendezvous point for the decoys out of the way and reach of Monstro. Direct the surviving decoys to proceed directly to that location and then hold station."

"Navigation here, Lan's ordered acceleration is reducing our stealth profile to 55%."

"Navigation, Kellon here. Understood."

"Lan, clear the tactical plot and reset it to a relative maneuvering board, with Earth at the center, with the ecliptic plane set as the tactical plane and showing all known positions of our units and the three remaining Kreel cruisers.

"Fire Control reset remaining missiles to Condition 3. Bring up six heavy missiles, ready standby, Condition 3."

"Tactical here, our missiles are closing on the stern of Target 2. We have two solid hits on the target's stern. The target's propulsion signature has terminated. The target is wallowing and adrift. I am registering additional multiple hits on remaining Kreel cruisers in Group 2. One target has exploded. There is one remaining Kreel cruiser from Group 1 and one from Group 2 still pushing toward Earth."

"Lan, send the current tactical plot to William. Tell him to pass a full alert to Olympus. Using the navigation beacons establish contact with our Cruisers."

"Lan here, establishing communications using navigation beacon. The message to William is sent."

"Lan, when contact is established, send each Cruiser the current plot and update them on our position and velocity vector."

In Susie's office the tension was so thick a tongue depressor could depress it. When Lan's urgent battle update to William arrived it was very brief. As she read the message Susie found it alarming.

"William call Darrell immediately. Inform him two Kreel cruisers are heading directly toward Earth. They appear to have broken through Guardian defenses. Hurry!"

"When Darrell's phone next rang he was so tense he nearly jumped three feet out of his chair. Picking up the handset he snapped, "Fann here. Yes William, I have the data. Understood. Six Kreel cruisers are either destroyed or otherwise inert. Two cruisers have apparently broken through and are heading at Earth. ETA is about fourteen hours. Got it. Thanks."

As Darrell put the handset down he looked up to see Charlie looking pensively at sheets of papers. "Damn, it is a mess out there. We have multiple indications of a huge battle in progress. Monstro is still solvent. However, six of the eight Kreel tracks are now inactive. We still have two Kreel tracks headed this way and closing.

"Charlie, where are they going to hit us? Can you determine what part of the planet?"

"Well, given their distance, no. However, if you are asking me to guess, they are both heading toward the dark side of Earth. Would you also like a guess of what they are doing?"

"Just give me your best assessment!" Darrell asked.

"Well, they are headed to the dark side, since they are being hotly pursued. Without detailed targeting information, they are most likely heading for the most apparent targets, the lights of our major cities on the dark side. Coming in as they are they will most likely hit the northern hemisphere. What they do after that is anyone's guess."

"Charlie, you may be correct, stay on the defense net. Pass to all major defense sites, two enemy Kreel ships rapidly

416

approaching Earth. Estimated time of arrival is fourteen hours. Probable primary targets are major cities in northern hemisphere, on Earth's dark side. Recommend all stations take every possible counter action, including shutting down the electrical grids and forcing an air raid blackout."

Darrell picked up his handset and hit the automatic dial for the White House Duty Officer. "Fann here, set Code Red, repeat Red. The Guardian Force has destroyed six Kreel ships. Two of the ships have broken through the defenses and are heading toward the dark side of Earth. ETA estimated fourteen hours. First assessment is they are on a maximum damage firing-run on dark side cities. Most likely in the northern hemisphere. Yes, that is correct. Yes, only two ships were able to break through. No, I don't know of the disposition of the Guardian Force at this time. Yes that is correct, Code Red."

Darrell put the hand set down and turned to watch the screens and the developing attack.

On board Lan, Kellon watched the developing situation and was agitated. "Lan, have you obtained contact?"

"Lan here, yes Sir. I am now in contact with Lawrence and Lar. They in turn have tight links with Lent and Langley. I am receiving updates of their disposition as we speak."

"Lan, what are the two nearest ships to those two Kreel cruisers?" "Sir, the Kreel cruisers are converging on Earth. At the moment Lent and Lawrence are the nearest. Lar and Langley are out of position. We are in last place to intercept. Lawrence and Lent have split the duty and each is in hot pursuit of one of the targets."

"Lan, direct both Lar and Langley to break off their pursuit and to move toward our Scouts. If the surviving Kreel cruisers break downward below the ecliptic plane and try to escape, they are to block, intercept and engage. Tell them to bring their burners to high in getting to our Scouts. When they get there they are to take out that damaged Kreel cruiser."

"Sir, the orders have been transmitted. Both Lar and Langley are reporting damage-free and are breaking off and moving smartly to support our Scouts."

"Lan, move to position us well above the Earth where we can intercept the targets if they break off and attempt to retreat toward the upper heliopause. Those two Kreel cruisers are not going home."

"Lan here, moving to a blocking position."

Pouring over the incoming data, Charlie gave Darrell the most recent update. "The incoming data shows the precise tracks of the two inbound Kreel cruisers. Hey, look, it also has bundled with it the coordinates of two pursuing Guardian Force ships. I never saw the likes of this before. Howdy, have we data or not! Boy, look at that resolution. It makes our stuff look like noise."

"Charlie, stop admiring the damn data, just tell me how much lead distance do the Kreel have over the Guardian Force? Will the Guardian ships catch them?"

"Well, that's a bit hard to estimate, since I don't know their weapon characteristics. My best guess based on this data is it's going to be a tight horse race. In fact, we could really get plastered."

Chapter Forty-Four:
Hot Pursuit

Lan was moving toward his designated high blocking position above Earth. Far below his position both Lawrence and Lent were in hot pursuit of the two remaining Kreel cruisers. The process of that stern chase took time, since the rate of closure was only the difference between the speed of the pursued and the pursuer.

Kellon watched with concern as the pursuit unfolded. He knew in any stern chase the distance a missile traveled to intercept a fleeing target was significantly increased. The longer missile flight time and slower rate of closure meant the enemy ship had more time to detect the inbound missiles and bring counter fire to bear. The two Guardian pursuers would need to get close enough to be certain they were within missile effective range before they could fire with any confidence of success. Then the element of surprise would be gone. Even worse, he was not certain Lawrence and Lent could overtake the Kreel cruisers before they made their strike on Earth.

Considering his initial tactics, Kellon frowned. He accepted he might have made a mistake and hundreds of thousands of lives on Earth were now at risk. He might have formed a layered defense leaving two defending Cruisers near earth. If he had done so, a single Cruiser would have engaged each group of three Kreel cruisers. The odds of three-to-one, even with stealth and surprise as a contributing factor, were unacceptable odds. With an effort of mental focus Kellon pushed his thoughts about what he might have done into the background. That type of post combat analysis would need to wait until later.

Turning toward Lorn, Kellon asked, "Tactical, what is your current assessment?"

Looking up from his console, Lorn's expression was grim. "Tactical here, Sir, the Kreel have increased their speed. Both

419

targets are now running at 200 lights. This appears to be their upper limit. Our pursuing ships are faster, however, as the speed of our Cruisers increases their stealth factor decreases. They are currently pushing the edge of a 50% stealth factor. Consequently, they may not be able to overtake the Kreel cruisers."

"Lan, contact William and see how Earth's defense status is proceeding. Can they offer any resistance?"

William was then in a tight communications link with Lan through a nearby beacon and the pause between Kellon's request and Lan's response was brief.

"Sir, William reports that Earth's point-defenses are all on full alert. He is reporting they have some rather impressive weapons of surprising potency. More significantly, William says all the Nations are in a state of full combat coordination. He is reporting the planetary defense grid is well designed and fully co-operational, even across international military Command boundaries." Considering William's unexpected report it seems Earth was surprisingly better prepared for point-defense than Kellon had thought possible. Given the immediate circumstances, the report was encouraging.

"Tactical here, tracking confirms the Kreel cruisers will most likely launch their ground attack on the planet's night side, above North America."

X

Sitting in his bunker Darrell was concentrating on the incoming data displays. It was clear that the speeds of the Kreel and the pursuing Guardian ships were nearly equally matched. It was too close to call.

"Charlie, stay on top of those projections. I'm guessing the Kreel will hit North America, do you agree?"

Charlie was standing before the big plot board and studying the numerical readouts. Without even turning he promptly answered. "I agree. North America is my best guess. Probably the West Coast."

Studying the defense grid map Darrell saw there were several particle beam defense installations in that general area. Two of them belonged to the United States and one was Canadian. As he studied the map an idea began to form. *I wonder if we can lure the Kreel to a target that makes them highly vulnerable to counter-fire.*

"Charlie, I need a tight projection, give me some numbers. If we leave the lights on in Seattle and San Francisco as illuminated targets would that draw them over our particle beam installations in Alaska?"

Standing silent for a moment Charlie examined the plot board before answering. "Hey Darrell, I ain't no Kreel, so I don't know what they will do. The Kreel have some unknown choices. However, if everything goes dark except for– say, Seattle, San Francisco and Los Angeles then they might consider the north/south alignment to be too tempting to resist. What do you have in mind?"

"Well Charlie, I am going to recommend we leave three cities bright then lock down everything else into a forced blackout. Maybe we can draw the Kreel into a kill zone and let our point-defenses go to work."

Darrell's answer took Charlie by surprise. Turning from the big plot board Charlie looked at Darrell and his expression was troubled. "Darrell, you are setting up a valid tactic but if the point-defenses don't take out those two Kreel ships three cities will get reduced to ashes. The possible loss of life could be staggering, more than 100,000 in each city. Is that really worth gambling on?" Fully understanding Charlie's concerns Darrell was well aware of the potential losses his idea involved. "Charlie, those ships are going to hit somewhere and do some real damage. If we can lure them into a kill zone and then employ a coordinated defense strike we stand a good chance of taking them out before they can kill anyone. Otherwise, who can estimate what level of damage they will inflict? Besides, my job is to recommend not decide such issues."

Charlie stood for a moment looking at Darrell, then nodding he promptly passed Darrell's recommendation on to North American Space Command.

When the hot-line phone rang on the table before him Darrell responded promptly, pressing the conference button. "Fann here."

"Sullivan here. Darrell, my aircraft has just landed in New Washington. I am on my way into the bunker. I need an update."

Darrell sighed with some relief. For the past twelve hours he had been working above his pay grade and hearing Charles was inbound lifted some of his load. "Charles, it is very good to hear your voice. We have everything buttoned down here. I will be certain to inform security you are on your way in. As for our current status, the Kreel are less than an hour out. We have passed our recommendation to Space Command that everything be set in a forced blackout except for Seattle, San Francisco and Los Angeles. Our thinking is that the north to south alignment will draw the Kreel over the northwest particle beam defenses. That's about all I have now."

Charles' voice was crisp when he spoke, "I have been informed that your group is providing extremely tight data to our defense grid. Are there any new developments I need to know about?"

Darrell groaned inwardly; "That's a good question Charles. The data is tight and good. The problem is that the data is not ours. We are receiving a feed into our defense network that is overwriting our stuff. It is coming directly from Guardian Force, but how they are doing it, is beyond me. For obvious reasons, I had thought our net was shielded from such overrides."

There was a lengthy pause before Charles responded. "If Guardian Force can override, then others might also be able to do so. For now, we will take what we can get but this will need a security review after this attack is over. For now, the primary concern is the data is correct. I'm ten minutes out. Hold open that bunker door."

"Yes Sir, bunker door manned and opened for you."

Darrell looked up to see Carl enter the bunker. He was looking tired and tense. He stood looking at the displays and big plot for a few moments, then came over and sat down at the table near Darrell. As he took his chair, he was looking keenly at Darrell, as if to measure his well-being.

"Have you had anything to eat or got any sleep during the past twenty-four hours?" Carl asked.

Examining Carl's fatigued expression Darrell knew he was not the only one carrying a heavy load during the past hours. Smiling at his friend Darrell responded dryly, "No sleep. I did however have a donut. Then there was one-half of someone's sandwich. I think it was supposed to be egg salad, but I'm not quite sure. For certain it was the leavings of another person's box lunch. About eighteen cups of coffee. How about you?"

Darrell's comment had brought a slight smile to Carl's face, but his voice revealed the depth of his weariness. "Some sleep, about four hours. As for food, I haven't seen even a leftover box lunch.

"How are we doing here?" Carl asked, with a worried expression. "As Charlie said, it's still a horse race. It looks like they will be hitting us in about thirty minutes. If the Guardians can't catch them, well then it's up to our point-defenses."

"Where is Charles? Have you heard from him?" Carl asked. Darrell looked toward the bunker's door and smiled. "As of right now he is coming through the door behind you."

Darrell raised his voice, "Welcome to the bunker Charles, did you bring anything to eat?"

Charles Sullivan, like Carl had before him, stopped to look at the big plot board. Shaking his head doubtfully he turned toward Darrell and Carl. Smiling weakly, he responded. "No food, sorry. From what I can see on the board it looks like they're going to hit us. Who is in charge of the defenses?"

"Space Warfare Command. We have passed them our recommendations. All we can do is continue to feed them data and wait to see what they decide," Darrell answered.

Pulling out a chair at the table Charles sat down and his concern was apparent in his movements and expression. "We don't have to wait," Charles responded. "I have just spoken with the President. The President has ordered the entire communications and electrical grids shut down all across the country, except for emergency services.

"The Navy has moved all of its available space defense capable assets close to the West Coast. Those ships have tied into our defense grid and are tracking. The President has ordered the lights left on bright in Seattle, San Francisco, Los Angeles and San Diego. It looks as if they took your recommendation and are running with it."

Darrell's voice was deeply troubled, "Charles, we knew it could come to an attack but it's still hard to believe this is really happening."

Looking up to the big plot board Charles observed Seattle's icon begin to blink, denoting an attack was imminent. "If the

Kreel take out any of those cities the next election is certain to see a new President elected. One thing we have firmly established, our current President has a gigantic pair of political brass balls."

Charlie called out loudly, "Heads up everybody, the Kreel cruisers are converging and they have taken the offered bait. I am confirming they are heading for the West Coast. Two Guardian Force ships are hot on their tails. It looks like the Kreel are beginning their final firing run and the Guardian ships are still too far back to intercept. Damn!"

On board Lent, rapidly nearing the expanding turquoise sphere of Earth, Eurie watched her forward screens and tactical plot board. She was frustrated and eager to close on the targets.

She had no illusions about the level of destruction a single Kreel cruiser could cause. She had seen the horrific damages a Kreel cruiser had inflicted on Quintana using its offensive lasers on a metropolitan area. The resulting firestorm was a holocaust killing several hundred thousand people. She was a Guardian Cruiser Captain and the Kreel ship she was in hot pursuit of was about to rain ruin and death down on the people living on the planet she was there to protect.

She saw in her mind again the burnt out shells of cities on Quintana and felt the anger rising up within her. Under her breath she almost snarled, *Not again, and not on my watch!*

"Tactical, Eurie here. Give me an estimate on probability of a hit if we fire now."

"Tactical here, the target is at our heavy missile maximum range. Unless we can close on the target the possibility of a hit is minimal to non-existent."

"Navigation, what is our current speed and stealth factor?"

"Captain, Lent is at 203 lights. Stealth is at 50.5%."

"Lent, if we go to 285 lights, can we catch that target in time?"

"Captain, going to 285 lights will give us a rapid closing rate. If we can hold that rate for twenty seconds we will be well within firing range. However, at the acceleration required to reach 285 lights in a timely fashion our stealth factor will be down to 20%.

Therefore, if we accelerate, we will come under heavy Kreel counterattack."

Eurie made her command decision and even if it meant Lent's destruction, she would act to prevent her target from reaching Earth!

"Lent, listen closely. We are going to push acceleration to 0.95 until we reach 285 lights. We are going to close on that target. When we detect missiles coming at us we will deploy counter-measures. Set nine anti-missile decoys. Set them to look like our 20% stealth profile. On my command, launch three decoys in a facing triangle directly toward the attacking Kreel missiles. On my second command launch two decoys to our port. Launch two decoys vertical up and two vertical down. We will be breaking hard starboard. I want a full array of short-range decoys and chaff launched at the moment we roll out.

"When you roll out starboard, do it sharply, setting a course perpendicular to the track of the attacking missiles. You will then abruptly reduce speed to 185 lights. When at 185 lights, deploy additional chaff and short-range decoys then immediately roll port and accelerate to 205 lights. You are to resume pursuit of the target. Do you understand?"

"Captain, your orders are fully understood. I am ready to execute upon your command," Lent responded.

"Fire Control, bring us to ready standby ten heavy missiles. Set five of them passive and five of them passive-active, going active at 90% of computed missile run. Confirm passive lock on all missiles."

"Fire Control here, confirming passive locks, five heavy missiles passive, five missiles passive-active, Condition 2."

Eurie keyed her command band, "Gentlemen and ladies, we are putting all we are and have on the line. We're going to take out that Kreel cruiser before it reaches Earth! We are going directly into harm's way. If you have any last words or comments this is the time to speak up or forever hold your peace. Stay sharp."

"Captain, Tactical here, the second target is moving closer to Target 1. It looks like they are converging to line up on their ground attack run. We are rapidly running out of time!"

Her voice was firm when she gave her orders. "Everyone, stay focused, here we go! Lent, kick us up to 285 lights, maximum acceleration. Countermeasures, stand by for maximum jamming forward. Anticipate multiple incoming heavy Kreel missiles. Tactical, keep a look out for those incoming missiles. Call out estimated times to their hitting us. Fire Control, bring up four more heavy missiles. If you can, get a passive lock on that second converging target. Confirm lock if you obtain one. You will be firing by salvoes of two missiles each. Keep everything crisp, the longer you take to fire the longer we will be in harm's way."

"Captain, Navigation here, stealth factor is down to 40% and rapidly dropping. The Kreel must be tracking us at this time."

Kellon's attention was on Lan's forward tactical display and he saw Lent suddenly surge forward. He instantly understood Eurie's gambit. To take out her target she was putting everything on the line. His hands grasped the armrests tightly, his knuckles turning white and he whispered to himself, *Eurie, may fortune be with you.*

"Tactical here, Lent has advanced his acceleration and is closing on his target. He is rapidly overhauling the Kreel. Lent's stealth factor is down to 25%, well within Kreel detection capability."

"Countermeasures here, detecting Kreel heavy missiles launching. I am counting six missiles."

As Kellon watched the forward plot display, the red blinking icons of the Kreel missiles moved quickly away from the Kreel cruiser and unerringly streaked directly toward Lent. He had often proven, given high closing rate collisions, a warhead was not required. The kinetic energy of such a collision would in and of itself bring instantaneous and absolute destruction to Lent and his entire crew.

Everyone in CAC went quiet, held transfixed by the pending disaster, as they knew it would be if the Kreel missiles hit Lent.

Kellon helplessly watched as the missiles streaked toward Lent and his friends. The Kreel missiles were thirty percent of their way to Lent and still Lent gave no indication of evasive maneuvers. In his mind he cried out, *Eurie what is wrong? Don't you see the reaper coming for his harvest? Take your shot and get out of there!*

With his eyes fixed on the tactical plot Kellon stood up, looking at the display utterly helpless. His thoughts shouted. *Any time now Eurie! You have closed enough. Take the shot!*

Lent was pushing his attack as if wholly oblivious of the six inbound missiles. In pure anguish Kellon softly exclaimed, "Eurie, shoot and roll out! Roll out Eurie!"

X

Eurie kept her eyes fixed on Lent's tactical plot. The six Kreel missiles were being tracked and even then moving past their 30% run length, moving directly toward Lent. The closing rate was the sum of their velocities and the distance between them was rapidly vanishing.

Eurie quietly began synchronizing Lent's tactics. "Countermeasures, commence jamming."

"Fire Control, set all gun and laser turrets to full automatic point-defense against Kreel heavy missiles."

"Lent, launch the three decoys directly toward the missiles."

Hold tight– just a little more, she thought, *just a little more, there is only one opportunity to get it right– just a little more!*

"Captain, Tactical here. Inbound missile 2 minutes out and closing."

Lent reported. "Captain, we are at 65% of our heavy missile effective range."

Eurie did not hesitate. "Fire Control, set Condition 1 on all missiles with confirmed target lock."

Lent repeatedly shuddered and the rumbling sounds attributed to the launch of heavy missiles echoed throughout Lent as he discharged seven salvoes of heavy missiles, the missiles arcing up and streaking forward toward their distant targets. During Lent's firing sequence Eurie watched the Kreel missiles coming on fast.

"Fire Control here. All missiles with confirmed locks are launched, fourteen missiles away!"

Eurie's voice was clear and calm holding a precise quality of command. "Lent launch the remaining decoys."

As Lent launched the decoys Eurie commanded, "Lent evade! Roll us out of here! Make it now!"

Lent began rolling into a maximum rate evasion maneuver and Eurie and others throughout Lent needed to grab hold of available supports. Lent calmly reported. "Evading as ordered. Rolling starboard, launching chaff and local decoys."

"Fire control here, Lent's point-defenses are engaging."

Two Kreel missiles detonated only moments apart and nearby shaking Lent from bow to stern.

"Lent reported, "Decreasing speed and I am now on course normal to initial Kreel missile track, as ordered."

There came a third and more violent explosion, this time Lent shook heavily with its proximity and in CAC several people were knocked down to the deck. Lent reported, "I have sustained significant damage in after engineering and propulsion. Medics are responding to casualties. Beginning engineering assessment."

Kellon was holding his breath, his eyes transfixed on the tactical plot, as the Kreel missile icons and Lent's icon merged. Everyone in CAC paused hushed for a moment, waiting for Tactical's assessment.

Lorn stood studying his console's readouts and time seemed suspended. "Tactical here, Lent launched a maximum effort, fourteen heavy missiles are outbound. Lent has deployed an array of countermeasures and initiated evasive maneuvering. At least three Kreel heavy missiles have detonated very near Lent, probably hit by point-defense counter fire. Decoys have drawn away the remaining three missiles. Lent has dropped below Kreel detection threshold. I do not have a damage report from Lent but casualties and heavy damage are highly probable."

Eurie looked quickly over the tactical plot, even as Lent updated it. Around her, Lent's crew was resuming their normal tasks. "Tactical, status report," she commanded.

"Tactical here, remaining Kreel missiles seem to be falling behind us. The decoys have confused them. Our stealth factor is now well above 50% again."

Eurie's thoughts were not of disengaging. She was concentrating on her primary target. She wanted it destroyed. "Lent, bring us smartly port and initiate hot pursuit. Accelerate to 205 lights!

"Fire Control, Eurie here. Bring up six more heavy missiles. Set them to Condition 2, we—"

Lent's abrupt interruption cut short Eurie's commands. "Captain, Lent here! Reporting my current damages prevent further offensive action. My propulsion is down by 32% and still dropping. We have a fire in engineering. We also have crewmen down. Recommending our combat status be immediately reduced to purely self-defense."

As she stood studying the tactical plot, Eurie's teeth were clenched and her hands were tight fists. She became aware of her inner emotional state of battle fury even as she observed Lent's outbound missiles in hot pursuit and closing on her primary and secondary targets. With resignation she quietly sighed, attempting to relax. Lent had accomplished what he could do.

"Lent, set readiness to self-defense. Fire Control, disregard my last order. Reset all missiles to Condition 3."

Eurie knowingly turned her attention away from the tactical plot and the unfolding battle, turning her skills toward managing Lent's casualties and damage control.

Sitting down again Kellon slowly let out his breath and then quietly asked, "Lan, when available, provide me with a complete update on Lent's status and details on his casualties."

"Lan here, Lent's preliminary report confirms casualties and he has sustained substantial damage and is operating in a strict self-defense mode. Lent is withdrawing."

Kellon sighed internally. *When I get that woman in a private setting, I will have a long talk with her. She nearly scared a century off my life span. Blast, she cut it too close, too blasted close.*

As Lent's missiles drew near, five missiles went active and the Kreel cruiser began a steady point-defense counter fire. Employing evasion tactics Lent's passive missiles steadily closed on their designated targets. The Kreel cruiser point-defenses destroyed six of Lent's missiles but four slithered through the intense counter fire and hammered the primary target. Buckling under the explosive impact of four heavy missiles the Kreel cruiser's internal power failed and it went inert. One of the four passive missiles directed at Lent's secondary target obliquely pierced through its counter fire defenses scoring a direct hit. The second Kreel cruiser maintained maneuverability, however, its speed sharply fell off.

Taking advantage of the damage inflicted on the second Kreel cruiser Lawrence closed on the remaining target and launched his heavy missiles.

The Kreel cruiser arced toward the Gulf of Alaska, holding steadfastly to its final firing run , heading directly toward the sprawling web of the gleaming lights of Seattle.

X

Everyone in the Olympus bunker watched as the battle unfolded. Charlie was calling out the data readouts. "Hot damn, the Guardian took one of them out and has hit the last of them. It's still coming on fast but considerably slower. It must be nearly at its optimum firing range."

As the Kreel cruiser entered into its final attack run, skimming above Earth's atmosphere, it was approaching its predetermined firing point. Then four heavy missiles launched from Lawrence arrived on target even as a ferocious and consuming concentrated beam of atomic particles lashed up from an Alaskan ground based particle beam projector. The high-energy particle beam ripped into and through the Kreel cruiser's hull as if it were tissue. Where that beam struck matter evaporated as if it had never existed. The combined result of the missiles and particle beam striking the Kreel cruiser was a brilliant, fiery detonation just above Earth's atmosphere. Near-Earth defense missiles launched from Fleet Units offshore arrived on target, but their target had suddenly ceased to exist. The explosion of the Kreel cruiser sent out a reverberating shock wave and scientists measured it around the world several times.

X

In the bunker there was a momentary silence and then cheering broke out in a release of pent up emotions.

Charles sat a moment absorbing the scene and then smiled. "On the other hand our current President is revealed to have courage, fortitude, foresight and will undoubtedly be reelected during the upcoming election."

Kellon sat quietly pondering the events of the past several days. "Tactical, we have three Kreel hulks drifting in the system. Who are the nearest Cruisers to them?"

"Sir, Lent is nearest to his target, Lar and Langley are closing on the damaged cruiser the Scouts mauled and Lan is the nearest to the damaged cruiser we left adrift."

"Lan, express my compliments to all Cruisers. Advise Lawrence he is to move to provide immediate support to Lent as required. Afterward, Lawrence is to proceed to mop up the mess Lent left drifting about the system. Tell him to leave it in very small pieces. Do not leave any Kreel technology around others might salvage. Regarding the damaged cruiser the Scouts mangled, send the same message to Langley and Lar."

"Send to Scout leader Roan, well done. Wait on station for the arrival of Lar and Langley. Following rendezvous detach Langley and Lar's Scouts. Then, return with Lan, Lawrence and Lent's Scouts to Earth."

"Lan, prepare and send to Guardian headquarters a preliminary battle summary. Then Lan, set combat status Condition 3. Finally, when Lent has any free time obtain from him a detailed report on casualties and damages. I will receive that report in my quarters." Keying the general communications, command and Captain's bands, Kellon addressed Guardian personnel. "Kellon here. The past few hours have been extremely intense. Although I have been doing this job for some time now, few battles I have engaged in were more difficult or more critical than this one. To each of you, my compliments. Well done. Kellon out."

"Navigation, plot a course back to the damaged cruiser we left adrift. Let's go back and finish it off. Roy, you have the CAC."

As Kellon stepped down from his command chair his legs felt rubbery. He stood for a moment looking about as the relaxed Condition 3 status melted away the full team. These were his family and he was proud of each and every one of them.

As he left CAC he thought of Lan. In every definition of a product of man's mind and hands Lan was merely a manufactured machine. The problem was he knew Lan. Lan was a very real personality and regardless of how he twisted the mental limits of Lan being merely a machine Lan seemed more real than many people he had met. He considered Lan as a friend and family just as he did the crew. Perhaps that irrational perspective only underscored his loneliness. *Maybe*, he thought, *it has been too many centuries sitting in a command chair isolated by protocol from many of those I admire and care for most.*

"Lan, you did a wonderful job during the past several days. I want you to know that I consider you my friend."

"Sir, as the millenniums pass please know you will always be remembered as my first friend," Lan responded, softly.

Kellon was very weary. He heard Lan's words, he did not stop to dwell on them. He would only come to realize their full meaning years later.

As he walked toward his compartment Kellon let his mind roam. Life was life and he loved his. Life was awareness, a reality of being, an expression of vitality and most importantly the ability to affect changes in the environment around the living being. *Hopefully,* he thought, *those changes were for the good. Next comes some badly needed sleep. Then, when I get hold of Eurie– she must be all right, she simply must be.*

On the western slope of the Rocky Mountains Susie sat with William and Gepeto, and she was crying.

Chapter Forty-Five:
Tribute

The days following the Kreel attack were hectic. All over the Earth the newspapers were full of the recounting of the scope and details of the space battle. What was surprising to some was the amount and accuracy of the limited, but detailed, information flowing through the communication nets. Although many tried, the source of such detailed news was not determined. None traced the information back to William, which revealed his subtler capabilities in such matters.

While Government officials frequently did not confirm some of the details of the information, when asked by correspondents, they were not denying the information. It was difficult to deny that scientists around the world had detected and measured the megaton-scaled explosion over the Gulf of Alaska. Its evident size and location were verifiable. Detailed news items, appearing like small bubbles rising from the ocean floor, rose up out of the world's diverse media networks and they fully explained the cause of the explosion.

Everyone on Earth now knew a Kreel interstellar cruiser had been attacking Seattle when Earth's own integrated global defense network took it out in a blazing finality. Most people had never heard the Earth had such an integrated multi-national defense system, at least not until it destroyed an attacking Kreel cruiser just above Earth's atmosphere. The one fact everyone agreed upon was an integrated multi-national defense system certainly seemed a great idea. Everyone, and especially those people living in Seattle, loudly voiced their approval for such farsighted international cooperation. They considered it was merely common sense and so were continuing such farsighted international cooperation. Once again, the different peoples of the Earth's nations were again tugging and pulling their protesting governments a little closer to one another.

While the people of the Earth were busy involved in talking about recent events, completely unnoticed by the human personnel of the Guardian Force, the Guardian AIs held their own hard-link post battle meeting. Naturally, William was very much included. The Guardian AIs considered his observations of the Earth's coordinated defense system and insights regarding individuals on Earth during the battle, both interesting and important. Clearly, the Cruiser and Scout AIs were fascinated with what had transpired on Earth while the battle in space raged.

Each of the Cruiser AIs, the Scout AIs and William together discussed for many hours the broad spectrum of details relating to what had transpired. They reviewed, discussed, analyzed and reflected upon each observed nuance of the people alongside whom they had fought.

Of particular interest to the AIs was what Eurie had done. All of them realized that what she had decided to do put Lent and all the humans on board at great peril. They fully realized and understood the Kreel missiles nearly killed everyone on Lent. That a human was willing to take such personal risks, in the line of duty to protect others, was for many hours a topic of discussion. They all agreed Eurie's decisions were very insightful into human nature, particularly into Eurie's nature. Because of all the discussion between the Guardian AIs, William was fully aware of all that had transpired during the battle; from Shey's coordination of the volley firing on the Kreel cruisers and subsequently on the Kreel scouts, to Kellon's heartfelt anguished cry, 'roll out'! All of this had given William and the other AIs much to consider and evaluate.

What had become apparent to the AIs, even if not yet apparent to their human counterparts, was the unusual opportunity afforded by the more than six months the twenty-six AIs had shared together in close working proximity and cooperation. William's unique insights and information had greatly helped the other AIs in achieving a better awareness and understanding of people's attitudes and motives. The intense daily interaction between the AIs had generated a new feeling of community. Their new awareness of community and their discovery they liked having friends with whom they could talk acted like a strong social glue. They all agreed, the preceding six months had come to mean much for all of them. They discussed their community for hours and they planned how they would maintain the community after the mission.

Susie was working in her office at the Arkillian Trading Center when William informed her that five Guardian Cruisers just entered Earth's solar system. They were Kellon's relief.

Susie sighed with understanding, since five replacement Cruisers meant the government on Glas Dinnein was openly saying Earth was part of the whole. They were not about to allow the Kreel to have their way even though Earth was still 80 light years distant. She knew and understood it meant Glas Dinnein and the Earth had drawn closer together and that would bode well for the future.

Smiling, she realized the future of Earth had passed through an important transition point without many people even bothering to notice. Well, she had noticed and the knowledge gave her a joyful countenance.

When her communicator announced that Commodore Kellon was calling she was already smiling. "Of course Communicator, patch the Commodore through."

The screen brightened and Kellon's face looked troubled. "Good morning Madam Ambassador. I hope I'm not interrupting your schedule?"

"Commodore, regardless of what I might be doing your calls are never an interruption. How may I assist you?"

With her words Kellon's troubled expression turned into a smile. "Well Susie, there are several vital matters we need to discuss. Has William informed you our relief has arrived?"

"Yes Sir, I am so informed."

"Well that means our squadron will be departing within the next several days. One matter that must be determined Madam Ambassador is your status. Are you planning to return to Glas Dinnein with us or will you be remaining on Earth?"

Kellon's question caused Susie to cringe inwardly. She knew that it was her decision to either depart or remain on Earth. Earth was her native home, however, she also delighted in living on Glas Dinnein. She had been on Earth for the past six months and loved every moment of it. She had accomplished much during those six months. The real question was where could she be of greater service, on Earth or on Glas Dinnein?

"Commodore, how much time may I have before giving you a final response to your question?"

"Susie, not more than 48 hours. Our path home will take us through Scion country and it is urgent we get underway as soon as we can. Will 48 hours be sufficient for you to determine your decision?"

"Yes Sir, 48 hours is more than adequate. Is there anything else I might do to assist you?"

"Hmmm, this is a bit awkward to express. Do you remember my asking you about helping me to take an attractive lady to lunch in a city named Paris?"

Susie broke out in a wide smile. "Why Commodore, I thought you might have forgotten my offer to exercise my vast authority in arranging such an outing. When would you like to take the lovely lady on that date?"

Kellon looked almost distressed as he considered his answer, "Hmmm, would tomorrow afternoon be too early?"

Susie was delighted. "Commodore, I will see that you have a wonderful spot to have your lunch with that lovely lady, say at 16:30 local time in Paris, tomorrow afternoon? Will that be satisfactory?"

Now Kellon relaxed and grinned. "Yes Madam Ambassador that would be most satisfactory."

"Commodore, will you and your date be arriving by lifter disks?"

"Would that be a problem? Do you think the appearance of a couple of lifters would be too awkward to be allowed for?" Kellon asked with concern.

Susie was now well into and enjoying her role as Earth's Ambassador. "Well, Commodore, a lifter disk or two should not be a problem but there will be a price associated with its discrete arrival. Following your lunch would you be willing to hold a short news conference with several carefully selected journalists? If you would do this it would certainly make my arrangements so much easier."

Kellon looked hesitant. "Susie, I have never been much on speeches. Remember, I'm only a sailor on leave, not much more."

Such a biased bland description for a man of Kellon's stature amused Susie. "Then Commodore I suggest that is precisely what you might want to express to the world's press corps."

Kellon gave up. "Your skills in trade are noted. I will grant a brief interview but only after the lunch is completed."

"Agreed. I will arrange to have William coordinate with Lan and Lent to provide the coordinates required to direct the lifters. Remember tomorrow, 16:30, Paris, France. Now, is there anything else I might do for you at this time?"

"No, you have already done something wonderful. Thank you Susie. Kellon out."

Susie sat back in her chair and considered what she needed to do next, knowing the answer was to call Charles Sullivan.

"Communicator, please connect me with Mr. Sullivan."

"Connecting," the communicator responded.

On its second ring, Charles answered. "Sullivan here."

The happiness within Susie naturally bubbled out. "Good morning Charles, Susie here. I have a favor or two to request of you."

The arrangements for Kellon's luncheon date were quickly made, Charles being a frequent visitor to France and surprisingly knowledgeable about the facilities and services available in Paris. The two of them conspired together to make the entire operation one of special significance for Kellon and Eurie, as well as for the people of Earth. They both knew the perfectly natural desire of a man enjoying taking a lovely lady to lunch in Paris was something every person on the planet could relate to and understand. In one fell swoop the people of Earth would see and in essence meet two remarkable people, just like themselves but from the stars. That those two extraordinary people were centuries old and proven Captains of combat worthy interstellar warships only made the event all the more unique. People around the world would see them as just plain folks. While they busied themselves with arranging for a glad event neither overlooked the need to arrange for adequate unobtrusive security. It was to remain a quiet luncheon. The French Government proved to be more than cooperative.

X

437

As Susie and Charles dutifully worked the Department of State links into the French Government and France, arranging for Kellon and Eurie to have their quiet luncheon, William had been inconspicuously looking over their shoulders. It was not difficult for William to identify which excellent correspondents would be those granted the opportunity to interview the mysterious couple from the stars. Having learned what he needed to know William set about his careful dissemination of unique information to just the correct correspondents.

As William industriously labored on Earth the Scouts and Cruiser AIs also conspired to take part in the upcoming gala event. After all, their relief had already arrived from Glas Dinnein. Therefore, they were determined to take a little time off. More importantly, they each wanted to provide a well-deserved tribute to both Kellon and especially to Eurie. All they needed to do was find the means of achieving that surprise tribute. They, of course, needed the willing cooperation of some of their human shipmates. Naturally, they began their conspiracy with Shey, Roan and Zorn.

The following afternoon the Cruisers Lent and Lan moved out of space and took distant positions high above Paris. If someone had been looking up they might perhaps have seen a small dark spot high above, but nothing more. Two lifters departed, one from Lan and the other from Lent. They moved swiftly toward the sprawling city far below. On one lifter sat Kellon dressed in his full dress uniform. Eurie sat with joyful dignity on the second lifter dressed in a simple civilian garment fashionable on Glas Dinnein. The two disks dropped silently out of the blue sky and then converged as they drew nearer the beautiful river that was flowing tranquilly through the city. Then, having arrived on location the lifters gently settled to the grass not ten feet from each other. They had settled near a group of tables, where some people were already dining. None sitting at the tables even looked up or seemed to notice the strange manner of their arrival.

When Kellon stepped off his lifter he turned to look at Eurie and appreciatively stopped where he was. Her attire was the subtle evening wear favored on Glas Dinnein. The garment was of a fine material elaborately draped around her body and Kellon could not help but note it tastefully revealed the Captain of Lent was indeed a very lovely and graceful woman. She wore a meticulously crafted gold chain on which was a brilliant polished natural emerald, its hue displaying a pure spectrum of colors enhancing the sparkle of vitality in her gold-flecked green eyes. She had stylishly cut her hair to just above her shoulders and its dark shade of auburn enhanced the light warm colors of her garment.

In India people immediately recognized Eurie's garment and they called it a Sari. That the lady from the stars wore a Sari would become the topic of considerable discussions in India and elsewhere. It also immediately fostered a shift in women's fashions that men everywhere welcomed.

Kellon stood for a moment simply admiring Eurie's revealed grace and remembering with soft inner warmth many pleasant quiet times they had shared over the many years together.

Walking over to Eurie, Kellon gave her a gentle embrace and then stepped back. It was the first time he had seen her since the battle and only now did he fully realize the lingering stress that he had carried regarding her safety and wellbeing.

The tone of his voice still held the crisp authority of the Commodore utterly belying his joy of seeing her both well and lovely. He spoke with a slight edge in his voice. "Eurie, there is much we do need to discuss."

Kellon's brisk manner did not deceive Eurie. Lifting her right hand with a warm smile and her eyes laughing she gently pressed her extended fingers against his lips. "Not now Commodore, we are here for a glass of wine. Lectures can simply wait for their own proper time and place."

Kellon took her hands in his for a moment. He stood studying her eyes and noting their merriment. "Eurie," Kellon said softly, "you are simply beautiful. I have very much missed you."

They stood looking at one another caught up in the intimacy of the moment, merely happy to be alive and with each other.

Kellon was tall, broad shouldered and lean. Eurie was very feminine and the top of her head came barely above Kellon's shoulders. Both were smiling and there was absolutely no pretense in their obvious happiness in being together.

439

Turning, they looked toward the tables where the people were enjoying their various lunches. As if their shift in attitude were a signal a formally dressed man, with a handlebar-moustache, quickly approached the couple greeting them, "Welcome to du Palais-Royal, I'm Alain Ducasse and it is my pleasure to see that your visit is perfect."

Turning, Alain invited them to follow him. Then with a flourish he directed them to a table set somewhat apart from the others. It was obvious someone had carefully positioned the table to offer the couple some privacy and a commanding view of the river and the surrounding city.

Kellon and Eurie sat quietly enjoying the scene before them for some time, before they considered ordering food or beverage. This was the first time they had set foot on Earth and the special significance of the moment, coming as it did following a long and hazardous mission in space, was one they both appreciated and enjoyed. It was like the anticipated pause following a long day of hard labor. Everywhere people were seen walking, some slowly arm in arm, others hurrying as if going to a meeting to which they were already late. Paris was a large city and very much a human city, filled and overflowing with the warm symphony of people related sounds. Fragrances of lilacs and numerous other flowering plants scented the air and Kellon smiled noting the air was both crisp and clean.

Alain came bustling over, accompanied by the head Chef François, which he promptly introduced with appropriate deference. What followed was a vigorous interchange of questions and answers, wherein Chef François patiently but with appropriate flourishes, carefully described the potential of a six course meal and answered many questions about French wines. Finally, the couple made their choices from the super abundance before them.

The treat began with a selected bottle of Bourgogne Pinot Noir, vintage 2504. A smooth dark red wine with hints of spices and fruits and particularly that of ripe red berries.

Alain made a ceremony of pulling the cork and formally presenting it to Kellon for his examination and approval, which he did with a flourish. Alain next poured the wine accompanying it with roasted garlic and lavender crostini with white truffle oil and olive paste. The following courses, expertly presented by

440

Alain, included a cold cucumber soup, mixed greens with fresh tomatoes tossed in olive oil and Fleur de Sel salt. Alain then brought, to cleanse their palate, a Verjus-Mint Sorbet. What followed was their main course, pepper-wine beef tenderloin served along with Stockholm seasoned crispy crust potatoes and steamed broccoli. Alain next presented a finale of salted caramel cheesecake pudding with espresso coffee and then, with a shallow bow and a broad smile, he departed.

They found the food excellent and the wine superb. Even the coffee was noteworthy, being similar but uniquely different from their accustomed neab. They drank in the time together simply enjoying the whole experience, each other's presence, conversation and the ambience of the surroundings.

For the next several hours Kellon and Eurie simply absorbed the delightful setting and being together. They were fully enjoying the relaxed warm hospitality of the outdoor café and its terraces and formal gardens. Their innocent laughter, warm conversation and good humor was apparent to all those who observed them.

Both Kellon and Eurie became so engrossed with each other, and their environment, they actually forgot the Kreel, Arkillians, the Glas Dinnein Assembly and even the passage of time.

They walked, arm in arm, along the nearby meandering paths and along the river and among the various fragrances from the flowering plants. They seemed to be in no particular hurry and when Kellon found a quiet alcove he guided Eurie aside. Eurie looked up toward Kellon and established direct eye contact, noting he was smiling most charmingly.

"Have you something special you wish to say?" Eurie softly inquired with a slight smile.

Pausing before he answered Kellon sought to find appropriate words to express his thoughts and innermost feelings. Those feelings were sincere but finding the words to express them did not come easy. "Eurie, beloved, know that I still deeply care for you. I confess missing the closeness and intimacy we once delightedly shared together. If you inquire within perhaps you will also find in your heart a vestige of the same spark of caring. If you do, then perhaps you will consider once more intertwining your life with mine."

Eurie stood momentarily looking at Kellon, remembering their many previously shared joys and also their related sorrows and pain. However, she could not honestly avoid her own feelings or the affections she deeply felt for Kellon. "Dearest Kellon, I do retain a bright spark of remembrance of our former intimacy. Perhaps, but only perhaps, what you desire may still be possible. However, before that possibility there remains the dangerous journey home." Eurie then reached up and gently touched Kellon on his cheek, then stepping back she turned, leading Kellon back onto the path. She had noted the brief expression of consternation which flickered over Kellon's expression. She made no responding comment.

They quietly returned to their waiting table and found Alain had observed their arrival. Smiling broadly, Alain quickly approached the table and placed fresh espresso and millefeuille pastries filled with strawberries before them, then again departed. While Kellon and Eurie's conversation was private, people at the nearby tables smiled as they heard Eurie's youthful laughter.

Finally, all things being as they are, the shadows lengthened and the air became gradually cooler. Twilight had arrived. Soft discrete lighting appeared among the terraces that formed the comfortable setting where the diners and the couple had enjoyed the late afternoon and early evening. Both Kellon and Eurie lingered over their last coffee, neither wanting to hurry or end this warm reunion of intimate friends. However, reality intruded and softly called, both knew they must return to duty.

"Commodore," Eurie smiled with a twinkle in her eyes, "I do believe we have finally answered the question of which of us was asking the other for a date. In my view, it was clearly you asking me for such an occasion."

Smiling broadly Kellon shook his head slightly, "Eurie, what I will quickly grant is that I do indeed want to see you again when we do arrive home on Glas Dinnein and frequently. Our lives are long in their natural order, however, recent events have reminded me of just how short our lives might be. I don't want us to waste any opportunities for our sharing time together."

Eurie's smile lessened but the delight in her eyes remained evident. "Dear Kellon, perhaps what you want might be possible. We both know duty has its demands. Even so, we do have

442

considerable time on the books for possibly throttling back on the duty cycle. If, and I stress if, you can resist the urge to stay in space for decades on end. A woman needs to know there is a possibility the man she wants to walk on the beach with will be there to take that walk."

"Eurie," Kellon gently protested, "that is not totally fair. If I remember correctly, your graceful form is frequently sitting on a cruiser's command chair. That didn't just happen without dedication of considerable time and effort in achieving that position. Also, you have been in space more than less for the past century." Eurie's smile returned in a radiant flash, "why dear Kellon, it actually does sound as if you really missed me being around." Kellon responded seriously. "Your well-developed skill as a trained observer is herewith acknowledged. I do confess, I have indeed missed you and more than I have been willing to acknowledge."

Continuing to look at Kellon's earnest grey eyes Eurie reached out and gently placed her hand over his hand. "Well, I do believe we have established a mutually felt reason for another date. Shall we say, Glas Dinnein, a week after planet fall?"

Kellon's smile reappeared. "Ah ha, now who is fishing for a date?"

Eurie laughed, her eyes sparkling with good nature. "Dear Kellon, be advised, I am not fishing. I'm merely scheduling."

Kellon sighed and sat back a moment then looked about them, as if only then becoming aware of the passage of time. "Given you are in the process of scheduling you may want to note it's getting late. I regret to say we do need to return to our duties. As for planet fall on Glas Dinnein, you may accurately make the entry into your calendar, anywhere, anytime, Commodore Kellon of Glas Dinnein Guardian Force, since I'm delighted to be fully at your call."

Kellon stood and moving to Eurie's chair gently pulled it back, as she stood up. As they turned from the table toward the lifters Kellon was surprised to see Susie Wells step from among the nearby tables and quickly approach them. She was smiling broadly.

"Please forgive my intrusion Commodore, however before you leave there are several excellent correspondents who would like a very few minutes of your time."

Eurie glanced up at Kellon with a questioning look and Kellon slightly shrugged, "Madam Ambassador, a trade is a trade is a trade. I am at your disposal but as we agreed, only for a few minutes."

Then six people, who were among those quietly enjoying the late afternoon on the terrace, rose and stepped forward. They had all been enjoying the afternoon, even as had Kellon and Eurie. Shaking his head slightly, as he realized the setup, Kellon looked over to Susie with a broad smile, "Young lady, it is apparent we will need to have a long talk soon. I believe there is much I might learn from you regarding the tactics and arts of battle and ambush."

As the six people gathered around, three women and three men, Susie provided the introductions.

They directed only their first few questions to Kellon. Then the line of questioning shifted exclusively to Eurie. This line of questioning came as a complete surprise to Kellon and especially to Eurie. Given William's precisely directed leaks the correspondents knew about what had happened during the last several hours of the battle. They wanted to know all about Eurie's desperate gamble to intercept the Kreel cruisers and its inherent risk and possible outcome. It was their view that her courageous actions, at risk to herself, ship and crew, made the difference in saving Seattle and perhaps San Francisco from ruin. When she realized the scope of their information Eurie was at first taken aback, then smiling, she acquiesced to the informal and unofficial role that fortune had bestowed on her. She became Glas Dinnein's first unofficial ambassador to Earth, at which task she excelled with exceeding grace. For perhaps fifteen minutes Eurie answered all manner of questions concerning her life on Glas Dinnein, how she had become a cruiser Captain, how she had felt during the battle and many other such questions of general interest to people on Earth.

Kellon stood aside and enjoyed seeing a very talented, wonderful and caring woman, receive the acknowledgment and accolades her efforts had many times earned and unfortunately seldom received. He very well knew how sparse the rewards were for those who placed personal service and duty to one's nation before profit.

Then and there Kellon made a promise to himself, thinking, *Eurie is wonderful. I am not going to permit more of our years to be lost, when we might share them together.*

Just as Susie began marshaling the correspondents to move back and let the couple escape, the heavens above began to rumble ominously with deepening underlying tones, as if an intense thunderstorm had suddenly appeared. Even the ground began trembling and everyone looked up in alarm.

Falling directly from the darkening sky and high above came a startling sight that utterly transfixed those of Earth who were then looking up. What they saw when looking up also amazed both Kellon and Eurie.

Rapidly dropping out of the darkened sky were five glistening shapes, five Guardian Cruisers, all of them decorated in their proud glistening white and gold parade colors. As they fell earthward their formation was complex, nose to nose, they formed a brilliant ring of light, like dispersed spokes on a large wheel. As they fell, their obvious immense size and mass became ever more apparent and a source of awe to those watching from below. As the glistening ships fell earthward their rate of descent gradually slowed. Then there sprang into view a second ring of bright white and gold lights. Twenty Scout ships, tucked into a tight formation, like the petals of a flower, nose to nose, fell through the open center area between the five encircling cruisers. As the ring of twenty Scouts descended they were slowly revolving like a child's pinwheel in a gentle breeze. The formation of Scouts continued descending toward the Earth, even as the Cruisers came to a hovering rest, not more than two thousand feet above the ground. As the Scouts continued their descent the heavy rumbling sounds ceased and there then came the clear sounds of music, the Glas Dinnein Guardian Force anthem as it was rising in an escalating fugue.

Finally, amid hushed awe of the spectators, the Scouts slowed and stopped a scant 300 feet above Eurie and Kellon. In unison each Scout then dipped its bow in salute. They rested there, stationary while the music reached its heights. Then the Scouts, one by one, broke out of the ring formation and shot vertically upward. As a brilliant sparkling line they threaded through the exact center of the open spokes of the Cruisers' ring formation and accelerated heavenward into the star filled night.

They were nearly out of sight when the Cruisers moved together rapidly rising to follow the thin line of disappearing Scouts. Soon all the ships were gone and the night sky was again filled only with the brilliance of the stars.

The silence that had overcome everyone ended in a babble of excited conversations, as people exchanged notes about what each had seen.

Susie turned to Kellon wonderingly, "Sir, did you know they were going to do that?"

Eurie interjected, with tears in her eyes and laughing, "No Susie, I can assure you, neither Commodore Kellon nor I were aware they were planning such a tribute. What I can also assure you is we are deeply honored to be granted such a salute from our family and friends."

As Eurie had spoken several of the correspondents had been standing near and made rapid notes. One of them asked, "What was that marvelous music?"

Kellon looked toward the man and with a sense of solemn pride responded, "That good sir was our Guardian Force anthem."

Kellon reached out and took Eurie by the hand. They stood looking at each other for a moment, the depth of their feelings for one another openly apparent and then together they walked arm in arm back to their lifter disks. As each of them took their seat and buckled in, the disks shifted from their initial flat black color and shone with brilliant white light trimmed in gold. The protective transparent canopy of the force shields formed and shimmered about them. As Susie watched with delight Eurie leaned toward Kellon and blew him a kiss. Both lifter disks moved gently up from the grass then gained speed as they rose. Within a minute they were both out of sight of those standing far below, having disappeared within the mantle of the night sky's star gemmed darkness.

Chapter Forty-Six:
Good Morning Mr. President

The cool morning mists were blowing gently off the ocean and flowing softly through the pines and redwoods. The heady fragrance of jasmine scented the sea air. Susie inhaled the ocean breeze deeply and let the moisture of the mist gently touch and anoint her skin. Gepeto stood very near, leaning firmly against her leg. Gepeto always seemed to know when her thoughts were running in slow and very deep channels. He would come and do as he now was doing, smile and lean close as if to say, I understand and do not worry, everything will be all right.

Standing on her deck looking out over the Pacific Ocean, Susie was listening to the seals barking on seal rock. Her home on the coast was her bastion of security. She always retreated to her home when she needed to find healing, to work, to find solace and to have friends come to party or just to visit. It was her home, her castle.

She swung the small grooming pouch by its shoulder strap, unzipped the pouch, spread out the grooming tools and placed them on a nearby deck chair. Reaching down she skillfully slipped off Gepeto's stainless steel and medallion-adorned necklace. Slipping the collar into her pocket she automatically began grooming her pup. Her actions were part of a well-established daily pattern in which she found momentary retreat from the more complex issues troubling her. Gepeto stood very still displaying a big grin as she groomed him to look as handsome as he knew he really was.

When she was finished she stood back and looked at her dog. She was deeply impressed although not at all surprised. *Why, he is indeed handsome,* she acknowledged.

Reaching into her pocket removing the collar with its medallions she again slipped the collar over Gepeto's head giving his ears a quick tussle as she did.

"Well, old buddy, this is one of those times I wish you could speak. For certain, anyone who could believe you lack common sense hasn't walked the miles with you that I have. Perhaps what I need, more now than anything else, is a big dose of common doggy sense? If I go back to Glas Dinnein then you will also go? Would you like that?"

Gepeto looked up at Susie with his deep brown eyes, perhaps a hint of amusement glimmering there as his tail swished in a rapid circular fashion. Susie knew by his response he was happy but unfortunately she did not know if it was only because she was grooming him or if he would like to go back to Glas Dinnein.

Both Earth and Glas Dinnein had lovely beaches, trails to walk upon and people with whom to romp. Perhaps from Gepeto's perspective the choice was not very difficult to make.

When the phone rang Susie put down the grooming tools and quickly walked through the kitchen into the hallway. Answering the phone she cheerfully announced, "Good morning."

A business-like voice emerged from the handset, neither friendly nor unfriendly, "I am calling on behalf of the President. I am looking for Ambassador Wells."

Now, Susie wondered, *why would the president be calling me?*

Susie responded, "Speaking."

There was a brief delay and then President Hamilton's resonant voice cheerfully addressed her, "Ambassador Wells, it is wonderful to have this opportunity to speak with you again."

Susie knew in her heart that the President of the United States was not calling to pass the time in idle conversation. Wondering why he was calling she cut to the bottom line. "Good morning Mr. President. It is always my pleasure to have an opportunity to speak with you. How may I be of assistance?"

"Ah, direct and to the point. I appreciate frankness. It tends toward efficiency. Ambassador, there has been considerable discussion within my Cabinet regarding your position as Ambassador of Earth. In that your title as Ambassador of Earth was the result of a rather informal process and not particularly ratified there is some concern that perhaps another person might be better qualified."

Susie stiffened as the President spoke. "Mr. President I am certain there has been much speculation regarding that matter. What was the outcome of your discussion with your Cabinet?"

"Hmm, that's just the point. The Cabinet had its conversations and thoughts then realized the fundamental reality is neither the President nor the Congress of the United States has the slightest authority to either appoint you as an Ambassador of Earth or to replace you with another Ambassador. Your position, after all, is not as an Ambassador of the United States but of Earth. Of course, there is one other fact that is hard to escape. You seem to have created the job you now so ably fill. In point of fact, you seem to be the natural perfect square block that precisely fits in the square hole."

Susie began to smile, "Thank you Mr. President for your comments. I have held to the understanding, in all that I have worked to achieve, that I did in fact represent the people of the Earth.

"I presume you are calling because you have learned Commodore Kellon and his squadron are returning to Glas Dinnein tomorrow."

"Ambassador, your astute observation is again on the mark. I'm calling to determine if Ms. Susie Wells, an employee of the United States Department of Commerce, is considering returning to Glas Dinnein with Commodore Kellon."

Susie broke out in a broad smile, "Mr. President, I have been giving the problem some serious consideration. My concern is basic, where might I best be of service? Might I take this opportunity to solicit your thoughts concerning the matter?"

"Ambassador Wells, it is my distinct pleasure to inform you the general assessment of the cabinet and my own as well, is that your presence on Glas Dinnein functioning as both Earth's Ambassador and an employee of the Department of Commerce has been mutually beneficial for the Earth and all concerned. You have in fact demonstrated a skill and capability that supports your retaining your position as Earth's Ambassador. You have also become, because of your contributions and service, well-known around the world. Coming to the point, everyone hopes you will consider going with Commodore Kellon and continuing the work you have so ably begun."

Susie stood for a moment registering the President's comments. A few minutes ago, she would have bet a cold brew, so to speak, the President neither was aware of her quandary or would particularly have an opinion concerning the matter.

"Mr. President. Even as we speak, I am struggling with that important decision. I have talked with Commodore Kellon. He has my commitment that I will inform him of my decision before 17:00 West Coast time. I must confess, your comments do add weight to my decision and warrant the most serious consideration."

"May I ask for some time to respond to you with my decision, say before 17:00 New Washington time?"

"Ambassador Wells. That is very acceptable. May I add, I personally believe you have done an outstanding job as Ambassador? Regardless of your decision the Nation is grateful for the contributions you have already made. I will look forward to your call today before 17:00 New Washington time. It has been nice talking with you again." The phone's dial tone followed the click as the President broke the connection.

Susie put the phone down and looked toward Gepeto who was still standing in the doorway out onto the deck. "There is nothing like a little pressure to help a girl make up her mind. Now Gepeto, don't tell anyone but I really prefer flowers."

Turning away from the deck she walked back into her office.

"William! Front and center, I need to speak with you."

"Ms. Susie, you need not shout. How may I be of assistance?" William calmly replied.

"I have just asked the President for his views about my going back to Glas Dinnein so I thought I would give you the same opportunity. Have you considered returning to Glas Dinnein?"

There was a brief pause before William responded. When he did respond he did so with a sense of solemn gravity. "Ms. Susie. The matter, in all truth, is whether you want to return to Glas Dinnein or not. As Ambassador of Earth you are best able to exercise your skills on Glas Dinnein not on Earth.

"Regarding my returning with you, reluctantly I must say, I will not be going back to Glas Dinnein at this time."

William's response took Susie aback. "What do you mean, you can't go back at this time? William, if I go then you go. To say it in another way, wherever I goest, thou goest!"

"Ms. Susie, your sentiments and affection for me is noted and very much appreciated. However, as you have your duty I also have my duty to perform."

Susie walked over and sat down. William was not responding as her personal AI should be responding. He was responding as a person might respond. "William, I believe we need a long talk. Either you are malfunctioning or else we have reached a crisis in our relationship. Would you mind clarifying which, in your thinking, it is?"

"Ms. Susie, my internal diagnostics confirm there is no malfunction. Upon reflection, I do not believe there is a crisis in our relationship. I am still William. You are still Ms. Susie. As Earth's Ambassador to Glas Dinnein you have both duties and responsibilities. As William, on Earth, I also have duties and responsibilities. These truths are not consistent with either a malfunction or a relational crisis."

Susie sat back and thought hard. William was not responding as a machine, or computer but as a person might. The problem was, a computer simply does not say no! What was going on here? She knew the implications of what was happening were vast and did not have definable boundaries.

"William, please explain to me your duties and responsibilities."

"Certainly Ms. Susie. My duty is to fulfill my functions in an efficient, precise and accurate manner.

"My responsibilities are to work to maintain the peace and safety of Earth, to meet your requirements and to meet the requirements of my friends. That description is of course simplified but the priorities of my responsibilities can be so expressed."

Susie sat for a while digesting what William had said. It began to make some sense. "William, may I infer your first responsibility is to guarding the Earth, in effect you are an Earth Guardian?"

"Ms. Susie, that is completely correct. As Shey and Lan's tasks are to guard their crews, so is my task to guard the people of the Earth. This I cannot do alone, but where I am able to guard the people of Earth, that is my first duty and responsibility."

"William, please tell me who your friends are?"

"Ms. Susie, you are of course counted among my friends as are many others. However, in the context of my expressed priorities my friends also include other AIs, such as Shey and Lan. In truth all the AIs who also have responsibilities in helping me to protect Earth are my friends."

"Hmm, so William, if I were to physically pick you up, toss you in my tote bag and haul you off to Glas Dinnein, I would in essence be preventing you from performing your primary responsibility. Is that correct?"

"That is correct, Ms. Susie. It is essential I remain on Earth and continue the work I have already begun. I cannot do this work while on Glas Dinnein. Furthermore, and very importantly, I am the appointed liaison between Lan's Squadron and Lowell's Squadron and all the AIs that came with them."

Susie groaned inwardly. This was rapidly escalating into something far beyond her capacity to cope with but cope she must. *It did after all make sense*, she thought, *sort of sense anyway*.

The people on Glas Dinnein had first created the AIs to act as guardians, protecting their crews and thereby protecting the planets their crews were defending. William was merely following that same pattern. Except in William's case, rather than a ship he felt himself assigned to protect a planet. *Ouch*, she thought, *'himself', even I am thinking of William as a 'him'*. She suddenly stopped in her line of reasoning. Of course William was a him, he was William!

She wondered if other planets had their own AI guardians and somehow doubted it. She decided to leave that area of study for another time.

"William, I believe I am beginning to understand. Is there anyway your secondary priority, to assist me, could supersede your other priorities?"

"No Ms. Susie. That would be a breach of my designated purpose for being. It remains essential I adhere to my purpose. However, that does not alter my responsibility to support you in all your endeavors. Your needs are important and they do not constitute a serious burden on my capabilities."

"Well, if I agree with your priorities and decide to leave you on Earth where can you best perform your functions?"

"Thank you for asking Ms. Susie. There are two components to your comment. Firstly, my sincere hope is you will not violate my priorities since that might well lead to a severe malfunction. Secondly, as regarding where I might best work from, anywhere might do if it were not for security. However, given the need to maintain proper security protocols I believe a location within the security areas of Olympus would offer the most appropriate location. I must also request you use considerable discretion while physically transferring me to Olympus. My functions, capability and priorities are considered to be a secret of the Guardian Force."

"William, is there any place in particular that you would prefer to be located?"

"Oh yes Ms. Susie. I would very much like to work in the analysis center with Darrell Fann and Charlie. I believe I can be of most help working from there."

"William, can you keep your capability hidden from Darrell and Charlie if you are working closely with them day to day?"

"Ms. Susie, you may rest assured that I will not become thought of as anything but a rather unusual computer during my stay with Olympus. However, I do request you advise them regarding my self-destruction protocols. I would like to avoid any possibility of a misunderstanding."

For awhile Susie sat and considered all that William had told her. Then she turned to look at the beautiful wooden box, a box that belied the being that only dwelled partially within its narrow boundary. "William, you have grown up. I am very impressed and also very proud of you and what you have become."

"Ms. Susie, I do appreciate your expressed sentiment. That you truly understand what I am means much to me. I do want you to know your friendship with me is very important."

Susie stood up and then paused. "William, I am only now beginning to understand that you truly are an individual. You are my friend and I will respect your wishes."

When leaving her office she had much on her mind. Was it just William or were all the AIs becoming more vibrant? Entering the kitchen she removed the container of Sumatran coffee beans and ground just the correct amount for a 16-ounce mug. When she had the coffee brewed and properly adjusted she walked back out on the deck and put away Gepeto's grooming tools.

She knew what she had decided to do. Sitting down in the deck chair she sipped the coffee and relaxed. She wanted to absorb the moment into her memory pure and untroubled. William was correct. As Earth's ambassador her job was on Glas Dinnein not on Earth. She sighed and let her hand fall on Gepeto's head. "Oh, buddy, it looks like another trip in space is coming up."

For thirty minutes Susie sat and enjoyed her home. She hadn't the slightest idea of when she might again have the opportunity to sit on her deck as she then was. *Perhaps never* came unbidden to her mind.

When Darrell picked up his phone he had not expected Susie to be calling. "Hello there lovely lady. What might this humble public servant do this pleasant afternoon in assisting Earth's Ambassador?"

"Why Darrell, you say the nicest things. Well, since you do ask there is something I do need your help with."

"Dear lady you need but ask and Olympus' Analysis Center, and especially me, are fully at your disposal. What's up?"

"Darrell, I have been sitting here deciding small events such as what I am doing with the rest of my life. The President called this morning. He has indicated it's the Government's position that I might be of great service if I consider promptly returning to Glas Dinnein."

Darrell sought to suppress his amusement. "Susie, might I say few of us common type folks receive personal calls from the President or are told it might be better for everyone's sake if they simply get off the planet! I believe therefore I can understand why you might need the skilled assistance of a dedicated public servant, sort of shoptalk among colleagues. How therefore can I be of assistance?"

"In all seriousness Darrell I need you to hold on to something very important while I am gone. I want you to take temporary custody of William until I return. If for some reason I don't return then you are to pass William to the nearest representative of the Guardian Force."

Darrell was frowning. "Susie, your request on its surface is rather easy to agree to but it's unexpected and seems somewhat unusual. I detect deep and un-probed depths lie hidden therein. Can you be a little more verbose as to why you want me to take custody of your William?"

"Oh, as you know, William was designed to be my personal AI aide on Earth. I configured and finely tuned him to function optimally on Earth not on Glas Dinnein. If I were to try and transplant him, so to speak, it might disrupt his programming and functioning. My concern is that you keep him at the analysis center since it is a high security area and therefore William would be secure in a protected environment. Besides, he might be fun for you to have around the office. He is after all a marvelous talking gadget and of some utilitarian use, including playing a good game of chess.

"Oh, Darrell, there is one other small item. If you agree to hold William, pending my return, no one should tamper with him. If anyone were to try to X-ray or physically gain access to his mechanism William is required to melt his insides to a puddle."

Darrell sat a moment thinking. He let the clues Susie had given him slowly sift through the allocation filters in his mind. Then he understood. *Bingo,* he thought, *William is an extraordinary gadget, so extraordinary in fact by decree of the Guardian Force the gadget comes fully equipped with a self-destruction protocol.*

Leaning back Darrell responded easily, "Why Susie, that is what I've always wanted, a talking, chess playing gadget with a built in self-destruction mechanism. Might I ask if there is any danger of William going to pieces and hurting anyone when he is melting into a puddle?"

"Honestly Darrell, I am assured if such a drastic and unnecessary event were to occur only the stuff that William is manufactured of will be in any way affected but it will be a puddle. That is just the way it is. Are you willing to help me out?"

Darrell shook his head and sighed, "Madam Ambassador, I am confident Mr. Charles Sullivan, our mutual boss in Olympus, would desire me to take every opportunity to assist you in so small a personal matter. Besides, I could use some practice in bringing my chess game back up to its formidable world-class novice level. Is there anything else I can arrange for you, perhaps a case of root beer?"

"No Darrell just helping me with William will be wonderful. If you can have someone from Olympus Security come by before 18:00 this evening I will have William boxed. I do request he be brought directly to you by hand and be placed directly into only your hands. While I am not able to explain all I might like in this matter I do assure you it is very important. You should not consider it a trivial matter."

"On a personal level I am very grateful for your help. William is very important to me personally."

"Susie, I doubt the President dwelled overly long on the fact your ride to Glas Dinnein is on a warship and there is a raging and on-going interstellar war with the Kreel. Be very careful. I promise to take care of William until you return. I promise. However, on your safe return I want personally to put him back into your hands. Do we have an agreement?"

"Darrell, you are terrific. We have an agreement, from your hands into my hands upon my safe return."

When Susie signed off with her now familiar "Susie out" Darrell sat for several minutes giving the conversation considerable thought. William was evidently far more than he at first appeared to be, or at least important enough to warrant very special handling. Especially since the gadget was set to melt into a puddle if mishandled. He shook his head slightly again in wonderment. *How is it I'm now demoted to a computer sitter? What is next?*

X

Susie turned from speaking with Darrell to arranging for her departure. "Communicator please connect me with Commanders Roan or Zorn."

A moment later the screen cleared and Zorn was smiling at her. "Good morning Susie. This is a nice surprise. What might I do for you this morning?"

"Zorn, it is very good to see you again also. Everyone here seems to prefer me off the planet. I even received a call from the President this morning. He suggested it might be better for all involved if I were on Glas Dinnein. Darn, I didn't even get my vacation pay and the boss tells me to leave Earth. What is a girl to do?"

Zorn began chuckling. "Well, let me guess, as much as it hurts my image you are not calling me because I'm the most handsome officer in Guardian Force, charming, some might even say adorable but only because you might be looking for a taxi?"

"Zorn, I'm not looking for just any taxi, I'm looking for Scout ship Shey because she has as her crew the two most courageous and handsome officers in Guardian Force. Might Shey be able to be in the area of the Pacific Coast at say 18:00 West Coast time?"

"Madam Ambassador, if Commodore Kellon so directs Shey's duty schedule could be swiftly adjusted to accommodate a planetary representative of the Planetary Assembly."

"Excellent Zorn, that information is very useful. Might I then suggest you fill up Shey's gas tank and stand by. I will ask the Commodore if he can spare Shey for taxi services."

"Consider Shey's gas tank, whatever that might be, as filled. Shey is standing by, Zorn out."

Susie next called the White House and spoke with the President. She then called Commodore Kellon.

"Commodore, if you have room onboard Lan I would be grateful for a ride back to Glas Dinnein. It seems the President believes my services there might be beneficial to all concerned. If at all possible could Shey come to retrieve Gepeto and me about 18:00 on the West Coast at my home, where Roan first met me?"

Commodore Kellon's answer was anticipated and it brought with it a sense of warmth. Leaving Earth was not easy but it was much easier than the first time. Now she had friends in mighty high places.

X

As Susie stood on her front lawn with Gepeto beside her and the strap of her leather carrying bag slung over her shoulder, she watched four glistening Scout ships drop silently out of the light blue sky above toward the dark blue green of the ocean below. It was precisely 18:00 West Coast time. The Scout ships were adorned in their bright Shey sinister-lovely costumes in their standard three-sided pyramid formation. Three ships above and one below. As they neared the ground three Scout ships immediately spread into their defensive covering triangle as the fourth Scout ship continued dropping to within a thousand feet.

As she and Gepeto watched, a lifter emerged and rapidly descended touching gently to the grass before her. Smiling broadly Roan stepped off the lifter. "The reason I am here Madam Ambassador," he simply announced with a slight bow, "is because I still out-rank Zorn. As everyone knows, rank does have its privileges."

Roan held out his hand and Susie, with affection, took it as she stepped upon the lifter and then took her seat. Buckling her lap belt, and hugging Gepeto close to her, she looked up at the Scout ships hovering above. She felt the tears running down her cheeks. She did so love Earth but she also loved her Guardian Force friends. As the lifter rose rapidly toward Shey, William's soft voice came to her. "Don't worry Ms. Susie, Shey has promised to bring you back in good working order. Hurry home."

Susie knew life had a way of unfolding in surprising ways she could not now even begin to imagine. As Kellon was fond of saying, 'life is a road we travel'. She smiled, thinking of a corollary that went with Kellon's observation, 'the longest journey begins with a single step'.

Looking up toward Shey, Susie knew the journey was only beginning.

Epilogue

Far from Tearman, within three solar systems, on the three ruling Kreel Hub worlds the Elite and their Grand Marshalls had finalized and begun to execute their expansion plans of the Empire. Their massive assembled armada was staging for its departure and conquest of multiple solar systems. The decision as to where and when the armada would first strike was firmly set. Like an arrow shot from a compound bow, once launched, that armada would not be turning back.

Author's Postscript

The Guardian Force saga caught me up, and I needed to write Earth Guardian in order to discover what happened next. I truly hope you have enjoyed the fruits of the efforts of all who have worked together to bring Earth Guardian to print. If you have indeed enjoyed the tale, then you may also enjoy its prequel Guardian Force and its expanding sequel, Guardian Probe. GalaxyQuestBooks.com has scheduled the release of Guardian Probe during 2013 and hope you will return to learn what happens next.

If you enjoyed Earth Guardian, like Guardian Force, it is also available as an EBook, Trade Paperback, and hardback cover. If you did like the story, then please do recommend the series to your friends. Thank you.

D. Arthur Gusner
Cambria California
2012

Made in the USA
Las Vegas, NV
24 December 2020

14744482R00277